KU-637-141

# SPRING

# SUMMER

# AUTUMN

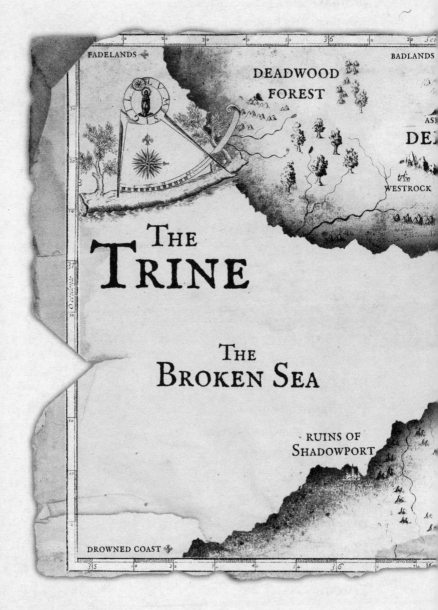

FADELANDS

BADLANDS

DEADWOOD
FOREST

DE

WESTROCK

# The
# Trine

## The
## Broken Sea

RUINS OF
SHADOWPORT

DROWNED COAST

# DEAD MAN'S
# STEEL

LUKE SCULL was born in Bristol and
lives in Warminster. Luke also designs
computer roleplaying games and has
worked on several acclaimed titles for
Ossian Studios and Bioware.

Luke's first novel, THE GRIM COMPANY,
was shortlisted for the David Gemmell
Morningstar Award, 2014.

Visit his website at: www.lukescull.com

WALTHAM FOREST LIBRARIES

904 000 00481926

# THE GRIM COMPANY

'The writing is incredible... *Sword of the North* is everything I'd hoped it would be, a deserving sequel to one of the finest fantasy novels of recent times – a rich and rewarding read told by a true storyteller.' SF BOOK

'Paced like a race, never a dull moment, extraordinary set pieces, bold and brilliant. A stellar exemplar of what the genre has to offer today.' TOR.COM

'An enjoyable romp at the heart of the genre.' INTERZONE

'Scull spins a gripping tale with expertise and relish.' GUARDIAN

'Packs an impressive amount of violence, hazy morality and betrayal, crafting an energetically cynical read. Showcasing thrilling action sequences alongside effective plot twists, it'll please fans of the darker edges of epic fantasy... An entertaining page-turner.' SFX

'If you like your gizzards glistening and your mages mean, this rollicking debut will suit. Hugely enjoyable.' DAILY MAIL

'One of the bright new voices in epic fantasy.' SPECULATIVE BOOK REVIEW

'A deftly crafted work that covers politics, betrayal, assassination, war, and frighteningly believable battles against enormous magical monsters.' WE LOVE THIS BOOK

THE GRIM COMPANY

# DEAD MAN'S
# STEEL

## LUKE SCULL

HEAD
of
ZEUS

First published in the UK in 2016 by Head of Zeus Ltd

This paperback edition first published in the UK in 2017
by Head of Zeus Ltd

Copyright © Luke Scull, 2016

The moral right of Luke Scull to be identified as the author
of this work has been asserted in accordance with the
Copyright, Designs and Patents Act of 1988.

All rights reserved. No part of this publication may be reproduced,
stored in a retrieval system, or transmitted in any form or by any
means, electronic, mechanical, photocopying, recording, or otherwise,
without the prior permission of both the copyright owner and the
above publisher of this book.

This is a work of fiction. All characters, organizations, and
events portrayed in this novel are either products of the author's
imagination or are used fictitiously.

9 7 5 3 1 2 4 6 8

A catalogue record for this book is available from the British Library.

Paperback ISBN 9781781851616
Ebook ISBN 9781781851623

Typeset by Ben Cracknell Studios

Printed and bound by CPI Group (UK) Ltd, Croydon, CR0 4YY

Head of Zeus Ltd
First Floor East
5–8 Hardwick Street
London EC1R 4RG

WWW.HEADOFZEUS.COM

For Rob

| Waltham Forest Libraries | N |
|---|---|
| 904 000 00481926 | |
| Askews & Holts | 26-May-2017 |
| FAN | £8.99 |
| 5409394 | |

# Contents

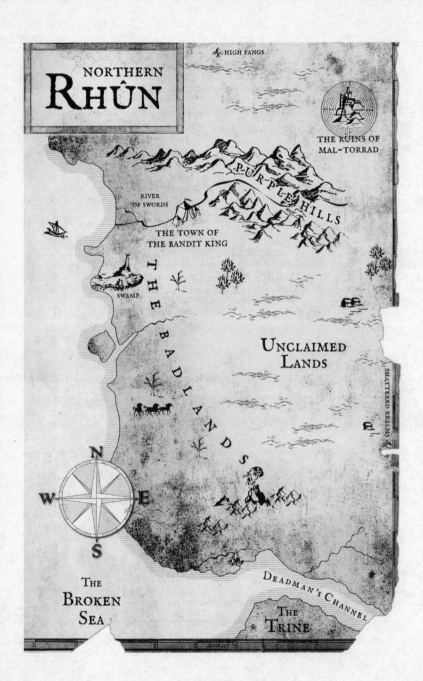

# DEAD MAN'S
# STEEL

# WINTER

# The Hunter

THE SINISTER GLOW in the distance was gaining on him again. His breath rasped in his chest. Blood ran down his bald head, matted his beard. There were other things in these ruins – twisted creatures that fed on human flesh. The first time he'd encountered them they'd been feasting on the corpses of Fivebellies' men. Pulling snaking entrails from chewed-open stomachs, scooping out clumps of gore from shattered chests and chomping on it like wild animals devouring prey.

The flesh-eaters had thought they'd spied fresh meat when he entered their domain. They'd rushed him, screaming for blood, mouths slavering thick drool: denizens of the darkness that hadn't seen the sunlight in years, if at all.

He'd left them broken on the ground, their stunted, twisted bodies hacked apart by his steel axes. They quickly discovered their mistake in seeing him as prey. Now they ran when they saw him. Feared him as much as they feared his pursuer. The gholam was relentless.

Then again, so was he.

He ghosted down streets that hadn't seen a living soul pass through in centuries. The dust was thick everywhere, made it impossible to hide his tracks, but that didn't worry him. His pursuer didn't hunt by smell or scent or sight. You couldn't lose something like that. Instead you went somewhere it couldn't follow. You trapped it.

Or you killed it.

He hadn't eaten or slept since entering the ruins and it was an effort to keep on moving, but he refused to feel sorry for himself. You make a promise, you stick to it. He'd said he'd buy them time to escape and that's what he would do. Difference between a man and a cunt is that a man sticks to his word.

He loped through the darkness, a single torch lighting his way, listening for sounds of the gholam's approach. Their game of cat and mouse had plunged them ever deeper into Mal-Torrad. He had to be close to the prison now. Close to somewhere the god-forged entity giving chase might be halted, if only for a while.

Structures of dark granite rose around him, as harsh and angular as the axes on his back. The underfolk hadn't been much for fancy designs. The buildings got bigger the lower he delved, giant stone rectangles with rusted iron doors that hadn't been opened since the civil war that had torn the kingdom apart. The orange light of his torch illuminated piles of gold glittering in the streets alongside countless squat skeletons: all that remained of the strange people who had called this city home. Didn't make much sense to him, but then not much in this world did.

Finally, he spotted what he was searching for. A palace, fronted by two huge statues of crowned underfolk who might've been the likeness of their king and queen. He headed towards the grand structure, sticking to the cover of the nearby buildings. His keen eyes noted the runes etched onto their doors, the scorch marks on the stone beneath his boots. A campfire had been lit here only a month past. Whoever had freed the gholam had entered the palace. Chances were the prison was within.

He stalked through the palace courtyard. Shadows flitted around the statuary lining the square and he could hear their chattering, their gibbering speech rising, getting higher, excited. *The flesh-eaters.*

They were working themselves into a frenzy. Preparing to attack. He ignored them, focused instead on the great iron gates ahead of him. They stood a little ajar.

He rested his torch against a wall and squeezed himself between the gates. The metal bit into his flesh but he ignored the pain, wedged himself firmly between them and pushed with all his strength. Teeth grinding together, every muscle in his body standing taut, he forced the gates apart with a screech that seemed to shake the very walls of the palace.

He stood panting and stared into the darkness between the open gates. There was a skittering sound behind him as one of the flesh-eaters, braver than the rest, made a move. He spun and caught the creature mid-leap, his hand closing around its throat and locking tight. It snapped at him, yellow fangs straining for his fingers, its luminous eyes near bursting with hatred.

He stabbed with the fingers of his free hand, forcing the creature's eyes back through their sockets and into its brain. Then he smashed its head against the iron gates until it was bloody pulp, and with a snarl flung the corpse back among the statuary. He heard the gnashing of fangs as its kin fell upon it.

He retrieved the torch and entered the palace halls.

The scorch marks on the ancient, dust-blanketed carpet guided him through the interior. He passed through the throne room, pausing for a brief moment to stare at the scene within – a slice of history frozen in time. Two skeletons sat on the thrones upon the dais, short and squat like the rest of the underfolk but wearing crowns atop their heads. Both underfolk had daggers protruding from their chests; the metal had long begun to rust. As he lifted first one crown and then the other to stare at the desiccated features beneath, he saw that they had once been male and female. King and queen.

Other skeletons littered the throne room: some were so small that they could only be those of children. A death pact between the ruling families, then. Else a ruthless coup in which none had been spared.

He spat and turned away. Some mysteries were better left unsolved, he reckoned.

The gholam's trail descended three more floors. He could hear the flesh-eaters piling into the palace above, the patter of clawed feet on the rafters.

On the fifth and lowest floor, he reached the prison.

It resembled a giant maze. The walls were thicker than a man was tall and covered in runes, as were the floor and ceiling. The runes glowed with magic; the whole prison throbbed with it. As he stalked through the corridors, he saw that certain runes had been intentionally hidden, concealed by a spongy material that clung to the stone like tar. He reached out and tore some off. Examined it with a deep frown and eyes as dark as coal.

It was flesh – the hide of one of the flesh-eating humanoids, stripped straight off the body. Whoever had freed the gholam had disabled the runes keeping it imprisoned, through the grimmest of means.

The light suddenly shifted and a malevolent glow washed through the prison. He spun, saw his implacable hunter as it began to flow towards him, leaving scorched stone in its wake. The gholam was shaped like a man but there was nothing human about the shadow wreathed in its infernal flame. Only the promise of obliteration in its embrace.

The gholam seemed to strike an invisible barrier. The runes covering the walls flared a bright blue and sparks hissed through the air. The gholam tried to move forward once again, only to bounce off something. The living weapon paused for a moment and then flowed back the way it had come, disappearing down another corridor. Seeking an alternative way to reach its target. Seeking a gap in the rune magic.

He knew what he needed to do. He began to sprint. As he ran he tore off the flesh covering the runes and replaced it elsewhere. Time and again the gholam got close, and time and again he exposed the runes and their warding magic seconds before its ruinous embrace could engulf him. Until at last there was no more room in which to run. His back was against a wall, the gholam opposite him, barely six feet between them.

The warding runes wouldn't let the god-forged horror reach him, but the thing filled the corridor, directly in his path, impossible to pass.

He was trapped.

With nothing else to be done, he sat down on the stone floor. This wasn't the kind of death he wanted, boxed into a corner and waiting for thirst or starvation to take him. Still, it was what it was. He'd kept his word. Kayne and the foundlings ought to have reached safety by now – if anywhere was safe from the unholy fucker opposite him.

He lost track of time as he sat there. The gholam didn't move. A day or a week might have passed.

He was starting to lose consciousness, his body beginning to close down. It didn't hurt much, but then pain had never hurt him. Not like the hurt of betrayal. Of being stabbed in the back by the only man he trusted.

Suddenly the gholam turned. Spun and flowed away as though it had given up the chase, or somehow found another target. Neither seemed likely to him, but he wasn't about to question his luck.

He waited a few hours to see if it would return. When it didn't, he climbed unsteadily to his feet, using the wall to support himself. The torch had long since died: the only light came from the soft blue glow of the runes around him.

He walked haltingly back through the prison, his vision blurring, making it hard to get his bearings. He reached a crossroads and stopped, blinking. An approaching cacophony of noise reached his ears: a rising tide of chattering, whooping, gnashing fangs. The flesh-eaters had come for him. Dozens of them, maybe hundreds, crowding the passageways on every side, clutching makeshift daggers of stone.

He paused for a moment and closed his eyes. He was so tired he could he hardly stand. Might be quicker to just lie down and let them get it over with. But he still had one promise left to keep.

His eyes snapped open. He unharnessed his axes. Readied himself.

The Wolf bared his teeth.

# Acts of Mercy

THE WINTER WIND howled through the meandering streets of the city, dusting the tall figure making his graceful way towards the harbour with fresh snow. He paused for a moment and tilted back his head, blinking obsidian-dark eyes against the spiralling flakes settling on his face. They were almost invisible against his ivory skin. A cloak of midnight blue billowed around his slender form, marking him as an Adjudicator – an elite officer among the invading army.

Isaac had walked these streets many times before, but only since the First Fleet's arrival had he done so without needing to conceal his true nature. The ability to beguile the lesser races was a rare skill he shared with his sisters: a blood-talent handed down by Zakarian, one of the original Pilgrims now lost to the Void. As he resumed his trek to the harbour, Isaac offered silent thanks for the Pilgrims' great sacrifice. A sacrifice made to prevent the extinction of their kind.

*Humanity will receive no such reprieve,* the Adjudicator thought grimly. He recalled when the land this grey city was built upon had been untamed wilderness. The kingdom of Andarr had been a handful of primitive huts when Prince Obrahim called the Great Migration and the fehd withdrew west. Isaac's kind had left the flourishing young race of man much of their knowledge. It was an act of monumental generosity, a parting gift for a people who would inherit a continent much changed following the titanic conflicts between the elder races.

Two thousand years later, the humans had sailed across the Endless Ocean and sought out their benefactors. Isaac's own sister, Melissan, had offered succour to the voyagers. She even consented to allow two of the fehd to accompany the humans back across the ocean. Aduana and Feryan were eager to learn about the lands over which their people had once held dominion.

Isaac's breathing quickened in anger. His hand inched towards the crystalline longsword at his waist; a weapon sharper than that forged by any man. He forced himself to calm, willed his anger to melt away like the snow flecking his golden hair. Such emotions were the mark of the lesser races. He was a fehd – and more, he was an Adjudicator.

He stared south beyond the harbour. Towards the flooded ruins of Shadowport where his kin had been imprisoned and tortured. Aduana and Feryan had been little more than children by the standards of his people, barely a few centuries old. The Magelord Marius had subjected them to horrors unimaginable.

Even across the vast distance of the Endless Ocean, Isaac and his kin had felt the deaths of Aduana and Feryan. Only a handful of the ageless fehd had perished since the Great Migration; now two had been murdered in the darkest of circumstances.

Two decades of mourning had followed. Two decades of grief before thoughts turned to vengeance.

Isaac stared at the humans cowering on the streets as he passed them on the way to the docks. Most were afraid to even glance in his direction. Some sobbed, while others turned and ran. Few had any place in which to seek refuge: rows of burned-out buildings led all the way to the docks, homes and offices reduced to blackened shells of melted stone by the First Fleet's artillery. Beyond the harbour, entire districts had been destroyed in the days following the arrival of the fehd army. A third of the city's population was newly homeless.

Dorminia's resistance had proved pitiful. The city's Magelord was dead and gone, its ruling council massacred by Isaac's sisters in public view. None among the humans could stand against even a handful of regular fehd soldiers, let alone elite Adjudicators. Their swordsmanship had been refined through centuries of practice. Their empathetic projection was strong enough to reduce hardened warriors to quivering heaps. And the weapons his people possessed were beyond anything humanity could muster in defence. Isaac and his sisters were as gods among these short-lived creatures. Gods, or something close to it.

Isaac felt the briefest flicker of sympathy when he saw the children draped in rags huddling in the ashes of what had once been their homes. The oldest of humans seemed to him ephemeral creatures, their lifespans a cruel joke. But these children, they were half-dead already.

*You chose,* he reminded himself. *You spent four years among these humans, judging them. Your verdict was harsh but it was just. Nothing less than utter annihilation. A purging of every human on the continent.* Beginning here, in this place men called the Trine.

The ten ships that comprised the First Fleet filled Dorminia's harbour. They were gunmetal behemoths all, each of them larger than the biggest human warship ever constructed and propelled not by oar or sail but by great engines that had eaten up the expanse of the Endless Ocean with ease.

Isaac's sisters Melissan and Nymuvia were waiting for him on the flagship's deck. The dark blue cloaks that marked them as Adjudicators fluttered behind them in the winter flurry.

'Brother,' Melissan greeted him as he joined them. 'You appear troubled.'

Isaac stood at the prow and watched the thralls milling around on the deck. There were hundreds of them, men and women he had kidnapped and smuggled into the city to hasten its fall. The implants within the flesh of the thralls overrode thought and emotion; forced absolute compliance with the directives given by Isaac and his two sisters. They would serve their immortal masters unquestioningly until death.

'Is it right to reduce them to... this?' Isaac said eventually. 'The Pilgrims taught that slavery was the greatest of evils. In the Time Before, to place a person in chains was to make of them a thing no better than an animal.'

Melissan came to stand before Isaac. They were of equal height – a head taller than any of the human thralls on the ship. Her hair was like spun gold, her eyes as black as ink. She was his full-blood sister, born of the same parents.

'They *are* animals.' She raised a delicate hand and frowned as a snowflake settled on her palm. 'They fight, they fuck, and then they die, and in their passing they leave nothing more significant than this.' She turned her hand and the thawed snowflake trickled to the ship's deck.

'Remember what they did, brother,' said Nymuvia, placing a hand on his shoulder. She was the youngest of the three siblings, and though she was born of a different father to Melissan and himself, Isaac cherished Nym more than anything else in the world. 'What they did to Aduana and Feryan. What the god-killer who ruled this city, Salazar, did to his neighbours across the Trine in his misguided effort to placate us.'

'They are poison,' Melissan added. Her voice was soft yet seethed with a great anger. The nearby thralls heard her fury and flinched away. 'A poison that must be purged from the land. How can a race so short-lived ever rise above the mud from which they crawled?'

'They are not all as you say,' Isaac replied. 'Not all. There are some worthy of our respect.' He knew whence his sister's anger came. She still blamed herself for the deaths of her kin. For saying 'yes' to Aduana and Feryan. That decision would haunt her for eternity.

Melissan brought her face closer, locked him with her gaze. 'You should dispose of the Halfmage, dear brother. I fear your fondness for that particular human clouds your judgement.'

Isaac returned his sister's stare. 'It is true he fascinates me. But I have known others among his kind who surprised me also.

12

Warriors loyal enough to die for each other, as any of our kind would. Is that not worth something?'

He recalled Brodar Kayne and his friend the Wolf. Very different men, but they had shared a bond that had seemed to him as strong as the steel deck now beneath his boots.

'Humans know nothing of true loyalty,' said Melissan. 'They are creatures of convenience, motivated only by greed and fear. They do not *feel* as we do. Their "love" is but a poor imitation of ours.'

At the mention of 'love', Nymuvia's eyes seemed to shine. 'I have news for you, brother. It is why we summoned you here. The Second Fleet's work at the Celestial Isles is finished. The general is coming. My betrothed is on his way.'

The smile on Nym's face almost chased away the shadow her words cast over Isaac's heart. 'Saverian,' he repeated. The general was a living legend among his people.

Isaac remembered the massacre of the humans at the Isles. A necessary act. One that Saverian had not shied away from. 'He will lead us to victory,' he said, though the words sounded inexplicably hollow.

'As he always has.' Melissan pointed towards the south. 'This "White Lady" is all that stands before the next part of our crusade. Her city will fall swiftly once the general arrives. When the last remaining Magelord of the Trine is dead, Thelassa will serve as our gateway to the continent.'

Isaac nodded. Magic was the one question to which the fehd had no easy answer. Their people stood outside the Pattern, outside the plan the Creator had designed for this world. Magic was as alien to Isaac's kind as their own abilities were to humanity.

But the fehd had equally deadly weapons. Weapons that had broken worlds. 'They will be Reckoned,' he said softly.

Nym's smile was proud. 'Like the elves before them.'

A thud and a scream shattered the brief silence that followed. One of the thralls had fallen from a mast. He lay groaning on the deck, his right leg clearly broken by the impact. Isaac recognized the man. It was one of the thralls he had captured near the city of Carhein in the first year of his return to these shores: a farmer who had been working the fields, oblivious to the true nature of the stranger approaching down the old dirt road.

'I will have a thrall bring him down to the medic deck,' Isaac said. 'That leg can be fixed—'

Melissan reached for her hip and drew the deadly weapon holstered there, the motion a blur. There was the harsh crack of a shot being fired and an instant later the injured man's head exploded in a splash of red spray. His body twitched a few times and went still. A puddle of crimson spread from the ruin of his neck, steaming in the winter air.

'Clean it up,' Melissan ordered, gesturing at the nearby thralls with her smoking hand-cannon. She replaced the weapon in its holster at her waist and turned to stare out across the city of Dorminia. 'That was an act of mercy,' she said. 'The Reckoning will not be as swift.'

Despite his unease, Isaac couldn't argue with his sister's assessment. When the general arrived, the time remaining to the humans in these lands would be measured in days.

Then again, to the fehd, such had always seemed the case.

# The Greater Oath

THE WORLD NEVER stopped changing, in Brodar Kayne's experience. Faster as the years went by. As he rode into the midst of Carn Bloodfist's great army camped west of Heartstone's walls and saw the unfamiliar faces of the young warriors sitting around the fires, most of them young enough to be his son, he felt like a relic belonging to another age.

He drew his mare to a halt and tried to ease the stiffness out of his legs. Then he dismounted, boots crunching on frozen ground, every breath sending out thick clouds of mist in the deepening gloom. He'd forgotten how cold it was in the High Fangs in the middle of winter. Forgotten how the bitter chill would force its way into his ageing bones and make it hard to crawl into his saddle in the morning and even harder to crawl back out.

He raised a hand to shield his eyes and squinted through the falling snow. His eyesight was worse than shit, but he thought he could make out the dark shadow of the chieftain's tent up ahead. He reckoned there were maybe fifty yards separating him and Carn Bloodfist. Fifty yards before he came face to face with the man whose father's head he had separated from his shoulders all those years ago.

Chances were Carn Bloodfist would attempt to do the same to Kayne before he could get a word in edgeways. Before he could explain that he was here to throw his sword in with the army of the West Reaching and retake the capital from that mad bastard Krazka. Chances were, Kayne was about to walk headlong into his own death.

That should have caused him to hesitate. To scramble right back on his horse and ride away before any of the faces peering up at him recognized the old greybeard who had just appeared among them. Instead he adjusted the greatsword strapped to his back and drew his filthy cloak tighter around his shoulders, fixed his blue eyes straight ahead.

Some things you just had to do, when the alternative was no alternative at all.

The smell of mutton cooking in the fire-pits nearby made his stomach growl like a Highland cat. There were other scents carried on the icy breeze: old leather, stale sweat, the acrid stink of piss. And underneath it all the familiar stench of war, the sickly sweetness of flesh gone rotten, of bad wounds festering and inviting death's shadow in.

Kayne knew all about death's shadow. He'd been living in it for the best part of his fifty-odd years. As he focused on the tent up ahead, he tried not to let his apprehension show. Ten yards passed. Twenty.

He almost made it. At the last moment, one of the warriors sitting in a half-circle around the furthest fire turned to utter something to a man behind him. His gaze settled on Kayne. For a second all was perfectly calm and the world seemed to hold its breath.

Then the warrior's eyes widened and the chicken wing he was chewing on slipped from his grasp, falling into the flames with a sizzle.

'*You.*' The word grated like a sword scraping against steel, shushing the chatter of the men around them. Silence descended like a shroud, broken only by the crackling of the campfires.

The warrior clambered to his feet. He was a little older than his compatriots, a tall man in his early twenties with a wine-coloured mark discolouring his right cheek. In his eyes glittered cold fury.

'You,' he repeated, his voice a harsh whisper now. 'You came back. Why the fuck would you come back? Here, of all places.'

Kayne spread his palms and held them out before him. 'I just came to talk. To speak with Carn.' He noted with despair that half the camp seemed to be watching them now.

'After what you did to his father?' The fellow was breathing hard, nostrils flaring. 'My brother was murdered that day. One of the thousands you ordered put to the sword.'

Kayne sagged a little. 'They were the Shaman's orders.' The words sounded pitifully small even as he spoke them.

A voice called out, 'Finn, what's this about? Who is this old shitbeard?'

The one called Finn took a step forward and spat. 'This man is the Sword of the North. Once the most feared killer in the High Fangs.' He paused a moment, weighing up his next words for maximum effect, and the undeniable truth of them was like a dagger in Kayne's heart. 'He led the massacre of Reaver's Gate fourteen years past.'

'I don't want no trouble. I just want to talk,' Kayne repeated. But an angry muttering bubbled among the warriors close enough to hear what was being said, and he knew nothing he could say would calm their rising fury.

Finn took another step forward. 'Someone hand me my sword,' he growled. Kayne could hear movement behind him, men rising and spreading out, inching closer.

He reached over his shoulder and drew his greatsword, three and a half feet of steel glittering red in the firelight. Then he knelt down, knees groaning in protest, and placed it carefully on the ground. 'Ain't a day goes by I don't regret what happened at Red Valley,' he said slowly. 'I got no intention of fighting you or anyone else in this camp. Well, excepting the Shaman if he's still around, but our feud can wait till after the war's over.'

Strong arms seized him, forced his arms painfully behind his back. He didn't protest. Didn't try to fight. He could smell the stinking breath of warriors behind him, feel the heat of their anger as they grasped him tight. Most were too young to have fought in Targus Bloodfist's rebellion, too young for their lifeblood to have joined that of their fathers and brothers and uncles in the great basin in the shadow of Reaver's Gate. The massacre at Red Valley was a scar that had yet to heal, a scabbed wound from which the hurt of a thousand sons of the West Reaching still bled. Especially now, with the man who had given the order to Krazka and his lieutenants standing right there before them.

Finn sneered, the birthmark on his cheek ugly against the paleness of his flesh. 'The Shaman's still useful to Carn. Don't reckon he's got any use for a washed-up old coward though.'

'I'm many things but a coward's never been one of 'em,' Kayne said, though the memory of Jerek's final goodbye surfaced to mock that claim, and his voice grew hoarse. 'Do what you have to do. Just be sure you keep your blades sharp for Krazka. Him and any who stand with that butcher.'

Kayne reeled as Finn punched him hard in the face. He spat blood and then a moment later heaved bile as a fist to the stomach doubled him up, or would have if his arms weren't pinned tight behind him. He tried to say something, managed only to slobber red drool over his chin and grunt as a vicious kick collapsed his legs, leaving him slumping forward, upright only on account of the men who had hold of his elbows.

Finn was standing over him. He'd finally found his sword and was pointing the sharp end right at Kayne's face. 'The Butcher King will get what's coming to him, don't you worry about that. As for you, it's time you answered for your own part in Red Valley, old man. You came back for vengeance? Looks like vengeance found you.' Finn grabbed a handful of his grey hair and Kayne's head was forced back, the edge of the sword shoved roughly against his neck. Could be the angry Westerman just wanted to give him a nice close shave, but the look in Finn's eyes suggested he had something more sinister in mind. Kayne blinked blood and snow and sweat out of his own eyes and waited for the end.

18

'Stay your hand, boy.'

The voice that thundered from the tent was deep and powerful. A hulking silhouette emerged into the waning light and Kayne felt his muscles tense, fought the urge to twist away from the men restraining him, pluck the blade from Finn and make his own bloody bid for revenge on the newcomer. As the light from the nearest campfire fell over him, though, Kayne saw that it was not the Shaman whose feet crunched over the snow towards them.

Carn Bloodfist was a hulking giant of a man – taller than Kayne by the entirety of his huge forehead, which jutted out above a visage that might've been carved from the jagged stone of the West Reaching's deepest valleys. His black hair had receded halfway down his massive skull and was gathered in a thick braid that reached as far as his beard, which was similarly braided. Whereas the Shaman was pure chiselled muscle, stretched to the limits of what his body could achieve, Carn was massive in that way of men who were simply born freakish big.

The chieftain of the West Reaching and leader of the resistance army loomed over Finn, who seemed to wilt in his colossal presence. Flint-dark eyes stared out from a face wreathed in shadow. 'I swore an oath fourteen years ago,' he rumbled. 'An oath to kill the man who slew my father.'

'Best get to it then,' Kayne rasped, hawking out a mouthful of blood. 'Before some other bastard with a grudge stakes his claim. This camp don't seem short of 'em.'

Carn gestured at Finn with a meaty hand, deep scars reciting a history of violence, a testament to countless battles won. 'Return to your fire,' he boomed. 'I will speak with the Sword of the North alone. Any man who dares disturb us or raises a weapon against him shall face my wrath.'

Finn's eyes narrowed, his jaw quivering in rage, but he dared not disobey his chieftain. Kayne finally drew breath as the blade was grudgingly withdrawn from his neck. The warriors behind him released his elbows and he toppled forward, swollen face thudding painfully into the frozen earth. Some remnant of the man he used to be wouldn't let him lie there; wouldn't allow further humiliation to be heaped upon him while warriors who once feared his name sneered, mouths twisting in contempt. He forced himself to stand, every joint screaming, until he looked up at Carn.

The great chieftain rolled his shoulders and pointed down at Kayne's feet. 'Pick up your sword,' he rumbled.

\*

The tent was larger than it looked on the outside and smelled faintly of mould. It was near pitch black within, a single candle set on an upturned crate in the centre providing the only illumination. Kayne scanned the makeshift table, hardly seeing the ink-stained map covered in scrawl, or the empty, half-cracked tankard. Instead his eyes were drawn to the broadsword gleaming orange in the flickering light. Carn walked slowly to the table, bent down and retrieved a battered shield propped against a travelling chest beside the crate. He strapped it around his wrist, then reached for the weapon.

'Here?' Kayne said wearily. 'You want to settle this here?' He still felt groggy from the beating he'd received a moment ago. Still couldn't seem to focus properly after that last punch. Nonetheless, the midnight runes covering the length of that gleaming blade were familiar to him.

'You recognize this?' said Carn.

Kayne stared at the weapon in Carn's hand. 'Aye. Your father's sword.'

'My father,' Carn echoed. 'Called the Bloodfist after he broke every one of his knuckles killing a giant with his bare hands. This weapon was a gift to him from a Lowland wizard just before he declared the West Reaching's independence. With it, it was said no man could face him in battle and live.' Carn was silent for a moment, stroking his great beard with fingers as thick as most men's wrists. 'They found it beside his body the morning he challenged you to a duel. I named it Oathkeeper.'

Kayne said nothing.

'Tell me how he died,' Carn growled, the words carrying a menace that seemed to chill the air within the tent.

There'd been a time when talk of past deeds swelled Kayne with pride. Now it just brought pain. 'He died like a warrior,' he replied honestly. 'Gave me a few scars to add to the others. One of the toughest fights of my life.' Not the toughest: the golden-armoured swordsman back in the Lowlands had been a true master of the blade.

And the toughest fight of all, one he wasn't sure he would've won, wasn't certain he'd wanted to win in any case – the memory of that fight was still as raw a wound as any of the physical hurts he carried.

*If I ever see you again, I'll kill you.* Jerek's words.

His hands were suddenly trembling, tears threatening his eyes. Carn must have seen his moment of weakness. Before he knew it the massive chieftain was barrelling towards him, faster than any man his size had a right to be. Oathkeeper hissed down, seeming to thrum with power as it sliced through the empty space where Kayne's head had been an instant before. The sixth sense that had saved his life on countless occasions saved him again then, and he rolled away just in time, coming back to his feet with his greatsword suddenly in his palms. The trembling of a moment before was gone. He was utterly still, as calm as the surface of Lake Dragur on a lazy summer morning.

The enormous figure of Carn Bloodfist faced him, seemed to fill half the available space in the tent. But Carn did not press the attack. Instead he grunted and gave a small nod, then turned and walked back over to the upturned crate. He removed his shield and placed it against the chest. Then he laid Oathkeeper carefully down beside the map and sat on the chest, staring into the darkness, a deep frown on his heavy brow. The flickering candlelight sent eerie shapes dancing over his craggy cheek. 'You remember how to fight, at least.'

'Ain't something you ever forget,' Kayne replied warily. 'If you've a mind to see me dead I reckon there's easier ways of going about it.'

'The Kayne I knew would never have submitted to my men so readily outside this tent,' Carn rumbled. 'I had to know if you were still the man I remembered. You are no use to me otherwise. Not if you have lost your appetite for killing.'

'I lost it long ago.'

'But not your skill.'

Kayne shrugged. 'I ain't what I once was. I'm old. The world leaves all men behind eventually.'

'Not just men,' Carn replied absently. 'Magelords also.' He raised a hand and pointed towards the deepest shadows in the corner of the tent. 'Witness the Shaman.'

'The Shaman's here?' Kayne rasped, his throat suddenly raw. He squinted into the darkness, thinking perhaps the Magelord had been observing them in one of his many animal forms. But as he strained his failing eyes, all he could make out was the vague outline of a hooded figure huddled on the ground. He took a few small steps closer, greatsword raised, fingers white from gripping the hilt so hard.

The head of the hooded figure was resting on its chest. As Kayne crept closer, the head lifted slightly. The motion was tortuously slow, as if even that simple act took a monumental effort. 'Greetings, Sword of the North,' said a rasping, paper-thin voice. It was the antithesis of the voice Kayne knew so well, the booming baritone of the man he had served for over a score years. But something in that pitiful utterance stirred old memories, and he knew beyond doubt that it belonged to the Shaman.

Kayne spun back to Carn Bloodfist, a hundred questions on his lips. The hulking chieftain merely shook his head. 'He grows weaker by the day. Krazka used some hellish weapon to inflict a

22

wound that refuses to heal. We thought him immortal, but all things die.'

Kayne stared at the hooded figure, his face hidden behind the cowl. He had once thought the Shaman a god, or the closest thing to a god that could still be found in the world. Now he could have simply reached out and snapped the Magelord in half. For all his dreams of vengeance against his former master, for all the fury that had given him purpose over the last few years, the realization unsettled him.

*The world never stops changing.*

'I swore an oath,' Carn said then, abruptly. 'I mean to see it fulfilled. But I also swore a second oath. I have difficulty deciding which is the greater.'

'What was this second oath?' Kayne asked quietly, though he reckoned he knew.

The chieftain's great fist clenched and he slammed it down onto the makeshift table. The crate cracked beneath the impact. 'To mount Krazka's head on a spike above Heartstone's walls. To drive the demons that now infest our land back to the Borderland.'

Kayne nodded, took a deep breath. This was the opportunity he'd been waiting for. 'Got a promise of my own to keep,' he said slowly. 'To keep, or die trying.'

Carn gave him a knowing look, dark eyes glittering. 'Your son still lives. Krazka placed him in a wicker cage at the summit of the Great Lodge, a warning to those who might seek to cross him. The Butcher King is fond of spectacle... as my people learned only too well fourteen years ago.'

Kayne grimaced. It all came back to that fateful day. 'I can't change what's done,' he said slowly. 'But I can offer my sword in the fight to come. Figure you need all the help you can get.'

The chieftain of the West Reaching turned Oathkeeper over in his hands, as if seeking an answer to the unspoken question in the runes etched into the blade. The silence stretched out, the tension so thick Kayne fancied he could reach out and touch it.

Until finally Carn grunted. 'We move on the gates at dawn,' he announced. He got up and opened his travel chest, began searching for something within. 'The battle for Heartstone will be as bloody as any ever fought in the High Fangs. Krazka commands demons. Heartstone's circle of sorceresses wields magic mightier than that of my own, for most were slain by the Butcher's Kingsmen the day the Shaman fell. Perhaps a legendary killer such as the Sword of the North can swing the balance in our favour.'

'I hope I can,' Kayne said evenly, though the other man's words hardly filled him with satisfaction. He didn't want to be a legendary *anything* any more. Only a decent husband and father, if the spirits would give him the chance.

Carn hardly seemed to hear him. 'I mean to keep one oath,' the chieftain rumbled. He'd obtained a whetstone from within the chest and ran it down the edge of his rune-etched broadsword, the steel shrieking like a host of doomed souls screaming for justice. 'And afterwards, I mean to keep another.'

\*

The snow had finally stopped falling by the time Kayne found somewhere to unpack his bedroll and set it down on the bitter earth. There were near ten thousand men in the great camp that had been erected west of Heartstone and he could feel the hostile eyes boring into him. Not a few of his new allies might have relished sticking a blade in Kayne in the middle of the night if the opportunity arose, but Carn had placed a guard to watch over him. Kayne gave the fellow a polite nod as he settled down to build a fire. The guard spat, then fumbled with his breeches and relieved himself, yellow piss steaming as it splashed onto the snow.

*Wish it were that easy for all of us*, Kayne thought glumly. His own bladder had been stubborner than an angry she-bear for days

# No Limits

KRAZKA YAWNED, STRETCHED, and then rolled over on the bed. He lifted an arm and placed it lazily on the figure beside him, absently stroked his lover's back. The flesh felt cool, in stark contrast to the endless burning in his face where the Shaman's fist had half torn it off. He'd grown to enjoy the barely concealed horror in the eyes of his subjects when they saw the shattered hollow of his cheek, the ear half hanging off his head. He even took a twisted pleasure in the throbbing agony. It reminded him he was alive.

After all, only the dead felt no pain.

The room was still dim, the single candle lighting the king's chamber casting only a meagre light into the grey gloom. Krazka always woke with the dawn: this was his favourite hour, the silent stillness before the sun bathed the world in fire and noise. The dawn was ripe with potency; in its heady embrace a man could dream that he might achieve anything, be anything.

*Reach for the stars.*

He dreamed of his mother often. Remembered her voice when the weight of the world began to wear on his shoulders and he needed a little encouragement to keep him on the path right and true.

*Reach for the stars.*

He sneered and his grip tightened on his bedmate's shoulder, his nails digging into skin. Of course, his old ma had never told *him* to reach for the stars. Only words he ever remembered uttered by the whore who had spilled him into the world were those she'd left him with as she let go of his feet and turned away.

*I don't love you. I'm sorry, I just don't love you.* Hard words for any babe to hear, not made any sweeter when it was his third naming day and he'd just been dropped head-first into a cesspit no less than twice a man's height and that was before you counted the huge stinking mound of shit at the bottom.

He hadn't cared about revenge at the time. That'd come after. But even then, barely able to walk even without taking into account the fractured leg he'd suffered in the fall, he knew that he had to climb up. To keep on reaching if he wanted to survive. So that's what he'd done, until he emerged from the pit three days later, covered in filth and looking like a demon crawled out of the abyss. Still, all that was the past. The future was what mattered now – and it belonged to *him*.

*Reach for the stars.* He heard the Herald's voice in his skull again, the hint of amusement in the demon lord's words, as if they held a double meaning, some joke only it was privy to. Krazka wasn't fond of anyone making jokes at his expense, but he figured a twenty-feet-tall fiend with razor claws and fangs could be excused. If only the Herald would hurry its scaly arse back to Heartstone and bring a horde of its kin with it, the situation with the three armies surrounding his city would look a good deal less vexing.

He yawned again, then gave the unresponsive figure beside him a shake. He stopped when he suddenly recalled the climax of last night's entertainment. 'On second thoughts, I'll let you rest,' he said wryly.

He turned the shake into a fierce shove and the corpse tumbled out of the bed. Lifeless limbs flopped around the man, whose head settled at an awkward angle, arched up to reveal the bright red maw in his throat. His dead eyes were still wide with shock. Krazka chuckled at that. 'They call me the Butcher King,' he murmured. 'What did you expect?'

He rolled from the bed and stepped around the body to retrieve his clothes, pleased to see they were unsullied by the blood glistening on the old wooden floorboards. He got dressed, threw the great white cloak made from the pelt of the Highland cat he had killed over his shoulders and fastened the clasp. The huge cat had ambushed him in a mountain pass many years ago. He'd ended its life armed with nothing but a pocketknife, though the fight had cost him an eye. You didn't take much out this world without giving a little in return.

He strapped on his sword belt, pausing a moment to draw the single-edged blade from the scabbard and admire the perfect balance. Demonsteel – or *abyssium*, as the Herald had named the metal from which it was forged. It could be found nowhere in the earth, for according to the Herald abyssium did not belong to this world. With it, no magic could harm Krazka. Carn's sorceresses had learned that lesson the hard way. The Shaman too, though it was a different, even more dangerous weapon that had done for their erstwhile Magelord.

Krazka reached down to the opposite side of his belt and caressed the hilt of the deadly tool holstered there. Then he rubbed his blind left eye with the back of his hand, wiping away the film of mucus that always formed during the night. Most would consider losing the sight in one eye to be a disadvantage, but Krazka found that it helped him focus. Helped him see through the web of a thousand lies men and women alike spun to fool themselves into believing the world was a better place than they knew to be true. That they were better than their actions said they were; that all the jealousy, all the cheating, and all the hypocrisy they despised in others was somehow justified in their own twisted little selves.

Krazka had no time for such deceits. He wielded only the truth with all its sharp edges, and if anyone had a problem with that they need only dig up the mountain of corpses he'd left at Beregund and Reaver's Gate and ask 'em why that might not be such a wise idea.

There was a clumsy knock on the door of the bedchamber and it creaked open. The giant bleached skull of a bear began to emerge into the room, but it was too wide for the gap and got wedged between the door and the frame.

'I'm stuck,' rumbled the deep voice of Bagha from beneath the skull. Krazka's eye narrowed and he idly considered drawing his sword and ridding himself of his lumbering oaf of a Kingsman once and for all. But the huge Lakeman had at least proved loyal to him. There was something to be said for loyalty after Wulgreth and the self-proclaimed knight Sir Meredith had upped and disappeared. Not to mention Shranree, his senior sorceress.

With a sigh, Krazka sauntered over to the door and removed the jamb. The door banged open and Bagha stumbled into the room clutching his ridiculous war mace in his ham-like fists.

'First things first, bearface,' said Krazka patiently. 'You knock before you enter the king's chambers. Second, when it comes to keeping a watch out for those who might mean me harm, wearing a fucking great bear skull over half your face don't strike me as perspicacious.'

'I don't know what that word means,' Bagha replied slowly. 'But if you want me to take this off, that's all right with me, boss.'

'If any other man dared call me "boss" instead of "my king" I'd see him lose his tongue,' Krazka said brightly. 'But seeing as you've got shit for brains I'll let it pass. Case you forgot, I crowned myself King of the High Fangs months ago.'

Bagha reached up to remove the skull covering his head. Then he took a step back and stumbled over the body beside the bed. There was a crack as four hundred pounds of hulking Highlander and a hundred pounds of iron war mace hammered into the wooden frame. The giant oaf climbed slowly back to his feet and stared down at the bed, which now sagged heavily on one side. 'Sorry,' he rumbled.

Krazka sighed and pointed down at the corpse. 'I'm gonna go take a walk. Get rid of that.'

Bagha stared at the naked body. His small eyes narrowed beneath his brutish brow.

'Something the matter?' Krazka asked.

'Why's he got no clothes on?'

'Why do people usually not got clothes on? Most times it's because they're bathing, fucking or lying in a hole in the ground. Maybe you could help expedite the latter instead of looming there like the unholy spawn of a she-bear and a tree trunk.'

Even a mind as ponderous as the huge Kingsman's couldn't fail to put the pieces together. 'Ain't right for two men to lay together,' he rumbled.

Krazka grinned. 'You got a man with his throat opened up bleeding out over the floor... and *that's* what's troubling you?'

'It's against the Code,' Bagha muttered, staring down at his huge feet.

Krazka's grin faded. 'The Code's dead,' he snarled. 'These are the new times. The old rules don't apply any more, not that they ever applied to yours truly in the first place. I fuck who I want. Fact is, man or woman, it's all just flesh to be used. Used and then tossed away.'

If a nefarious former outlaw like Bagha – a man who often spoke casually of how he had murdered his own wife – could look uncomfortable at talk of killing, the hulking Kingsman managed it just then.

*

The cold no longer bothered Krazka. Since his bargain with the Herald thirteen years ago – shortly after the massacre at Reaver's Gate – the self-styled Butcher King found himself unaffected by the extremes of both the harshest winter nights and the hottest summer days. His fortieth year had been and gone, but as he marched along the battlements running the perimeter of Heartstone's great wooden palisades Krazka felt stronger than ever. The Herald had told him he would retain the vitality of a man half his age for the rest of his life: one of the many gifts the demon lord's mysterious master, the Nameless, had bestowed upon the one-time chieftain of the Lake Reaching.

Krazka's lone eye swept the snow-covered hills to the west, where Carn Bloodfist's host was encamped. After weeks of skirmishing in the Heartlands, the civil war tearing the High Fangs apart would finally converge on the capital and the fate of the country would be decided. The chieftain of the West Reaching and his vast army would fall upon Heartstone's walls in a great tide. When they did, Krazka intended to be ready.

He had ordered archers posted on the battlements. They bowed as he passed them, though few dared meet his gaze. In truth they hated him almost as much as they feared him, but so long as they did what they were told Krazka cared not. Reasons had never interested him so much as results. Men liked to rationalize their decisions in a thousand different ways, but in his experience the world functioned much the same when you ignored the 'why' and focused only on the outcome.

At regular intervals along the western palisade were hung huge iron cauldrons cast by the smithies at the Foundry. They were suspended over large braziers by chains connected to winches. As soon as Krazka gave the order, the cauldrons would be filled with oil and the braziers lit. The defenders on the battlements would then hoist the cauldrons up to the walls and rain boiling black death down on those on the other side. It was a nasty way to die, though Krazka could think of worse.

*I been blessed with a vivid imagination in that regard.* He reached his destination and stared up at the wicker cage swinging from the gallows above the west gate. He couldn't claim the credit for that particular implement; the Shaman had devised it. The occupant was slumped as far as the prison's wicked design would allow, his body locked in perpetual discomfort. He'd been a hearty young man only three months back; now the former king of the High Fangs looked as frail as someone thrice his years.

Krazka grinned at the sorry sight. A sudden gust of wind set the prison to creaking and he raised his voice to be heard above the noise. 'Enjoying the new view? I reckon you'll do well to survive until Carn's men get here. The winter ain't getting any warmer. 'Course, your old man managed a whole year in one of these things, but then I figure he was made of stronger stuff than his son.'

'Why?' The voice was rasping, broken. 'What... did I do to you?'

Krazka stared out across the vast expanse of the King's Reaching. Just outside the walls, feline shapes patrolled the snowy ground. Occasionally one would disappear and then materialize twenty yards away. The blink demons were few in number but even the Brethren had been unable to cope with their strange abilities. Further distant, lines of squat figures stood unmoving, waiting for the enemy to arrive. Demonkin were the weakest of demons, but the fear they inspired could cause a seasoned warrior to shit his breeches as surely as that of any other fiend.

'You, personally?' Krazka said eventually, when he was satisfied all was in order. 'You ain't done anything to me, save take what was rightfully mine.' Krazka drew his abyssium sword and examined the edge in the light of the nearby torch. 'It should've been me that was made king after Jagar's heart finally gave out. Your dad's favour with the Shaman meant you got the crown instead. Now, your pa might've been my match with a sword or he might not –guess we'll never know, what with him long gone. But he never knew his head from his arse when it came to tactics on the field of battle. It was me that saved the day at Red Valley. Didn't get any thanks for it either.'

From up in the cage there was a harsh sound that might have been choked laughter. 'You're jealous? You did all... *this* because you wanted to be king?'

Krazka's eye narrowed and the world seemed to flicker red. Before he knew it he was pointing the barrel of his deadly weapon up at the cage. He checked himself at the last moment and instead spun the weapon three times before replacing it on his belt. 'Ain't so much jealousy as disgruntlement,' he said. 'I'm sick of *privilege*. Bastards getting something they don't deserve because they was born in the right place or their face fits the image of the man other men want them to be. Take the Sword of the North, your old pa. Got a nice story, I'll admit: sole survivor of a demon attack that massacred his village, goes on to become some great Warden over in the Borderland. Don't hurt that he looks the part, what with those blue eyes. Men need their legends and I guess he fit the Shaman's bill. Still, the thing about legends is that legends cast shadows. I got caught up in his. Krazka One-Eye, the man who crawled up out of a cesspit and fought his way to the top of the pile to become chieftain of the largest of the Reachings. Kayne got to be the hero. I got to be the butcher.'

'You... wanted to be a hero?'

'Naw. I want to be a *legend*. Heroes got a nasty habit of dying before their time. I want to get old and die happy with my name carved into history – a name bigger than any before me. I want the High Fangs, and the Lowlands, and the lands across the great ocean the Herald sometimes whispers of. You got to keep reaching, see. If you're not climbing you're falling and there's only ever death waiting for you at the bottom.'

'But... *demons*...' The voice was growing fainter, the effort of uttering so many words having already exhausted the prisoner.

'You work with what you got. I ain't no great Magelord or Lowland prince. The gods are dead and the darkness of infinity waits for us all in the end. No point living a life with limits. Sentiment's worth nothing. Look what it got your dad. A year spent caged and hounded till the ends of the earth because he let family get in the way of business.'

A weary voice called out, 'For a man who prides himself on action, you talk a lot. The boy's dying. Let him be.' Orgrim

Foehammer, chieftain of the East Reaching and second-in-command of Heartstone's army, joined them on the battlement above the west gate. His face was haggard above his beard, his eyes midnight-dark from lack of sleep. Rana trailed a little behind Orgrim. The thin-faced sorceress seemed uncomfortable in her new role as leader of the town's circle.

'You two make for a sorry sight,' Krazka said jovially. 'And you're late, woman. I said the crack of dawn, not the crack of whenever-the-fuck-you-feel-like.'

'Forgive me, my king,' Rana said, her voice trembling slightly. 'My nephew disappeared last night. I've been searching for him, to no avail.'

'Ah.' Krazka studied the woman's features for the first time. The nose surely bore a resemblance. Hadn't the lad he brought back to his chambers last night mentioned his aunt was a sorceress? He gave her a big grin. 'Let's hope he turns up safe and sound. Right now we got other things demanding our attention.' Krazka reached under his cloak and withdrew the steel tube Wulgreth had brought back with him from the North Reaching. At least that was the story the strange warrior had told Krazka: a lot of things about Wulgreth failed to add up.

The Butcher King raised the looking tube, brought the narrow end up to his good eye. He watched the world dramatically shift in size, bringing into sharp focus pine trees armoured in frost and frozen streams glistening in the maiden light of a new day. And cutting across a sheet of blinding white snow, the dark line of an army on the march.

'They're on the move,' he growled.

Orgrim frowned. 'You said reinforcements would be here by now. If Mace's forces arrive before Hrothgar's men, we're screwed. And the army of the Green Reaching inches closer by the day.'

'Brandwyn's men are more familiar with the wrong end of a sheep than the right end of a sword.' Krazka's voice was thick with contempt. 'I slaughtered all the true warriors of the Green Reaching during their rebellion four years back. Just ask our boy there.' He nodded up at the wicker cage, where Magnar Kayne was as silent as a ghost. Then he drew his long-barrelled projectile weapon with his left hand and his sword with his right and spread his arms towards the approaching army as if preparing to embrace his enemies. 'Let them come,' he snarled. 'I'll build a mountain out of their corpses. Tall enough to storm the heavens a second time.'

Despite his show of bravado, inside he felt the tiny seed of doubt beginning to grow. He didn't like uncertainty, except when it was him inflicting it on others. He closed his eye and focused his thoughts, reaching out for the demon lord whose mind had been linked to his these last thirteen years.

*When?* he demanded silently, not confident he would receive a response. The Herald had been awful quiet of late. *I've sacrificed as you asked. I need backup. Now.*

*Soon*, replied the Herald's voice in his skull. It was a strange sensation, akin to a dozen different voices all whispering at once. The ruined side of his face throbbed wildly, as if something were trying to crawl through his skin. *An old foe has returned and the attention of the Nameless is required elsewhere.* The disapproval in the demon lord's next telepathic sending instilled utter fear in Krazka's heart before the red rage that lived inside him – his own inner demon, that had seen him climb from a cesspit to the throne – flared and burned it to ash. *That hand-cannon you hold... you were told to rid yourself of it.*

Krazka stared at the weapon in his hand – the weapon with which he'd brought down a Magelord. A 'hand-cannon', the Herald had just called it.

*I answer to no one and nothing!* He sent his thoughts with a rage to match that of any demon lord's. *Not you and not this Nameless you serve. Best you remember that. I doubt even your scaly hide could withstand this weapon if it came to it.*

36

Utter silence greeted his outburst, and he wondered if he might have gone too far.

A harsh sound snapped his attention back to the here and now and he realized he was grinding his teeth together. Orgrim and Rana were watching him as if he'd gone mad.

'Well?' he barked. 'The fuck you two doing just standing there? Go organize the town's defences. Hell's about to come to Heartstone.'

# Beyond Redemption

Eremul the halfmage stared at the wreckage of the depository and tried not to choke on the bitterness that welled up inside him.

His life's work was reduced to ash. Thousands of carefully catalogued tomes and scrolls had been burned to cinders. The building was a blackened and charred ruin of collapsed kindling and shattered stone, levelled beyond any hope of repair. The impact of the blasts from the First Fleet's artillery had produced a crack that divided the street itself, a fissure from which smoke still occasionally drifted. This wasn't a temporary inconvenience like in the aftermath of Salazar's destruction of Shadowport, when the waters of Deadman's Channel had risen and flooded the harbour; this was utter annihilation.

*No matter how pitiful that which is lost, the pain is never less than devastating when it is everything you have.*

Once more his tired eyes scanned the rubble for signs of Tyro. The dog was gone. He knew that. Nothing could have survived the onslaught when the devastating cannons opened fire from the warships. The Halfmage had thought a Magelord's power obscene; the realization that every single one of the invaders carried a weapon similar to those cannons in reduced form, small enough to fit in the palm of a hand and capable of enacting instant murder from a hundred yards, made him feel more impotent than he had even sitting opposite Salazar in the Grand Council Chamber.

'We had some good times here, as I recall.' Isaac's melodic voice drifted up from behind him and the fehd officer appeared beside Eremul's chair. Like the rest of his people he stood a head taller than all but the tallest of men, his slender limbs more graceful than those of the nimblest human dancer. The smooth, silver armour Isaac wore covered every inch of him up to his neck. Though it appeared as thin and as flexible as cloth, folding with his movements, the Halfmage had witnessed it turn aside a sword thrust on the night of the First Fleet's arrival. Isaac stared down at the wreckage with eyes like mirrors of purest obsidian, so ancient that, even now, weeks into the invasion, Eremul felt awed and terrified to behold their splendour.

The Adjudicator held up the end of his blue cloak with one hand to avoid getting it smeared with filth. With the other he scooped up a handful of ash. 'I spent many a day sweeping the depository clean. I fear that even with my lifespan, that task would be beyond me now.'

Eremul frowned at the Fade officer, or 'fehd', as he had learned the ancient race more accurately referred to themselves. Isaac had used his strange powers to masquerade as the Halfmage's manservant for years, all the while performing reconnaissance for his people and making preparations for their invasion. Even with the occupation well under way, Isaac still found time to humour his erstwhile master.

'There will be no need for books when your kind is done here,' Eremul said grimly. 'You told me yourself: no exceptions can be made in your crusade.'

Isaac's angular features shifted marginally into what might have been a frown. He fished around the wreckage some more and withdrew a human thighbone. It looked as though it had been gnawed on – an odd detail that made little sense to Eremul. The Adjudicator tossed the bone away and then stared south towards the harbour, where the most gigantic vessel the Halfmage had ever laid eyes upon was sailing into port. 'Saverian arrives,' Isaac announced.

'This general of yours, I assume,' Eremul said bitterly. His heart sank. He knew what this latest development meant. Now the assault on Thelassa would begin in earnest. Once the City of Towers had fallen, as it surely would, the fehd would have no further need of Dorminia as a base from which to launch their invasion of the continent. The Grey City would become expendable, and all within would perish.

'The general,' Isaac agreed, but the music in his voice seemed off-key, strained. 'You shall escort me to the harbour. I want you to witness something. The reason, in the end, why I decided humanity must be expunged from this continent.'

'You sister Melissan already clarified that matter. Right before she blew Timerus's brains out and your *other* sister relieved Marshal Bracka and Spymaster Remy of both their positions and, perhaps even more regrettably for them, their heads. Poison, I believe she called us. A poison that must be purged.'

'She is fond of that particular expression.' The pain in Isaac's voice brought involuntary tears to Eremul's eyes. 'The crimes committed by the Magelord Marius hurt my sister more than any other among us. In her grief she blames herself for the deaths of Aduana and Feryan.'

The Halfmage wiped one of the sleeves of his robe irritably across his face. 'Must you do that?' he said exclaimed angrily. 'Keep your emotions to yourself.'

'Empathetic projection can be difficult to control,' Isaac replied. 'Besides, there is no shame in mourning such a tragedy.'

Eremul's thin lips curled. 'I barely shed a tear when my legs were taken from me. Neither did I cry when your ships destroyed my home and business.' His next words came out as a rasp, and the renewed dampness in his eyes almost turned them into a lie. 'Why, I couldn't even muster a single, solitary tear for the woman I loved.'

He hadn't seen or heard from Monique since the day Timerus had had him falsely arrested for treason. The Grand Regent had promised that Monique was alive and being held somewhere safe, and in return for the Halfmage accepting his execution she was to be released and all charges against her dropped. Whether Timerus had intended to keep his word Eremul would never know, as all hell had broken loose when Isaac's sisters unleashed an army of concealed thralls upon the gathered crowd. Timerus had been among the first to die – and with him the knowledge of Monique's fate.

*That Ishari snake lied to me. He had her killed. Either that or she fell victim to the riots. My one true chance of happiness, torn away. Like my legs. Like my dignity. Like damn near everything.*

Isaac was watching him strangely. The slight twist in his angular features could have been mistaken for sympathy, if the idea were not so preposterous.

*They feel nothing for humanity. We are but a plague to be exterminated.*

'We should proceed to the harbour,' the Adjudicator said. He hesitated before adding, 'I can assist you with your chair. It will be like old times.'

'I can manage,' Eremul snapped back. 'I made it this far by myself.' That wasn't strictly true; Isaac had shadowed him all the way south from the Refuge, the block of warehouses near the Hook where Dorminia's homeless sought shelter. A merchant from the Grey City Cartel had taken it upon himself to arrange the sporadic delivery of food parcels to the most needy. The bread was stale and the soup tasted like something scooped out of a latrine, but it was nonetheless a surprising display of civic-mindedness. Unfortunately, whatever generosity the people of Dorminia could muster in these desperate times did not extend to him. Eremul was now a pariah. Accused of aiding and abetting the city's invaders due to his misguided association with Melissan, he had been attacked on three separate occasions, escaping thanks only to some quick thinking and a judicious display of magic. Without

Isaac to guarantee his safety, there was a good chance he would have been set upon by an angry mob on the way to the docks. Yet another injustice to add to the many that had been heaped upon him.

*If the gods weren't long dead, I might accuse them of lining up to take a shit on me.* It was he who had come closest to uncovering the fehd plot. He who had uncovered the true nature of the mind-controlling mechanical spiders implanted in the thralls. No one on the Council had believed him. Now most of the magistrates were dead, their estates seized by their inhuman invaders. Only the fehd and their thralls were allowed within the Noble Quarter: the foolish few who had attempted to infiltrate the enclave, possibly with delusions of heroism in mind, had been immediately slain. Their occupiers had no interest in torture or grand gestures of intimidation, it seemed. Not when ruthless efficiency worked just as well.

As he and Isaac made their way down to the harbour, Eremul watched the conquered citizens of Dorminia go about their daily lives as best they could. It was a sorry facsimile of normalcy. As he trundled over the crumbling cobblestones and the stench of the wharfs assaulted his nostrils he was reminded of a dead fish he had espied once, its body still flapping in the fisherman's net even after its head had been removed.

*It is the nature of living things to cling to familiarity until the bitter end.* The corpse of Dorminia and its people would continue to twitch in predictable patterns until that end came. 'The Reckoning,' Isaac had called it. *Whatever that may involve, I suspect it does not include a nice cup of tea and a slice of cake.*

The ships of the First Fleet had arranged themselves in a crescent moon formation within the harbour. As the Second Fleet drew into port, the vessels of both fleets formed a great circle around the gigantic flagship that brought up the rear. A hissing noise erupted and the great iron turret that towered almost to the height of the masts at the centre of the ship shook and belched forth a great cloud of steam.

'In the Time Before, ships such as these were considered long obsolete,' Isaac said. 'Almost all of the knowledge of our ancestors has been lost. We are but a pale shadow of what we once were.'

'*Obsolete*,' Eremul echoed, remembering the pant-shitting terror he had felt the night the First Fleet's artillery opened fire. 'If this is what you consider "obsolete" then I hope you never stumble across this lost knowledge. What do you mean by the "Time Before"? Before *what*, exactly?'

The Adjudicator held up a hand to silence Eremul. 'I have said too much already.'

The circle of ships eventually parted to allow the great warship to dock. The flag hoisted from the towering mainmast nearest the prow displayed a blue sphere stained with green patterns and surrounded by an unbroken band of gold. Eremul glanced at Isaac, thinking to ask about the flag's significance, but the fehd officer shook his head, forestalling further questions. He appeared troubled.

A bridge was lowered from the main deck to the dock platform. Soon those aboard began the task of disembarking. There were dozens of the immortals, males and females in equal number, marching in single file with their silver armour glinting and their grey cloaks flapping, revealing the crystalline swords and deadly hand-cannons at their hips. Eremul was surprised to see that not all the fehd were pale of skin and golden-haired: some were as dark as ebony with hair to match, others a lighter shade of brown or with hair as red as a sunset. All were taller than most men and possessed the perfect complexions and too-angular features of their kind.

The procession of fehd slowed and then stopped. A reverential silence settled over the harbour. A moment later, a fehd who could only be their celebrated general stepped onto the bridge.

He was taller even than Isaac, pure white hair framing a face so severe it would make Salazar look grandfatherly by comparison. He moved with astonishing grace, every muscle displaying absolute mastery of his form. The way he carried himself spoke of a singular arrogance – or perhaps certainty – that there was nothing this world, no threat or danger he had not already faced and conquered. He wore a black cloak threaded with silver, and as his penetrating gaze swept over the Halfmage, Eremul wanted to shrivel up and die.

'That… is Saverian,' Isaac said quietly. In contrast to those of his newly arrived commander, the Adjudicator's eyes *did* carry a hint of uncertainty – or so it seemed to Eremul.

*Perhaps this time it is I projecting my emotions upon him.*

'An impressive figure,' Eremul muttered, feeling sick.

'Saverian's legend is second only to that of his brother, Prince Obrahim,' Isaac explained. 'He is of the First Blood, ancient even by the standards of my people. For five thousand years he has led us in times of conflict. Saverian drove the dragons from Rhûn when my kin were still finding their place in this world; Saverian defeated the king of the elves in single combat to mark the end of the Twilight War – a duel that lasted three days and three nights. It was he who imprisoned the entity that followed the Pilgrims to these lands. The nameless horror.'

Eremul stared at Saverian, appalled that such a being could walk among them, in this very city. It seemed that every time he thought he understood the measure of power in the world, some new bastard turned up to ridicule his assumptions.

A crowd of human onlookers had gathered to witness the arrival of the Second Fleet. Most dared not venture too close – the Halfmage saw furtive faces staring from within the shadows of the backstreets and alleys near the edge of the harbour. One of the faces he thought he recognized; it belonged to an unpleasant fellow who kept eyeballing Eremul with undisguised hatred. The Halfmage was still struggling to remember how he knew the man when further movement on the bridge caught his attention. He stared, confused by the unexpected sight.

More fehd were disembarking from the ship. Each of these new arrivals escorted another fehd seated on a wheeled chair much like Eremul's own. The seated fehd were covered head to toe in the most bizarre garb the Halfmage had ever seen – a ludicrously well-padded suit of white fabric, or perhaps leather, which swathed their bodies up to their necks and incorporated thick boots and gloves, as well as a curved glass helmet that entirely covered their heads. Behind the glass, the faces of these seated fehd were incredibly gaunt. They stared blankly with obsidian eyes darker than those of their kin, so black they resembled empty holes in their faces.

The attire looked far too encumbering to be of much practical use. Upon further observation, however, the Halfmage concluded that this hardly mattered. 'Are they *dead?*' he wondered aloud. The strange fehd might have been breathing under their suits, but it was impossible to tell. They were utterly motionless.

'Not dead,' Isaac answered. 'Lost to the Void. All sixty-six of the Pilgrims who survived the voyage that brought us to these lands. Their journey poisoned them all eventually. Neither age nor illness will claim their bodies, but their minds are elsewhere and so they will remain until the end of time. Their sacrifice will never be forgotten. *We* do not abandon our own.' Isaac's obsidian eyes flicked to the small group of homeless orphans watching from a nearby alleyway.

'You wish to teach me a lesson about how fucked-up humanity is? I've already received an extensive education in such matters.'

'The measure of a people is found in how it treats those who have sacrificed for its survival. How it heeds those lessons and applies them for the betterment of those who come after. My kind learned those lessons an eternity ago. We call it the Time Before. Since then, no fehd has intentionally harmed another. No fehd will turn away from another when they are in need. We are all one – and together we live and die as one.'

The Halfmage stared at the orphans. There were fewer of them in the city these days. They were the weakest, the most vulnerable; they had been first to perish when famine had come to Dorminia.

*Those not already dead of the poison introduced into the streets by the White Lady's agents.*

He had to look away. His eyes settled on his reflection in the harbour, and he stared at his broken body in the water. The dying sun bathed the city in blood as Isaac's words stabbed through the blanket of despair that engulfed him.

'The day before Dorminia fell to the White Lady, I took my leave of the city's "liberators". I wandered these streets, searching desperately for a sign that humanity was not beyond redemption. Do you know what I found? Children starving in the Warrens, innocent of what was about to befall them. While in the Noble Quarter, those most capable of averting the tragedy that followed expressed the sentiment that *"at least a brief war might serve to clean up the streets"*. You remember what happened to the Warrens when the White Lady's forces arrived. The devastation wreaked by the trebuchets. The bodies.'

'I remember,' Eremul said, but his voice sounded strange and this time he wasn't sure if it was Isaac's empathetic projection or simply his own dark memories that brought fresh tears to his eyes. 'I was born with little magic and littler capacity to sway the minds and hearts of my fellow man. I am broken and bitter and I would not piss on most of this city's human filth if they were on fire. But if I had it within me to change the fates of those children, whatever it took, I would do it. You have to believe me.'

'I do,' Isaac said quietly. 'And that is why I will weep for you.'

# Going Nowhere

$S$*he was running from the tower, the snip of iron scissors chasing her through the darkness. To either side of her were vast tanks filled with blood. She could hear the thump of tiny bodies within scraping against glass. Revulsion overcame her and she failed to see the turn in the corridor, instead colliding against one of the tanks. She staggered back and stared at the woman within. The naked body floated in the vile liquid, turning slowly, lit by a baleful red radiance emanating from the blood. The woman's eyes shot open and Sasha ran. Ran out of the tower and back into the rain.*

*She was standing on the docks again. The rain poured down, forming a grey shroud over Thelassa's harbour as the fleet of the dead sailed slowly into port. Thousands of eyes stared from severed heads stacked high with architectural precision. Ship after ship emerged through the mist, all bearing the same grisly cargo. Some of the faces she recognized in spite of them having started to rot: neighbours, occasional colleagues, regular Dorminians like her: people with hopes, dreams and ambitions. Everyone in the city had lost someone they once knew. There were too many for it to be otherwise.*

*She stared back at those faces, struck dumb, wondering who or what could have carried out such a ruthless massacre. The putrefying visage of one head in particular seemed to draw her gaze. It was her sister, Ambryl, her blonde hair now lank and shedding out of her desiccated scalp. Flesh sloughed off her sister's once-pretty face. Suddenly Ambryl's eyes shot open, and her mouth formed a name—*

*'Sasha!'*

*Her sister's desperate scream tore her gaze away from her brother's body. Blood still streamed around the handle of the knife embedded in his throat, but it was the way his eyes bulged out of their sockets that held her in a horrified trance. She made a choking noise, turned to Ambryl, who was reaching for her with a trembling hand. Sasha started towards her sister, desperate to get away, to flee the horror of what was happening around her, but just then her father released an agonized roar and the next thing she knew she was knocked to the floor as he charged the men standing over her dying brother.*

*Everything blurred together. Her father's outraged howls. Her mother's sobs. Ambryl's screams, slowly fading as the coward who had brought these killers into her home dragged her outside.*

*Her father staggered away, hands pressed tightly against his stomach. Dark liquid streamed between his fingers. The rebels immediately encircled him like a pack of rabid dogs, beating him down, punches and kicks shattering this proud man who had never bent before anyone. The last thing she glimpsed before she squeezed her eyes shut was his ruined face, crimson tears trickling slowly down his cheeks.*

*It seemed to last an eternity but finally the terrible cacophony of violence subsided, leaving only her mother's muffled crying and the harsh breathing of her father's killers. One of the rebels spoke, grunting out his words in between gasps. 'Stubborn old prick. If he'd done what we asked none of this would've happened. What about the wife and daughter? They're Reds too.' There was something terrifying in his voice. Something hungry.*

*'The Watch will be here soon. Forget them,' replied another of the rebels.*

*'But they're Reds. Loyal to that bastard up in the Obelisk. What mercy did Salazar ever show his enemies?'*

'He's right,' said another voice, in a tone that seemed to suggest the opposite. 'They deserve to be punished too.'

'How old do you reckon they are?'

'The old one? Too old. Her? Old enough.'

'She's just a girl...' said the second rebel half-heartedly – but by then it was too late. She kept her eyes squeezed tightly shut as a rough hand grabbed hold of her ankles and something inside her seemed to explode—

\*

Sasha's eyes shot open. Pain. Her world was filled with pain.

She elbowed and spat and unleashed a volley of curses that would have made a sailor blush. The hand on her thigh released its grip immediately. A moment later a voice groaned, 'Ouch! Damn it, Sash, that hurt. What the hell was that for?'

She blinked the crust of her tortured sleep from her eyes and stared at the wounded expression on the face of Davarus Cole – childhood friend, comrade, and fellow captive atop the Tower of Stars on another bitterly cold night in Thelassa.

'Sorry. Bad dream,' she said.

Cole rubbed his forehead where her elbow had left an angry red mark. 'Which one?' he asked miserably.

'All of them. I think you knocked my ankle again.'

'Sorry,' he said glumly.

She reached down, gingerly prodded the splint supporting the fractured bone. She gave him a look of mock anger. 'Forget that. I don't remember saying you could grab my arse.'

Cole's pale face blanched further. 'I didn't mean to. I was fast asleep. Besides, it was you who suggested we keep close for warmth.'

Sasha immediately regretted waking her companion. Cole looked exhausted. Sleep had been hard to come by for both of them since their imprisonment, but there was a deep weariness in Cole's grey eyes that she had never seen before. Weariness, and also anger. He'd suffered in the last few months. She just wished he would open up to her. It wasn't as if they didn't have all the time in the world to talk, stuck up here on top of this damned tower. She decided to try one more time.

'Are you ill?' she asked softly. 'You don't look right. What happened in the Blight?'

He sighed and looked away. 'I'd rather not talk about it.'

She grabbed a stick and poked irritably at the embers of the small fire they'd managed to build from the possessions the tower's previous guest had left behind. His naked body was still sprawled in the spot where they'd discovered him, stripped of anything they could use for kindling. The freezing conditions had preserved his flesh and he wasn't yet showing significant signs of decay. As far as blessings went it was a decidedly minor one, but right now Sasha would take what she could get. 'Time to stretch our legs again,' she said. 'Give me a hand.'

Cole climbed to his feet and helped her up. Together they walked the tower's perimeter, Sasha with one arm thrown around his shoulders. The merciless stars glittered cruelly in the night sky above, while a dark bank of cloud on the horizon warned that fresh snow was on the way. 'This is bullshit,' Cole said, emptying a mouthful of spit over the side of the tower and watching it fall hundreds of feet to the broken streets below. 'She could've just killed us. Better that than waste away up here like that poor bastard.' He jerked a thumb towards their cadaverous companion.

'I think the White Lady has bigger things to worry about than us,' Sasha replied.

Cole sighed in frustration. 'I just hope the streets don't collapse and take this tower with them.'

Sasha risked a glance over the edge and swallowed the vertigo that threatened to overwhelm her. On the first day of their imprisonment she couldn't get within ten feet of the edge of the tower without feeling faint. Boredom had since largely superseded her fear. 'The foundations will have settled by now,' she said, taking in the view below. 'It could've been a lot worse.'

Great cracks disfigured the once-perfect marble streets of Thelassa. A colossal spider's web of fractured stone coiled away from the monstrous pile of rubble at the centre, the shattered remains of the tower the White Lady had hurled at Thanates during their monumental battle. A few sections of street had plunged into the ruins of the ancient city of Sanctuary beneath Thelassa, but it seemed Thelassa's supports had by and large held firm in the wake of the Magelord's fury. As Sasha scanned the city, she noticed a strange glimmer above the harbour: a white luminescence that hadn't been there a few hours ago. 'What do you figure that is?' she asked, pointing.

Cole stared. 'It looks like some kind of magic. Maybe it's supposed to protect the city from whatever killed all those people aboard the ships.'

Sasha crossed her arms and frowned at the shimmering barrier. *The Fade. Ambryl and I were sent here to warn the White Lady of their coming. The Halfmage wasn't mad after all.* Every one of the hundreds of men and women who had sailed to the Celestial Isles in search of riches had been slaughtered, their heads stacked in neat piles on the ships and sent back to the City of Towers.

Cole shook his head. His face was gaunt, his skin astonishingly pale even taking into consideration the biting winter cold. 'What did you say to the White Lady back in the throne room, anyway?'

Sasha winced. 'Just some home truths.' *I slapped her and called her a cunt. The White Lady. The most powerful wizard in the world.* She remembered the look of disbelief on Ambryl's face then and almost smiled, so absurd did it all seem. Then she remembered her sister's sacrifice and her amusement faded. Ambryl had pushed her away from a falling house and, instead

51

of burying Sasha, the falling stone had claimed her older sister.

'Your cold's getting worse,' Cole said. Sasha blinked away the tears threatening her eyes and wiped her weeping nose with the back of a hand.

She didn't have a cold. What she had was a nose ruined from too much *hashka* and whatever other narcotics she could get hold of. She kept her habits hidden from him, which wasn't hard. Cole was as naïve as a newborn babe when it came to reading other people.

'I still can't believe that Three-Finger tried to rape you,' he muttered, as though he had heard her thoughts. 'I knew he was coarse, but I always thought he had a heart of gold beneath it all. If I ever see that son of a bitch again I'll kill him.'

While she shared Cole's sentiments, the venom in her friend's voice unsettled Sasha. She'd never seen him so angry before. Vain and boastful and, yes, maybe even faintly endearing in a ridiculous sort of way, but never *murderous*. She didn't like this change in him. 'Sometimes people are exactly what they seem to be,' she replied. 'And sometimes they're actually the opposite.'

*The White Lady. She's a monster wearing the face of an angel. Or Brodar Kayne. I could have sworn he was a soulless killer until I got to know him better.* She frowned. Kayne's friend Jerek had threatened to kill her, only to turn into her protector on the battlefield outside Dorminia. Though he might still want to kill her. Some men were just confusing. Some women, too.

*Ambryl.* She had thought her elder sister hated her. Instead she had given her life for Sasha.

'Someone's coming,' Cole hissed, interrupting her thoughts before they could whisk her away to a dark place – or a darker place, at any rate. Sasha strained but couldn't hear a thing. 'The White Lady's handmaidens,' Cole added. 'The Unborn.'

Sasha had just opened her mouth to ask how he could be so sure when the steel grate set into the tower's roof slammed open and two of the handmaidens climbed out. They were followed by four more. The half-dozen Unborn moved to surround Cole, paying Sasha no heed.

*Why would the White Lady send six of her handmaidens to deal with us? One is more than a match for most men.*

'The Mistress commands us to bring you to the palace,' said one of the Unborn, in the emotionless monotone of her kind. She reached into her white robes and withdrew a collar forged of a dark metal.

'For fuck's sake. Not this shit again,' Cole growled. He placed a hand on Magebane's jewelled hilt. 'We'll take any reason to leave this damned tower,' he spat. 'But not with those collars around our necks.'

Sasha stared at the object. The collar was connected to a chain of interwoven links and was clearly designed to allow the holder to lead their captive like a dog on a leash. She might have considered them an affront to her dignity, had she any left. Instead she placed a hand on Cole's arm. 'Relax. It's not worth dying over. We will go quietly.'

The handmaiden stared at Sasha with its dead eyes. 'There is no "we". The Mistress requested only Davarus Cole. You are to be disposed of.'

'*Disposed of?*' Sasha repeated, aghast. She heard the sound of a steel blade sliding from its sheath and in the blink of an eye Cole had positioned himself protectively in front of her. Magebane glowed an angry blue, but there was something else emanating from the blade, a shadowy essence she had never seen before. The air around them seemed to grow even colder.

'The first one of you to make a move, I'll send her head back to the White Lady as a warning,' he said, voice full of fury. Coming from the old Cole, the words would have sounded ridiculous, an idle threat without a rat's turd of weight behind it. Yet as Sasha stared at her childhood friend, she didn't doubt him for a second.

Even so, one thing the Unborn did not fear was death. There was a white blur as the handmaiden closest to Cole darted for Sasha, who froze, knowing she could never hope to escape these creatures. Not in any circumstances, but especially not with a broken ankle and trapped atop the tallest tower in the city.

The handmaiden – incredibly agile, the unholy creation of the White Lady's secret laboratories – stumbled, Magebane sticking out of her side. Cole's arm was around the creature's neck in an instant. With his free hand he tugged the weapon loose and, in a shower of black gore, sliced open her throat. The stench hit Sasha's nostrils and she gagged, though there was nothing in her stomach to puke up.

'That's one less of you,' Cole said, pushing away the twitching creature. Sasha had witnessed first-hand how tough it was to stop the handmaidens; she had seen them fight on with broken spines during the battle outside Dorminia's gates. And yet her friend had ended the handmaiden's unnatural life with an ease that shocked her. The Unborn twitched a few more times and then lay still.

'You are stronger in our Father's essence than we, brother,' said one of the remaining handmaidens. 'Yet we still outnumber you five to one.'

*Brother?* Sasha had no idea what the creature meant – but her surprise immediately turned to astonishment as the tower's previous occupant began to stir, climbing slowly to its feet, limbs cracking and lolling head turning to face the Unborn.

'Five to two,' Cole said. His colour had returned a little. It was as though killing the Unborn had restored some of his vigour.

There was a pregnant pause as the five surviving handmaidens inclined their heads. They seemed to be listening to something. Receiving instruction, perhaps.

'The girl lives,' said one of the Unborn, eventually. 'For now.'

A small part of Sasha wanted to take umbrage at being referred to as 'the girl' in this city, a matriarchy ruled by the most powerful woman in the world. But all things considered, she was too relieved to care.

*

The White Lady's palace was still being repaired: the gilded doors to the throne room lay where they had been blown off their hinges during her showdown with Thanates. Sasha's heart thundered at the sight of the twisted metal. As she and Cole were led across the threshold and the eldritch ruler of the city bled into view, sitting atop her ivory throne, violet eyes staring straight ahead, she wanted to turn and run. But there was nowhere to flee.

The Consult was already assembled. Rows of women and the occasional man were seated on the benches below the throne, all dressed in white ceremonial garb and forced to stare up at their mistress as if she were one of the dead gods depicted upon the mosaic overhead. But she was not a god – she was a killer of gods. Once high priestess of the Mother, one of the thirteen Prime gods, Alassa – as Thanates had named her during their confrontation – had switched sides from the religious Congregation to the wizardly Alliance after her own child had died in her womb. And after watching her hurl a tower at Thanates, her former paramour, Sasha understood an alarming truth: this Magelord's wrath was singularly terrifying once unleashed.

*And I slapped her across the face and called her a cunt. Oh, shit.*

The White Lady rose to her feet as Sasha and Cole were brought to stand before the dais. 'Leave us,' she ordered, her soft voice perfectly serene, her purple gaze still unreadable. 'All of you.' She nodded at the Consult, who quickly rose and departed the chamber.

In the silence that followed, Sasha could hear her own heartbeat thundering in her chest. She kept her eyes fixed on the marble floor; she dared not look up and meet the Magelord's gaze.

Cole wasn't so awed. 'Why have you brought us here?' he demanded.

'I ask the questions, child,' the Magelord replied. 'You are no less impertinent than the last time you stood before me. More so.'

'Well, things have changed,' Cole replied. His voice was grim. He placed a hand on Magebane's hilt. 'Where are my friends?' he demanded.

'Your friends?' echoed the White Lady.

'Derkin and Ed. They were at the docks when you had us arrested.'

Sasha finally risked a glance at the Magelord. Her beauty was stunning – platinum blonde hair and perfect features unmatched by any living woman Sasha had ever laid eyes upon. But inside, Sasha knew, this woman was monstrous. Worse than Salazar, if such a thing were even possible.

'I care nothing for your friends, child of death. You are less important than you seem to believe. Even with a stolen god's essence residing within you.'

*Child of death? A stolen god's essence?* The Magelord's claims hardly seemed credible. The Cole of old would have shouted something like that from the rooftops at every opportunity, yet now he winced with what appeared to be shame. 'I'll answer your questions if you help me find my friends,' he replied. 'One is a hunchback. The other is big and childlike. They're both good men.'

A hint of anger hardened the Magelord's voice. 'The first time you set foot in this city you brought a rapist with you. The second time, you brought Thanates. Do not talk to me of good men, child.'

'I was wrong about Three-Finger,' Cole admitted. 'But Thanates – the Crow – he saved us at the Blight. You wanted to have us all killed. Just like you tried to have the Darkson assassinate me. Well, he didn't succeed. I slew one Magelord. Perhaps I can kill another.'

Sasha stared at Cole in shock. There was no bravado in that utterance, none of the cockiness that had somehow propelled Cole through the direst of situations through the sheer power of his own bullshit. The threat was delivered with the gravity of a man telling his wife he'd caught cock-rot from the local streetwalker.

The White Lady frowned and then raised a slender hand. Cole responded by reaching for Magebane. There was a scraping sound; something huge and golden slammed into Cole from behind and suddenly he was pinned to the floor by one of the gilded doors, some unseen force pressing the full weight of the ruined metal down upon him.

The White Lady stepped from her dais. Ignoring the stairs leading to the throne, she floated gently down to stand beside Cole, who appeared to be struggling for breath. He met Sasha's eyes and the desperation on his face snapped her out of her shocked stupor.

'Stop! You're killing him,' she pleaded. 'Please... You summoned him here for a reason. Kill me if you have to. I'm no use to anyone.'

The Magelord ignored Sasha. She ran a strand of platinum hair through her fingers and stared down at Magebane, clutched uselessly in Cole's pinned hand. 'You overreach yourself, child. Your weapon may protect against magic, but it holds no sway over that which magic can manipulate. Your share of the Reaver's divinity, while significant, establishes you as nothing more than a talented tool. I hold the essence of no fewer than *five* gods within me. Only Salazar held more.'

'I'm not a tool,' Cole managed to hiss.

'Please,' Sasha begged again. 'Let him breathe.'

Another few seconds passed. The Magelord appeared to be deliberating. Finally she unwound the hair from her finger and flicked it behind her shoulder. The door shot up and flew out of the throne room, hitting the far wall with an almighty clang. Cole groaned and gasped for breath as the White Lady frowned down at him with her purple eyes.

'True power must be seized with both hands,' she said levelly. 'Do not run from what you are, child. You cannot serve our cause by refusing your true nature. Submit to the hunger and it shall empower you.' The White Lady turned to an attendant waiting nervously by a far door. She pointed at Magebane and beckoned the attendant over. 'Pick that up and keep it safe. It will be returned to him once he has departed the city.'

The Magelord turned to Sasha, who wanted to cower away. Instead, after a glance at the stricken Cole, she met the White Lady's gaze with a loathing she couldn't disguise.

'I have not forgotten your error. No one has dared speak to me in such a manner for five hundred years. Much less lay a hand upon me in anger.' Remarkably, the White Lady's purple eyes glittered with something that might have been amusement. 'I had thought your sister the interesting one, but you surprise me. I shall overlook your outburst this once. Now, help your friend up. His journey will take some days and time is of the essence.'

Sasha knelt beside Cole. He was in some pain but didn't appear badly hurt. 'Where are we going?'

'*You* are going nowhere, at least for the time being. Davarus Cole, however, will be heading south. The Shattered Realms must be informed of the imminent threat to our species.'

'Threat?' Sasha whispered, though deep down she knew. The Halfmage had been right all along.

'You recall the warning you brought me. The massacre of the workers at the Celestial Isles was but the beginning. While you were imprisoned, the Fade arrived in the Trine. Dorminia has fallen. I am all that stands between the Ancients and the end of mankind.'

# The Right Tool

COLE NARROWED HIS gaze and stared at his reflection in the extravagant mirrored basin. The Consult chambers on the upper level of the White Lady's palace were richly furnished, luxurious enough to make Garrett's mansion look threadbare in comparison. How he wished his foster father and mentor were here now.

'It's all bullshit,' he whispered. He began to turn, but in a moment of sudden rage spun back and struck the mirror with his bare fist. The glass shattered and a shard sliced his knuckles, raining blood down into the basin. It stung, but the pain felt familiar, natural. It helped take his mind off the insidious hunger within him.

The urge to kill was growing stronger. It was always present, goading him. The Unborn he had killed had barely sated it; the creature was more dead than alive. He couldn't shake the memory of watching Sasha sleeping atop the Tower of Stars. Having to resist the desire to draw Magebane and do something unspeakable. It made him sick to remember. Sasha – his best friend and the girl he loved more than anything in the world.

He leaned over the basin and dry heaved, horrified at the memory. *What am I becoming?*

The essence of the Reaver dwelled within him. The Reaver, the Lord of Death. When Cole killed and fed the dead god's hunger, he became faster. Stronger. Almost unstoppable, an assassin without peer. But when he refused, as he had since the rebellion at Newharvest, it took a toll on his body. The hunger grew worse until it was all he could focus on. When he slept, visions of a great disembodied skull and rivers of blood tortured his dreams. He avoided sleep when he could.

He pressed his uninjured hand against his forehead and squeezed his eyes shut in despair. He had wanted to be a hero. Now he stood on the precipice of becoming a monster.

'Cole, it's time.' Sasha limped into the chamber carrying the bags she had helped prepare for his journey south. She stopped when she saw the shattered mirror and the mess he had made of the basin. 'What happened?' she demanded.

'I had an accident,' he mumbled.

'Let me see that.'

Cole refused to meet her eyes as she grabbed his hand and began rummaging around in the bags for something to stem the bleeding. 'Carhein is a day's ride east, once you've docked in north Tarbonne,' she said angrily. 'You won't get far if you bleed out before you make it out of Thelassa.'

'Why Carhein?' he grumbled. 'Why not somewhere on the coast? I hear Djanka is already warm this time of year.'

'You're not going on vacation! You're to bring word of the Fade invasion to the Rag King and plead with him to send reinforcements. Tarbonne is the most powerful of the Shattered Realms. They say the Rag King and his Companions were once like us, before they won the throne. Perhaps they will listen where others won't.'

Cole grunted. He wouldn't have minded jumping aboard a ship and sailing south to the Sun Lands to seek out the Darkson. The scar on his stomach still ached, the legacy of his former mentor's betrayal. He wanted payback on that smooth Shamaathan bastard.

'Cole?' Sasha's voice dragged him away from thoughts of revenge. 'What did the White Lady mean, about the Reaver's divinity? And about you "feeding the hunger"? How *did* you bring that body back from the dead?'

Cole heaved a sigh and examined the bandage Sasha had just wrapped around his hand. 'You remember Garrett's history lessons?'

Sasha rolled her eyes. *So lovely*, he thought, before looking away. 'You know I was always the studious one,' she replied. 'You were more interested in being the hero.'

*A lot of good that did me*, he thought bitterly. He cleared his throat. 'Well, you know that when Salazar, the White Lady and the other Magelords stormed the heavens, they didn't just kill the gods. They stole their power. That's why Magelords don't die of old age. They carry the essence of the gods within them.'

Sasha nodded. Her dark brown hair fell prettily around her shoulders. He swallowed before continuing, his mouth suddenly dry. 'Salazar and I shared a connection through Magebane. You see...' He took a deep breath. 'My father wasn't really a hero, Sash. He was an *Augmentor*. Salazar's most feared killer.'

Much to his surprise, Sasha nodded again. 'I kind of figured as much. The other Shards were careful not to discuss it around me, but it wasn't difficult to piece it all together.'

*Maybe not for you*, Cole thought, anger warring with admiration. She was smarter than him; perhaps the smartest person he knew. 'When I killed Salazar, I absorbed the essence of a god he carried within him.'

'The Reaver,' replied Sasha. 'The Lord of Death.'

'Yes. I feel him inside me, Sash. Hungering. Eager for me to kill. I'm not sure I can control it. I'm scared.'

He closed his eyes and therefore could only hear Sasha's surprised intake of breath. 'I never imagined I would hear you say those words.' Suddenly she embraced him and he sagged in her arms, lowering his head to rest against her shoulder. He could hear her beating heart and smell her sweet scent. He lifted his head and gazed into dark eyes filled with concern. He felt irresistibly drawn to them, and below them, her soft lips—

'*You're an arsehole, Cole. Garrett would be ashamed of you.*'

Sasha's parting words before the siege of Dorminia rose painfully in his skull, as did the memory of his tortured nights watching her sleep atop the Tower of Stars, and he quickly drew back. 'Right,' he said abruptly. 'That's enough feeling sorry for myself. I'd better get ready to sail. Are you going to be safe here alone?'

Sasha looked a little hurt by his sudden withdrawal. 'If the White Lady wanted me dead, I wouldn't be here now. I'm more concerned about you.'

'You shouldn't be. I'll return safe and sound, I promise.'

There was a moment of awkward silence before Cole's enhanced hearing picked up a faint whisper of movement in the corridor outside and one of the White Lady's handmaidens appeared in the doorway. Unlike with Sasha, whose heartbeat was a persistent throbbing rhythm in his ears, he could detect no pulse from the creature. 'We leave now,' said the Unborn in its deadpan voice.

Cole collected the bags Sasha had prepared for him and gave her one final hug. 'Time to be a hero,' he muttered to himself.

\*

*Why me?*

The question had been dancing around his brain since the White Lady had revealed her plans for him. Maybe she'd been quietly impressed by his success in assassinating Salazar and escaping Newharvest and considered him the most capable man for the job. Maybe she feared his powers and this was merely an excuse to send him away. Most likely it was just the fates conspiring to once again take a cosmic shit on him and force him into all manner of crazed situations that left him bitter and broken. What was it Thanates had said?

'*You have an uncanny knack of finding yourself at the heart of events.*'

As Cole made his way through the twilight streets of Thelassa, silently escorted by a trio of the White Lady's handmaidens, he wondered what had become of the Dalashran wizard-king. He somehow doubted Thanates had perished as a result of his battle with the White Lady; the grim wizard seemed like the type of man it would be unwise to pronounce dead until his corpse had been observed rotting in a morgue for at least a week. Among other things, Thanates had survived being flogged, hanged, having his eyes pecked out, and spending the best part of five centuries trapped in the body of a crow. It was comforting to know there were still a few folk who had had it worse than Davarus Cole.

The operation to repair Thelassa's streets was well under way. Even at this late hour, the wide avenue leading to the harbour was teeming with citizens clearing away rubble and fortifying the city's damaged foundations. He watched a team of workers haul a statue of a winged, angelic creature upright. The tip of one of the wings had broken off and Cole spotted it lying near a shrub. He scooped the fragment up from the marble streets and handed it to the forewoman, giving her what he considered his most charming smile. She snatched it from his hands and turned away with a scowl.

'A thank-you wouldn't have hurt,' he mumbled, unable to stop himself.

She spun back towards him. 'What did you say?' she demanded.

'I said, a little gratitude wouldn't hurt.' He hadn't wanted to make a scene, but recent events were starting to get the better of him.

The forewoman looked as though she was about to launch a tirade until she noticed the Unborn lurking nearby. She blanched and quickly returned to her work. Cole shook his head, remembering how women used to flock to him in the good old days, eager to share a smile and sometimes a bed. Not now. Not with him disfigured by a badly healed nose and scars from his various escapades. He was a monster, inside and out. No better than these Unborn. Except at least they were still relatively attractive, in a corpsey kind of way.

*A corpsey kind of way... What does that even mean?* He shook his head, disgusted with himself, and almost tripped over a crack in the street he had failed to notice, lost as he was in his thoughts.

'You should concentrate on where you are going,' said the nearest of the Unborn.

'That's easy for you to say. Some of us have actual worries to distract us.' Cole's eyes focused on the handmaiden. He remembered something Thanates had told him about; the sight of Captain Priam and his Whitecloaks lurching around Newharvest as though they were drunk, or drugged, or both. 'You feed on the living,' he said accusingly. 'You drink their blood. Don't you?'

'It is necessary in order for us to exist.'

'Then you shouldn't exist. You're abominations! And not the abominations created by wild magic. You're a worse kind.'

The Unborn tilted her head slightly, watched him with those strange, colourless eyes. When she eventually spoke Cole was shocked to hear the slightest tremble of emotion in her voice; as faint as the ripple caused by the wings of the smallest insect passing over a stream. 'We *know* what we are, brother. The child inside us – the child we all once were – is not entirely gone. It knows what it is we do.'

Cole passed the remainder of the journey to the harbour in a horrified silence.

The White Lady was waiting at the docks when Cole and his escort finally arrived. The entire harbour was lit by the silvery glow of the magical barrier Cole and Sasha had first spied from atop the Tower of Stars. It surrounded the city's port as far as the eye could see: a faintly glimmering, translucent wall. Thelassa's fleet was arranged in a defensive line opposite the barrier. The navy looked formidable in the ghostly light; like a spectral armada descended from the heavens themselves.

'Davarus Cole,' the Magelord greeted him. 'I trust you are prepared. You will sail aboard the *Caress*.' The Magelord gestured to a small caravel Cole knew well: it was the same ship he and his small group of companions had used to escape Salazar's justice in the weeks before the assault on Dorminia. That seemed like a lifetime ago, but in fact by Cole's reckoning it had barely been four months. He looked up at the flag flying from the mainmast, saw the outstretched palm of a woman cradling seven towers. The meaning was clear: this was the White Lady's city, built in her image and fostered by her immortal grace. It seemed impossible anything could threaten her here – and yet the single bead of sweat that rolled down the Magelord's brow, the slight tremble of her lips, proclaimed the severity of what she now faced.

'Seek out Zatore in the palace,' the Magelord continued. 'She was once my apprentice and now advises the Rag King. Deliver her my message. Tell her the need is great. She alone can convince the king to send every soldier Tarbonne can muster, and those of other Realms over which he holds some influence. I will lower my barrier to allow the passing of the ship that will carry you south.'

'Why me?' Cole dared ask, finally giving voice to the question that had been nagging at him all day.

The Magelord raised a perfect eyebrow. 'I believe you are a catalyst for events that will shape the world. A marker in the Creator's grand design. What mages refer to as "the Pattern". Put simply, you are chosen.'

'*Chosen?*' Cole echoed. He once had believed himself chosen, destined for great things. Lately, though, it seemed all he had been chosen for was endless bad fortune.

'No more questions. My handmaidens are needed elsewhere, and so you will sail with a human crew. Your friend, Sasha, convinced me to place one of your "associates" among those on board. Do not make me regret my beneficence.'

Cole was led onto the caravel. He took one final look at Thelassa as he walked across the bridge connecting to the deck.

He could see the palace in the distance, framed by soaring spires, like fingers reaching for the stars. The city was indeed beautiful. Despite the horrors of Sanctuary that lurked far below, despite the Unborn, despite its enigmatic and possibly crazed ruler and her monumental crimes, Thelassa was a city of mostly contented men and women. Cole had once thought of the world as black and white, composed of good and evil, heroes and villains. Now he realized that no one man or woman could lay sole claim to either extreme. Life was complicated and filled with shades of grey.

He stepped onto the deck – and was immediately swept up into a giant hug that lifted him right off the wooden boards and left his feet dangling. The happy moaning sounds and overripe stench that washed over him could only belong to one man. Cole finally prised his head away from the big hairy chest and stared up into the grinning face of his friend Dull Ed. The huge halfwit released his bear-like grip and Cole dropped to the deck, wincing at the pain in his chest.

*Between Ed's crushing hugs and being pinned under a door, my bruises will be blacker than a Sumnian come tomorrow.*

'Ghost!' exclaimed Ed, in his ponderous voice. It was his nickname for Cole from their time together at the Blight, and in a strange way he rather liked it. He doubted Ed would have remembered his real name in any case.

'Midnight's here,' Ed said happily.

'Who's Midnight?' Cole asked. He stared around at the small caravel's crew. There were a dozen of them, men and women in equal number. The captain gave him a welcoming nod. The man who appeared to be her first mate busied himself checking the sails. It was probably a trick of the light, a reflection of a fire in one of the houses nearer the docks, but the first mate's gaze seemed to burn red for the briefest of moments. Something small and furry skittered across the deck and Cole leaped back in surprise.

'That's Midnight!' Dull Ed exclaimed with delight. 'I brought her with me in case she gets lonely. Her brothers and sisters died, just like mummy cat.' Ed's face grew sad.

Cole remembered finding Ed nursing the corpse of a burned-up cat the night of their return to the City of Towers. One of the ex-prisoners from Newharvest, Smokes, had senselessly set the cat on fire during the riots. Ed had rescued her kittens just before Cole showed up. He stared at Midnight, now curled up in Ed's big hands, and felt a stirring of sympathy for the animal. Just like Cole, she had no family. She was alone. 'I promise you I'll help take care of her,' he said, and gave his friend a pat on the shoulder. 'But right now we should get some rest. I'm looking forward to sleeping in a real bed for a change.' It was a sorry state of affairs when a cramped cabin bed aboard a caravel was a welcome comfort, but anything beat sleeping on the hard stone roof of the Tower of Stars in the middle of winter.

As Cole went to investigate his accommodation for the journey south, he had the uncomfortable sensation someone, or something, was watching him.

\*

*He was spinning again. Spinning through the darkness, his arms and legs locked in place. Even attempting to move his facial muscles was a torturous struggle that seemed to last an eternity. He knew it was a dream; he had endured this same nightmare many times. It did nothing to lessen the terror he felt.*

*He could smell the rancid breath. It enveloped him like a disease, a pestilence. He knew what awaited him at the end of this journey. It was always the same. He didn't want to open his eyes, didn't want to see that dreadful visage again. But he had no choice. He opened his eyes.*

*The skull-planet filled his vision. The maw gaped, teeth like mountains yellowed with the decay of millennia. He saw the god's own eyes then – like twin moons, putrid, the colour of*

*curdled milk. They glowed evilly, a green radiance that filled him
with nausea.*

*And then the god spoke.*

*'Child.' The voice seemed to echo from an impossible distance.
It filled his ears, as deep as the deepest abyss, so powerful it
seemed to reach beyond space and time. 'You resist me.'*

*'I don't want to be a killer,' he tried to say, but his mouth
might as well have been stuffed full of rocks.*

*'You are a killer, child. Death is what you are. My chosen
implement. The one who shall open the door to my return. To the
return of all of us. Prove yourself worthy, child.'*

*Cole tried to scream, to shout for help, but his moans sounded
pathetically weak. No one could hear him. No one would come
to his aid.*

*He was almost inside the cavernous maw now. The Reaver's
hot breath burned like a furnace. But then in an instant it was
snuffed out, and the gargantuan disembodied skull disappeared,
leaving only blackness and its final words drifting out of the
ether.*

*'Prove yourself...'*

*

Cole's eyes snapped open. His heart was hammering. He lay
paralysed for a moment, trying to distance himself from his
terror, reminding himself it had all been a dream. Slowly the
familiar sensations returned to him. The smell of oiled wood.
The slightly musty odour of his mattress. The sound of seawater
lapping against the hull. His eyes began to adjust and he made
out the faint outline of the door to his cabin. It was slightly ajar,
which struck him as strange. He remembered closing it and
pulling the latch—

There was a dark blur and he jumped, almost banging his
head against the ceiling above. A warm bundle of fur rubbed

against him and a soft *meow* caressed his ears. He grinned ruefully, cursing himself for a fool. Once upon a time he would boast that he possessed nerves of steel. Now he was scared of a kitten. He could hear its heartbeat, soft and rapid. He closed his eyes again and took a deep breath, praying that this time his sleep would be free of the nightmarish visions.

Then he heard the other heartbeat.

This one was human, and getting nearer. It was extremely soft, as if whomever it belonged to had mastered the calming techniques the Darkson had taught Cole during his training in Sanctuary. An assassin, then.

He reached out, felt the cold hilt of Magebane beside his bed. The captain had returned the weapon to him shortly before their departure.

The shadowy outline of a man ghosted through the door. Cole remained perfectly still, faking sleep, waiting for the moment.

Two pinpricks of red stared at him through the darkness. The intruder whispered something unintelligible and they flared a brighter red.

Cole gasped as Magebane grew hot in his fingers, absorbing the hostile magic that had just been directed at him. He dived from the bed, heard a curse from his would-be killer, who turned and fled back through the door. Not just an assassin. A mage also.

Cole was up and after the man in an instant, naked feet pounding across the cold floorboards. The door leading up to the deck was wide open, letting in starlight from the night sky above. Cole hurtled up the stairs, dived into a roll and came out on the deck with Magebane held before him, preparing for an attack.

The deck appeared to be deserted. Where the helmsman ought to be there was only a dark smear. The ship's wheel creaked gently of its own accord. Cole's eyes narrowed. There was something *dripping* from it. He heard a creak—

Cole somersaulted away at the very last moment as the assassin dropped from the rigging above, landing with catlike grace in the spot he'd been standing. The figure straightened. In his hands he clutched a long, leaf-bladed spear he had procured from somewhere. His gaze burned even brighter now – like two red rubies caught in a fire. Around his neck glittered a golden key.

'Lord Marius sends his regards,' said the assassin. His voice was velvet-soft. 'The master didn't mention that you wielded abyssium. It does not agree with the laws of our own world. Simply put, it breaks magic. But that is of no consequence. I have had three hundred years to learn many other ways to kill.'

'Who are you?' Cole asked. 'Where are the crew?'

'I am called Wolgred, also the Wanderer by my peers. Those crew who were sleeping are still in their beds. Those who were not...' The assassin gestured with his spear at the dark smears on the deck. 'The blood calling is never sated for long, alas. One learns to drink when the opportunity arises.'

Cole took a deep breath and tried to focus himself the way the Darkson had taught him. As he stared at this Wolgred, he knew he was over-matched. This assassin was not just a masterful fighter; he was some kind of demonic wizard possessed of powers Cole had never encountered. He considered hurling Magebane and hoping for the best, but without the magical resistance the dagger provided he would be dead in an instant, turned into yet another smear on the deck.

Cole's indecision was resolved for him. Wolgred leaped at him, impossibly high, his leaf-bladed spear angling downwards. Cole rolled out of the way just in time and dived behind a crate, almost crashing into the body of one of the crew, which was crumpled in a heap. Cole placed a hand on the corpse. It was warm. 'Rise,' he whispered. 'Rise up and help me.'

With an unintelligible moan, the corpse began to climb to its feet. Wolgred's soft laughter reached Cole from the opposite side of the crate.

'You think a *zombie* holds any fear for one such as I? You'll need to do much better than that, boy.'

'I'm not a boy,' Cole hissed. He tensed, then sprang over the crate, aiming a kick at the assassin's head. He'd hoped the corpse he had just raised would distract the assassin enough for the attack to connect, but instead the haft of Wolgred's spear batted aside his foot. The butt of the spear rose and thwacked him in the stomach and then he was knocked back against the crate, Magebane slipping from his grip to clatter to the deck several feet away.

Wolgred levelled his spear. 'I confess I am disappointed,' the assassin said. 'The master indicated you might prove a more formidable adversary. I will deliver him your shrivelled heart after I have emptied you.'

Wolgred pulled back his spear. Something tiny darted past the mage, but all Cole could focus on was that deadly leaf blade poised to skewer him.

'*Midnight! Come back!*' Suddenly Ed was barrelling towards Wolgred. Cole glimpsed Midnight scampering away and racing up the mast, but the halfwit was unable to change course. He slammed right into Wolgred, whose spear plunged into the halfwit's stomach and went straight on through, bursting out of Ed's back. The big man stood dumbfounded as Wolgred tried to pull his weapon free.

Cole's fingers closed around Magebane. He lined up the dagger and threw it.

It struck the assassin in the chest and sank deep. Wolgred fell to his knees and almost immediately the assassin's flesh began to wrinkle. He screamed and dropped his spear, grasping desperately at the ruby hilt sticking out of his chest. There was a moaning sound and the corpse Cole had brought back from the dead stumbled into the assassin, bit down hard on Wolgred's shoulder and then dragged him to the deck.

Cole ignored the sounds of tearing flesh and Wolgred's screams. Instead he rushed over to Ed, who was still staring at the spear impaling him, red drool hanging from his chin. 'G-ghost,' he stuttered. 'I'm cold...'

'It's okay, Ed. I'm here.' Cole choked back tears as his friend sagged in his arms, his wet breathing becoming weak and laboured. Once, Cole had been able to heal Derkin's mortally wounded mother by channelling the life force of a man he had killed into her body. He lacked any such stolen vitality to channel now. He looked at Wolgred, but the assassin was a husk, whatever magic had kept him alive for three centuries stolen by Magebane, returning his body to its natural state. The dead crewman Cole had raised loitered uselessly nearby.

'I'm sorry, Ed,' Cole sobbed, his voice cracking. His friend's eyes were beginning to glaze over. That hated presence within Cole, the voice of the Reaver, urged him to retrieve Magebane and consume Ed's life force before it fled completely, but he ignored it. Instead he laid his friend down on the deck and knelt beside him.

Ed's eyes fluttered open. 'Midnight?' he asked, his voice paper-thin.

'She's here, Ed. She's here. I'll look after her like I said I would. I promise you.'

Ed smiled. And then his friend's eyes closed for the last time.

Cole remained there for a while, his own eyes squeezed tightly shut, hot tears running down his cheeks. Finally he rose and walked over to Wolgred's withered corpse. He bent down and placed a hand on Magebane's hilt. The dagger came free of the assassin's desiccated chest with a dry snap.

He drove his boot into Wolgred's fleshless face as hard as he could. He felt bone crack and he stomped again, crushing the assassin's skull, grinding it down until all that remained was the golden key he had worn around his neck. Cole picked it up and stuffed it into a pocket, then sat down on the deck and stared up at the stars. Shouting began to erupt on the deck as the rest of the crew, woken by the noise, came to investigate, but he ignored their questions. Yet another person close to him was dead, and all he could hear were the Reaver's words echoing endlessly around his skull.

*Death is what you are.*

# A Good Day For Killing

THE DAWN BROKE bright and blood-red.

Brodar Kayne stared up at the sun and blinked away the sleep that gummed his eyes half shut. He was aching all over: from the long ride north from the Green Reaching, from the shitty sleep on uncomfortable ground, from the beating he'd received from Finn and his friends. Even his brief encounter with Carn had resulted in him pulling a muscle in his leg. He stretched it out painfully, then climbed to his feet and took stock of the camp. All around him, men were preparing to march. Within an hour they would reach Heartstone's walls.

He grabbed a bowl of steaming hot stew from a mess pot and wolfed it down. The day promised to be clear but ball-shrinkingly cold. In Kayne's experience, a good day for killing.

He finished his morning exercises and decided to take a walk around the perimeter of the camp. As he'd noted the previous day, most of the warriors were very young. He saw two boys in their mid-teens sparring and resisted the urge to wade in and show them the correct way to parry an overhead slash. It was too late to matter now, and chances were no one would be of a mind to listen to what he had to say anyway.

It was a funny thing, fame. Nothing made a man feel quite so important and welcome when it was the right sort of fame. Nothing made him feel quite so isolated and alone when it was the wrong sort – and sooner or later it always ended up being the wrong sort.

*Killing only ever begets killing. Ain't nothing good ever came of knowing how to use a sword to murder a man.* Mhaira had told him that. She had wanted him to retire, to become a shepherd and shear sheep. Instead the Shaman had summoned him to Heartstone and the next thing he knew he was cutting throats. Got him even more fame than serving as a Warden for ten years, and a nice farmstead for his family out in the Green Reaching, but he lost everything that made him proud to call himself a man.

He wasn't much for prayer – certainly not to the gods down in the Lowlands. A dead god seemed even less useful than an absent one. But he still believed in the spirits. A wise man, a *veronyi*, was leading a ritual over by a small formation of stones often used for such purposes. Kayne loped over to join them.

He knelt down and took a handful of earth in his battered hands, then sent a quick prayer to the spirits of earth to keep his wife safe until he could return to her. It'd been a few years and he was doubtless even uglier now than before he left, but he hoped she would welcome him back with open arms.

*She will. Of course she will.* Mhaira's love was purer than anything he had ever known. But he needed to keep his promise to her. The promise he'd made the day they fled the Shaman and split, him attempting to lead the Brethren away while she made for the Borderland.

*They caught her in the Devil's Spine, or at least that was the lie they told me.* In actual fact, Magnar had made a desperate deal with the Shaman to spare Mhaira, while her cousin Natalya took her place on the Magelord's pyre. The Shaman used magic to alter Natalya's appearance in order to fool Kayne into believing it was Mhaira who burned. To teach him a lesson, or so the Magelord had since claimed.

Kayne rose and dusted off his hands, a deep frown on his weathered brow. He was half of a mind to turn right around, burst back into Carn's tent and take his revenge on the Shaman for all the wrongs the bastard had done him. That had been the plan before Krazka had stolen the throne and made a pact with a demon lord. Since then, Kayne's priorities had changed and now he found himself once again on the same side as the Magelord of the High Fangs. He heaved a weary sigh. Alliances changed so swiftly up in the Fangs; all he could do was cling onto what to seemed the right thing at any given moment.

Kayne resumed his walk around the camp, but he was soon struggling for breath and had to stop. His chest hurt again and the familiar tingling sensation in his arm had returned. He was so damn exhausted he found himself bending over, hands on his knees, shaking and sweating despite the cold.

*The hell is wrong with me?* he thought furiously. He could've gone to seek out a healer and asked them that very question, but that might mean receiving an answer and he wasn't sure he was ready to hear one just yet. He needed just a little longer, in any case. Just a little more time to rescue his son and find his wife. Then at least if his heart gave out it would give out full.

A man couldn't ask for much more.

'You're the Sword of the North, aren't you? Come, have a drink with me.'

Kayne slowly straightened, taking deep breaths. The tingling began to subside and he took a few halting steps towards the young fellow who had just hailed him. He was a handsome chap with a brown beard and short, curly hair. He was sitting by a campfire and warming a mug of mead over the flame, watching Kayne with a curious smile.

'Nice to see one friendly face,' the old warrior muttered. He settled down on a rock beside the fire and grimaced at the stiffness in his knees. 'Some warriors snort *jhaeld* before a fight,' he said. 'Reckon mead's always a safer bet.' He accepted the offered mug and took a long sip.

The curly-haired fellow nodded. 'They say that about you. That you never bothered with the fireplant.'

Kayne raised an eyebrow and wiped his beard with the back of one hand. 'Who says what now? *Jhaeld* can lend a man courage, but not skill, and it impairs his judgement. In my experience a clear mind is worth more than hot-blooded fury. That ain't to say there's not a time and place for both, mind. Eh, who are you again?'

'My name's Shakes.' The fellow held out a hand, which Kayne grasped. It trembled slightly in his grip, but Kayne was polite enough to pretend he hadn't noticed.

'Strange name. There a story behind it?'

'Well now,' the fellow said. He glanced down at the spear at his side and looked embarrassed. 'That was the nickname my brothers gave me. I get the shakes in battle, you see. Can barely hold a weapon without accidentally stabbing the man next to me. Figured I wouldn't make much of a warrior, so I decided to become a bard instead. Lend better warriors courage through my song.'

'A bard, eh? You mean like the warrior-skalds of legend?'

'Aye. Except I prefer to avoid fighting entirely if I can help it. I spent some time down in the Lowlands learning from the virtuosos of the Garden City. Only a few merchant caravans ever made the journey over the years. I couldn't pass up the opportunity when it arose, though that's one trip I never want to make twice.'

'You can say that again,' replied Kayne. 'What are you working on now, if you don't mind me asking?'

'I figure we have enough songs about Grazzt Greysteel and the heroes of the Golden Age. I intend to pen a new epic, one for the Age of Ruin. A saga to make future generations look back and wonder if perhaps it wasn't all grimness and darkness after all. That there are and were some things worth fighting for.'

Kayne nodded. 'Seems a noble enough goal. Got any subjects in mind?'

'I want to write a song about your deeds.'

'My deeds?' Kayne spluttered. 'I ain't ever done much worthy of song. Not since I was young, anyway. The less said about the latter years the better, I reckon.'

Shakes stroked his chin thoughtfully. 'May I ask about your companion? They say the Wolf never leaves your side. Yet I don't see him here.'

Kayne flinched as if struck. 'Jerek is... we parted ways back in the ruins of Mal-Torrad. Don't reckon we'll see each other again. Probably for the best.'

*If I ever see you again, I'll kill you.*

Kayne took another sip of the warm mead and grimaced. It was too sweet. Too sweet for the sudden bitter taste in his mouth.

Shakes didn't appear to notice his discomfort. 'Then let me ask about your relationship with the Shaman.'

'We ain't got no relationship.'

The bard stuck a hand in a pouch on his belt and rummaged around. He withdrew a quill, some ink and a sheet of parchment. 'It is said you were once close. You were his chosen champion, they say. Why did he turn on you?'

Kayne shook his head. 'It's a long story.'

'You can make it short. Or you can march alongside me and tell me everything. It might help take our minds off what awaits us at Heartstone.'

Kayne glanced at the parchment trembling in the bard's hands. He blew out his cheeks, blinked his blue eyes and took another sip of mead. 'Well,' he said. 'I ain't much of a storyteller, but I could use the company. It happened like this...'

\*

*The expression on his son's face told him immediately that something was wrong.*

*The Sword of the North bowed slightly to Magnar, and then to the Shaman, who was watching him from behind the throne, massive arms folded grimly in front of his chest.*

*'I came as soon as I received the summons,' he said uncertainly. 'Your mother's been unwell, son. It's the sickness*

*in her lungs. The sorceress you sent says she has something there, a growth of some kind. She says there ain't no magic that can stop the body attacking itself.' He glanced at the Shaman, looking for some kind of confirmation, but the glacial blue eyes of the Magelord of the High Fangs were narrowed in a fashion that cut that path of conversation off dead.*

*'The Green Reaching has declared independence,' the Shaman growled. The vein in his thick neck looked fit to burst. 'Brandwyn had the note delivered by raven this morning. He disputes the new tax on the winter harvest. Decries it as unjust. This is my domain, yet he dares reject my terms?'*

*The scraping sound in the throne room was the Magelord's teeth grinding together. Kayne met his son's iron gaze, dread rising within him.*

*'I told you we couldn't trust Natalya, Father,' Magnar said quietly. 'She manipulates Brandwyn. You know she's been sharing his bed since her husband Gared passed.'*

*Kayne shrugged helplessly. 'What do you want me to do, son? Kill her? She's your mother's sister.'*

*'She is a traitor!' the Shaman boomed. 'I have granted you too much leeway to deal with this situation as you deem fit, Sword of the North. You also, Magnar Kayne. I made you king. The youngest since I came to these lands. You disappoint me.'*

*Kayne swallowed hard, his mouth dry. Maybe he'd been too soft, allowed matters to get out of hand. Brandwyn declaring independence? That was madness! He remembered what happened the last time a Reaching had attempted to secede. He remembered Red Valley, the blood that had been spilled the day the West Reaching had surrendered.*

*'I will make amends,' Magnar said. 'Father will travel to Beregund and execute Brandwyn.'*

*Kayne nodded slowly. 'Aye, I can do that.'*

*'And Aunt Natalya,' Magnar added. Kayne's gaze locked with his son's, eyes of blue meeting those of grey, his mother's*

eyes. He wanted to protest, but his son, the king, gave a tiny shake of his head.

'And Natalya,' Kayne said, in a strangled voice.

'No.' The Shaman pronounced the word like a hammer striking an anvil. 'There will be no half-measures. Beregund must be put to the sword. Everyone in the town shall be executed.'

Icy claws seemed to pierce Kayne's flesh. He shook his head furiously. 'Why?' he demanded. 'There ain't no justice in that. Punish those responsible, aye. But I ain't hurting no more innocents.'

The Shaman's voice dropped to a low rumble. His muscles tensed, rippled like there was liquid iron dancing beneath his bronze flesh. 'Are you refusing me, Sword of the North?'

The younger Kayne spoke before the older could. There was a desperate edge to his voice that made his father flinch. 'The Green Reaching is too important to allow rebellion to fester. Without the food it produces, the High Fangs will starve. Removing Brandwyn will only delay the problem. You have to see that, Father.'

'No more innocents,' Kayne growled.

The Shaman took a step towards him.

'Wait,' Magnar said, pleading with the Magelord, begging him. 'Let my father have a day to think on all of this. You know he has friends in Beregund. This isn't easy for him.'

The Shaman took a deep breath, visibly forced his rage under control. His massive chest swelled like a bellows. 'Very well,' he said grudgingly. 'A single day. For loyal service rendered. But know this, Kayne: to defy me is to commit treason, and to commit treason is to die by my hand. None are above this law. Not even you.'

'Krazka stands ready to move,' Magnar added. There was shame in his grey eyes. 'His army will join ours at the border of the Lake Reaching. I'm sorry, Father.'

Kayne turned away. 'A day,' he echoed. 'You'll receive my answer then.'

'The answer was no?'

'Aye, it was no. I rode straight back home to Mhaira and we fled the Green Reaching as soon as we could saddle another horse. Didn't make it far before the Brethren caught up with us.'

Carn Bloodfist's great host had finally come to a halt. Heartstone's thick wooden walls were just ahead, the height of three men, teeming with archers on the battlements and, if Kayne knew that bastard Krazka, nastier surprises for the approaching army.

Shakes placed his quill, ink and parchment back in his pouch. He hadn't stopped scribbling for the entire hour of their march. 'This has the makings of an epic tale.'

'I got the feeling it won't have a happy ending.'

'Perhaps not. But I'm rather fond of tragedy.'

There was the sound of snow crunching behind them and the two men turned. A warrior approached, trailed by a group of his comrades. Kayne's heart sank when he saw that it was Finn, the angry Westerman with the birthmark on his cheek who had roughed him up the evening before. He shot Kayne a look of utter loathing. 'The chieftain demands you join him at the van.'

Kayne's eyes narrowed. 'Carn wants me at his side? Strange place for a man he swore to kill.'

Finn spat. 'Krazka's sent his demons out to play. We need men with experience fighting fiends.'

At that, Kayne nodded. It'd been a while since he'd tested his sword against a demon. Though it wasn't an experience he was eager to repeat, he had to admit he found a joy in killing fiends; he had never experienced killing men, save maybe that bastard Skarn.

Kayne bid farewell to Shakes, then set off to find Carn and his entourage. He'd only gone a few steps when someone tripped him from behind and for the second time in as many days he fell flat on his face, scraping his chin painfully on frozen snow. He looked up to see Finn glowering down at him. The young Westerman jabbed Kayne painfully in the ribs with a boot. Finn's friends looked on with amusement.

'I saw you clutching your chest back there, old man. I don't know how you fooled the chieftain into believing you're worth keeping around, but I see the truth. You're a washed-up charlatan with nothing left except a reputation as false as a whore's screams. Stay out of my way once the fighting starts or next time you won't get up. That's a promise.' Having said his piece, Finn stormed off.

Kayne climbed slowly to his feet, waving away Shakes' efforts to help. He spat out snow and shook his head ruefully. 'I got the feeling that one don't like me.' A crowd of warriors had watched his humiliation from over by a small stand of trees. There was something disturbingly familiar about one of them, a broad-shouldered warrior with a hood pulled over his head. Kayne blinked and the man was gone, if indeed he had ever existed. Old age and bad eyes could play all sorts of tricks on the mind. As could nerves.

He squinted up at Heartstone's walls, and then at the sun one final time. It was a good day to kill. A good day to die.

# A Good Day To Die

'To the walls!' Krazka screamed. The tide kept coming, a flood of men throwing up grappling hooks and ladders, desperate to scale the palisades with scant regard for the arrows and boiling oil raining down on them. Many died, but more kept taking their place.

*It's the demons*, he realized. The supernatural fear that radiated from the demonkin had initially driven the first wave of attackers back towards the hills, only for the deserters to be swiftly thrust forward again by those marching behind them. With their countrymen blocking off their retreat, the panicked warriors had rushed headlong towards Heartstone with the kind of conviction a whole plant of *jhaeld* couldn't instil.

*Turns out fear and courage are two sides of the same coin when you spin it right.*

Krazka was angry now. Spitting furious, in fact. The Herald had gone silent and Hrothgar's men had failed to arrive as promised. Krazka had already sliced an ear off Hrothgar's eldest and had it delivered by raven as a warning some weeks ago. It seemed the chieftain of the Blue Reaching had been unmoved. With no reinforcements forthcoming, Krazka resolved to remove the boy's head when the opportunity arose. True, it would put him in a poor bargaining position if there had simply been an unexpected delay, but he reckoned they were past that now. It would feel pretty fucking good, that was a fact. He'd be damned if he was going to endure the stresses of kingship without letting his hair down every once in a while.

He reached the western wall just as a terrified Westerman began hauling himself over, the metal claw of his grappling hook wedged firmly in the wall. Krazka cleaved the top half of the man's skull off, then yanked the grappling hook free and choked another man with it, pulling the rope so tight around his neck the bastard's face turned blue. He kicked that corpse from the battlement too, watched it tumble to the snowy ground below. Westermen were milling around down there, readying ladders for another foray.

'Somebody bring me a cauldron,' he bellowed. 'I want those fuckers boiled alive.'

A group of defenders rushed to obey. As they were positioning the cauldron, however, one of the men slipped and it upended inside the palisade, raining bubbling oil down on the warriors below. Their screams did a grand job of unsettling everyone around them, and Krazka's good eye narrowed in fury. He whipped out his hand-cannon, as the Herald had referred to it, and shot the clumsy son of a bitch square in the face. That didn't really improve matters much, but at least there was now one less incompetent fuck around to make a mess of things.

'Where's Orgrim?' he roared.

'Here,' came the answering bellow from Foehammer. The big chieftain of the East Reaching was down by the gate directing a last-ditch defence. Already the gates were hacked and splintered in a dozen places. Bagha was with him, making even Orgrim look small beside his colossal frame, the great war mace he carried splattered by the blood and pulverized brains of the Westermen he'd killed.

'Why aren't the demons holding them off?' Krazka barked. He hadn't expected his fiendish allies to be so ineffective, not after the carnage they'd wreaked the last time Carn's army had come calling.

'The demons met with unexpected resistance,' answered a thin Lakeman who was leaning on the battlements. He was tossing daggers in the air and catching them by the hilt. Occasionally he would peer over the wall and heave one at the attackers down below. Krazka recognized him as Lenka, one of three brothers from his neck of the woods. All ruthless killers; the best kind.

'This will be the part where you elaborate,' Krazka said, when Lenka failed to add anything more. 'If I wanted a juggler, I'd hire one.'

Lenka shrugged. He had a languid manner, gave the impression there wasn't anything in the world important enough to demand more than half his attention at any given time. 'Most men shit their pants at the thought of fighting a demon, but there's a few out there that seem to have it down to an art. One's a big bastard with a magic sword, looks like. Screams whenever it strikes flesh.'

Krazka scowled. 'That'll be the Bloodfist himself. Got one of these tiny metal shots with his name on it. Be hard to miss with a forehead like his.' Suddenly there was a whooshing noise followed by an explosion of heat. The walls shook and fresh screams cut through the morning air.

'Breach!' someone yelled. 'Magic!'

Krazka cursed. 'Someone fetch Rana,' he barked. He raced down the battlements towards the melee that was taking place just inside the newly opened gap in the wall. Flames licked the jagged edge of the opening and several bodies smouldered on the ground nearby, caught up in the fireball that had blasted a hole in the palisade. A dozen defenders were facing off against a similar number of Westermen. The latter looked to be getting the upper hand as the Butcher King arrived and so he drew his single-edged sword, his demonsteel blade, and spun into battle. He flowed like a dancer, twisting and turning, cleaving off limbs before pivoting around and dashing back to finish off his opponents. One bald fucker with a mace tried to crush his head with a wild swing; Krazka leaned back and watched it swing harmlessly wide, then stepped inside the arc of the man's clumsy effort and casually placed his hand-cannon against the fool's skull. An instant later his brains were painting the shocked faces of the Westermen to either side of him. Krazka wasted no time in cutting them down while they gawked.

In less than a minute it was over. The bodies of the Westermen littered the snow in a spreading pool of crimson, Krazka standing casually at the centre, beads of blood dribbling from his sword onto the snow. A sudden gust of wind howled through the gap, clearing the smoke beyond and sending his fur cloak fluttering behind him. His good eye narrowed. On a slight rise just beyond the town's walls was the sorceress, her hands raised in the act of casting another spell. The Butcher King grinned and stalked towards her.

Before the woman could notice him, something dark and vaguely feline materialized out of the air behind her. She jerked suddenly, her arms flopping uselessly by her sides, her magic disrupted. A barbed tongue burst from her stomach, tasting the air. Then it slowly withdrew, leaving the unfortunate woman staring down at the blood and viscera now pumping from her gut. A moment later the blink demon pounced, rending the sorceress apart with its razor claws.

There was a flutter of movement behind him and Krazka turned. It was Rana, the leader of his own sorceresses. Her face was pale; she looked like she might retch. 'Let that be a lesson,' Krazka said, gesturing at the pile of human flesh that had so recently been a living woman. The blink demon had already departed in search of new prey. 'Always watch your back.'

Rana swallowed. Either spit or vomit, it was hard to say. Like most women, Krazka thought, she had a weak stomach. But when she finally gathered herself enough to speak, it was *her* words that somehow left a knot in Krazka's gut. 'Brandwyn's forces have arrived at the south gates. They have sorceresses with them. And there is something else, my king. The Sword of the North is here.'

*

Brodar Kayne had seen some carnage in his time, but the initial assault on Heartstone was as bloody as anything he could remember. His countrymen weren't much for tactics, and with the demonkin waiting for them on the approach to town the fighting erupted into chaos almost instantly. This wasn't like the carefully planned assault on Dorminia back in the summer: this was wild butchery.

Carn's men numbered ten thousand strong, fully twice the number Heartstone had within its walls. But if the siege of the Grey City had taught Kayne anything it was that defending a city was a hell of a lot easier than attacking it. Fact was, the Sumnian army that took Dorminia would've made easy work of Heartstone. The army of the West Reaching had none of the great siege engines the dark-skinned people of the south had brought to bear. It was a sobering realization – that for all his people's renowned ferocity they were hopelessly behind the times.

*It ain't familiarity that breeds contempt,* Kayne reckoned. *It's progress.*

His thoughts were interrupted as a fleeing Westerman clattered into him. Kayne barely kept his feet before grabbing the man by the jerkin and spinning him around. His eyes were mad with terror and Kayne knew the demon-fear had him in its thrall. Nothing he could say or do would quell the fellow's terror and so he offered him a sympathetic pat on the shoulder and let go of his jerkin. The warrior sped off, so manic with fear that he almost immediately collided with a stray boulder and knocked himself cold.

Moments later Kayne saw the source of the Westerman's terror. Two demonkin were moving, gibbering, towards the group of warriors Kayne had attached himself to. Their elongated arms flailed around their squat and hairless bodies and their shapeless faces yawned wide to reveal needle-like teeth. They had no eyes: demonkin were blind. Still, their ability to sniff out warm blood was like nothing natural. As Kayne watched they each bore a warrior to the ground, their teeth biting down, chewing through bone as if it were paper.

He fell upon them, his greatsword slashing down. He heard leathery hide split, felt their skeletons buckle beneath the force of his blows. Demons didn't die nearly as easy as men and they continued to snap at him, claws raking at his flesh, their razor nails carrying the demon-rot: a terrible sickness that caused a man's skin to blacken and fall off. He winced as he felt their dagger-like fingers scrape along his leather vest, seeking the softness beneath.

With a grunt he crushed the skull of the remaining demonkin and then stood there gasping for air, ichor dribbling off his greatsword to fall steaming to the snow. He glanced towards Heartstone's walls, saw the first wave of warriors trying desperately to scale the palisades as arrows rained down. Demons patrolled the town's perimeter, locked in battle with groups of Westermen brave enough to stand their ground. An ear-piercing shriek cut through the cacophony of battle and Kayne saw the towering figure of Carn Bloodfist wading his way through a group of demonkin. The chieftain cleaved left and right with his magical sword, Oathkeeper. Where it bit into flesh the demons seemed to explode, body parts raining down everywhere, the enchanted rune-etched steel emitting a high-pitched whine as though it were screaming for vengeance.

'Keep up, old man,' grated a voice beside him and Finn sped past, his comrades in tow, making their way towards Carn. A group of warriors had formed a shield wall around their great chieftain. Kayne made to join them, but then stopped dead in his tracks as a nightmare materialized right in front of him.

The blink demon melted out of thin air, bloody drool slobbering from its oversized mouth. There were clumps of hair still stuck in its claws – a woman's, by the look of it.

It had a been a blink demon that had massacred Kayne's village as a child. Killed his brother Dannard while Kayne cowered in fear. The tricky, catlike demons had earned a prized place of hatred in his weary old heart.

The demon's tongue shot out, probing towards Kayne, who raised a hand. The tongue wrapped around his wrist and the old warrior gritted his teeth as the serrated edge began slicing into his flesh, but he didn't slow, didn't deviate from what he knew he had to do. When you made a choice to do something in a fight to the death, you did it right and you did it quickly. Hesitation had killed more men than the plague.

He levelled his greatsword in his free hand and then stabbed straight ahead, driving the tip into the fiend's sole central eye. The steel pierced the surface and went in a good few inches before the demon realized what was happening and tried to use its tongue to tug Kayne towards it. Rather than try to resist he drove forward instead, using the creature's own momentum, shoving his sword deep into the demon's flank and giving it a cruel twist. It tried to fade away, to escape somewhere where it didn't have three feet of iron lodged in its body, but by then it was too late. It died thrashing and screeching, Kayne trying his best to avoid getting mauled by the demon's claws as it perished right there on the snow.

Once the demon had finally stopped twitching, Kayne unwound the fiend's tongue from his wrist and examined the damage. It was bleeding heavily, hints of bone exposed in parts. He tried flexing it, noted with relief that his hand still seemed to be working. Pain was just pain. Pain he could tolerate, though there'd been times when he thought death might've been preferable. Fact was, a greatsword wasn't much use with only one working hand.

He half stumbled and half ran towards Carn and the others at the wall. The city's attackers were finally breaking through the western gate. Eldritch energies lit the morning sky to the south, where Krazka's circle and the handful of sorceresses Brandwyn had brought with him from Southaven were engaged in a magical duel.

Carn noticed Kayne's arrival. The chieftain's cavernous voice boomed above the din. 'Krazka's demons are routed. Now the battle truly begins. They say you've taken the lives of more men than winter itself, Sword of the North. Now is the time to keep your promise.' The chieftain of the West Reaching pointed at the top of the wall, where Kayne's failing eyes could make out a gibbet hanging near the gate. His heart, already hammering after his struggle with the blink demon, felt like it would explode.

It was the wicker cage he knew so well. The cage in which he had spent a year of his life. The cage in which he had been told Magnar had spent the last few weeks.

It was empty.

*

'Escort the boy out of the east gate,' Krazka ordered. 'Don't be gentle, but don't kill him. Not yet. Got a feeling he might be a useful bargaining chip if needed.'

Lenka and his two brothers leered at Magnar Kayne, and Krazka felt a hint of envy. No one had leered quite as well as he had before the Shaman had fucked up half his face. He wondered what had become of their erstwhile Magelord. Feeding the worms, hopefully. The Butcher King might just go down as the first mortal to slay a god-killer, and wouldn't that feat look mighty fine in the telling of his legend?

'Will do, boss,' said Lenka. His brothers grinned, their lips bright red against their pale skin. Krazka had heard they liked to drink the blood of their slain enemies. They reminded him a little of Ryder, before old dogface had disappeared down in the Greenwild weeks ago. The three brothers were terrible men, the worst of men: perfect henchmen, in Krazka's estimation. Good men tended to let their consciences get in the way of what needed to be done. Besides, loyalty was something that existed only in fantasy. Fear ruled the hearts of men and women alike: fear and greed. *Give 'em enough of both and you have them in the palm of your hand.*

Magnar stirred in Lenka's grip. The deposed king of the High Fangs was wasting away. His skin was covered in sores and he had numerous scars where Krazka had cut chunks out of him. Even so, Magnar had proved tougher than he looked; most men barely survived a week in a wicker cage. He gave the prisoner a kick in the ribs to rouse him, though the young Kayne was so weak he hardly made a sound. 'Heard a rumour your pa is here,' Krazka said cheerfully. 'Don't expect any grand rescue. Today is a day for burying legends.'

*And birthing new ones. Aye, when we move on the Lowlands the world will know the name of Krazka One-Eye. From the furthest reaches of the High Fangs down to the Sun Lands of the black men. Always wanted to see a black man in the flesh.*

There were renewed shouts from the west gate, followed by a sudden increase in the sounds of clashing steel and men dying. Orgrim Foehammer hurried over. Behind him was Rana, as well as a sorceress Krazka thought might be named Polga or something equally provincial.

'They've broken through,' the chieftain of the East Reaching growled. 'We're outnumbered.'

Krazka sighed and examined his reflection in the mirror-like blade of his demonsteel sword. 'How badly?'

'Two to one.'

Krazka turned to Rana. 'Reckon you can spare a few sisters?'

Rana looked skittish. She always looked skittish, Krazka noted. It annoyed him. She was a woman, not a fucking horse. 'We can perhaps spare one or two, but if Brandwyn has any sorceresses in reserve—'

'Send three of your best here. Tell them to wait until the fighting has intensified near the western gate. Then burn everything.'

Rana blinked. 'Burn everything?'

Krazka tilted his head and cupped a hand to his ear. 'There an echo somewhere? Aye, everything. Burn the western gate and everyone around it to ash.'

'You can't do that,' Polga spluttered. She was a middle-aged woman of unremarkable appearance. Could be someone's mother or grandmother, except sorceresses were forbidden to marry. Krazka sometimes amused himself by wondering how they satisfied themselves in the absence of a man. Right now he had the sudden urge to see how this sorceress liked two and a half feet of steel shoved up her arse. 'Why's that?' he asked, his voice a dangerous whisper.

'You'll kill the town's defenders,' she replied slowly. As if speaking to a child.

The world began to turn red. Krazka scowled at Orgrim. 'How badly we outnumbered?' he asked again.

'Two to one,' repeated Orgrim.

'Well then, we'll kill twice as many of them as our own. That's how you win wars.'

'You can't,' repeated Polga. 'I won't do it.'

Krazka raised an eyebrow and turned to Rana. 'What d'you say? You gonna refuse your rightful king?'

The leader of Heartstone's circle stood there stupidly, mouth flapping like a fish out of water. 'Here,' Krazka said. 'Let me help you make up your mind.' Three steps were all it took for him to reach Polga. Three seconds were all it took for her unremarkable face to strike the snowy ground after he cut her head off. Blood fountained out of the corpse, covering the shocked Rana head to toe before the body crumpled to the snow.

A moment later the Butcher King's sword was at the neck of his most senior sorceress. 'Choose,' he said evenly. 'Obey or die. Them's the only two options. What'll it be?'

Rana's face was as white as a ghost's. 'Obey,' she squeaked.

Krazka nodded. 'You tell the other sorceresses what I just told you. Anyone who argues will end up like Polga here: meat for the crows.' He turned to Lenka. 'Once my predecessor is safely away from the fighting I want you and your brothers back at the west gate. Wait till the magical assault is finished and then pick off any survivors. Move fast and kill quick.'

Lenka raised a lazy eyebrow. 'Sounds dangerous. What's in it for us?'

Krazka grinned. He liked the man's backbone. To a point. 'Double the share that was promised once Carn is routed. A realm to share between the three of you after we conquer the Lowlands. Me not cutting off your ugly heads right here and now.'

Lenka exchanged a look with his older brothers. 'Done,' he said.

*Fear and greed*, Krazka thought. *Fear and greed. Every time.*

*

Kayne charged shoulder to shoulder with the Westermen through the breach, greatsword held aloft. Bodies littered the ground around him. Nearby, a blackened mass of flesh still steamed from the boiling oil that had been poured over the town's attackers by the defenders on the battlements. Their charge carved right through the initial wave of defenders, Carn's magical sword leading the way, slicing down men left, right and centre. Kayne leaped a corpse, sighted his target and prepared to cleave the man's head off. At the last second the man – more accurately, Kayne saw, a boy – turned and saw his death approaching. His eyes filled with terror.

Kayne's sword swept low, flat of the blade leading, and knocked the boy's legs out from under him. He stared down at the youngster, greatsword suddenly trembling in his hands.

'The fuck you doing old man?' said a familiar voice. Kayne barely heard it. He was held fast by the fear in this boy's eyes. Unable to deliver the killing blow.

'He's lost his courage, Finn.'

'Out of the way, I'll take care of it.'

Kayne was pushed to the side and then Finn took his spot, his own sword preparing to finish off the fallen lad. 'What did I say you were?' Finn sneered, lining up his blow. 'A washed-up charlatan.'

Before even he knew what he was doing Kayne spun Finn around. A right hook dropped the Westerman where he stood. Finn's friends rushed in and Kayne disarmed two of them before the third had even joined the fray. All around them the fighting was raging, but he was oblivious to it. He couldn't explain why it was so important to him to stop them killing this boy. All he knew was that he would die before he let that happen.

'Kayne.' It was Carn Bloodfist. The chieftain of the West Reaching waded out of the carnage like death itself, Oathkeeper streaming crimson droplets. 'You disappoint me.'

'These are our people. Our countrymen.' Kayne's voice was thick with grief. 'They fight because they're scared. We butcher them like animals then we ain't no better than monsters. Than demons.'

Carn's dark eyes narrowed beneath his large brow. 'You were not lying when you said you had lost your appetite for killing.'

'I'll kill when I have to. Just not like this.'

Carn shrugged his great shoulders. 'I will spare this one – but *only* this one. I will not risk our victory for sentiment. Not from you, Sword of the North.'

Kayne nodded. Carn would keep his word. Strange though it was, if Kayne had to trust any man to do what he said he was going to do, his sworn nemesis staring across at him just then would be near top of the list. There was something comforting in that; in men saying a thing and then actually doing a thing. Even if that thing was seeing him dead.

*If I ever see you again, I'll kill you.* There'd never been a man truer to his word than Jerek. Not even Carn.

He left the fighting at the gate behind him, made his way east along the wide dirt road that ran through Heartstone. Memories came flooding back: old streets he had walked a hundred times before in his younger years; the smoky smell of the Foundry. Far ahead of him the hulking edifice of the Great Lodge loomed in the centre of town. It seemed the most likely place to search for Magnar so he headed towards it, hoping beyond hope that he wasn't too late.

A moment later a trio of sorceresses rounded an apothecary shop and almost collided with him.

Common wisdom had it that a warrior stands no chance against a mage. That magic conquers steel every time. And Kayne reckoned that when it came to the Magelords, that might well be the case. They could kill with a thought. Turn a man inside out in the time it takes them to blink.

But those who weren't Magelords, regular wizards and sorceresses – their weapons shared the same weaknesses as everyone else's. They had to choose their spells. Ready them, target them correctly. Most of all, they required the will to look a man in the eye and take an action that would snuff out his life, and that's a hard thing when you haven't ever killed before.

But *he* was Brodar Kayne, and for him killing came as easily as breathing.

He was already launching himself into a roll as a bolt of flame sizzled from the fingertip of the nearest sorceress, by far the quickest to react. It missed him, struck the earth nearby in a minor explosion of flame and dust. He plucked a stone from the ground, launched it and heard the satisfying crack as it dropped her unconscious. The second sorceress watched numbly while her brain attempted to catch up with what was happening. Kayne was on her in an instant, the pommel of his greatsword knocking her senseless. That left the third and final sorceress – and whatever time a man might be able to create for himself in that vital moment between thought and deed, even it had its limits.

The sorceress whispered a word and instantly Kayne's body refused to obey him. A creeping paralysis began to take hold, locking his head in place, then running down his arms until his greatsword tumbled from his nerveless fingers. This was the moment where it all ended. Where he died, along with his promise to Mhaira.

He summoned all his stubbornness. All the anger within him, rage that had been building since he'd learned of his son's fate south of the Greenwild. He willed himself to act with every screaming fibre of his muscles.

He shifted slightly. Bumped an arm that felt like a lead weight against his waist and dislodged the knife there. Magnar's knife, fashioned by Brodar Kayne for his son's fourteenth naming day. It tumbled towards the ground.

The paralysis spell had reached his waist now. The tops of his legs. Down, ever down. But not quite far enough.

He hooked a foot under the knife as it fell. Kicked out. Watched it spin in the air, gleaming from the light of the fires raging through town.

It hit the sorceress in the throat and stuck there. She choked, her spell broken, and in an instant Kayne was beside her. He grabbed her as she fell, held her close and lowered her gently towards the ground as she died in his arms, suffocating on her own blood. 'I'm sorry,' he whispered. 'I'm sorry.' He thought he might have recognized the woman's face. He remembered her treating Mhaira when his wife was sick.

He carefully removed the knife from the woman's throat, and then closed her eyes one final time. He retrieved his greatsword and checked on the other sorceresses to make sure they were breathing. Eyes red from smoke, tiredness and grief, Brodar Kayne continued towards the great edifice at the centre of Heartstone.

*

Krazka stood at the summit of the Great Lodge, the highest point in Heartstone, and stared out over town. 'This is it,' he said, spreading his palms wide, encompassing the hell playing out on the streets below. 'Everything I've worked so hard for. Everything I've lied, murdered and raped for. On the verge of ruin.'

Beside him loomed the monstrous figure of Bagha, nearly seven feet tall and nearly the intellectual match of a seven-year-old. Dumb though he was, the massive killer was perceptive enough to spot the flaw in Krazka's argument. 'You'd have lied, murdered and raped anyway,' he rumbled.

'Aye. True enough. The rest was a bonus, but I was feeling maudlin.'

Krazka narrowed his lone eye and surveyed the wreckage of his plans. To the south, Heartstone's sorceresses were still holding off the army from the Green Reaching. It seemed Brandwyn the Younger was as cowardly as his father, whose head Krazka had made great sport of after he had cut it from his shoulders during the sacking of Beregund. It was west where his troubles lay. The magical assault on the western gate had not materialized; the sorceresses had failed to show. The town's defenders were being driven back by superior numbers. Very soon the invading army would reach the Great Lodge itself.

'The Herald fucked me,' he declared bitterly.

There was a confused moment of silence as Bagha attempted to process this information. 'Huh. Didn't know it had a cock. Figure that might hurt. The Herald's really big.'

Krazka's eye narrowed further. 'That weren't meant literally, bearface. The Herald was meant to send reinforcements. Hrothgar was supposed to send men, too. Neither delivered. If you can't trust a demon lord and a blackmailed chieftain, you tell me who I *can* trust.'

Bagha pondered this for a moment. 'Your nana?' he volunteered.

*I climbed up out of a cesspit with my bare hands*, Krazka thought bitterly. *I ain't gonna die here next to shit-for-brains.*

'Follow me,' he barked, storming over to the stairs that led back down to the ground floor. He strode through the throne room and then out through the hall of heroes, where the arms of legendary warriors and Wardens decorated the walls. He kicked open an oak door, grabbed a torch off a sconce on the wall opposite and handed it to Bagha.

'Oil,' he said, pointing at the huge wooden barrels lining the room. 'I want you to burn this place down.'

'Burn down the Great Lodge?' Bagha repeated.

'You know, people might understand me better if I started painting my orders in their blood when they don't get the message. Aye, I said *burn the fucking place down*. I need a distraction while I make a break for the east gate. Reckon I'll lay low in the Lake Reaching for a while until I can start afresh.'

'What about me?' Bagha asked.

'Come join me when you're done. Round up Rana and Lanka and his two brothers as well. They might prove useful. I'll be waiting on the western shore of Lake Dragur.'

'What do I get out of all this?'

'I'll quadruple your pay.'

Bagha thought about this for a moment, the ridiculous bear skull atop his head bobbing up and down as he attempted something approximating a calculation. 'Triple,' he demanded.

Krazka blew out his cheeks, then added a wince for good measure. 'You drive a hard bargain. Triple it is. Out of curiosity, how many men you killed so far today?'

The giant Lakeman frowned at the gore-splattered war mace resting on his enormous shoulder. 'I lost count,' he admitted.

'That figures. Remember, Lake Dragur. Kill anyone who tries to stop you.' That said, the Butcher King spun on his heels and stalked out of the Great Lodge, cloak billowing behind him, one hand on the hilt of his demonsteel sword, the other on the hand-cannon holstered on his belt. Things hadn't worked out this time around – but when you fell down, you got back up and started climbing again. He would find more men loyal to him in the Lake Reaching. Seek out a new demon lord, if one existed. Maybe holding the former king of the High Fangs hostage would grant him leverage to parley with the other chieftains and maybe it wouldn't. It didn't matter. Life was a vast tapestry of possibilities and he wouldn't rest until he had rewoven it into his own image, or else burned the whole fucking thing to ash.

He was almost at the east gate when the ruined side of his face began to throb. The Herald's voice suddenly burst into his head, a cacophony of voices howling like a gale inside his skull.

*The Legion comes.*

*Nice of you to think of me.* Krazka hurled the thought at the demon lord like a spear. *It's too late. Heartstone is lost.*

*Heartstone is of no consequence.*

*It is to me. A king needs a throne.*

*You misunderstand. You have served your purpose. Your people have been destabilized. Weakened. Now the Legion comes.*

Krazka's eye narrowed. *You saying our alliance is ended?*

*There was never an alliance. You were a tool to be used and discarded.*

The world turned red. Scarlet. Crimson. 'You treacherous, scaly motherfucker,' Krazka snarled aloud. 'Once this is over I'm coming for you. That's a promise.'

The Herald's voice sounded almost amused. *You need not trouble yourself. The seal placed upon us by the Ancients millennia ago is finally broken. The Legion cannot be stopped. The Nameless will have this world. You will be meat. All things will be meat.*

Krazka screamed in fury and tore at his face, where the scarred mass of his cheek was pulsing in time with the howling laughter now tearing through his skull. He stumbled forward. The gate was just ahead.

'Where are you going?' The powerful figure of Orgrim Foehammer intercepted him. The chieftain of the East Reaching was covered in sweat and blood, the maul he carried in his ham-sized fists red from recent use. 'You ain't fleeing what you've wrought here, Butcher King. We've lost. It's time to face the music.'

'Out of the way, Foehammer.'

Orgrim shook his head. 'I was a fool to throw in with you,' he said, his voice heavy with despair. 'Better to have died honestly with my people, defending the Fangs from the demon invasion. I thought you offered a way out.'

'Well now, let that be a lesson. There is only ever one way out.' Krazka was moving before the words left his lips, his demonsteel sword flashing in the morning sun. Orgrim had been a warrior of great renown once, his fight with the Sword of the North on the banks of the Icemelt years ago the stuff of legend. But now he was old and fat.

Still, he almost got his hammer up in time. Almost, but not quite. *And almost ain't never been good enough.*

Orgrim stared down at the hole Krazka had just opened in his stomach. Blood flooded out and the Foehammer sank to his knees, the maul after which he was named toppling to the snow with a thud. Outraged shouts split the air and two of the fallen chieftain's men charged, swords raised. Krazka shot one in the head, his brains exploding out of his skull. The other he cut down in the blink of an eye.

Then he was through the gates and out onto the road heading east. He only glanced back once after leaving – which was how he spotted the blink demon emerging behind him an instant before it pounced.

*

The Great Lodge was a raging inferno.

Kayne stared numbly at the flames that engulfed the largest building in the High Fangs. There was no sign of Magnar. No sign of anyone except a few corpses littering the ground nearby, their heads smashed in by something large and blunt. Kayne's own greatsword was dripping red – the fighting had caught up with him on his way to the centre of town. He'd been forced to kill many men. He didn't want to think about that. Didn't want to think about anything except his son and the promise he'd made Mhaira in the final moment before they'd parted.

There was movement behind him and he turned. It was Carn Bloodfist. 'The town is won,' the chieftain announced. Despite this, his heavy brow was furrowed with concern. 'I have received troubling news from Mace. The army of the Black Reaching was intercepted north of here. Mace brought five thousand men with him. Less than a thousand still live.'

'*How?*' Kayne whispered.

'A horde of demons fell upon them. A horde the likes of which the High Fangs has never seen. Thousands. Tens of thousands. They filled the horizon, a teeming mass large enough to overrun the north.' Carn turned away and stared out across the city. The fighting had died down; now the survivors were gathering the injured and wounded on both sides. The civil war was over. All thoughts had turned to survival. 'We must abandon the High Fangs. Every one of the ten Reachings. Only death awaits those who remain.'

'Abandon our home? Where will we go?' Kayne's voice was heavy with disbelief. Thick with despair.

'The only place we can go. The Lowlands.'

Kayne squeezed his eyes shut. It seemed history had a habit of repeating itself. The southern Seer, Shara, had told him he was a marker in the Pattern, whatever that meant. Seemed to him that this Pattern had become a twisted, knotty thing. He stared at the wreckage of the Great Lodge. 'I need to find my son,' he said, half-choking on grief, knowing it was too late, that Magnar had been burned alive. 'I promised her. I promised Mhaira.'

'We will pass near Beregund on the way. You may find your wife there. As for Magnar, it seems it is too late to fulfil this promise, unless you wish to gather his bones from the ash. The demons will not wait for you, Sword of the North. We must begin preparations to leave immediately.'

'Then I'll find Krazka,' Kayne snarled. 'I'm gonna make that fucker pay.'

'He left through the east gate. Your son was taken the same way earlier,' announced a powerful voice that stirred old memories.

Both Carn and Kayne turned as the newcomer approached. The years had stolen much of his hard muscle but the figure of Orgrim Foehammer was unmistakable. His beard was matted with blood, and he held a hand over his stomach, wincing painfully with every breath. 'I tried to stop him fleeing when I saw we'd lost. A sorceress found me and did what she could, but damn, it still hurts something fierce.'

'Foehammer,' grated Carn. 'You stood with the usurper. I should kill you now.'

Orgrim bowed his head, deep shame in his eyes. 'Aye, you should. I wouldn't try to stop you, not that I maybe ever could. But I wanted to bring word to an old friend first.' Orgrim reached out a hand. After a moment's hesitation Kayne clasped it. The two had been close once. Orgrim had saved his life on the banks on the Icemelt. Guided him through his Initiation to become a Warden.

'You're hurt too,' Orgrim observed.

Kayne glanced at his mangled wrist. 'No time to find a sorceress,' he grunted. 'I need a horse.'

'You do this, you do it alone,' Carn rumbled. 'My responsibility is towards my people. The demons will be here within a day. We must be moving by then.'

Kayne nodded and blinked something out of his eyes. A snowflake. 'I'll catch you if I can.'

Orgrim shook his head. 'Krazka has hired killers with him. Some of the most vicious men I've seen in my near sixty years. And his sole surviving Kingsman is a giant of a warrior.'

'I've killed giants before. Real ones.'

'He's got a sorceress with him as well, not to mention some kind of weapon that can blow a man's head off from a hundred yards. It floored the Shaman, who we once reckoned immortal. You'll die, Kayne.'

Kayne glanced up at the sky. Iron clouds had gathered. The air was heavy with anticipation of a coming storm. 'I can live with that,' he said. His knees hurt, his wrist hurt, his chest hurt. But he had a promise to keep. 'Besides,' he muttered to himself. 'It's a good day to die.'

\*

'Fucking snow.'

Krazka shielded his good eye with one hand and wrapped his new cloak tighter around him with the other. The pelt of the Highland cat had served him well for a decade, but there was something very satisfying about wearing the hide of the first demon that had attacked him since the Herald's betrayal. It was said the Sword of the North had killed a blink demon single-handed back in the day.

*And now the Butcher King has, too.*

'Almost had me, didn't you, boy?' he said jovially. He reached down and patted the feline-shaped carcass beside the fire. He'd had to carry it some way to the shore of Lake Dragur. Truth be told, it'd been a real bitch to skin the fiend, but Lenka and his two brothers had lent him a hand. They were sitting opposite him across the fire while Bagha kept watch. Not that the massive warrior could see much through the snowstorm, but it pleased Krazka to make the man suffer.

'Your brothers don't talk much, do they?' he said to Lenka. The thin Lakeman shrugged. Beside him his elder siblings stared balefully at nothing in particular. Krazka turned to the fifth figure beside the fire. Thick rope secured the wrists of Magnar Kayne behind his back, but in truth it wasn't needed.

The lad was closer to dead than alive. Krazka hadn't been able to get much out of him all morning, no matter how and where he poked the grey-eyed former king. 'We'll get you talking before this storm's over. Well... I say "talking", but I reckon "squealing" might be closer to the mark. Lenka, you wanna have a go? A gold coin if you can get him to scream.'

The killer got to his feet and padded over to their prisoner. White sheets fell around them, blown in by freezing southern winds. The waters of Lake Dragur lapped softly against the shore just to their left. Unlike the Icemelt, which froze in late autumn, the lake was fed by heated springs originating in the volcanic peaks of the Black Reaching. The water was rarely cold enough to freeze, and even when it did the ice was easy enough to break. It would provide a handy source of food until a better plan presented itself.

Lenka bent down and examined the knives at his belt. 'This one,' he said finally, withdrawing an exceptionally thin blade with a wicked edge. 'I call it the skin-peeler.'

'Imaginative,' Krazka drawled. The sixth and final figure beside the fire whimpered and he turned to her in annoyance. 'Don't get teary on me now, sweetheart. You didn't have to come.'

'What's she doing here?' grumbled Bagha from where he kept watch. He shifted his head a little, as though he might have spotted something of interest.

'That's what bitches do,' Krazka sneered. 'They follow their master. Women are like dogs, bearface. You make them fear you; you show them the consequences of disobedience and they're yours for life.' He patted his demonsteel sword. 'You know what happens if you don't obey, don't you?'

Rana went white and nodded. Krazka grinned and turned back to Lenka. The thin-faced killer was busy cutting Magnar, his tongue poking out in concentration. The boy gasped a little, but still no scream.

'Someone's out there,' Bagha rumbled. 'I can see a horse. There's a man riding it.'

Krazka was on his feet immediately, sword in one hand, hand-cannon in the other. 'You sure it's a horse? Not a demon?' A single man held no fear for him, whereas a demon might be anything. He doubted the Fangs had seen the worst of what the Devil's Spine would spit out now that the Legion, or whatever the fuck the Herald had called it, was on the move.

'It's a man,' Bagha repeated. 'He's getting off the horse.'

As he stared into the blinding snow, Krazka could make out a tall figure walking towards them. There was something about the way he moved that was troubling; when you'd killed as many men as he had, every movement told a story.

'Boys,' he grated, waving at the brothers. 'We got company.'

Lenka and his siblings got silently to their feet and padded over. Rana sat where she was, her eyes fixed on Magnar. On the hilt of the knife sticking out of his ribs.

The figure drew closer. Through the thick sheet of snow Krazka could make out greying hair with a slight widow's peak, the jagged scar on one weather-beaten cheek. Blue eyes gleamed like a glacier on a cold winter morning, speaking only of death. Unique of all the warriors in the High Fangs, they had more to say on that subject than Krazka himself.

'He's old,' Bagha said, his blunt face breaking into a grin. 'He'll die fast.' The massive warrior hefted his iron war mace.

'Thing about getting old,' Krazka said quietly, feeling a tingling excitement in his veins. A promise made long ago about to be realized. 'It means you're good at *not* dying.' He holstered his hand-cannon and raised his sword in a mockery of a salute. 'Looks like Daddy's come for his boy.'

\*

Mhaira stumbled *again. Her breath rasped in her chest. He saw the blood flecking her mouth and wanted to scream in anguish. He ran to her, pulled her up and hugged her tight. In the distance* the howls and grunts of the Brethren were growing nearer. They couldn't outrun the Shaman's servants. He knew that. Had always known it.

'I'm sorry,' he said brokenly. Tears almost choked him but he knew he had to be strong. This was their only chance. Mhaira's only chance. 'Go on without me. I'll try and slow them.'

'Brodar—'

'I love you, May.' He leaned forward and kissed her forehead. 'You warned me. This is what comes of killing. But I was too weak to say no.'

'You were never weak,' she replied. 'And you said no. When it mattered, you said no.'

'I brought us to this,' he said, cursing himself. Hating himself. 'I should have just done what he asked. I should've gone to Beregund and—'

'No,' she interrupted gently. 'You did what was right and I would have it no other way. Just promise me one thing. Please.'

'Anything,' he said, his voice a strangled rasp.

She placed her hands on his cheeks and held his gaze. Her soft grey eyes were the most beautiful thing he had ever seen. Didn't seem right they should exist here, in this world of ugliness and violence. 'Promise to protect our son. He always wanted to be like you. Always feared he would live in your shadow. He is only doing what he thinks is right. Promise you will forgive him. That will you protect him.'

'I promise,' he said. He steeled himself for his next words. 'I have to go now. Run on ahead. Don't wait for me, and don't look back.'

'I love you,' she whispered.

'I love you, too'.

Kayne blinked snow from his eyes. Snow or tears – it was hard to say which. Either way it wasn't doing much to help as he tried to focus on the trio of evil-looking warriors spreading out to surround him. Behind them loomed a monster of a man, bigger than Carn, as big as the armoured giant Jerek had killed down in Dorminia months past. The giant wore the skull of a great bear on his head. The mace he clutched in his huge fingers likely weighed as much as Kayne himself.

Behind the giant, grinning widely at the scene playing out before him, was Krazka.

Kayne's fury rose. That leering eye had haunted his nightmares. One of them wouldn't be leaving here alive, and a quick glance at the odds arrayed against him told him it was almost certainly going to be Kayne. But he would fight with his every last breath to bring that murdering, raping piece of shit the end he deserved.

*Fight or die.* There was something in that simple truth that had always sung to him. He could hear it now, the first refrain of a song he'd danced to a thousand time before.

He brought his greatsword up in a fighting stance. The greatsword Braxus had forged for him as a wedding gift half a lifetime ago. A lot of men said you couldn't fight effectively with a weapon that size, that it wasn't possible to move fast. But you didn't need to move fast. You needed to move *right*.

The warrior directly in front of him, the one with the dozen knives at his belt, sneered and then plucked a dagger free, hurled it in one smooth motion. Kayne twitched slightly and felt it whistle just wide of his neck, then adjusted his greatsword as a second knife flashed through the snow. He felt it bounce off the steel, but any satisfaction he might've taken from that was short-lived. The two brothers were on him in an instant, their thin-bladed swords darting in, stabbing and slashing. Moving on instinct, Kayne parried one sword, twisted out of the way of the other, the pelting snow all around them making it near impossible to see. He felt his blade connect with flesh and was rewarded by one of his opponents stumbling away. An instant later he felt a stinging pain in his arm and realized the other's sword had bitten deep into his own body.

He didn't hesitate. Didn't even flinch. Instead he twisted with the blow, following the path he knew the swordsman's momentum would take him along. He swung hard, felt his greatsword cleave through skin and muscle. He heard a wet sloshing sound and blinked snow from his eyes to see the man staring down at his stomach. Snaking intestines were spilling out of the wound, steaming gently where they touched the snow. The man's sword was dripping with Kayne's own blood, but the Sword of the North paid it no mind. He grabbed the dying fellow and pulled him close, spun him around just as the knifeman's third effort came twirling through the air. It hit his brother dead in the chest. The younger man screamed in rage.

White-hot, blinding pain exploded in Kayne's side and he gasped. He glanced down to see a spear lodged there. The second brother had blindsided him. With a snarl he reached around to the chest of his human shield and yanked out the knife buried there, twisted and hurled it at the limping figure still grasping the spear. At this range he couldn't miss. The point slammed into his face, burying the knife up to the hilt. The spear went slack as the man died and his hands slipped away from the haft. Gritting his teeth, Kayne tugged the steel head free of his flesh.

He almost passed out from the agony. He didn't have time to feel sorry for himself though – the sole remaining brother was on him in an instant, thin face contorted in rage, incoherent screams rising above the howling wind. Kayne grabbed his arm an instant before it plunged yet another knife into his chest, twisted it as far as it would go and was rewarded by the sound of bone breaking. The screams of outrage turned to screams of agony and the knifeman reeled away and fell to the snow cradling his fractured arm, sobbing like a child. Only the gentle lapping of Lake Dragur against the shore broke the silence that followed.

Kayne's breath rasped in his chest. He could feel the blood welling from his arm and leaking down his wounded side to patter onto the snow. The pain was starting to fade. Somewhere deep in his subconscious he knew that was dangerous. Pain was useful. Pain kept a man alive.

A voice called out, 'Finish him, bearface.' Another enemy lumbered through the snow towards him and he knew he needed to focus, but it was hard to care, hard to think at all. Something hit him in the mouth and he heard his jaw crack. Then he was lying on the snow, spitting out blood and teeth. Still, the snow felt pleasant. He needed to rest. Had needed to rest for years, that was the truth.

*It's a good day to die.* The words floated idly through his skull. The great bulk of the warrior above him moved closer, mighty war mace raised for the killing blow. Kayne's blue eyes began to feel heavy. They settled on the campfire, on the woman sitting there.

On the young man tied up beside the fire. Kayne hadn't noticed him before. There was something sticking out of his chest. Grey eyes met his own, the shadow of death heavy over them. Kayne knew that face.

Like an erupting volcano, hot fury surged up. Pain flooded back. The war mace descended and at the last possible moment Kayne moved, rolled under the mighty arc of the weapon, which struck the ground in an explosion of ice. He snarled, hot blood filling his nose, filling his mouth. He spat it up into the face of the giant above him, then reached out, grabbed the haft of the spear nearby and plunged it straight into the monster's gut. He gave it a cruel twist and then used it as leverage to haul himself slowly to his feet, every inch pure torture. Fury drove him on until he was standing once again. Gasping, covered in blood from head to toe. He released the spear and tugged the bear skull from the warrior's head with a grunt, spraying crimson everywhere. He raised the skull and smashed it down onto the pinned giant's big lump of a head. Once, twice, three times, until the man's face was a gory mess and he finally toppled onto the snow.

Kayne dropped the broken skull and walked over, swaying with every step, to where his greatsword lay. He bent down and retrieved the weapon. The knifeman was still sobbing nearby and Kayne followed the sounds until he was standing over the youngest of the three brothers. The only one still drawing breath. 'You tried to gut my son,' he whispered, blood spraying from his mangled mouth with every word.

The reply was a pitiful sob – but the Sword of the North was out of mercy.

A moment later he turned and tossed the man's severed head at the feet of the last figure standing opposite him.

Krazka, the Butcher King, who had betrayed his own people to ally with a demon lord, brought his hands together in a slow clap. He stood casually, purple hide cloak fluttering behind him and single-edged sword clutched lazily in a gloved hand. He beckoned Kayne forward, mouth twisting in an evil grin.

Kayne raised his greatsword. Tried to take a step towards Krazka. The world seemed to rock wildly and he had to stop, fighting desperately not to fall. He knew he wouldn't get back up if he did.

Krazka examined his own wicked sword in the light of the campfire. 'They say you were the best. You never faced me on an even footing, but after that I might grudgingly accept you as my equal. Don't matter now, though. Reckon you're done. You can't even move.'

Kayne didn't reply. He didn't have the breath to waste. Barely had any breath at all. The world grew darker. He was only dimly aware of Krazka striding towards him, sword held with consummate skill. 'You got close, but close ain't never been good enough. I ain't hiding in your shadow no longer, Sword of the North. Time for one legend to die and another to take its place.' Through his failing eyes, Kayne could see Krazka's face. That leering eye, making a mockery of the world. Of everything Kayne had ever loved. 'Fitting you die here with your boy. Don't you fret – he'll follow you shortly.'

Krazka went for the killing blow. The sword danced in his hands, quick as a snake. It was an extravagant move. An executioner's move.

Kayne twisted. The smallest of movements. But sometimes that was all that was needed. The right move. The right move at the right time.

The Butcher King's demonsteel blade sailed out of his hands, tumbling to the snow twenty feet away. Kayne tried to follow through but his strength was gone and he could barely hold his greatsword aloft. Krazka caught the blade between his palms six inches from his chest. The sardonic humour of a moment ago was instantly replaced by shocked fury.

'How the *fuck* did you manage that?' Krazka spat. He tore the sword from Kayne's unresisting grip and hurled it to the snow. Kayne sank to his knees, utterly spent. Krazka loomed over him and Kayne felt something cold and metallic pressed against the side of his head. The Seer's words floated to him from somewhere in the recesses of his fading mind.

*You knelt before the Butcher King.*

There was a click from above him, followed by a savage curse. 'That chamber was empty. The next one won't be. I ain't leaving no survivors. No witnesses. You humiliated me. I'm the gods-damned *Butcher King*. I climbed out of a cesspit with my bare hands. No one humiliates Krazka—'

Kayne waited, but only silence followed.

And then a soft voice spoke, feminine and seething with fury. 'You betrayed our people. You sacrificed the town's children to a demon. You tortured that poor girl, Yllandris. *You murdered my nephew.*'

Kayne tried to open his eyes. The silhouette of a woman was moving closer. She carried a torch in her hand. She raised the flame towards Krazka. 'You thought me your bitch. A coward. But I was waiting. Waiting for the moment I could get close to you and work my spell. The women of the High Fangs are not weak creatures to be raped. To be murdered. *To be abused.*'

Kayne smelled burning flesh. A moment later something warm and wet struck his brow and trickled down. A tear, perhaps.

'Now *you* are the one who is helpless. You will hurt no more innocents. Terrorize no more of my sisters. Shranree was a cruel woman. I am not, but this you deserve. On behalf of Yllandris. On behalf of Polga. On behalf of my nephew and all the victims of your wickedness, may you burn forever more.'

The woman's hot breath whispered in Kayne's ear, the words getting fainter as the life slipped from him. 'I wish I could help you and your son, but your wounds are too great and I am no healer. I will tell them you died well. That whatever your sins may have been, you died fighting to keep a promise to a woman you love. There is nothing more precious.'

Kayne heard footsteps crunching on the snow, moving away from him.

Then, finally, his eyes closed.

# Small Blessings

THE HALFMAGE HAD never been afraid of the sea. There was something comforting about the predictability of the tides, the endless cycle of nature at work. Even the Broken Sea, with its natural properties altered by the wild magic that swirled within its depths thanks to the fallout from the Godswar, largely adhered to a familiar pattern. It was something knowable to cling to in a world of uncertainty. Perhaps not for much longer, in this Age of Ruin. But it was something.

No, what Eremul was afraid of wasn't the sea.

*It's sailing on a ship the size of a small town towards a city governed by the most powerful wizard in the world. A ship carrying enough firepower to blow us all to the Confederation and back.*

Eremul glanced at the churning waters far below and tried to steady his nerves. Deadman's Channel was narrow at the best of times, but it seemed that no sooner had Isaac assisted the Halfmage aboard the Second Fleet's titanic flagship than Thelassa was drawing into view. It cut a markedly different sight to Dorminia – a pale and beautiful twin to the stunted, grey dreariness of its counterpart across the channel. Given the choice, Eremul would choose the latter every time.

*After all, 'stunted' and 'dreary' are what I'm all about.*

Following behind the flagship were the magnificent vessels that made up the Second Fleet. Each was crewed by a small team of fehd as well as a much larger team of thralls. The general himself, Saverian, stood only thirty feet away from Eremul at the very front of the flagship. The white-haired general's forbidding presence was a large reason for the Halfmage's anxiety. He wondered how a Magelord would fare in the face of this legendary immortal.

*Perhaps we are about to find out.*

As they drew closer to Thelassa's harbour, a strange sight greeted them. A shimmering wall appeared, rising from the sea to tower hundreds of feet above Thelassa's fleet just beyond. Eremul could feel the monumental magnitude of the magic emanating from the magical barrier; a colossal undertaking that rivalled the great spell Salazar had cast to crush Shadowport for sheer audacity.

The fehd appeared disconcerted by the unexpected obstacle. The flagship dropped anchor and the rest of the fleet followed suit. A vast cloud of steam hissed forth from the great turrets on the ships, turning the chill winter air momentarily sticky. Following a brief exchange between Saverian and his officers, the flagship turned sharply and the Halfmage was forced to grab hold of a metal railing to stop his chair being propelled down the deck. Having presented its side to the magical barrier ahead, rows of artillery began to click into place on the ship's weapons deck.

Isaac approached Eremul and pointed at the silvery barrier just ahead of them. 'I don't imagine you are able to dispel this?' he asked, apparently in earnest.

Eremul stared at the ancient creature who had once masqueraded as his manservant and tried not to laugh in his face. 'This wall was conjured into being by perhaps the greatest living master of magic in the known world,' he said sardonically. 'You might as well ask a fisherman to reel in one of the great whales that are said to dwell within the Endless Ocean. I am half a man and half a mage. The White Lady is a repository of the divinity of the gods.'

'They were never our gods,' said Isaac. 'We do not understand this thing you call "magic". It did not exist in the place from which my ancestors came.'

Eremul's eyebrows rose. 'Well, it manifestly exists *here*,' he said. 'Besides, what do you call the feats your people can perform, if not magic? Your agelessness. Your ability to beguile.'

'The Time Before was a wonder of artifice and invention,' Isaac said, as he and Eremul watched the cannons preparing to fire. 'Our ancestors discovered how to permanently alter their bodies. They eliminated diseases. Grew taller and stronger with every passing generation. The wealthiest among them had new powers and abilities implanted directly into themselves; traits such as empathetic projection, that could be passed down to their children, and their children's children. Eventually, they unlocked the secret to eternal life. It proved their undoing in the end.'

Eremul was suddenly overcome by a great sadness. He frowned up at Isaac. 'I asked you not to do that,' he said.

The Adjudicator reached out and, much to the Halfmage's surprise, clapped him on the shoulder. 'As I said, it is difficult to control. Ours is a story of triumph won through tragedy.'

The mechanisms driving the gigantic cannons ceased their whirring and clicking. A pregnant silence settled over the harbour. 'You should cover your ears,' Isaac said calmly.

Eremul did as the Adjudicator suggested. It wasn't a moment too soon. A cacophony of explosions suddenly shook the deck beneath him and a fiery rain of death exploded from the flagship's cannons. The sky was lit up as the loads from the cannons hurtled towards Thelassa. As the deadly storm descended on the City of Towers, it struck the translucent barrier and was thwarted, bursting apart, the explosive projectiles detonating in mid-air. The heat from the failed assault washed back over the ships and Eremul choked on air suddenly hot enough to burn his throat.

'Cease the assault.' General Saverian's voice rang out like a clarion call, the command as irresistible as the tide. 'The lady of the city approaches.'

The artillery went silent. For a long moment smoke wreathed the harbour, making it difficult to see beyond the barrier ahead of them. When it finally cleared, it revealed the shimmering wall of magic to be utterly intact.

Floating safely behind the barrier, her white silk robes dancing around her in the breeze, was the Magelord of Thelassa.

General Saverian raised a gloved fist in greeting. His voice was like iron, gripping all present in its power. 'I am General Saverian,' he boomed. 'You will lower this barrier.'

The White Lady's response was perfectly modulated, carried on the wings of her magic. 'Turn back, Ancients. You will not harm my city or my people.'

Eremul looked from the White Lady to Saverian and back. He could never have imagined he would live to see this day: a Magelord, an immortal wizard, made to look vulnerable in the face of something even she could not understand. Saverian was five thousand years old. He had been conquering the worst of what the Age of Legends could throw at his people before humanity had even learned to crawl.

*To me the White Lady is inhuman. Terrifyingly ethereal, a figure to fear and look upon as something almost divine. To Saverian she is simply another buzzing insect. A queen bee, perhaps, with a dangerous sting – but inconsequential nonetheless.*

The white-haired general crossed his arms in front of his chest and narrowed his ruinous gaze. His black cloak flapped around him in the salty breeze. 'There will be no exceptions in our crusade, killer-of-gods. Your city will be destroyed and your people exterminated. Such is the fate of those we judge unworthy.'

'And who are you to judge what is worthy?' the White Lady asked softly. 'It is as you said, general. Even the gods could not judge *me*.'

Saverian's voice rose until it thundered across the deck. 'Your gods were the only entities with the power to oppose us! Yet your kind slew them, just as you murdered two of our people. For that, there can only be one answer.'

'You will not pass this barrier,' the White Lady declared again. But there was a strained quality to her voice now; perhaps even a hint of doubt.

Eremul turned to Isaac beside him. 'What would happen if the White Lady were to unleash her magic against Saverian? She could destroy your general here and now.'

Isaac shook his head. 'We are not of the Pattern, and its rules govern us only loosely. For the eldest of our kind, magic runs off us like water. The resistance fades the further one is removed from the bloodlines of the blessed Pilgrims – but even one possessed of only a few centuries can withstand a great deal of magic. The elves, too, thought to bring their sorcery to bear against us during the Twilight War. It availed them little.'

Saverian drew himself up to his full height – over seven feet of harsh lines and too-angular limbs encased in that near impenetrable silver armour that flowed like cloth. 'I chased the great serpents from Rhûn. I slew the king of the elves in single combat. I was ancient when your forefathers were scrabbling in the mud. I am General Saverian, and I declare now that you will be Reckoned. There is no shield, magical or otherwise, that will protect you from it.'

Having made his declaration, the general turned his back on the White Lady and gave the signal for the fleet to turn around. The Magelord watched the ships depart in silence. Then she turned and drifted back towards her city.

As the great fleet returned across Deadman's Channel, Eremul summoned his nerve and asked the question that had been troubling him since he had first heard Isaac use the term. 'What does it mean,' he asked, 'to be Reckoned?'

The Adjudicator stared into the distance. He seemed troubled, and for a moment the Halfmage wondered if he had pushed his luck too far.

Then Isaac told him.

'Dust,' he whispered. 'Everything will be dust.'

Eremul sat in the dreary room in the Refuge that he shared with two other refugees. Ricker and Mard were poor company but at least they didn't despise him like many in the city did. Sleep had eluded the Halfmage again this night. In all likelihood it would elude him every night from now until the moment General Saverian utilized the unspeakable weapon Isaac had described. The weapon that had broken worlds. Isaac's words twisted around and around in Eremul's skull.

*In the Time Before, we called it the last resort. All nations had it come the end. The desperate scramble for immortality made rulers mad. Once one committed to using the weapon, they all did. Those who weren't killed instantly were poisoned. The land, too, felt the effects of what we had done. The Pilgrims were our last hope. They left in search of a better place. Their journey lasted untold millennia, until eventually they found somewhere. A new land to call home.*

*The elves were the first to be Reckoned, their great forest cities reduced to blackened wastelands of ash and bone. The second Reckoning occurred far to the south, when an empire of scaled folk we named the saurons threatened to unleash their deadly poisons upon our people. We chose the lesser evil. I chose the lesser evil.*

As an Adjudicator, Isaac – together with his sisters – was one of the select few entrusted with the moral conundrum of deciding when a civilization merited the use of the ultimate weapon.

The Halfmage's hands shook as he opened the hidden box attached to the underside of his chair and removed the bottle of Carhein white he had purchased weeks ago. It had been meant as a gift for Monique; her favourite wine from her homeland in Tarbonne. But Monique was gone, and the clear liquid in that bottle might be the only thing that would allow him to forget the imminent destruction of the city and its people, at least for a time.

Then a rough hand darted in and snatched the bottle from his grasp. The broken smile of Ricker leered down at him. 'Think I'll be having that,' he said. He popped the cork into his mouth and attempted to leverage the cork out with what few remaining teeth he had.

Eremul stared up at Ricker as he struggled with the bottle. 'I *am* a wizard, you know,' he said slowly. 'I can't help but think it might be wiser for you just to ask.'

'Don't care,' Ricker mumbled around the cork. 'Ain't got nothing to live for. You want to take this off me, you kill me first.'

The Halfmage sighed. After a brief moment of deliberation he waved a hand at the fellow to continue. 'Enjoy it,' he said. Then Eremul wheeled himself over to the corner of the squalid little room he had claimed as his own and closed his eyes.

*So much for a quiet drink.*

A moment later there came a knock on the door.

'Who's that?' growled Mard. The old man hardly moved from his spot on the floor. In his more lucid moments he had claimed that he used to work the docks before his house was burned down and his family killed by Melissan's thralls. The Halfmage suspected the tragedy had driven him mad.

The door opened and the outline of a woman appeared in the doorway. She hovered there uncertainly, cloaked by the darkness of night outside.

'I told you,' Mard yelled angrily. 'I don't want no cock-rot. My wife would kill me.'

'Your wife is dead,' Eremul said gently. 'And we have bigger things to worry about than the cock-rot. Trust me.' He frowned at the woman. Streetwalkers were common enough in the Refuge; everyone did what they had to in order to survive. But this woman wasn't dressed for the job, so to speak.

He wheeled himself closer. 'Do you need something?' he asked irritably. Then he smelled her perfume and a soft gasp escaped his lips. He knew that scent. She moved closer and the moonlight caught her, revealing her features. The Halfmage's heart seemed to explode in his chest.

'I don't want no cock-rot,' Mard barked again, but Eremul hardly heard him. He stared at the face before him, the sleek black hair, the reading lenses perched on her perfect nose.

'Monique?' he said, his voice catching in his throat. An instant later she threw herself on him, wrapping her arms tightly around his body, her warm breath in his ear and her warm tears sliding down his cheeks.

'I found you,' she sobbed. 'My love... I've found you.'

Eremul stroked her hair, hardly believing what was happening, scarcely daring to imagine this wasn't all some great joke designed to rub further shit into his wounds. But it wasn't. Monique was here. The only woman he had ever loved had tracked him down.

'I don't want no—'

'Shut the fuck up,' Eremul whispered savagely. Mard fell silent with a whimper.

'They sent me to Westrock,' Monique said, her lilting Tarbonnese accident thick with emotion. 'I was kept imprisoned there. When the invasion began everyone in town fled east, but I couldn't leave. Not without you.'

The Halfmage held Monique as she sobbed. For the first time in years, he had the strange sensation he wasn't entirely worthless after all. He actually *mattered* to someone.

He knew the gods were dead and the Creator long gone but nonetheless he offered up a prayer of thanks to whomever might be listening just then.

The fehd might be planning a Reckoning, but until it happened, he would count every minute a blessing.

# Sidetracked

D AVARUS COLE STEPPED off the *Caress* and took a deep breath. He turned back to the caravel and gave a small wave to those aboard. No one so much as nodded in acknowledgement. The captain blamed him for the loss of four of her crew, he knew, and no sooner had his boots touched down in the port of Ro'ved than she was making preparations to depart. Ed and the other dead would be taken back to Thelassa for burial. Cole wished he could be present to bid his friend a final farewell, but the urgent mission he had been entrusted with could allow no delays.

The streets of Ro'ved were little more than mud. The dockhands glared at him as he passed. He ignored them and made his way towards the stables as he'd been instructed. The writ of passage he carried was signed by the White Lady herself and requested that he be given whatever he needed, with the promise of full recompense in future. If the frowns on the faces of the Tarbonnese who were watching him were any indication, they weren't likely to take kindly to a foreigner turning up and making demands.

*It can't be helped. I'm here on a mission of utmost importance. The future of the Trine could depend on my success.*

He wandered narrow streets, looking for any sign of a stables. The wooden buildings were crowded tightly together and he soon became lost. The smells of baking bread assaulted his nostrils and hunger stirred in his gut; the right kind of hunger.

He entered a bakery and was about to hand over some coins for a fresh loaf when he remembered the White Lady's writ. He presented it to the gap-toothed old woman behind the counter. 'My name is Davarus Cole. You see this? It's an official document signed by the White Lady of Thelassa. She requests you render me whatever aid you can.'

The woman squinted at the parchment. 'Who's a white lady?' she asked, in a strong Tarbonnese accent.

'Not who. *The*. The White Lady. You know, the Magelord.'

The woman shrugged. 'Never heard of her. I never cared much for politics. That was more Sebastian's thing, before he was lost to the dreams. I miss my husband.'

Cole blinked. He knew a little about dreams himself. 'What do you mean? What happened to him?'

The woman's eyes grew moist. 'After our son died in the wars he became depressed. He started muttering about a three-eyed demon that haunted his nightmares. Soon he wouldn't talk except to mutter about the blessed embrace of the Nameless. One morning I woke up and he was gone.'

'Gone? You mean he's dead?' A tear rolled down the baker's cheek and Cole felt vaguely embarrassed, standing there waving a note in the old woman's face.

'Not dead. That might've been easier to bear. No, he's *gone*.'

'Right.' Cole very carefully placed the note back in his pocket and stepped back. The last thing he wanted was to get involved in whatever strangeness was going on with this old woman. He put the bread down and turned to walk away.

'Wait,' said the baker. 'Take that. Don't worry about payment. You remind me of him. My son, I mean. Times are hard since he and his dad left me alone here, but you look like you could use something in your belly.'

Cole hesitated. He took in the shabby building, the cracks in the walls that had been left unfixed. The deep lines of grief beneath the baker's eyes. 'How much is a loaf of bread?' he asked abruptly.

'Fifteen coppers. But you needn't give me anything.'

'A Dorminian always pays his debts,' Cole said brightly. 'It seems a little expensive, but I'll make a note here in case I forget. Fifteen *silvers* to be owed to...' He trailed off, waiting expectantly as understanding dawned on the woman's face.

'Why... it's Renée. Look at you taking pity on an old woman! Are you some sort of hero?'

Cole winced at that. 'Not a hero,' he replied. 'Definitely not that. Tell me, do you know where I can find a stables? I need a horse.'

*

*You'll be a great man one day. Like your father.*

Garrett had uttered those words to Cole often when he was a boy growing up under his care. That simple truth had shaped young Davarus Cole's formative years. Given him the confidence to be braver than anyone else. Better than anyone else. To be a *hero*.

'I'm not a hero,' he said bitterly to himself for the third or fourth time that morning. 'My father was a killer. My mother was a harlot.' He kicked his horse and it responded with a slight whinny. The road east to Carhein from the port town of Ro'ved had given him plenty of time to ponder his miserable life; a life that until recently had been built on a foundation of lies.

Cole tugged Magebane free of its scabbard and glared at the dagger. The winter sun gleamed prettily off the blade and caused the ruby set in the hilt to burn brightly.

*Like the eyes of the bastard who attacked me on the* Caress. The bastard who had killed his friend Ed. Cole fingered the golden key now hanging around his neck. He had no idea what purpose it served, but it was a tiny measure of satisfaction to have taken something from Wolgred after he died. Taken something from the assassin who had taken Ed's life.

He stared at the glowing blade in his hand, disgusted. 'I never had a choice, did I?' he muttered. 'This was the path laid out for me. All because of a stupid weapon.' He was half tempted to toss Magebane in a bush and ride off without a backward glance. It would be practically impossible to find the dagger again if he did. Tarbonne was a lush and verdant country, even in winter. He rode past gently rolling hills covered in naked trees, gurgling streams and pastures of many shades of green that formed a pretty tapestry.

Cole glared at Magebane again. The truth was that he would be nothing without his birthright. Without the enchanted dagger that his father, Illarius Cole, had bequeathed to him with his dying breath.

*Magebane is who I am,* he realized with despair. *Everything I am.*

The terrible curse he carried meant that he would waste away and eventually perish unless he killed with the dagger, and killed often. The vitality he had stolen from the Unborn on the roof of the Tower of Stars had faded. Already his skin was pale and his hair flecked with grey. If he didn't feed the divine hunger soon, it would feed on him.

*Why am I even doing this?* The only thing of any value in his life was Sasha. The day he finally summoned the courage to tell her how he truly felt would be the day all his hopes and dreams were forever shattered.

*She's smarter than you. More attractive than you. She doesn't have a hopeless addiction that will eventually destroy her.*

Sasha had always been the better of them, that was the truth. There was no chance she'd want anything to do with a whore-spawned killer; she deserved better.

He felt the lightest of touches and twisted his head slightly to see Midnight pawing playfully at his neck. The little black kitten was nestled comfortably inside the backpack thrown over his shoulder. He reached into a pocket and withdrew a tiny piece of fish he'd pilfered from the ship just before disembarking. He had no idea how to look after a kitten, but he'd made a promise to Ed to keep her safe and that was that.

His arse began to ache and he wondered how much farther it was to Carhein. Tarbonne's capital was one of the oldest cities north of the Sun Lands. Reportedly neither as large as Dorminia nor as secretive as Thelassa, it had once been known as the Jewel of the Nine Kingdoms before the Godswar had changed the face of the region. Though it was apparently now only a shadow of its former glory, Carhein was nonetheless celebrated as a centre of art, culture and commerce.

Not that Cole would have time to sample any of that, particularly not the bordellos for which the Pink District was so famous. No, it was *his* lot to once again play errand boy for the powerful. He had no idea how he would go about gaining entrance to the palace and meeting with this Zatore. The White Lady had handed him a letter for him to present to the king's advisor. That struck him as an artless means of communication when both were mages and could presumably send a message through a dream or magical familiar or some other arcane bullshit, but then who was he to question a Magelord?

*I only kill them from time to time. When they're bored enough of life to decide death might be worth a shot.* Cole had the feeling that even with Magebane in hand, Salazar could have swatted him like a fly if he had really wanted to. Certainly the White Lady had not broken a sweat putting him in his place.

Without looking, he turned and spat and almost hit a passing rider on the other side of the road. The man shook a fist at Cole, who waved an apology. A few minutes later Cole spotted a wagon approaching. The teamster brought the wagon to a halt and beckoned Cole to do the same.

The wagon-master looked friendly enough, and Cole hadn't spoken a word to anyone since bidding farewell to what remained of the crew of the *Caress* at Ro'ved. Curious, he trotted over to the man.

'Well met,' he said, bringing his horse around. 'I'm Davarus Cole. Something you need?'

'These are dark times,' the wagon-master said, in a thick Tarbonnese accent. He was a wide man with a thick moustache. 'Take care on the road. The Cult of the Nameless preys on unwary travellers. They have eyes everywhere.' He cast a furtive glance around, as though they could be being watched at this very moment.

'Thanks for the warning,' Cole offered. The teamster was watching him expectantly and he felt obliged to continue the conversation, though he would just as soon be on his way. 'Tell me more about this cult,' he obliged. He recalled the baker woman back in Ro'ved mentioning something about this 'Nameless'.

'You know of the disappearances in recent years? Fathers, mothers leaving their families never to return. The wars that tore this kingdom apart before the Rag King won the throne have bred despair and that despair has found a voice. The Cult of the Nameless. They preach that love is weakness. That if we submit to the darkness we will know pain no more.'

'Sounds like a bunch of shit to me,' Cole said angrily. 'I've been to some dark places this last year and trust me when I say the pain never goes away. You just learn to live with it.'

The teamster shrugged a thick shoulder. 'I bring fair warning, is all. You are a foreigner in this land. Better to walk with your eyes open.'

'I appreciate the advice,' Cole lied. 'How much farther to Carhein?'

'Ride fast and you will be there by nightfall,' replied the teamster. He looked around fearfully one last time before going back to his wagon.

Cole waved farewell and decided to follow the wagon-master's advice and maintain a brisk pace. As his horse cantered down the road towards the capital, he passed only a few folk travelling the other way. Several wore fearful expressions. A few gave him curious glances. None were pretty or interesting enough to pique Cole's curiosity and so he paid them little mind.

A few more miles passed before he became aware of just how thirsty he was. The conversation with the teamster had dried his throat and his waterskin was down to a few trickles. As luck would have it, he noticed a white brick building on the side of the road just ahead. The signage outside indicated a tavern: the Farmboy's Folly.

Cole hesitated a moment. The White Lady had specifically told him to make for Carhein with all haste and not to become sidetracked. The insinuation that he couldn't be trusted made him bristle with indignation. *After all that bitch has put me through I'll be damned if I'll go thirsty because of her!* He glanced at Midnight and reasoned she must be thirsty too. If there was one character flaw that could never be levelled against Davarus Cole it was a disregard for the welfare of animals.

At least that's what he told himself as he handed his horse's reins over to the stable boy and pushed open the door to the tavern. It was pleasantly warm within. A log fire blazed in the hearth and the smell of roasting meat wafted through the air. There were a score or so of locals lounging around the tables. In the time-honoured tradition of alehouses everywhere, they all turned to stare at Cole as he wandered in. A few of them were playing cards, while in the corner of the tavern a group of young men of a similar age to Cole were laughing and pointing at something on the wall.

'Just some water,' said Cole as he approached the bar. The barman looked slightly taken aback, and when Cole added 'and a saucer of milk', the disapproval in the man's glare could have stripped paint off the walls. Over in the corner, the group of young Tarbonnese were jeering at Cole and joking among themselves. Something about that stung. After all he'd been through, he deserved more respect.

'What are they doing?' he asked the barman, pointing a finger towards the snickering men.

'Playing knife toss,' the barkeep replied, with a sniff. 'It is a tradition in these parts. A game for real men,' he added, casting a dark frown at Midnight. The kitten was perching on the bar, lapping up the milk from the saucer.

'*Real men*, you say?' Cole shot back, trying unsuccessfully to mask his indignation. He walked over to the group. One of the men threw a knife at the wooden board hanging from a rusty nail on the wall. Painted circles covered the board, one inside the other, getting progressively smaller towards the centre. The man's throw landed in one of the outer circles. Despite his poor effort, his friends clapped him on the back as though that were some kind of impressive achievement.

'Mind if I try?' Cole asked. He took a nonchalant sip from his glass of water.

One of the men nudged another, who grinned and took a swig of his ale. He handed Cole a knife and gave him a wink. 'It is simple,' he said. 'You aim for the brown hole in the centre. I am sure you are familiar, yes?' His friend chuckled and made a gesture involving a finger and a certain part of the anatomy that filled Cole with anger. He lined up the knife and threw it, barely looking. It stuck in the board, far closer to the centre than the other knives.

'You mean like that?' he said sarcastically. He turned as if to walk away, but then plucked Magebane from its scabbard, twisted around and hurled it in one smooth motion. This time it hit dead centre, quivering there like an exclamation mark. 'Or is *that* how a real man does it?' he asked loudly, spreading his palms.

There was a stunned silence and then a chorus of cheers burst from the small audience that had gathered to watch the show. The men who were but moments ago questioning his masculinity were now patting him on the back and extolling his virtues. Cole unstuck Magebane from the board and thrust it inside its scabbard. He gracefully accepted the plaudits and went to fetch Midnight, who had finished her milk and was curled up around a bottle of Tarbonnese red wine, snoozing happily.

'A toast!' cried one of the knife-tossers. 'To our new friend from the Trine!'

Cole grinned and shook his head. 'I can't,' he protested. 'I have somewhere I need to be.'

*Besides. After what happened back in the Blight, I can't allow myself to let my guard down ever again.* The last thing he wanted with all this talk of a cult was to get careless. He had learned his lesson.

'He throws like a man but he drinks like a girl!' someone yelled. Cole couldn't help but bristle at that. His drinking prowess down in Dorminia's grimiest dives had been legendary. It hurt to have it defamed by a bunch of smelly foreigners.

'Another time and I'll drink you all under the table,' he snapped back. He placed Midnight carefully in his backpack. She purred softly. 'Some of us have matters of great importance that demand our attention. The fate of the world could well rest upon my shoulders.'

'Oh, will you listen to him,' said one of the serving girls. He hadn't noticed her before. She had pretty eyes – but even those weren't her most obvious assets. Somehow her alluring accent made her words all the more arresting. 'If he wants a go under the table I've a mind to say yes!'

That brought a fresh chorus of laughs and Cole found himself stopping halfway to the door. Every instinct was telling him to leave, save for one. Unfortunately, it was a rather pressing instinct. 'Oh, all right,' he said, turning back to his new friends and giving them a big grin. 'I'll accept a toast. But just one drink,' he added in a stern voice. 'Just one.'

*

All was darkness.

Blinding pain assaulted his skull, as though there was a host of tiny men inside bludgeoning it with tiny hammers.

He could smell vomit. Sour and acrid. The smell was so strong that his clothes must have been covered in it. His eyes were open, but all he could see was blackness. Panic seized him. Panic, and fresh nausea. His mouth tasted foul – ale and wine and spirits mixed with the bitter taste of bile.

'Where am I?' he rasped. He could feel motion beneath him. He was lying on a moving object, being taken somewhere. He tried to move his arms, to reach up to his face, but his wrists were tied. He tried to move his legs, but they too were secured.

*What happened?* He struggled to piece together his memories. They were like shattered glass, confusing and incomplete. He had the mother of all hangovers, he knew that much. Even thinking hurt.

'Where am I?' he said again, louder this time, his voice cracking with desperation.

He heard movement nearby. Smelled the sour stench of someone's breath as they leaned down. A sack was pulled from his head and then he was staring up into a hooded face. Dark eyes glittered with sinister fervour beneath the hood.

'You are on a wagon. You and your friend from the tavern. The Cult of the Nameless has you now, child. Do not resist. Submit to the darkness. Soon we will reach our destination and then your pain will be gone.'

The cultist placed the sack back over Cole's head. He closed his eyes and let his head slump back against the wagon. 'For fuck's sake,' he whispered.

# An Unexpected Ally

A WEEK AFTER THE White Lady's confrontation with Saverian outside Thelassa's harbour, the *Lady's Luck* entered the last stretch of her desperate voyage to the Celestial Isles.

Sasha wiped her mouth with the back of her hand and spat out what little bile she hadn't already vomited over the edge of the carrack.

*Gods, I hate this ship*, she thought angrily. The trip across the Broken Sea to the flooded ruins of Shadowport had been painful enough, but this was torture. The Unborn crew clearly didn't feel the effects of such things as seasickness – not even when the terrifying waves that surged across the Endless Ocean threatened to capsize the ship on occasions too numerous to count. She, however, had puked up her guts so often it hurt to breathe.

She wondered to what depths the dark grey water beneath her reached. Once or twice she'd glimpsed gigantic shapes surfacing in the distance, only to dive back into the water seconds later in gigantic explosions of spray that surely would have flooded the *Luck* had the ship been anywhere near them.

Perhaps worse than her seasickness was the sense of boredom. Her shipmates were not very communicative – with one unfortunate exception.

'A beautiful morning, is it not?' Fergus asked as he came to stand beside her at the prow. A tall, sharp-nosed man with a prominent widow's peak, Fergus might be considered handsome and distinguished – at a distance.

*Before you see the void behind his eyes. The emptiness where a soul should be.*

The truth was, Fergus made Sasha's skin crawl. He seemed devoid of human emotion, even more so than the Unborn around them. The difference, perhaps, was that while the Unborn had never developed to a stage capable of feeling, he had simply bypassed it completely. He was a whole man, except he lacked the parts that made a man a person. At one time each of the Unborn aboard the ship had been a baby girl. They had Fergus to thank for their unnatural existence, for it was he who pioneered the unholy creation of the White Lady's handmaidens.

Sasha turned her back on Fergus, but it seemed he was unwilling to take the hint. Unwilling, or unable to comprehend her body language.

'The Isles are only a few miles ahead of us now.' The self-proclaimed 'man of progress' ran a long-fingered hand through his grey hair. His eyes always seemed to be calculating, analysing, stripping things apart and refiguring them. She remembered the *snip* of his scissors back in the tower of horrors in Thelassa and suppressed a shudder.

'I told you not to talk to me,' she spat. 'You're a monster.'

Fergus gave what for him passed as a smile – a slight twitching of his lips. 'No, my girl, you are mistaken. *These* are monsters.' He pointed at the handmaidens on the ship's deck. 'I am a man of progress.'

Sasha squinted across the endlessly rolling waves, hoping to spot land. Anything to give her an excuse to busy herself away from this sociopath. Fergus was a high-ranking member of the Consult, who governed the city in the name of the White Lady, and hence held seniority over Sasha, who was still confused about her own role aboard the *Lady's Luck*. The Magelord had inexplicably taken a shine to her, magically fixing Sasha's fractured ankle and giving her a living apartment in the Consult chambers. Fergus had personally requested she be part of the crew to travel to the Celestial Isles.

'I hope there is yet something to be salvaged from these Isles,' Fergus commented. 'They were the greatest source of untapped magic in the known world. Who knows in what ways the Ancients may have desecrated them.'

*May have desecrated them? They murdered hundreds of Dorminians here!* Sasha wanted to scream at the man. Instead she took a few breaths to calm herself and wondered how Cole was faring down in the Shattered Realms. Knowing him, getting himself involved in ridiculous escapades and pissing folk off left, right and centre. She also knew that if there was anyone who could succeed in spite of all that, it was Cole.

She felt something being pressed into her hand and glanced down. It was a pouch; a small brown pouch. She glanced up to see Fergus's thin face twitching in another mockery of a smile. 'A little something for you. To help with your seasickness.'

Sasha untied the cord and peered inside. It was filled with a silvery powder.

'I don't need this,' she said, thrusting the pouch back at him. But she didn't thrust it all the way back, and as it hung from her twitching fingers she wanted nothing more than to tear it open and snort it all up her busted nose. And that bastard Fergus knew it. He was watching her as though she were a curious insect, dissecting her thoughts, her emotions. Her needs.

'Very well,' he said and took the pouch from her, stashing it in his coat. He glanced out over the water and his lizard's stare lit up. 'Ah-ha! I do believe we near our destination.'

Emerging out of the mist ahead was the dark outline of a coast. Even at this distance Sasha could sense that something was amiss. The air felt heavier, *fertile*, as though there were vast energies at work that could not be seen or felt or heard but which might manifest themselves in unexpected form at any moment.

The Unborn captain of the *Lady's Luck* joined them at the prow, moving as silently as a ghost. 'The Celestial Isles were torn from the heavens during the Godswar,' said the handmaiden. It was unclear if the words belonged to her or if she were merely acting as a mouthpiece for her master in the City of Towers. Sasha had already witnessed the telepathic link the White Lady and her minions shared. 'What you can feel is the raw essence of magic. The potentiality of creation. This place is dangerous – perhaps even more dangerous than the Swell. Even the local wildlife is touched by its aura.'

A dark shadow engulfed the deck and Sasha glanced up to see a colossal eagle fly past, its wingspan wider than the ship below it. It screeched once and turned slightly, as if contemplating whether those on the ship might be prey. Evidently it decided not – or perhaps the unnatural presence of the Unborn disturbed it; either way it changed course and soared back towards the Isles.

Fergus steepled his fingers together and made a *hmm* sound. 'An impressive specimen – and quite unnatural, of course. During the Age of Legends there was said to be a bird so large its shadow could encompass a town. A "roc", I believe it was called. I've always wondered what would happen if one were to encounter a dragon in the skies. I suppose we shall never know.'

As they sailed nearer to the Isles, the strange feeling in the air grew stronger. Sasha heard a thump on the deck behind her and turned to see what she at first assumed to be a fish lying on the deck. On closer examination she saw that the fish was strangely shaped, with a large blunt head that tapered smoothly to the tail and unusually intelligent eyes. There was something unsettling about the animal.

Fergus bent down to examine it and murmured in delight. 'My, my. A *whale!*' he exclaimed.

'A whale?' Sasha exclaimed. 'Those massive creatures I glimpsed a while back? They were huge. Bigger than a house.'

'This whale is touched by the magic of Isles,' Fergus said. 'Not every such touch is a welcome one. It is said that a whale's brain is close in size to that of a man, in relative terms. How fortuitous that one should find itself stranded here, and in such... agreeable form.' His eyes seemed to light up as he stared at the creature. It didn't flap as a fish might but rather lay there mournfully, as if it knew its fate. Fergus reached into his coat and withdrew an extremely sharp-looking knife.

'What are you doing?' Sasha asked, though the glitter in the man's eyes told its own story.

'I am going to experiment,' Fergus replied. 'I wish to see this animal's brain for myself. The search for knowledge is never-ending. I am after all a man of progress.'

An hour later they finally got close enough to the coastline to begin looking for a place to dock. It was then that the bodies began thumping against the hull.

Sasha stared overboard, fresh bile rising in her throat. There were hundreds of them floating in the bay: the headless corpses of the Pioneers who had sailed from Dorminia with dreams of returning rich, or at least something more than destitute, bright in their minds. The fehd had slaughtered them all.

A sudden overwhelming need to blunt the horror seized her and her eyes alighted on Fergus. He had that shit-eating smile on his face already, as if he had known exactly how all of this was going to play out. She hated him for it, despised him.

But that didn't stop her going to him and thrusting out a hand. He passed her the pouch of *hashka* without a word.

*He doesn't see people*, she realized. *He sees projects. Puzzles.*

She had the cord half undone when a cry went up from the lookout. Sasha managed to avoid fumbling her precious cargo and stowed it in a pocket just as tiny shapes became visible on the coast. They were still too small to see in any detail, but seconds later she heard a sharp cracking noise and the decking just to her right shattered, fragments of wood and dust exploding into the air.

The Unborn beside the forecastle jerked suddenly. Black blood began to ooze out of her chest, smelling foul, causing the humans aboard the *Luck* to reel away in disgust or hold their noses. All save for Fergus, who merely watched with interest. The handmaiden didn't seem unduly concerned by the wound, but there was another cracking sound moments later and her skull fell apart like a melon, rotting brains spraying the mast behind her.

Sasha threw herself to the deck as further cracking sounds split the air, one after another. Chunks of wood and flesh and rancid black blood were flying all around her. She saw several Unborn plunge over the ship's railing and dive into the ocean, making for the Islands, trying to reach their assailants before the ship was sunk.

*How are they are attacking us?* she thought desperately. *They're hundreds of yards away!* The sound of thunder shook the skies above and black lightning arced down from the clouds to strike the coast in a small explosion of stone and spray. The assault on the ship stopped momentarily. Sasha climbed back to her feet, wiping putrid gore off her face. The scene aboard the *Lady's Luck* was utter carnage: dead and wounded crew were sprawled against crates, flopping on the deck or staring numbly down at jagged holes in their bodies. Though only a few of the Unborn had been destroyed, many were missing limbs. Sasha could see the ripples made by those that had leaped overboard still swimming towards the coast.

More lightning lit the sky, spearing down to strike the section of coast where their attackers had been spotted. The cloud of dust thrown up by the lightning made it hard to see exactly what was happening, but the cracking noises swiftly returned. Strangely, none of this newest wave of attacks seemed to target the ship.

Fergus ambled over. He appeared unhurt, and indeed mostly unmoved, by the madness playing out around him. 'It seems we have an unexpected ally,' he mused. He pointed up at the sky. 'There is a mage in the clouds above. A mage, or some other being capable of summoning and directing lightning.'

Surely enough, more lightning forked down. It was answered by those below, a renewed burst of cracking, whistling shots sent up into the clouds.

Sasha's heart was already hammering in her chest, and when she spotted the huge vessel ghosting out of the mist around the side of the coast it almost burst. This new ship was unlike any she had seen before: a metallic, angular behemoth the colour of a leaden sky. The *Lady's Luck* was perhaps the finest vessel in the Trine but even the White Lady's flagship was small and primitive in comparison to this.

'We must flee,' announced the captain. 'The fehd have not abandoned the Isles. We cannot survive a confrontation with that ship.'

The *Lady's Luck* was brought around with all haste and the sails hoisted as they turned and fled the approaching vessel. Surprisingly, it didn't immediately attempt to give chase. Lightning tore through the sky behind them and Sasha saw the fehd warship outlined in black fire.

*The mage is attacking the ship. He's trying to slow its advance.*

They sailed at full mast, knowing that if the pursuing ship caught up with them they were all doomed. Somehow they lost sight of the fehd vessel and in the early evening the captain announced that it was not evidently giving chase. Sasha was halfway through her pouch of *hashka* by then and so when the harsh croak of a crow interrupted the stillness of the night, she didn't immediately make the connection. All she could think of was mighty magic being unleashed, of harsh words being tossed at the most powerful woman in the world. Of her sister, Ambryl, sacrificing herself to ensure her younger sibling survived. Somehow everything connected in her delirium and the identity of their unexpected ally dropped like a stone in her *hashka*-addled mind.

'*Thanates*,' she whispered.

The crow fluttered down out of the night sky and landed on the deck. The bird began to glow and change shape and then he was standing before them: a tall man sporting a black overcoat, tattered and torn in a hundred different places. The red rag he had once worn to cover his missing eyes was gone, stripped away by the White Lady during their duel. In their empty sockets burned black fire.

There was a moment of stunned silence and then one of the Unborn leaped at Thanates. He raised a gloved hand and she was flung overboard, plucked off the deck and dumped into the churning waters below like so much flotsam.

The grim wizard took a step towards the crew. He smelled of black powder, and ash, and death. 'Servants of Alassa,' he snarled. 'Where is your mistress?'

'Protecting her people,' replied the ship's Unborn captain. 'You are not welcome here, Crow.'

Thanates laughed, an ugly sound like a bird's caw. 'You misunderstand. I do not ask your permission. Your mistress and I have unfinished business. She had me flogged and hung from the walls of her city. She even stole my memories. Now I am here for vengeance.' The wizard raised a fist wreathed in black fire.

'Wait.' Sasha stumbled forward, falling to her knees and scraping them painfully on the deck. 'You were fighting the fehd. Why?'

Thanates paused. 'The Ancients murdered hundreds of innocents here. A wizard-king of Dalashra does not allow an injustice to pass without answering in kind. *This I remember.* You, servants of Alassa, will now answer for the crimes of your mistress.'

'Wait,' Sasha said again. 'You know me. I'm Sasha. Davarus Cole spoke of me.'

Once again the mage hesitated. 'Davarus Cole? Ah. The child of murder. You are the girl he professes to love.'

*Love? No one could possibly love me.* Sasha blinked desperately, willing away the *hashka*-induced fog clouding her mind, knowing this was one her one chance to avert a catastrophe. 'He said you were a good man. We are not responsible for what the White Lady did to you. We came to these Isles seeking magic to help combat the fehd.'

Thanates grimaced. 'I thought to do the same. The Ancients will allow no one close. The weapons they carry reach further than any bow or cannon.'

Unexpectedly, Fergus cleared his throat and raised a thin hand. 'Excuse me. Allow me to posit you a question, if I may. Does a thirst for vengeance outweigh a duty to mankind?'

Sasha stared at Fergus. The man's eyes glittered. There was no fear, no sense that he understood how close he was to magical evisceration. Only curiosity at yet another mystery to untangle.

The self-proclaimed wizard-king of Dalashra frowned. 'Speak not to me of duty. A king's duty is always first to his people.'

Fergus nodded. 'Then your duty must be to put aside your vendetta against my mistress and help us fight the fehd. For if you do not, all of humanity is doomed.'

The black fire surrounding Thanates' clenched fist flickered and died. He scowled. 'Easy to say. Alassa cares nothing for duty. Deepest of all her desires is to be a saviour. That was what drove her rage as much as the loss of our child: the denial of her wish for us to unite the Congregation and the Alliance. Instead, we doomed it.'

'You can still save us,' Sasha whispered. 'You and the White Lady. Please. There's no one else.'

For a long time, silence reigned. Thanates stared around the ruined deck as though he could see the damage wrought by the fehd. 'I have learned of what the Ancients did here. The bodies. I do not care for it.'

'So you'll help us?' Sasha pleaded.

Thanates gave a heavy sigh. His jaw set, and he stared seemingly unseeing at the sky, until finally he nodded. 'You must arrange a meeting between us. I cannot promise we will not kill each other. But if Alassa and I are able to put aside our hatred, I will tell her of my time in Dorminia and an individual fehd I grew to know well. His name was Isaac.'

# Transcendence

THE HALFMAGE STROKED the hand of the woman beside him, marvelling at how soft it felt. She rewarded him with a smile that in the circumstances almost broke his shrivelled excuse for a heart.

The thundering blast of a horn split the air and the giant transporter ship carrying the weapon that heralded Thelassa's Reckoning crawled into harbour. It was almost of a size with the two great flagships of the First and Second Fleets – but this vessel carried no artillery and only the most skeletal of crews. Most of the main deck was occupied by a metal cylinder so vast it rivalled the towers Eremul had glimpsed from Thelassa's harbour: a monstrous barrel of steel that pointed towards the heavens. Isaac had referred to it as the 'Breaker of Worlds' and had intimated that in this mysterious Time Before it could be deployed in much more compact form; a factor that ultimately led to the mass devastation of their ancestral homeland when thousands were utilized at the same instant.

*The Fade and mankind. We both share a proclivity for mass murder that would humble the gods, except we killed them too.*

The Halfmage felt Monique's fingers squeeze his hand. He tore his gaze from the harbinger of their doom and met her gaze. 'Will it hurt?' she asked him. 'When it is our turn, will it hurt?'

Eremul shrugged helplessly. 'I do not believe so. It will be instantaneous, or so I understand. We will not have time to feel pain. One second we shall exist. The next...' He trailed off, unwilling to finish the sentence.

'But you are a wizard. Your magic can protect us?' The hope in Monique's voice made him feel six inches tall.

*And I am barely three feet on a good day.*

'My magic will not protect us,' he said weakly. 'Even the White Lady's magic will not protect her city or her people. The weapon that will be deployed from that ship, the Breaker of Worlds, unravels the fabric of all things. The explosion will be vast. Nothing will survive for miles around.'

A trumpet sounded and the Halfmage stared down the docks to where a procession of fehd approached to meet the incoming vessel. General Saverian strode purposefully along at the front of the group. At his side was a female fehd whom Eremul remembered being present at the bloodbath on the day of his intended execution. Isaac and his sister Melissan – whom he had once known as Lorganna – followed behind, a score more of the Ancients marching behind them. Resting over Saverian's right shoulder was a much larger and bulkier version of the deadly hand-cannons the Ancients employed.

'Time for us to go,' Eremul muttered. They had needed a break from the Refuge, not to mention Mard and Ricker's endless litanies of crazed bullshit. Privacy was a luxury afforded to no one under the current occupation of the city. Strange though it seemed, the harbour was about the safest place for a notorious pariah. Unlike his fellow Dorminians, the fehd bore him no particular ill will. No more ill will than Eremul had for the rats that infested the Refuge. He would be Reckoned when the time came, and that was that. Petty cruelty was, it seemed, for the lesser races.

As Eremul and Monique departed the harbour and began the trek back to the Refuge, a melodic voice the Halfmage knew well called out his name. He twisted around to see Isaac gesturing at him to remain where he was. To Eremul's rising panic, the Adjudicator uttered something to General Saverian. Sudden dread turned to pant-pissing terror when the two began making their way towards him and Monique. Not only them, but Isaac's sisters also.

*Shit*, he thought, trying not to let fear master him. *Keep calm. If they wanted you dead you would already be in a hole in the ground. Or, more likely, ash drifting in the wind.*

Monique clung to him and he knew he had to keep it together for her. Isaac and his sisters he could somewhat countenance; it was the white-haired general who utterly terrified him.

'So this is the human,' uttered Saverian, staring down at the Halfmage with eyes blacker than despair, older than the land itself. It might have been a question – except that the cold certainty in Saverian's voice left absolutely no room for doubt. 'Your pet.'

'I would not word it that way, sir,' replied Isaac.

Melissan laughed, a sound like the tinkling of a hundred silver bells. 'I fear my dear brother is quite besotted with his little project. I dare say he might even consider him a friend – preposterous though the notion is.'

The other female at the side of Saverian raised a perfect hand and flicked away a strand of golden hair. The Ancients were a uniformly beautiful people – tall and slim and with features that might have been carved by the most skilled sculptor. But this particular fehd was truly beyond words. 'Is this its life partner?' she asked curiously, giving Monique a tiny nod.

'"It" is a "he", Nym,' Isaac said gently. The look he gave her was one of pure joy. Eremul had never had a brother or sister. Whether it was the Adjudicator's empathetic projection or just the expression on his face, he knew for that one instant the intensity of the love one sibling might feel for another. The passing of it left him empty. As it always did, bitterness welled up to fill the void.

'Humans rarely have life partners as we understand them,' Melissan interjected. The Halfmage could *feel* the venom dripping from her voice. 'They are like dogs. They rut and then leave to find another with whom to share their seed. A consequence of their minute lifespans.'

The Halfmage wanted to spit his anger in the arrogant face of the fehd who had manipulated him so effortlessly. It had been Melissan's doing that he had come within seconds of dying at the end of a noose. And now she dared insult the only thing that gave his life any meaning?

*I have spent my thirty-five years on this earth being ridiculed, spat upon and made to feel utterly worthless by my own kind. I can tolerate whatever you can throw at me. But don't insult her.* The four perfect immortals were staring down at Monique as if she were a fly-speckled piece of shit. *Three,* he corrected himself. Isaac seemed discomfited by the whole situation.

General Saverian placed a gloved hand on the shoulder of the female named Nym. 'For a thousand years Nymuvia has been promised to me. One day we will lifebond and spend the rest of eternity together. I pity you transient things and your illusions of relevancy. Of permanency.'

*Don't do anything rash. Don't do anything rash.* Eremul repeated it over and over, the gnashing of his teeth his only, pathetic, outlet for his rage. He so desperately wanted to unleash his magic against this Saverian, but fear stopped him. Fear, as well as Isaac's words.

*Magic runs off us like water. The elves, too, thought to bring their sorcery to bear against us during the Twilight War. It availed them little.*

Saverian was five thousand years old. If killing this legendary general with magic were easy, it would have happened a long time ago.

'The Breaker of Worlds awaits our inspection,' the general announced, repositioning his shoulder-cannon and spinning on his heel. 'We have wasted enough time on these animals.'

Eremul finally snapped. 'Don't call her an animal, you arrogant fuck!' he snarled.

Saverian paused. Melissan whirled around, mouth twisting

in anger. Nym gasped softly. Isaac just closed his eyes, as if he had half expected this outcome but hoped tragedy might be avoided nonetheless. The general turned slowly.

An arrow struck Saverian.

It hit him in the chest and skittered off his silver armour, though judging by the pain that flashed in his obsidian eyes, the impact hurt. Eremul, too, squealed in pain – a result of Saverian's emphatic projection, stronger even than Isaac's.

Battle cries tore through the air. Pouring out of an alley came a mass of armed men. There were ex-Crimson Watch, militiamen – veterans of the brief wars with Shadowport and Thelassa – as well as common citizens brave enough to pick up a sword in a desperate last stand against the city's occupiers. The ambush had been planned perfectly, or else had proved incredibly fortuitous: the rest of the fehd party was hundreds of yards away, leaving the four officers utterly exposed.

'For Dorminia!' and other largely uninspired but commendable cries went out. In spite of everything Eremul felt a small surge of pride. Someone in the city had organized a last-ditch resistance. He was shocked to see a familiar face among the rebels – Lashan, the one-time harbourmaster and a man Eremul had humiliated twice in the recent past. Lashan's eyes locked on the Halfmage as he charged, a shortsword clutched awkwardly in his recently healed hand. Eremul had broken his fingers beneath the wheels of his chair back in the summer. The man had been a coward among cowards then, but he had found his courage from somewhere.

'Traitor!' Lashan screamed, spittle spraying from his mouth.

*It's not what it looks like*, the Halfmage wanted to protest. Clearly whoever had organized the attack had not trusted *him* enough to be involved in their plans. He understood that. He didn't even care if they killed him while taking down the fehd command. But Monique was in their path, too. There were at least thirty armed men already within bowshot, and more behind them.

The three Adjudicators stepped out to defend their commander – but Saverian raised a hand and they fell back. Alone, the white-haired general took a single long stride towards the massed ranks of the ambushers.

What happened next caused Eremul to freeze in disbelief halfway through mumbling a protective spell intended to shield Monique. General Saverian leaped impossibly high, spinning in mid-air just as the first wave of arrows descended. The projectiles bounced off his twirling cloak, batted aside as though the black fabric were woven steel. Halfway through his mighty leap Saverian somehow levelled his shoulder-cannon with one hand. The noise that followed was like a row of black powder barrels exploding one after the other. An endless stream of tiny metal projectiles tore through the air, punching holes in Dorminian bodies and leaving them reeling away spraying blood, or collapsing stone dead to the cobbled streets.

Like a miniature whirlwind Saverian hit the ground. Now his crystalline longsword was in his hand, and he covered the remaining twenty paces to the rebels in a straight dash that seemed to bend space and time. He slashed one way and then the other, all perpetual motion, his translucent blade hacking off limbs and cutting men in half like a great whirring saw, so fast the Halfmage couldn't even begin to follow his movements. Lashan was one of the last to die, his sword hand sent flying in one direction while his head soared off in another.

In fewer than ten breaths it was over. The docks were a red mess of hacked-apart bodies and spreading pools of blood. Saverian bent to retrieve his shoulder-cannon, then straightened and sheathed his sword in one perfect motion. He blew softly on the smoking tip of the barrel and strode over to Eremul.

'Anger is the hallmark of the lesser races,' he stated. 'Of the animals and beasts. True power is obtained through *transcendence*. Your words mean nothing. They are the bark of an angry dog. Tomorrow the city of Thelassa will be Reckoned. This city will follow it. Make the most of your final days.'

General Saverian turned and strode towards the waiting ship. Melissan and Nym quickly followed behind him. Isaac hesitated, then with an apologetic glance at Eremul he joined the rest of his kind in inspecting the Breaker of Worlds, the terrible weapon that would finally be employed on the morrow.

The Halfmage stared straight ahead. Towards the north of the city, and the Refuge. 'We are leaving now,' he said hollowly. In his shame he couldn't look at Melissan. The dampness of his robes told its own story.

He had pissed himself.

# Bent, Not Broken

HE AWOKE TO the sound of lapping water. He opened his eyes, stared up at the iron sky. It was still snowing, but nightfall was close now. A thick layer of snow had settled on his body and he shook it off, wiping flakes away from his face. Magnar was beside him, his son's chest rising and falling in an easy rhythm beneath a blanket of white. Kayne cleared it away, terrified of what he would find beneath. But there was no sign of the knife that had been embedded in his son's chest.

Kayne examined his own body. He had raw scars on his wrist, on his arm, on his side where the spear had entered him. He poked around his mouth. One or two teeth were missing but his jaw was unbroken.

'I am reminded of the first time we met. You killed to win my favour. I healed you then, as now.' The voice was paper-thin, as ancient as the trees scattering the hills around them.

Kayne shot up from the snow, clambering to his feet. His body still ached something fierce, but by any measure he should be dead from the wounds he had taken before he had collapsed. He looked around for the source of the voice. For the man who had saved his life and that of his son. Found him standing beside the lake, his back to Kayne. A frail figure, child-thin beneath the robes.

The Shaman.

The Magelord turned slowly. Reached up with wrinkled, age-spotted hands and threw back the cowl.

Kayne's breath caught in his chest. The Shaman looked ancient. He looked like a corpse, or as close to a corpse as something that still drew breath could get. The only feature of his appearance that was in any way reminiscent of the imposing immortal Kayne had once known were his blue eyes, though even they were dulled by age now – rheumy and covered in cataracts.

'What happened to you?' Kayne whispered.

'This.' The Shaman pulled open his robe, revealing a chest more shrivelled than an apple left out in the sun for a month. Beneath the wrinkles, near the heart, was a festering hole. The flesh was black and leaked pus. The smell was terrible even from this distance, and Kayne had to turn away or gag. 'A projectile cast of demonsteel. Fired from the fehd weapon this usurper somehow discovered.' The Shaman nodded at the smouldering skeleton standing in a pool of meltwater beside the remains of the campfire.

The paralysis spell that had frozen Krazka in place while he burned alive continued in death. The expression on his fire-blackened skull was one of bemused fury. The bones of his fingers still clutched the weapon in his charred death grip, but the strange object was ruined now, the metal barrel bent and blistered. 'Demonsteel is anathema to magic,' the Shaman continued. 'The metal lodged within me is a poison I cannot survive. You should take the usurper's sword, Kayne. It is a formidable weapon.'

Kayne bent down to retrieve Krazka's demonsteel blade. He hesitated. Then he picked up his old greatsword, the battered blade his friend Braxus had forged for him all those years ago. He stared at both and frowned. 'It ain't the weapon that makes the man. It's the man that makes the weapon.'

He spun and hurled Krazka's sword over the lake. Watched it disappear beneath the water to sink to the depths, an evil weapon that if the spirits were kind would never surface to take another life.

He sheathed his own greatsword and went to check on Magnar. His son was still unconscious, awful thin and badly scarred from all kinds of torture Kayne didn't even want to think about. But at least he was alive.

He turned back to the Shaman. 'Why?' he asked simply. 'After all that happened between us. Why save our lives?'

The Shaman was silent for a moment. When he replied, it was in a whisper so strained Kayne struggled to hear it above the wind. 'I loved a woman once. In the time before the war on the gods, the Congregation caught her and burned her alive. They used demonsteel to defeat our magic. It broke me. I was weak then, Kayne. I thought to become someone else. So I came here, to your country, a place no other Magelord cared to claim. I made myself a god. A god whose dominance could never be questioned. Those who did not heed my laws, I broke.'

'You tried to break me.'

'Yes. Yet *you* could not be broken. I was the weakest of Magelords. But you, you were always the strongest of men. Your people need you now, Sword of the North.'

As if to illustrate his words, the Magelord pointed a shaking finger across the lake. Kayne squinted, trying to see through the snow. He could make out shapes. Profane shapes. Hundreds of them, crawling and slithering across the snow. He recognized demonkin and blink demons, but there were other, even fouler kinds he had never before set eyes upon in all his time as a Warden.

'They'll catch us before we've made it a mile,' Kayne said. 'We're too late.' He bent down and scooped up Magnar, shocked at how little his son weighed. There was nowhere to flee, nowhere they wouldn't be hunted down within the hour.

Then Kayne became aware of movement around him. He turned slowly as clawed feet padded across the frozen ground the length of the lake. A menagerie of beasts melted from the snowstorm: bears and wolves. Elk and reindeer. Highland cats, their fur as white as the snow, near invisible save for their yellow eyes.

'The last of the Brethren,' the Shaman explained. 'They will make their final stand here.' He lifted his arms, arms so thin they made a mockery of the bulking biceps the Magelord had once boasted. 'I was always the weakest of Magelords, and to create a Portal is one of the hardest feats of magic. I have little magic left, and so I give myself. My divinity. The stolen essence of the gods. My gift to you, Kayne. My apology.'

There was a great tearing sound. The air around the Shaman began to waver, ripples of air forming and distorting the lake beyond until it was no longer a lake but the rolling hills of the Green Reaching. Through the magical doorway Kayne could see a great train of folk fleeing south: a vast diaspora of Highland people fleeing the demon horde rampaging through the Fangs.

'Go,' the Shaman whispered. Motes of gold and silver were streaming from him. He seemed to shrink and then fold as he struggled to maintain the Portal. 'Take care of your son and find your wife. Lead our people to safety.'

Kayne stumbled towards the wavering image of the Green Reaching. He glanced back just before he crossed the threshold. 'What about you?' he asked.

The Shaman's blue eyes blinked once. 'All things die,' he said simply. Then he began to break apart, streams of divine energy shooting out of holes in his body where his flesh had begun to crack; returning to the heavens from where it was stolen centuries ago. 'Go,' commanded the Shaman's fading voice one last time.

Gripping his son tight in his arms, Brodar Kayne plunged through the Portal.

*

'Even with the healing magic I have administered, his body is weak. But he will survive.'

He breathed a sigh of relief and ran rough, callused hands down his face, feeling the month's worth of beard, the scars and hard lines carving a history of violence in his features. The cold water might've washed away some of the grime but these scars would always remain, a constant reminder of what he was. Who he was.

He looked up at the young sorceress who had just brought him the news. She was one of the few survivors of the magical contest between Heartstone's circle and the Green Reaching's cadre of sorceresses – a tragic waste of life. He remembered the knife quivering in the throat of the sorceress he'd killed, and winced. 'I'm sorry about your friend,' he said. 'I just wanted to find my son.'

The sorceress shrugged coolly. 'You found him.' Having delivered her update on Magnar's condition, the woman turned and walked away. Kayne might've settled some personal business with Krazka but no one was celebrating him as a returning hero. This wasn't a time for heroes and, besides, there was no outrunning the shadow of the things he had done. No outrunning the shadow of Red Valley or a score of smaller crimes.

A familiar voice called out, 'It is time.' Kayne got up from where he'd been kneeling by the icy stream and exchanged a single nod with Orgrim Foehammer. The gathering of chieftains was about to start.

The narrow valley in which the Shaman's Portal had opened was only a few miles from the modest farmstead Kayne and Mhaira had lived for the best part of their married lives. He was desperate to take a horse and ride there now, but Carn had insisted he be present for a brief gathering between the chieftains of the West, Green and East Reachings. Soon the exodus would reach the Greenwild and inevitably the vast host of fleeing Highlanders would begin to spread out.

Kayne made his way towards the looming figure in the middle of the snow-blanketed vale. Warriors streamed past, women and children too, everyone heading south. Towards the Lowlands. Tens of thousands of his people, chased from their homes by the invading demon horde.

Carn was waiting, Oathkeeper's point planted in the ground before him. Kayne and Orgrim arrived just as Brandwyn the Younger appeared out of a crowd of his countrymen. The chieftain of the Green Reaching stepped forward and immediately grasped Kayne's hand, his skin softer and smoother than any warrior's had a right to be. But then Brandwyn wasn't truly a warrior: he was a governor and a councillor, more at home with numbers and politics than with a sword and shield. Brandwyn the Elder, his father, had been a true warrior. But he had also been a headstrong fool and his stubbornness had got a great many folk killed.

Brandwyn the Younger smiled at Kayne from beneath a rust-coloured beard. He had small eyes and a weak voice. 'Brodar Kayne. The Sword of the North. I hardly knew you growing up, but my father always spoke highly of you as his good friend.'

'Aye. Your pa and me were close once,' Kayne replied. Maybe they were too close. Maybe he should have swayed Brandwyn from his path long before it got to the point where he decided to break the Treaty and declare independence for the Green Reaching. Still, life had a lot of *maybes*; the only thing that really mattered was the certainty of the now.

'Tell me how that son of a bitch died,' Brandwyn the Younger said softly.

Kayne blinked, a little taken aback. 'Krazka or the Shaman?'

The young chieftain's eyes glittered. 'Both.'

Kayne thought for a moment. 'Like they deserved,' he answered.

'To business,' Carn rumbled, forestalling any further questions. 'The bulk of the demon legion is still in the Heartlands. Once they are done killing all in their path, they will spread to the furthest Reachings. To the Sky Reaching and the Blue Reaching. To the Deep Reaching and the North Reaching.'

'There any hope for them?' Kayne asked.

Carn shrugged his massive shoulders. 'Perhaps some may make it to safety. Hrothgar is a canny leader. But Narm

Blacktooth hasn't been heard from in many days.'

'What of Mehmon?' The chieftain of the North Reaching had been another friend of Kayne's back in the day.

Orgrim cleared his throat. 'Frosthold was burned to the ground. I carried out the orders myself. Me and Krazka. Mehmon's dead.' Orgrim's eyes filled with shame.

'*Dead*,' Kayne echoed. Mehmon had been a man of honour. There weren't many of them left, seemed to him.

'We all die eventually,' said Carn. The look he gave Kayne was heavy with meaning. 'But if we wish to save our people, we must forget those it is already too late to help.'

There was a commotion just to the north and a squat, thickset warrior shouldered his way forward.

'Mace!' Orgrim exclaimed. 'You made it.'

The chieftain of the Black Reaching looked utterly spent, his dark hair matted to his head with sweat and his hairless chin scabbed from countless minor cuts.

'By the skin of my balls,' he snarled. 'The demons caught up with us a few miles from Heartstone. We thought we was marching south to help retake the capital from the Butcher King. Instead, we walked into a fucking massacre.'

'You did well to make it this far,' Carn growled, holding out a hand in greeting. Mace grabbed it, the chieftain of the Black Reaching a foot shorter than but maybe just as wide as his counterpart from the West Reaching.

'I had help,' Mace said. 'The Forsaken showed up. Turns out they abandoned the North Reaching weeks past. No one's been sending supplies to the Icespire since Mehmon's death.'

*The Forsaken*. Kayne had only met a few members of the order in the past. They rarely left their fortress, the Icespire, which perched on the very edge of the frozen wastes. Those accepted into the ranks of the Forsaken tended to die on the job, alone on the tundra battling ice ghouls or worse. With one notable exception, they were the forgotten heroes of the Highland people.

'There was another fellow too,' Mace was saying now. 'A

lone warrior. Showed up halfway through the fighting. Killed more demons than any other three men combined. Wouldn't lower his hood but his axes sang of death like the Reaver himself.'

'Axes?' Kayne repeated. He felt a chill run down his back. 'He survive?'

Mace shrugged. 'Wouldn't have thought so. Last I saw he was hopelessly surrounded.'

'If the demons follow us here,' Carn said, 'it will be slaughter. We are spread out, our women and children vulnerable.'

Orgrim hefted his great warhammer. 'I'm gonna round up some warriors. My bravest and most loyal. I surrendered the East Reaching thinking to spare my people, but I see now the demons will spare no one.' The big chieftain's voice grew hoarse, the weight of his mistakes evident in his haunted eyes. 'I let them in – and now my people, my countrymen, are dead. Let me die with them. Buy you what time I can.'

Mace spat again. The good kind of spit that announces grim work needs doing and a man isn't going to shy away from it. 'I'll gather my warriors and join you. Any who want to flee south are free to go. Those who want to stay and die like Highlanders can come with us.'

'I fear no demon,' Carn said. 'But my people need a leader. I must stay with them.'

Brandwyn rubbed his beard thoughtfully. 'The demons have yet to enter my own Reaching. I will not sacrifice myself or my people. Besides, I need to organize our food supplies. Those we can transport south with us. It will be a long road to somewhere hospitable.'

That left Kayne, who flexed his recently damaged wrist and stared into the distance. 'Don't reckon I fancy another trek south,' he said slowly. 'It'd be easier and maybe nobler to die fighting demons alongside the Foehammer. Like in times gone by.' He nodded at Orgrim, who gave the ghost of a smile despite the tragedy on his face. 'But I can't stay. I made a promise to keep my son safe, and I ain't going anywhere without Mhaira.'

Carn tugged Oathkeeper free of the earth, shook the snow off the rune-etched blade. 'You know the Lowlands better than any of us,' he said. 'I will see your son is cared for until you catch up with us. The Sword of the North is needed in the south.'

They exchanged farewells, Kayne gripping Orgrim's meaty hand in his own one last time. 'Remember on the banks of the Icemelt, when you told me I had fire and steel? We were young then. Well, the fire's gone out and I reckon the iron's gone brittle with age, but you can't say we had a bad run. Kept the Fangs safe from demons for thirty years.'

'I broke,' Orgrim said. 'In the end, I broke.'

Kayne shook his head. 'You didn't break. You bent. I reckon you can forgive anyone one moment of weakness. You're a good man, Orgrim. One of the best I know.' He reached out and clapped the big chieftain on the back. 'Die as you lived. Defending our people.'

Kayne watched his old friend depart, knowing this was the last time he would ever see him. Yet another face soon to belong to the past. The Shaman's words came to him. *All things die.* Even a Magelord, a man whom he also might've called a friend once. Maybe the last of them.

He went to check on Magnar. His son was sleeping on a pallet in the care of the healers. A sorceress placed a finger to her lips as he drew near, giving him a shake of her head, and so he quietly snuck away to find a horse. Just as he'd managed to convince someone to let him borrow their mare for a few hours Shakes approached. He already had his parchment and quill in hand. 'Brodar Kayne,' he greeted him eagerly. 'I understand momentous events took place on Lake Dragur. The Shaman is dead. You must tell me everything.'

Kayne smiled. 'Maybe later,' he said, climbing up onto his borrowed horse and raising a hand in farewell. 'I got more important things to do right now. I'm going to find my wife. I'm going to find Mhaira.'

# Carhein

*There's always light at the end of the tunnel*, Garrett had told him once.

As Davarus Cole lay trussed up on the back of a wagon, like a corpse in one of the Collector carts in Dorminia, he wondered if that light might come in the form of a blazing fireball tossed by an angry Magelord, or perhaps a vast explosion courtesy of the Fade weapons he had heard rumour of. It sure as hell wasn't going to be anything positive, he knew that much.

Someone must have poisoned his beer back at the tavern. He couldn't remember drinking that excessively, though in truth he couldn't recall much of anything at all.

The wagon bounced suddenly, causing his left knee to bang painfully against the side. 'Shit,' he hissed.

'Quiet, child,' commanded a voice. There was something familiar about it. Belatedly, and with growing anger, Cole realized that it belonged to the wagon-master who had offered up a warning about the Cult of the Nameless just before he'd stopped at the Farmboy's Folly for a drink.

'You,' he spat. 'You're one of them. One of the Nameless cultists.'

The sack over Cole's head was pulled off. Despite the dimness of the covered wagon, he had to blink tears from his eyes as they adjusted from hours spent in utter darkness. If the light leaking through the cracks in the canvas above was any indication, he'd been trussed up on the cart now for a night and half a day.

The cultist reached up and pulled down his hood. The ruddy face and heavy moustache beneath confirmed Cole's suspicions. 'Not merely *one* of them,' replied the man, eyes glittering. 'I am Nadap Naif. I am deputy leader of the south cell in Carhein.'

'Did you plan this?' Cole demanded. 'Did you know I would stop at the tavern?'

'On the contrary,' sneered Nadap. 'I wanted you well away from the area before night fell. I suspected a meddlesome foreigner like you would stick your nose where it wasn't wanted – such as in the Folly on the night of the full moon.'

Cole took a quick look around. The hangover he still nursed caused his head to swim. Just behind Nadap was another cultist, also draped in black robes, hood pulled over his face. It was he who had spoken with Cole when he had first awoken. On the other side of the wagon bed, the serving wench – her name eluded Cole – was tied up, a sack pulled over her head. Still, those soft curves were unmistakable. He remembered warm hands on his body, hot breath on his neck…

'You kidnapped the waitress from the Folly!' he exclaimed.

'The harlot was crying out for the embrace of the Nameless! Her wantonness was clearly a call for help. We found you with her in her room, the two of you passed out from drink. Unlike this girl, you will not be granted the opportunity to seek solace in the darkness.'

'I won't?'

'No. You, child, you have been chosen.'

'Chosen for what?' Cole asked, though as the wagon clattered over a hole in the road and sent sharp pains up his arse, he had a sinking feeling he knew what was coming.

'*Death*. Your sacrifice to the three-eyed demon will help hasten this world towards the blessed embrace of darkness.'

Cole heaved a deep sigh. A moment later he stifled a yawn. Nadap frowned. 'Does the knowledge of your impending death bore you?' The cultist reached into his robes and withdrew

Magebane. He waved it before Cole's nose. 'Perhaps I will use this pretty dagger of yours to cut out your eyes.'

Cole settled back down, once again silently cursing his ill fortune. He was supposed to be delivering a message to the Rag King's advisor. Every second he spent tied up on this wagon was time wasted. 'Where are you taking me?' he demanded.

'We are almost at our destination. There you will see – assuming you wish to keep your eyes.'

Cole nodded meekly. Once again he tested his bonds. There was a jagged piece of metal sticking out of the wagon nearby; in days gone by he would already have been furtively working the rope against it, preparing to make a grab for Magebane just as soon as the fibres parted and his hands were free.

That was then, back when he'd thought himself a hero. Now he was more likely to get himself killed. And chances were he'd bungle things so badly he would probably get the girl killed as well.

Despair washed over him. The pleasant, earthy smell of the countryside slowly faded to be replaced by the stench of a big city and a voice called out at the front of the wagon, 'We are almost at the west gate. Gag the prisoners.'

Nadap stuffed a filthy rag into Cole's mouth and he wanted to puke. The cultist went to examine the girl, who was still sleeping, her ample chest rising and falling in an easy rhythm. He shrugged and turned to address the driver. 'The Trineman is gagged. Charmaine will not be a problem.'

*Charmaine?* Cole stared at the Tarbonnese girl and wondered what had happened in her room in the tavern before whatever poison had been slipped into his drink had knocked him unconscious. Guilt surged up like a geyser. Had he taken her to bed? He thought of Sasha and how she would react to the news. True, they weren't officially a couple, but her lack of male companions could only mean she was saving herself for him. Cole wished he'd had the willpower to return the gesture, but it felt wrong to deprive the world's women of

Davarus Cole. At least until he'd put a ring on Sasha's finger.

He caught a faint *meow* and remembered that Midnight was stowed away in his backpack. The cultists hadn't yet discovered the kitten, it seemed.

He heard voices outside the wagon. They were muffled and he was unable to make out what was being said. He tried to cry out for help, but the gag drowned his words and all that escaped was a moan. The wagon lurched forward again. Soon the murmur of the city reached his ears. A smorgasbord of smells made him simultaneously hungry and nauseous.

*We're in Carhein*, he thought. The wagon abruptly stopped again and a trumpet sounded.

'Soldiers,' hissed the driver at the front of the wagon. 'The Rag King sends more men south to war.'

There came the drumming of marching feet outside. Cole could hear the thumping of hundreds of heartbeats as the soldiers passed before the wagon. They soon receded into the distance and once again they began to move. Minutes passed and sweat beaded his brow. It was stifling within the confines of the wagon. Eventually the sour stench of shit reached his nostrils and Nadap moved to remove his gag. 'We are here,' he growled.

The girl, Charmaine, began to stir then, lifting her head groggily and staring around with wide eyes. She opened her mouth to say something but Cole met her gaze and shook his head.

The canvas covering the wagon was pulled back and grimy daylight flooded his vision. They were in a narrow alley crowded by discarded rubbish and the turbid overflow from a blocked sewer. The wagon blocked his view of the city beyond the alley, but Cole was reasonably certain they were in one of the poorer parts of Tarbonne's capital; the slums, in all likelihood.

One of the cultists untied his ankles and grabbed his arms, while the other took hold of Charmaine and hauled her up. Nadap rapped out a complex sequence on the nearby door of a building so dilapidated it looked fit to collapse. Moments later the door swung open and Cole was pushed through into the darkened interior of the cultists' hideout. He was led through a nearly pitch-black corridor. They turned a corner and then approached another door, beneath which bled a sinister green light. He could sense death in the air; it permeated every inch of the wooden floor and walls surrounding him. Behind him, Cole heard Charmaine sobbing.

The door creaked open and the two captors were shoved into a large room lit by a brazier burning brightly in each corner. The cultists were burning a strange substance to lend the flames their green radiance, and the sulphurous smell made Cole's eyes water.

'You return,' whispered a cowled figure sitting cross-legged on the floor in the centre of the room. 'You brought the girl. And an unexpected guest.' The cultist climbed slowly to his feet. He pulled down his hood, and Cole recoiled slightly at the visage that greeted him.

The old man had cut out his own eyes, judging by the jagged scars surrounding the empty sockets in his face. In the centre of his forehead, a huge incision in his flesh revealed bone beneath. The cut was shaped like an eye; the effect of the self-mutilation was unsettling.

'Yes, Dreamer,' answered Nadap. 'A sacrifice to the Nameless. A Dorminian.'

'A foreigner?' said the one called Dreamer. He smiled, revealing brown teeth. His breath was rancid. 'Convenient. The city guard will not be searching for him.'

'What do you want with me?' cried Charmaine. The girl was pale with terror. Cole tested his restraints again, but there was no chance of slipping his bonds – the rope was knotted tight around his wrists.

'Ask not what we *want* with you, child – but rather what we can *do* for you.'

'You can let me go, you sick fucker!' the serving girl screamed, much to Cole's shock. Charmaine had shifted from afraid to spitting furious in an instant.

Dreamer placed a wrinkled hand on her cheek. She spat and tried to twist away but Nadap, the false teamster, held her firm. 'There is a turmoil within you, girl. A hurt you seek to salve by whoring yourself indiscriminately to every man who lays eyes upon you.'

Cole wanted to protest at the 'indiscriminately', and especially the 'every man', but the glimmer of steel at Dreamer's waist and the evil look that flashed across the face of Nadap as the cultist stared at him quashed that desire like a turd caught under a wagon wheel. He understood now the peril he was in.

'You lost someone close to you,' Dreamer continued. 'Your sister. She was one of those who disappeared just before the Rag King won the throne. I know your pain, child. My own son perished in the wars. But then the three-eyed demon came to me in my dreams and spoke of the Nameless.'

If there was one thing a fanatic could be relied upon to do, it was expound in detail about whatever bloodthirsty cause got them out of bed in the morning, whenever the opportunity presented itself. Cole figured the best way to buy time to come up with a plan was to keep the man talking. 'The three-eyed demon spoke to you,' he repeated, trying to instil some measure of awe into his voice. 'Why you?'

'Not just me. There are other Dreamers throughout the Shattered Realms. We speak for those who are lost. Those who have nothing, made homeless and destitute by the civil wars that have torn this kingdom apart. The Nameless offers us succour. Solace in oblivion.'

Cole stared around furtively, searching for anything he might be able to use to free his hands. Nadap still had Magebane stashed somewhere under his robes, but there was no chance of getting hold of it with his wrists bound and the other cultists sticking to him like scabs to a wound.

'The Nameless ushers forth a new age,' the Dreamer continued, warming to his subject. 'There will be no more inequality when the Nameless walks among us. No longer shall the rich lord it over the poor. No longer shall sons and daughters die in pointless wars, or disappear in the middle of the night, never to return.'

'You're mad,' spat Charmaine.

Dreamer chuckled. 'A certain amount of madness is the first step towards salvation. It is time you learned this particular lesson. Nadap, unlock the Contemplation Chamber.'

The other cultist took a key off a hook hanging on the wall beside a door and opened it, taking a step to the side. The body of a man tumbled out, emaciated to the point of starvation.

'Alas, the last occupant of the Chamber resisted deliverance,' said Dreamer. 'He refused to pluck out his eyes and see the truth as I have done. Now the only truth he will ever know is the finality of death.'

Cole stared in horror at the Contemplation 'Chamber'. In actuality it was little more than a cupboard, with hardly room enough to stand. The inside of the door was gouged and scratched and covered in rust-coloured stains; Cole's horror grew when he saw the ruined stumps of the dead man's fingers. The prisoner had tried to claw his way through the door before he perished from lack of food, water or both.

'Put the girl in there,' Dreamer ordered. Charmaine immediately began to scream and struggle as Nadap dragged her towards the nightmarish cell. Cole stared at the body, Dreamer's words echoing in his skull.

*Now the only truth he will ever know is the finality of death.*

Suddenly he had an idea.

'Rise,' he whispered. 'Rise and attack these men.'

The corpse began to shift, unleashing a ragged moan just as Cole's head connected with the face of the cultist behind him. The man fell away with a howl and Cole made a dash for the nearest brazier. He placed his bound wrists over the flame, gritted his teeth stoically and prepared to accept the agony. It was only pain, and flesh would heal. If he could just hold the rope there long enough for it to burn through—

'Shit,' he hissed, jerking his hands away involuntarily. 'That's hot.'

The prisoner he'd raised from the dead lunged at Dreamer, sinking its inhumanly strong jaws into his neck and tearing out his thin throat in a gout of blood. Charmaine brought her hands together and elbowed the wagon driver in the stomach, spinning away to stand beside Cole. That left Nadap, who stared wide-eyed at the corpse chewing on the head of his fellow cultist and then turned and fled.

*

Cole stumbled out of the building, Charmaine behind him, the two cultists hot on their heels. He slowed when he saw the line of pink-plumed guardsmen waiting before the wagon. Nadap was sprawled dead on the ground, three quarrels sticking out of his back.

'Stop where you are!' barked the apparent captain of the guards. 'Put your hands where I can see them, dogs!'

Cole wasn't in much of a mood to oblige, what with two murderous fanatics right behind them, but it was either that or suffer the same fate as Nadap. He skidded to a halt and raised his bound hands before him. A second later, Charmaine followed suit.

'Now get down on your knees—'

The guard captain was interrupted as the fanatics barged through the door, both brandishing wide knives. Cole flinched, expecting a blade in the back at any second – but there was only a tiny delay before the click of many crossbows filled the air, and the cultists hit the ground in a one-two of dull thuds.

'Are there are any more of them inside?' the captain demanded.

Cole shrugged helplessly. 'I don't think so.'

The captain turned and spat. 'Rabid dogs. I'm tempted to put this whole section of slums to the torch. Flush them out like the rats they are!'

'I found the contraband, sir,' said a female guard. She stepped out from the behind the wagon, a small, dark, furry bundle in her arms.

'*Midnight*,' Cole whispered. He'd forgotten about the kitten.

'You are familiar with this vermin?' barked the captain.

'She's not vermin!' Cole replied, trying not to let his temper get the better of him. 'She's my cat.'

The guard captain's hand shot out and slapped Cole painfully across the face. Shocked, he had to resist the urge to pluck the man's rapier from his belt and drive it through his pulsating throat. It wasn't just shocked outrage behind that desire – it was *hunger*. The Reaver hadn't fed in many days. 'Your arrogance offends me, Trinesman! Are you not aware that such animals are banned from Carhein? Fortunately for you the cat escaped the wagon and one of my officers followed it to this hideout. Are you not familiar with the story of the Rag King?'

'I'm afraid not,' Cole replied, as diffidently as he could manage in the circumstances. 'I didn't have much time to ask questions before I was drugged and bundled off in the back of a wagon.'

The guard captain turned to Charmaine. 'Is this true? Were you drugged by these cultists?'

The Tarbonnese girl shook her head. 'I think we just had too much to drink. This Dorminian passed out.'

'Well, that's bullshit,' Cole muttered. The captain scowled at him and he swallowed his anger, forcing himself to remember the reason why he had come to this country. 'I need to deliver a message to the king's advisor,' Cole replied. 'It's of the utmost importance. I've wasted enough time here already.'

'Pass me the message and I will be the judge of its importance.'

Cole sighed in annoyance. 'It's in my backpack,' he said, gesturing at the wagon.

'Captain,' said a guardsman. He straightened up from inspecting Nadap's body and Cole saw that he held Magebane

163

in his hand, its soft radiance casting a bluish sheen on his ratty features. 'Look at this.'

'That's mine,' Cole said, trying to keep his voice casual.

The captain retrieved the dagger from his colleague and examined it with wide eyes. 'This is magic. Why would a boy like you own a weapon like this?'

'I'm not a boy!' Cole said hotly. He forced himself to calm down. 'It was passed down to me by my father. Its power works only for me.'

*Magebane's magic will only work for those possessing the blood of a true hero.* Another of Garrett's lies. The blood of a murderous, Magelord-kissing Augmentor was the real truth.

'Prove it,' demanded the captain.

'I can't. Not unless you know any wizards nearby,' Cole replied.

'Only Zatore.'

'Yes,' Cole exclaimed. 'Zatore. The king's advisor. That's what I've been trying to say. I need to bring a message to Zatore.'

The captain went to Cole's backpack and opened it. He removed the scroll and examined it with a deep frown. 'It's blank,' he said. 'Do you take me for a horse's arse?'

'It's magically encrypted,' Cole explained. 'Here. I have a writ from the White Lady of Thelassa herself explaining the situation. If you'll just loosen these bonds…'

Grumbling, the guard captain drew a dagger from his belt and sliced through the rope binding Cole's wrists. He flexed his hands, forcing the blood back into them, and then reached into a pocket, relieved to find that the writ was where he'd left it.

'Here,' said Cole, thrusting the writ at the guard captain. The officer scanned it, his eyebrows rising slightly.

'You'd better come with me to the palace,' he said finally. 'The king and his Companions haven't been themselves of late, but if this signature is indeed that of the Magelord of Thelassa, they must be told. The girl stays here.'

'Fine with me,' Cole said, ignoring the slightly hurt look that passed across Charmaine's face. He glanced at her and hesitated. 'Did we... back at the Folly...'

'No,' she said, a little angrily. 'We didn't.'

*I knew it. I knew I couldn't betray Sasha. Not even after my drink was poisoned and I didn't know what in the hells was going on.*

'Don't take it personally,' he said cheerfully. 'I'm keeping a promise to a girl I love.'

Charmaine's voice was flatly matter-of-fact. 'That's funny. I remember you being as desperate as a dog on heat. You just couldn't keep it up once we got down to action. You were too drunk.'

'Ah,' said Cole. He turned back to the guard captain and cleared his throat. 'Shall we go now?'

# The Thin Line

SASHA FINISHED EMPTYING her stomach and stumbled away from the chamber pot, wiping drool from her chin with the back of her hand. She blinked a few times, attempting to chase away the demons of purple and gold that her *hashka*-fried brain summoned up and then shredded in an endless mind-bending cycle that had become as familiar to her as an old boot.

'You asked me for...?' she slurred, stumbling into Fergus's offices in the uppermost part of the Consult chambers. He was sitting at his desk, poking at a soft lump of spongy material with a pair of scissors. *It's the whale's brain*, she realized through the fog that clouded her mind. Not an unwelcome fog; it helped shield her from the true depths of her revulsion.

'Ah, Sasha,' said Fergus with a small smile. *Snip snip* went the scissors and she froze in panic. He placed them in a drawer under the desk and beckoned her closer. 'I require your help. I understand you have quite the aptitude for operations. You used to be a key part of a rebel group opposed to Salazar, if I am not mistaken.'

Sasha squinted at Fergus. He seemed to split into two people before they merged again to become one. 'What does it matter to you?' she asked, willing herself to think clearly, to shake off the effects of the drug commonly referred to as moon dust because of the lunacy it provoked. This was a dangerous man.

'I require someone to organize the next round of Harvesting.'

'Harvesting?' Sasha echoed, hating every syllable of the

word, knowing it would lead to an even darker place than the one she currently found herself in.

Fergus gave a sharp nod. 'The Mistress has lost many hand-maidens since the war with Dorminia. Their numbers must be replenished. You are familiar with the Unlife chambers, are you not? There are five throughout the city. There is no need to be quite so conservative with our production of new Unborn. Not in these desperate times.'

'You want me to kidnap more women and steal their babies?' Sasha asked, utterly aghast. The wild bursts of colour crawling across her vision formed horns above the man opposite her. 'I won't do it,' she spat. Literally spat, saliva slobbering out to cover Fergus's face. 'You're evil.'

Fergus reached into his coat and withdrew a handkerchief. He carefully wiped away the spit, displayed no signs of consternation at her outburst. 'To men of progress, evil does not exist,' he stated. 'It is a manifestly false concept. When there are no gods to judge, who can say what is right or wrong? There are animals in the wild that kill and eat their young. Are they evil?'

'That's not—' Sasha began, but Fergus continued over her, delivering his lecture with such utter conviction that a shred of doubt began to creep in.

'Is it *good* to practise restraint and leave the city under-prepared in the face of our immortal foes? What then of all the children who will die should the Fade breach the barrier? Many more so than my programme calls for. Many thousands more.'

'You can't just kidnap people and steal their children!' Sasha was screaming now. Other members of the Consult turned to stare but she ignored them, focused her anger on the man seated before her.

'Those were the Mistress's words, when I first proposed my plans many years ago,' Fergus said. He smiled that small, self-satisfied smile of his. 'Eventually she saw the merit in what I proposed. For you see, there is no good and evil. There is only necessity. The mother of invention and the keystone of survival.'

'Fuck you,' Sasha whispered. 'I'm not doing it.'

Unperturbed, Fergus nodded and then reached into his desk drawer again. 'Talking of necessity, perhaps this will change your mind.' His eyes glittered as he lowered the bag to his desk. He pulled it open a little, revealing the silvery contents.

Sasha swallowed, her throat suddenly as dry as the vast deserts of the Sun Lands to the south. Her hands shook. Hating herself, she reached towards the bag.

'There will be more waiting for you when you bring me a plan to increase our output of Unborn by a further half,' Fergus said. 'I will give you until midday. My staff will provide all the necessary details.'

Sasha squeezed her eyes shut. She had been a hopeless junkie ever since her first taste of the silver powder at Garrett's estate as a teenager. At first it had helped ease the pain. Soon it had become a vice she found impossible to resist. It had been easy enough to get her hands on whatever she needed: her unsuspecting foster father rarely questioned how she spent his coin and her Shard colleague, Vicard, had kept her well supplied until his death at the Wailing Rift.

*There is no good or evil.*

Who was going to judge her? Her parents? They were dead. Her foster father? Garrett was dead. The other Shards, her sister Ambryl? All dead. She was utterly alone.

Utterly alone except for one person. And if anyone had ever known the difference between good and evil, it was Cole.

She grabbed the bag of *hashka* and hurled it at Fergus. It struck him on the nose and the powder exploded all over him, covering him head to toe. He didn't react, just sat there stunned, as though a calculation he had been confident would be proven correct had turned out to be terribly wrong.

Before anyone could react, there was a loud series of explosions from the throne room, where the White Lady and Thanates had been locked in furious discussion since the *Caress* had docked in Thelassa.

Sasha hurried through the Consult chambers, dodging around men and women dashing in the same direction, all heading for the stairs leading to the lower levels. Sasha joined the stampede, trying not to trip and break an ankle in her hurry. She doubted the White Lady would be as accommodating with her healing magic a second time.

Sasha was among the first to reach the throne room and therefore had the perfect view of the disaster about to unfold. Thanates was pinned to the ceiling, the White Lady directly beneath him, silver fire dancing around her hands. Somehow the ivory throne atop the dais had been torn in half. Most of the statuary leading to the throne was also destroyed, as though one of the mages had taken shelter from a magical assault behind the assorted depictions of beasts from ages past. Judging by the precarious state of Thanates, Sasha expected that was exactly what had happened.

'I warned you,' the White Lady was shrieking now. 'When I accepted your truce and allowed you into my city, I *warned* you not to speak of him!'

'Release me, Alassa,' Thanates commanded. 'Do not throw away your city because you cannot control your pain.'

'Throw away my city?' the White Lady sneered. 'I *am* my city! I am the light in the darkness! I am the last guardian!'

'You need me,' Thanates grated.

'I've never needed any man!'

Sasha watched the back and forth between the two wizards, while all around her the Consult cowered in fear and the Unborn awaited instruction from their furious mistress. Sasha thought of Fergus still seated at his desk covered in *hashka* and wanted to laugh. Then she realized how badly she needed another hit, and understood that her only line of supply was probably cut off forever now, and wanted to cry.

She wondered how Cole was faring down in the Shattered Realms. No doubt he would soon make his triumphant return, army in tow and bursting with a dozen stories about his latest escapades. What would she tell him when he asked about her contribution to the city's defence? *Oh, I went on a failed voyage to the Celestial Isles, then lounged around the palace getting doped up to my eyeballs.*

'Five hundred years,' the White Lady was snarling now. 'Five hundred years and you still know how to push me past the edge of fury, Thanates. I will end you now!'

'Kill me and your hopes of saving your city die with me,' the Dalashran snapped back.

*Do they actually* want *to kill each other?* It seemed to Sasha that if one of the mages truly wanted their former lover dead, it would have happened long ago. Even now, with the Magelord clearly in a dominant position, she seemed to seek out further lines of argument with Thanates rather than finishing him off.

The White Lady's purple eyes narrowed, her platinum hair dancing behind her. Once more Sasha was awed by this woman's beauty. A terrible beauty, intoxicating to behold.

'I will end you now,' the White Lady repeated.

Whether or not she meant those words would forever be a matter of conjecture, as at that moment there was a great tearing sound and a hole seemed to open in the centre of the throne room. The air wavered, shifting and distorting to show another throne room on the other side. This one was much different to the White Lady's. Jade statues of strange creatures lined a scarlet carpet leading up to a great golden throne. Bronze-skinned men dressed in golden armour formed a guard of honour. There was a flicker of movement as someone, or something, stepped into the magical doorway—

'A *Portal?*' the White Lady whispered in utter fury. 'Here? Who dares?'

A moment later she received her answer.

The man who emerged into the throne room was tall, thin and extravagantly dressed in flowing golden robes. A magnificent crown studded with emeralds sat perched atop his head, while black hair streaked with grey reached down to his shoulders. He too was bronze-skinned and dark-eyed. The impressive beard and moustache he wore down to his chest were braided in a complex pattern, a fashion unfamiliar to Sasha. The man – *a king?* – bowed slightly to the White Lady, crossing his hands in front of his waist as he did so. It was clearly not a gesture of subservience but rather a mark of respect between equals.

'Hiakara?' the White Lady snarled. 'You broke the agreement. To Portal into the city of another Magelord is forbidden.'

'There was no time for a more formal visit,' said the foreign Magelord. He spoke with a strange accent, as though the language didn't come naturally to him. 'I had to Portal.'

'You wish to offer us aid? I thought you cared not for the west.'

Hiakara shook his head. 'It is not that I do not care, queen of Thelassa. The Jade Isles has its own problems and you and these invaders are a world away.'

'Then why are you here?'

Hiakara's voice grew grave. 'There is another threat, one for which I feel responsible. The gholam has been activated. A thief broke into the imperial treasury and stole the key.'

'The *gholam?*' exclaimed the White Lady. She sounded aghast. 'I thought the imperial treasury impenetrable.'

'As did I. The thief used a strange flavour of magic to gain access. Somehow the defences were not triggered.'

'Do you know the identity of this thief?'

'We do not. I sent one of my agents to hunt them down. Her mission was not a success.'

'The gholam,' the White Lady repeated, rising dread in her voice. 'One of the three god-weapons. Even our magic could not harm it. Do we have any idea where the thief or the key may be found?'

Hiakara shook his head. 'In the absence of a living target, the gholam will always seek out the bearer of the key. In doing so it will kill anything in its path.'

The White Lady's obvious discomfort was more terrifying to Sasha than her earlier rage had been. 'Thank you for the warning, Hiakara. You will not change your mind about sending aid?'

The eastern Magelord shook his head again. 'I cannot. But I wish you luck, queen of Thelassa. From a purely selfish perspective, I hope you stop these invaders before they can threaten the Confederation. As I said – we have our own troubles to deal with.' Hiakara seemed for the first time to notice Thanates pinned to the ceiling. He raised a hand slightly in a gesture of acknowledgement. 'Once-king of Dalashra,' he said.

'Wizard-Emperor,' said Thanates, from his corner of the ceiling.

Hiakara turned, and in a flurry of golden robes he stepped back through the rift he had opened. It pulsed a few times and then contracted, growing smaller until, with a popping noise, it disappeared completely. The White Lady's throne room was restored to normalcy; or at least as close to normalcy as it ever was.

There came a thud. Thanates picked himself up off the floor and dusted off his tattered coat, a deep frown creasing his scarred and eyeless brow.

For a long while the Magelord of Thelassa stood silent and unmoving. Then the White Lady turned her back on the Consult. 'Leave me,' she commanded, her voice shockingly subdued. 'I need to be alone.'

# The Rag King

'THE MISTRESS TRUSTED you to deliver her letter to me personally. She does not trust easily. I am impressed.'

Zatore stared at Cole over the small rosewood table in her study in the Royal Palace of Carhein and raised an eyebrow in approval. The Rag King's advisor took a sip from the glass of wine she was holding and Cole couldn't help but notice the soft shape of her lips. Zatore was just the right side of mature, with long black hair touched by only a hint of grey and the olive skin of Espanda complemented by a green dress that accentuated the fullness of her figure.

Cole raised his own glass of water and swallowed a mouthful. He'd decided to pass on the wine after his latest adventure.

*I won't leave myself open to being poisoned ever again.*

'You needn't be impressed,' he replied modestly. 'The truth is, I'm nothing without my birthright.' He nodded over at Magebane, which was currently in the possession of the captain of the palace guard – a stern-faced man who hardly seemed to blink. He was stationed by the door to Zatore's chambers.

'You understand why I had Eric confiscate your dagger?' Zatore said, with a gracious smile. 'I can take no risks. Your reputation precedes you.'

Cole nodded solemnly. 'I can't say I blame you. I'm just glad to have finally met someone in this country who respects me.'

Zatore smiled again. Her shoulders were bare and the figure-hugging dress she wore didn't leave a great deal to the imagination.

*Focus, Cole. Focus.* He was here on a mission of vital importance. He couldn't afford to get sidetracked, not this time. The future of the Trine, of humanity itself, might depend on his success.

'I studied under the Magelord of Thelassa for twenty years,' Zatore mused. 'She took a new apprentice after me, I believe. Brianna, perhaps.'

Cole nodded. 'A fine figure of a woman.' *Though not as fine as yours – Damn it, focus Cole!* 'She died helping to overthrow the tyrant Salazar,' he continued. 'She sacrificed herself to disrupt his magic.'

Sasha had become very emotional telling him the story of Brianna's death while they were sitting atop the Tower of Stars. It sounded like she had admired the woman a great deal.

'Sacrifice,' Zatore repeated in her husky voice. 'It is sometimes necessary.'

'I know all about sacrifice,' Cole said darkly. He stared around the lushly decorated study. The guards had brought him straight to the king's advisor and he hadn't had the opportunity to scout the rest of the palace, but if it was as opulent as Zatore's chambers then Tarbonne was doing a good deal better for itself than Dorminia. Even before all the recent trouble in the Trine.

'Indeed?' Zatore rose from her chair and moved across the table to place a delicate hand on his arm. 'Tell me what you know about sacrifice.'

Cole glanced down in mild alarm at the uncomfortable stirring in his breeches and cleared his throat. 'The truth is I'm always getting myself into trouble doing what I think is best. I spent years trying to be a hero and lost everything dear to me. I've hardly slept in months.'

*Though that has little to do with lack of opportunity and*

*everything to do with the divine hunger devouring me from within.*

'You do look unwell,' Zatore observed, stroking his arm. 'You are so very pale, and your hair is thin for one so young.'

'Lack of sunlight,' Cole answered quickly. 'It's grim up north.' A sensation other than the obvious was making him uncomfortable. There was something disturbing about the way Zatore was looking at him. She was regarding him with an intensity that seemed almost... *hungry.* 'Perhaps we should deliver the White Lady's message to the king now?' he suggested.

'Patience, Davarus Cole.' Zatore moved around him, twisting like a serpent to stand behind his chair and stare over his shoulder at the blank parchment resting in the centre of the table. It was covered in a soft glow. 'The Mistress encrypted the message and it will take some time for my own magic to decipher its words. Whatever she wishes to say, it is highly sensitive. Perhaps she feared her message would fall into the hands of these inhuman invaders from across the ocean you speak of.'

'The Fade,' Cole agreed. 'Do you think your king will send aid? I hear Tarbonne has the largest army in the Shattered Realms.' He stiffened as one of Zatore's fingers stroked the back of his neck. He met the eyes of the captain of the guards – Eric? – and was struck by how vacant they seemed.

'It has the most *divided* army,' Zatore purred. 'The duke yet holds out in the south and a third of Tarbonne's men-at-arms swear fealty to his banner. But you are a charismatic man, Davarus Cole. Perhaps you can yet convince the king it is in his best interests to commit soldiers to the north, if the letter from your mistress does not have the desired effect.'

'She's not my mistress,' Cole said. He relaxed a little. He *was* charismatic, that was the truth. Perhaps it wasn't so surprising Zatore was smitten with him. She wouldn't be the first older woman he'd had that effect on. Her hand continued to caress his neck, working its way to the front. Suddenly the king's advisor froze, one finger hooked beneath the golden key hanging under his shirt.

'What is this?' she asked, her voice changing from sultry to sharp in an instant.

'Just a gift from one of my many lovers,' Cole said, thinking to make the lie as convincing as possible.

'This was Wolgred's,' she hissed.

*Wolgred. The Wanderer. The mage who attacked me aboard the* Caress! *How does Zatore know of him?*

Cole twisted to stare up at the king's advisor. Her eyes were narrowed in fury. For the first time he noticed their slight reddish tinge and dread filled him. He remembered Wolgred's eyes burning like rubies in the assassin's skull.

He sprang out of the chair, making a dash for the captain of the guard across the chamber, desperate to get his hands on Magebane before Zatore could work her magic against him. But he'd only gone three strides when his legs suddenly refused to respond. Every one of his muscles seized up. No matter how he struggled, he couldn't twitch even a solitary finger.

Utter panic gripped him then, as tightly as Zatore's magic.

Zatore moved to stand before him, the words of the spell she had just cast to paralyse his body dying on her lips.

'Everything in order, milady?' Eric called out from his post by the door. For a moment Cole dared hope the man might help him – but that hope was quickly dashed.

'Quite perfect, thank you. Would you go and fetch us more wine? I should like a few minutes alone with our guest.'

'But, Lady Zatore, that is against protocol—'

The king's advisor raised a finger and pointed. 'Go,' she commanded, and her brown eyes seemed to flash crimson for the briefest of moments.

'Yes, milady,' the guard replied emotionlessly. He turned and departed without another word and Cole knew that he too was under Zatore's spell.

*I'm going to die.* Without Magebane he was just a man, and not a particularly smart or skilled one. If the look on Zatore's face was any indication, it wouldn't be a quick or easy death.

'I don't know how you came by this,' the king's advisor said, examining the golden key with a deep frown. Cole could smell the cloying sweetness of her perfume but it masked something else – a hint of something charnel, *rotten.* 'I must assume Wolgred is dead. He would not free the gholam only to carelessly relinquish the key. The master would skin him alive.'

Cole fought Zatore's magic with every shred of willpower he possessed, but it was hopeless. It was an effort even to blink. The realization that he would never see Sasha again brought tears to his eyes and they rolled down his cheeks unchecked; a final, pathetic show of weakness.

'Did the White Lady send you here to assassinate me?' Zatore mused, knowing he couldn't respond. 'Or does she truly believe the king would weaken his own army merely to delay her destruction? The Ancients cannot be stopped by men with swords and arrows or even a Magelord with the stolen power of the gods.'

The king's advisor moved closer to Cole. Her lips parted, and her eyes burned with hunger. Not the wanton desire of lust; no, this was a ravenous, obscene hunger that sickened him. 'When Eric returns, I will tell him you were an assassin sent by the duke's men,' Zatore whispered. 'I would devour your blood here and now, but to magically manipulate the Companions undetected is a delicate task and explaining your desiccated remains to that grey-haired bitch might expose me. I will drink you later.'

*Drink me?* Cole managed to widen his eyes ever so slightly in horror.

Zatore turned and walked across to the table. 'The White Lady's message is ready,' she said. 'Let us see what my erstwhile mistress has to say. Before I dispose of this document and haul you before the king.' As Cole watched transfixed, Zatore lifted the scroll. 'The fehd?' she muttered, reading from the document. 'That is their true name? The coming of the Ancients was predicted by the Master, though none of his apprentices know the full scope of his designs. There has never been a more brilliant man. It is my privilege to serve, and to learn. One day I will stand at his side for eternity.'

Cole wanted to close his eyes. To block out the sight of the woman who only minutes ago had been distracting him with all kinds of shameless thoughts.

'"*You were a faithful and talented apprentice.*" How generous of her to say so! Yet the White Lady could never give me what I wanted. Eternal beauty. Eternal *life*. All that blood magic offers. Wait – there is more: "*I know, Zatore. I know. Consider this my gift to you.*" What gift? What does that cunt know—'

The parchment suddenly glowed a brilliant silver, so bright that Cole's eyes wept fresh tears, blinding him for a moment.

When his vision cleared, Zatore was shaking like a leaf caught in a gale. She gasped and then her body began to contort grotesquely, limbs cracking, bones snapping in a hideous dance as the silvery glow rose from the parchment and enveloped her. First her arms fractured like dry twigs. Then her legs split, white bone poking through ruptured skin. Finally her spine snapped and she jerked horribly, like a marionette twitching to the strings of a ruthless puppeteer. With a blood-curdling shriek Zatore crumpled to the floor.

Cole was suddenly free to move, the magic that had frozen him in place shattered like the skeleton of the woman just opposite. He hurried over to the table, trying not to vomit at the sight of the shapeless mass of flesh that had moments ago been a living woman. He grabbed his backpack, quickly checked inside to make sure Midnight was fine, and then made a dash for the door.

*To hell with the White Lady's message. I'm getting the fuck out of here.* If he could just remember the way out of the palace—

The door to Zatore's chambers opened and the captain of the guard, Eric, barged straight into Cole. In his surprise the guard dropped the bottle of wine he'd been holding and it shattered into a thousand shards of glass, the produce of Carhein's finest vineyards splashing all over Cole, who managed to keep his feet. The guard's eyes widened when he saw the corpse of the king's advisor. He reached for the sword at his hip. '*Murder!*' he screamed. 'Guards, to arms!'

Cole glanced wildly around, but there was nowhere to run except straight at the helmed figure blocking the door. He charged and caught the man with a boot straight to the face. Eric crashed to the floor and Cole was beside him in an instant, prying Magebane from the guard captain's belt. It came free in a whisper of steel and immediately a blue glow sprang up around the blade.

Cole leaped the fallen guard and plunged into the corridor beyond.

A trio of guardsmen came sprinting towards him, spears raised. Cole backed away but felt an arm grab him from behind. It was Eric, the man's nose a bloody mess. Desperate and out of options, Cole spun and drove Magebane into the guard captain's neck. Warmth filled him as Eric's life was leached away, transferred by the dagger into his own body. It felt terribly wrong. Terribly wrong, and yet rapturously good.

The first of the spearmen lunged and Cole twisted, his reflexes razor-sharp, his movements effortlessly fluid compared with the lumbering guard. Magebane stabbed out again, opening the man's throat. More strength surged into Cole's body.

*Yes,* boomed a voice from somewhere deep inside. *Kill them. Kill them all, child.*

The two remaining guards tried to catch him in a pincer movement but he was unstoppable now, a killing machine. A crazed grin split his face and he batted aside one spear, stabbed out and heard a gasp as warm blood washed over his hand. He sensed movement behind him but it was laughably ponderous, like the guard was moving through tar. The Reaver opened the remaining guard's face and then stabbed him through the heart before his scream could even escape his ruined lips.

A chorus of heartbeats thundered in his ears. He twisted to see more guardsmen sprinting towards him. He didn't count them. There was no need.

He kicked off the wall and reversed momentum, stabbing one in the side of the neck and dropping him like a stone. He leaped again and somehow he was running *along* the wall, the thrusting spears of the guards around him like stalks of corn swaying lazily in the wind while he was the scythe, irresistible and unstoppable. In moments they were all dead. Inside he was raging fury but outside he was shadow, a darkness stalking through the corridor, smiling savagely, leaving only bodies in his wake.

The Reaver flowed into a large rectangular chamber; the throne room judging from the high-backed chair on the dais. It was occupied by a man covered by a patchwork cloak stitched from hundreds of scraps of cloth of all shades and colours. He wore a silver crown atop his head. *The king,* said a tiny and desperate voice. *Stop!* But it was drowned out by that relentless refrain.

*Kill them all. Kill them all, child.*

A half-dozen guards formed a protective wall before the throne, crossbows raised. He heard a series of clicks and saw the bolts flying towards him, twisting in the air.

The Reaver willed the shadows cloaking him to intercept the projectiles. Tendrils of darkness flowed outwards, plucked the bolts from the air, sent them clattering uselessly to the floor. Then he was upon the guards, stabbing and slashing, crimson droplets raining down all around him.

*I am death.*

'Lady Steel!' shouted a barrel-chested warrior just to the left of the king. He carried a monstrous shield protectively before him. To the king's right, a lean woman with long grey hair and dressed in full plate armour raised her longsword in salute.

Together the pair strode from the dais. They reached the Reaver just as he finished off the final guard, a fountain of red spray exploding from the man's torn throat.

He sprang at them, his dagger trailing scarlet beads. They would all perish here, fuel for the infernal hunger raging within him.

Somehow the shield-bearer blocked his attacks. The iron-haired woman took a step forward and launched a furious series of slashes and the Reaver was driven back, the edge of his steel striking sparks off her armour but failing to penetrate to the sweet flesh beneath.

He snarled and spat and fought with redoubled fury. Time and again the male managed to raise his shield just in time to turn aside an otherwise fatal blow, while the woman with the iron hair fought with supreme skill, dodging away from Magebane and riposting with such precision that, somehow, he found himself being driven back.

The fury began to fade, the edge of madness slowly receding as the Reaver fought these masters of sword and shield. The king merely watched from his throne, unmoving, chin resting on one scarred hand.

The Reaver grunted as the iron-haired warrior scored a small nick on his arm. The sudden shock of pain cut through the red haze and like the first green shoots of spring poking through the earth after a long winter, Cole's consciousness forced itself out. The supernatural rage driving him faltered and the big shield-bearer knocked him backwards with a fierce shove. Cole was forced to scramble away, blood dampening the spot where the woman's dancing sword had cut him.

'Wait,' he managed to rasp, dodging the arcing blade of the woman – *Lady Steel?* – and raising his hands before him in a placating gesture. 'I need to speak with the king.'

'Demon,' growled the grim warrior with the great shield. 'You will get no closer to him! The Companions have defeated worse than you.'

'I'm not a demon,' Cole said desperately. The shield pummelled him again and he staggered, almost tripping over the body of one of the guards he had killed. 'The White Lady sent me to deliver a message to Zatore,' he said in a mad rush. 'She was some kind of blood mage. I think she was controlling the king. I didn't mean to kill the guards.'

'Enough,' the shield-bearer spat. 'Don't think your lies will save you now, assassin.'

Lady Steel said nothing, though one grey eyebrow rose slightly.

'I swear, I'm telling the truth—'

The shield struck Cole painfully on the head, cutting him off mid-sentence.

'Hold,' said a gravelly voice that carried effortlessly from the throne. 'Let him speak with me.'

Uttering a string of curses, the shield-bearer stepped back and glowered at Cole. Lady Steel sheathed her sword, though her eyes didn't leave him for a moment.

Cole rubbed at his bruised skull and lowered Magebane. The blade was dripping red and as he gazed around at the carnage in the throne room, a sick feeling rose in his stomach.

*I did this. All these guards, dead. All because of me.*

'You will surrender your weapon before approaching the king,' growled the shield-bearer. Cole licked his lips, his mouth suddenly dry, and did as the man commanded, handing over Magebane, trying not to look at the blood-smeared hilt. He approached the throne. There was a squelching sound and he realized his boots were wet; soaked through with blood. The nausea rose again and he swallowed it down.

The Rag King watched him. As Cole drew closer he saw the man's face was as patchwork as his cloak, a hundred scars crisscrossing it from chin to brow. 'Zatore is dead?' the king asked, once Cole was standing before him.

'Yes,' Cole, replied. 'Her death was...' he was going to say *horrific*, but everything that had occurred since Zatore's chambers had been horrific. 'Colourful,' he finished lamely.

'You killed her?'

Cole shook his head. 'The White Lady gave me a message to give to Zatore, who triggered some kind of spell. A trap placed on the scroll. It shattered her. Broke every bone in her body.'

'Where is this message now?' the king asked softly.

'In Zatore's chambers. On her table.'

The Rag King nodded at the shield-bearer, who scowled at Cole before striding out of the room, presumably to retrieve the note.

The king looked at Cole. 'What *are* you?' he asked curiously.

*A killer. A murderer.* 'I'm... just a man.'

'The thing that entered this throne room and killed my guards was no man. It took two of the Companions to hold you off. Are you a mage?'

Cole shook his head. 'No. I...'

*What* am *I? A whore-spawn bastard. A child of murder and an heir to murder. A monster.*

'I'm cursed,' Cole finally managed.

The Rag King's eyes narrowed. They were different colours, Cole noticed: one blue, one green. The myriad scars on his face seemed to dance as he scowled. 'I know a little about curses myself.'

'They're all dead! He murdered them all! Even Eric.' The thundering voice of the big warrior announced his return before he stormed through the doors. He made straight for Cole, huge shield clutched in one hand, battleaxe in the other, violent intent written all over his face.

The Rag King raised a hand and Lady Steel moved to intercept him. 'Easy, Jax. We are no longer on the road. I alone pass judgement in this hall. Do you have the White Lady's message?'

'Here,' growled Jax, shoving it at the silent swordswoman blocking his path. She took the proffered parchment and brought it to the king, who began to read, his mismatched eyes scanning the document. 'The Magelord of Thelassa wants my help? She should know I have scant men to spare. Not for any cause, least of all to combat mysterious bogeymen from across the sea. What is this? "I know, Zatore. I know. Consider this my gift to you".' The Rag King chuckled suddenly. 'I believe the last line was addressed directly to me. It appears the White Lady's gift came in the form of an execution – hence freeing me of the machinations of my duplicitous advisor. I confess to not feeling myself as of late. Now I know why.' The king sighed and placed the parchment down. 'Sir Meredith warned me about Zatore. He was wrong in ways too many to list, but in this matter it appears he was correct.'

Cole had no idea who Sir Meredith was – but if the man was as formidable as the king's other former companions here in the throne room, he could count himself lucky that Sir Meredith was not among those present. Lady Steel was watching him with an intensity that could have boiled ants. The woman didn't seem to blink.

'The people of the Trine need your soldiers,' he said, thinking it best to get to the heart of the matter before the rising sickness in his gut ended with him humiliating himself. 'Dorminia has already fallen.'

The Rag King leaned back slightly on his throne and folded his hands on his lap. They too were massively scarred. 'Forgetting the fact that you have just slaughtered a score of my guards, how does this concern Tarbonne?'

'They wish to destroy all mankind,' Cole said, trying not to glance at the bodies littering the hall behind him. 'Once they've conquered the Trine they'll move south. The Fade wield weapons beyond our understanding. If Thelassa falls, no one is safe.'

'I have no soldiers to spare. The war with the duke demands every fighter I can muster.'

'You can convince the other realms to send aid,' Cole argued. 'This is bigger than a conflict between men. This is a battle for *survival*. The Fade don't care who sits on the throne in Tarbonne or any other kingdom. If we don't work together, everything we know will be dust.'

'Sounds like a loud of horse shit to me,' the big shield-bearer, Jax, muttered. 'Invaders from across the ocean? We should summon the inquisition and have this assassin put to the question. Wring the truth out of him.'

The Rag King glanced at Lady Steel. The silent swordswoman stared at Cole for a moment and then gave a slow nod. 'I believe he speaks the truth,' the king replied. 'The White Lady thought to buy my favour by ridding me of Zatore's influence.' The king frowned at Cole. 'Why she chose to send you of all people I cannot say. Whatever curse you carry that caused you to become... whatever it was you were, it does not change the fact that she is desperate, nor that your desire seems genuine. If these invaders do indeed move south, I will deal with that when it happens. I did not win this throne by neglecting the more immediate threat.' The king reached up and ran a scarred finger along the grisly tapestry of his face. 'As to the other realms,' he continued, 'my influence has waned. Many have their own troubles. They will not listen to me.'

'Then I came here for nothing,' Cole said bitterly. 'Nothing except to take the lives of innocents.'

'Lives you must answer for,' Jax growled. He took a step towards Cole. The Rag King made a soothing gesture and the big man turned away in disgust.

'It is true you should die for your actions here,' the king said. 'Curse or no curse, you have murdered enough of my men to hang many times over. A younger and more impetuous me would have seen to it myself. Still, I would not make an enemy of the White Lady. Jax, hand this young man back his weapon.'

There was a curse followed by a clatter as the king's companion tossed Magebane at Cole's feet. He stared down at the ruby-hilted dagger, filled with loathing for himself, and for this weapon that had taken so many lives.

*I wanted to be a hero. I never wanted to be a killer. It's not what I am.*

But it was exactly what he was. And without Magebane, he wasn't even that; without Magebane, he was worthless, a nobody.

Hating himself, he bent down and retrieved the dagger. 'Now what?' he asked numbly, meeting the king's mismatched eyes, Lady Steel's implacable gaze, Jax's angry glare. He had failed in his quest. He wished Sasha were here instead of him. *She* would have convinced this strange king to send men in response to the Fade threat.

'Now you leave,' the Rag King said simply. 'Do not return to Tarbonne. Attempt to do so and you will forfeit your life. Just as these men gave theirs in my service.' He pointed a scarred hand at the butchered remains of the guardsmen, their lifeblood oozing out to form puddles that glistened in the torchlight. Once again Cole's gorge rose.

He turned and ran from the palace, one hand pressed firmly to his mouth. He almost made it outside before the first mouthful of vomit burst through his fingers.

# Weapons

O N THE MORNING of Thelassa's Reckoning, the skies above the Trine opened.

Eremul frowned up at the dark clouds overhead and let the bitingly cold rain wash over his face. It was a grim day, befitting the even grimmer events that would play out later. He could see the ship that would launch the Breaker of Worlds undergoing some final checks in the harbour. He doubted the downpour would prove any impediment to the fehd's plans.

Despite the rain, a small crowd had gathered to watch the terrible weapon being readied aboard the ship. Perhaps it was fatalistic interest; perhaps some thought their occupiers planned to set up a permanent base in the Grey City and were preparing to remove a rival most held no love for. Dorminia had endured three tyrants in as many months and the White Lady's brief reign might have been the worst of them – at least until the Ancients got around to Reckoning the Grey City and everyone within.

*Strange how everything happens in threes. The three cities of the Trine; the three Adjudicators. The White Lady's handmaidens always seem to come in a trio. Perhaps the Creator had a fetish for the number. Or perhaps it is a cosmic rule that possibility will always fill a vacuum, and three is the number from which possibility spirals.*

It was a day to be philosophical, Eremul mused. Tens of thousands of lives were about to be snuffed out like candles. It paid to focus on the greater questions when the lesser ones gave answers that made him want to slit his wrists.

He wondered how Monique was faring back at the Refuge. He had concluded it was probably safe to leave the woman alone with Ricker and Mard. One of the men was permanently so drunk he couldn't raise his head, never mind his cock, while the other was more terrified of the cock-*rot* than possible destruction at the hands of a world-breaking weapon.

A light hand fell upon his shoulder and Eremul almost jumped out of his skin – or at least gave what passes for a 'jump' for a man with no legs. 'You will join me at the Obelisk,' said Isaac's sing-song voice behind him. 'The view will be spectacular.'

'Must you sneak up on me like that?' the Halfmage snarled. 'Besides, I've already witnessed the devastation of one city. You recall when Salazar crushed Shadowport beneath the waves.'

Isaac shrugged. 'Life is a series of experiences. Take what you can before you can take no more.'

Eremul frowned. 'Thelassa is many miles away. Even from the Obelisk we won't be able to see a thing. Unless your eyes have hidden uses beyond unsettling the... *lesser races*.'

The Adjudicator smiled, seemingly enjoying the Halfmage's barb. 'Our eyes are indeed able to see further than yours, but it is different eyes we shall use. A surviving remnant of the wonders we possessed in the Time Before.'

'I'm not pushing this thing all the way up to the Obelisk,' Eremul said, tapping the wheelchair Isaac had contrived for him years ago. 'It's a long trek uphill and I have little desire to be set upon by an angry mob in the middle of a downpour.'

Isaac's obsidian eyes seemed to glitter as he took hold of the handles on the back of Eremul's chair. 'I shall help you.'

\*

The Obelisk was the tallest building in Dorminia – a monolith of dark stone towering over the nearby estates that once were home to the city's nobles and magistrates. Now that Eremul had laid eyes upon the City of Towers and its delicate spires for the first time, the Obelisk didn't appear half so impressive. Then again, many of the things he'd once considered impressive were rather less so since the Ancients had arrived in the Trine.

*That is one of life's great lessons. The more you learn of the world, the less you matter. When we are young we are at the very centre of the circle of Creation. As the years pass we drift to the edge until, when it is our turn to fall into oblivion, we accept it with nary a whimper.*

The Halfmage wondered if time changed the fehd as it changed men. Staring around the Noble Quarter and meeting the gazes of the immortals who now claimed it as their enclave, he suspected not.

'How many of you are there?' he asked Isaac, as the Adjudicator wheeled him through the Obelisk's courtyard, drawing curious glances from his kin.

'A thousand of us made the voyage across the Endless Ocean,' Isaac answered. 'In our homeland we are twenty times that number. A fraction of what your people can muster even in this small pocket of the continent, but propagation is less of a concern for those who do not age. Endless breeding is the hallmark of...' He trailed off.

'*The lesser races*,' Eremul said, mimicking Isaac's lyrical voice. The fehd officer smiled at that and for a moment it felt like old times, the Halfmage and his trusty manservant indulging in some idle banter – or at least a one-way stream of sarcasm and invective on Eremul's part.

*Isaac is not a manservant,* the Halfmage reminded himself. *He is a seven-feet-tall immortal. And he is about to bring me into the very heart of fehd command here in the Trine.*

They passed the Crimson Watch barracks – now empty – and approached the Obelisk's iron gates. The fehd on duty threw Isaac a salute and gave Eremul a questioning look, but the Adjudicator motioned for him to open the gates and his kinsman immediately complied. The last time Eremul had visited the Obelisk the gates had been secured by a great padlock. As the Halfmage watched, the fehd guard moved to a strange panel that had been recently installed on the wall. It was covered in what appeared to be a grid of numbered buttons. The guard tapped out a sequence with his slender fingers. A moment later the gates clicked and slid open of their own accord.

The Halfmage raised an eyebrow, but Isaac merely motioned him to follow.

The entrance hall was much the same as the Halfmage remembered. As he trundled down the carpeted foyer he heard a whirring noise and glanced up to see a series of mechanical objects that looked a little like the fehd hand-cannons affixed to the ceiling. They moved as he did, tracking his path, tiny eyes of red fire winking down at him.

'They are not dangerous,' Isaac said, noting Eremul's discomfort. 'They only observe. In the Time Before, these could be found on every building, or so the legends say. They recorded everything.'

Eremul slowed as they approached the steps leading up to the Grand Council Chamber. 'If you wish me to escort you to the top floor, you will have to carry me,' he said bitterly. 'I am allergic to stairs.'

Isaac said nothing. Instead, the Adjudicator turned to a section of wall just to the left of the steps. The fehd officer pressed a silvery button in the centre of another panel that had been installed three feet above the floor. Suddenly the wall slid open, revealing a small, empty room beyond. Isaac entered and beckoned Eremul to follow him.

'Is this a joke?' the Halfmage asked. He thought perhaps his one-time manservant had decided to imprison him; payback for all the humiliating labour he had forced Isaac to undertake during his four-year tenure at the depository.

The Adjudicator turned to another panel just inside the room. There were six buttons arranged vertically on the panel.

*One for each of the Obelisk's floors?* Eremul mused.

Isaac pressed the button at the very bottom of the panel. 'Brace yourself,' he said, something like anticipation in his musical voice.

Eremul opened his mouth to ask why – but stopped in amazement as the door suddenly seemed to disappear into the floor. He had the sensation of being lifted into the air. It went on for several seconds.

'We made a few improvements when we moved in,' said Isaac wryly.

The queasy sensation stopped and the door opened with a sharp ding not unlike the tolling of a small bell. Isaac took hold of Eremul's chair. 'Try not to say anything,' he advised, and wheeled the Halfmage into the newly rebuilt top floor of the Obelisk.

The sight that greeted Eremul wasn't at all what he had expected. General Saverian and a half-dozen officers were sitting on high-backed chairs arranged in a circle around a slightly raised platform. Floating above the platform were several three-dimensional images of Dorminia and the surrounding region, depicted in breathtaking detail. As Isaac wheeled Eremul closer, the Halfmage's mouth dropped open in shock. There were tiny figures milling around the deck of the largest of the floating, ghostly dioramas, which was a perfect representation of the ship carrying the Breaker of Worlds.

'Is this magic?' he said in wonder.

'Not magic,' replied Isaac quietly. 'What you see is the harbour as it exists at this moment. The images are transmitted here through vista-spheres – one of the few surviving wonders from the Time Before. They float high in the skies above. Think of them as similar to Salazar's mindhawks.'

Saverian turned and frowned at the Halfmage. 'Adjudicator,' he said, the hint of annoyance in his voice sending tendrils of fear down Eremul's spine. 'You appear to have brought a *human* among us. May I ask why?'

'I wanted to show him a fragment of the glory of what our people have achieved, sir,' replied Isaac, diffidently. 'While I still can.'

'You are too indulgent, brother,' said Melissan from her seat beside the general.

'I fear that is the truth,' replied Isaac, with a small smile.

'We near launch,' Saverian announced in an iron voice, his eyes focusing on the diorama before them. Sheets of rain battered the virtual deck of the ship, dripped from the colossal cannon that was moments away from reducing the thirty thousand inhabitants of Thelassa to ash. At the general's announcement, the cannon began to shift position.

Beyond the raised platform around which the fehd were seated, clear glass ran the circumference of the Obelisk's top floor, providing a perfect view over Dorminia's Noble Quarter. Rain crawled down the glass to the courtyard far below. Salazar had met his end on those cobbles months ago; a kinder death than the people of Thelassa would receive.

For a brief moment Eremul considered unleashing his magic against those present. Perhaps he could destroy whatever strange items Saverian and his officers were using to communicate with the fehd operating the great cannon aboard the ship. At best, he might buy a small delay. Was it worth the cost of his own life?

*No one in Dorminia would piss on me if I were on fire. In Thelassa, why, they might just go and fetch some oil.*

Saverian raised a hand and adjusted something in his ear. 'Initiate the Reckoning on the count of five,' he announced. 'One... two...'

Unable to watch, Eremul closed his eyes and waited.

'General,' said one of Saverian's officers, his skin as dark as the others' were pale. 'Take a look at this.'

The urgency in the fehd's voice was enough to snap Eremul's eyes back open. Saverian motioned with one hand and the ethereal image of Dorminia's harbour on the platform was suddenly replaced by a panorama of the Demonfire Hills north of the city. Broken peaks of granite rose up from the ground to stab at the heavens.

The Halfmage's brow furrowed. There appeared to be an outpost stationed there – a small camp of the immortal fehd and their thrall helpers, nestled within a hollow between two particularly large hills.

'What is *that*?' Melissan asked, pointing a slender finger at something making its way down the northernmost hill.

It was neither human nor fehd. It looked like a man made of shadow and fire – and as it flowed across the rock, it left scorched stone in its wake. The unidentified horror was heading straight towards the fehd outpost.

'Focus on it,' ordered Saverian. 'I want a closer look.' The black-skinned officer twisted a dial on a panel to the side of the platform and the panorama shifted, narrowing and increasing in size and detail as the fehd relic transmitting the image moved closer to the interloper. As those gathered in the Obelisk watched, a dozen human thralls converged on the foreign invader, weapons raised. The unknown horror met them, lashed out with nebulous limbs composed of flame and shadow. Where they struck, the unfortunate thralls burst apart, bodies collapsing into ash, alive one instant and obliterated the next.

'Give me sound,' Saverian barked. The officer flicked another dial and then they could hear the screams, the harsh bark of hand-cannons exploding. The horror flowed into the camp, ignoring the tiny metal projectiles raining down upon it, tearing a path through the thralls as it closed on the handful of fehd beyond. One of them Eremul knew: a female, blue cloak fluttering behind her.

'*Nym*,' Isaac gasped. He turned to Saverian. 'Sir, you sent Nym with the reconnaissance mission?'

The general's teeth were grinding together as though he were chewing steel. 'Yes. That is my prerogative, Adjudicator.'

Nym held something clutched in a slender hand – a spherical object similar to the firebombs the rebels had unleashed in

Dorminia. She tossed it. There was a concussive explosion and for a moment the panorama was covered in thick dust.

The nightmare of shadow and fire rose from the crater that had just been blasted out of the hill, utterly unharmed. It reached the first fehd, who leaped at it, crystal sword slashing. He moved incredibly fast and fought with inhuman skill. But his blade passed right through the apparition, which surged forward and engulfed the Ancient. White skin began to smoke and the fehd's hair caught fire.

'It seems not to feel pain,' said Melissan, sounding dismayed. 'What manner of being *is* this?'

'A weapon,' Saverian growled. 'One of three, created by the gods in the time humans call the Age of Strife. They feared a mage uprising. This was their response. The gholam.'

There was a blood-curdling shriek and then the fehd burst apart.

'General, how do we stop it?' Melissan begged, voice rising in panic. Eremul found himself shaking with fear, fresh sweat soaking his robes.

'It is impervious to steel,' said Saverian grimly. 'It is unaffected by magic. Even our conventional weapons will not suffice. There is but one course of action. We break it.'

*Break it?* Eremul's mind whirled. *The Breaker of Worlds. He means to Reckon it.*

Saverian reached up to his ear. 'You are to adjust targets,' he commanded. 'I will give you the new coordinates.'

'General,' Isaac cut in desperately. 'Our kin are there. Nymuvia is there!'

The mighty white-haired general rose from his chair. His face was implacable, his voice as hard as iron. 'It is the only way, Adjudicator. I will not allow it to reach the city. It must be stopped now.'

'General,' Isaac said again, pure agony in his voice. 'Nym is my sister! Your betrothed!' He started towards Saverian, but Melissan laid a hand upon his arm.

'Stand down, brother,' she whispered.

Saverian stared beyond Isaac, out into the pouring rain battering Dorminia's streets. 'I am the shield that defends our people from harm,' he said, biting off each word. 'I will do whatever it takes. Understand this, Adjudicator. Whatever it takes.'

The Halfmage spun his chair to follow the general's line of sight. Saverian raised a hand to his ear again and spoke a series of numbers. Moments later a flash lit up the sky. An arc of light shot up into the heavens. Far above the city it suddenly changed course, veering off towards the north.

*Towards the Demonfire Hills.*

An oppressive silence fell over the room. Saverian's jaw was clenched, his face unreadable. Melissan held Isaac close, whispering something in his ear. The other fehd looked anxious or afraid.

The Halfmage focused on the ghostly panorama of the Demonfire Hills. The world seemed to hold its breath, every second bursting with unspeakable tension. Melissan let go of Isaac and he turned away from her, a single tear rolling down his cheek.

The image of the Demonfire Hills suddenly flickered and died. From somewhere far, far away, there came the sound of an unimaginably large explosion. The room shook as the Obelisk swayed alarmingly.

Then the heat hit them.

# Promises

He shifted slightly in the cage, the accumulated sores of a year of imprisonment sending waves of agony through his body. He hardly felt the pain. Hardly felt anything at all except numbness.

He'd just watched his wife burned alive on a pyre. All he wanted now was death. An end to it all. His body was wasting away and every breath was a struggle, but the emptiness in his heart hurt worse than anything he had ever known.

He heard footsteps outside the cage. Maybe it was Borun, come to apologize again. His closest friend had turned his back on Kayne when he needed him most. Said he had a wife and daughters to think about.

Could be it was Orgrim. But he was a chieftain now, and though he'd expressed regret at what had happened the big Easterman wouldn't sacrifice his duty to his people for his duty to a friend.

Or perhaps it was Magnar. His son had watched his own mother die in the flames. The boy he had raised to be a man.

He wanted to die. Prayed for it. But the Shaman wouldn't grant him his wish until he was good and ready. Chances were he would burn just as Mhaira had burned. Even the rage inside him had turned to ash. He had nothing left. Not strength enough even to lift his head.

'Kayne,' rasped a voice. A voice he knew from years gone by.

'Jerek?' Kayne tried to say, but only a hoarse choking sound emerged.

*'I'm getting you out of there. The Shaman wants to get to you, he'll have to go through me first.'*

*'I'm done,' he managed to say. 'Go. Don't worry about me.'*

*'I made you a promise, Kayne.' There was the sound of steel striking wicker. 'After you pulled me from the fire.'*

*'Go,' Kayne said again. 'Or you'll burn too.'*

*'Burned once already. Didn't finish me, did it?'*

*Kayne said nothing. He had no more energy with which to speak. He heard the cage splintering just to his left. Heard the snap as the grim warrior they called the Wolf grabbed hold of his prison and began wrenching it open.*

*'Go,' he managed to gasp, one last time. He didn't want another death on his hands. Another life lost because of his actions.*

*For a moment there was nothing but grunting and the snapping of wicker. Then a strong hand grabbed hold of him and pulled. Agony exploded as his broken body was dragged from the ruined prison.*

*'I gave you my word,' Jerek said. 'Got myself exiled from the Forsaken when I heard what the Shaman done to you. Only way to leave the Icespire, short of death. But a man says a thing, a man does a thing.' Kayne grunted as he was lifted and tossed over a burly shoulder like a sack of potatoes. 'I'll be there when you need me,' Jerek rasped. 'And that's a fucking promise.'*

He slid slowly from his horse. His boots crunched on the snow and his breath misted in the chill morning air but inside he burned, feverish with excitement. He took a breath and tried to calm his beating heart. He didn't want to drop dead before he made it to the door.

He was home. He was home, and Mhaira was waiting for him.

Everything was just as he remembered it. The house looked like it had in his dreams, a place that held some of the best memories of his life. Some of the worst too, but those also had to be embraced because without them you never really understood what was important. Not until you almost lost it.

Kayne made his way to the door, noting the tidy fields, the neatly trimmed trees that lined the path. Proof that his wife was here, living under the same roof she'd lived under for the last twenty years. He had thought her dead. Horribly murdered, burned to ashes on the Shaman's pyre three years ago.

But she was alive, and she was waiting for him.

He ran a hand down his face, suddenly conscious of the scars, the month's growth of beard, the filth that caked him from neck to toe. Mhaira had always complained that his stubble tickled her, though she'd always had a twinkle in her eyes when she said it.

He grinned, imagining the look on her face when she saw him. That had been the only thing that kept him going at times: the memory of her smile when he woke in the morning. And the lingering image of her putting Magnar to sleep. Not grand events like the day of their joining, though those were precious in their own way. It was the simple things, the everyday moments that were no different from what any other man and woman shared the length and breadth of the High Fangs, except Mhaira had chosen to share those moments with *him*.

He slowed as he approached the door. The wedding wreath that had always hung there was missing. Mhaira sometimes brought it inside when the weather got too cold, even though the blessing of the spirits had meant it had endured the passing of seasons and years intact. So long as their love remained true.

He hesitated, then knocked twice on the door, his body shivering with anticipation, tears threatening his eyes. He shook his head ruefully. There'd been too many tears recently. He didn't want Mhaira to think he was going soft.

He waited, and then waited some more. There was no answer. Brow creasing in confusion, he knocked one more time. There was still no answer. He tried the handle and found the door unlocked. Maybe Mhaira was sleeping. The truth was she wasn't getting any younger, though to his eyes she never seemed to change despite the passing of the years. She was always just as beautiful as the day he'd married her.

He entered the house, seeing the hole on the wall he'd repaired years ago, noting how clean and tidy everything was. He tiptoed over to their bedroom door and pushed it quietly open, expecting to find her sound asleep. The bed was empty, though her clothes were still there. He saw the scarf he had bought for her as a naming day gift and raised it to his nose. It still smelled of her.

He wandered the house, searching for any sign of his wife. The rooms looked recently lived in, though there was no food in the larder. He popped his head outside, certain he would find Mhaira tending the garden, but that too was empty. Though it was covered in snow, the garden wasn't overgrown. Someone had been here not long ago.

'May?' he called out, beginning to grow worried. He left the house and crossed the field to the other house, where Mhaira's cousin, Natalya, and her husband had lived before Gared's passing. When he was only a few feet from the door, it thudded open. An elderly woman hobbled out, supported by a walking stick. She squinted up at Kayne. 'You here to help me south along with the rest of our folk? I was expecting someone younger.'

Kayne stopped and stared at the wizened old crone. 'Who are you?'

The grandmother tapped her stick against the snow. 'My name's Gabs. Young king Magnar sent me here some months back.'

'He did?' Kayne asked, confused. 'Why?'

Gabs shook her head. 'The lady of the house weren't well. The young king sent me to make sure her needs were being seen to. Poor thing could hardly get out of bed come the end.'

*Come the end.*

'Where is she?' Kayne asked, his voice suddenly trembling so badly he could hardly force the words out. 'Where's Mhaira?'

199

The old woman shook her head sadly and finally Kayne understood, and all colour seemed to fade from the world.

'She passed last week. It was the illness in her lungs. I buried her by the bench in the garden, like she asked. You knew her?'

Kayne barely heard. He turned away, the ground seeming to lurch beneath him, his heart a lead weight in his chest. He walked back towards the house in a daze, legs feeling as though they belonged to a different man.

'Here now, what are you doing?' came Gabs' voice behind him. He ignored her, crossed the field and entered the house. Walked down the hallway and out into the garden. He saw the shallow mound beside the bench, then. It was covered in snow.

'May,' he whispered brokenly, collapsing to his knees and scooping away snow with his bare hands, not feeling the cold, not feeling anything except an emptiness so deep he might sink into it and never find his way back out.

His hands closed around something. It was their wedding wreath. He shook it softly with trembling hands, and as the snow that clung to it fell away he saw that the leaves were as green as the day he and Mhaira had wed, the interweaving branches that symbolized their joining as strong as ever.

He knelt there, staring up at the grey sky. Snowflakes began to drift down to settle on his face, another storm gathering overhead. He looked down at the wreath. A moment later a sob escaped his lips and hot tears rolled down his cheeks. All the pain surged up, began to burst from him.

Footsteps crunched on the snow behind. He didn't turn, didn't want Gabs to see him in this state. Didn't want to hear the old woman's awkward questions.

He just wanted to be left alone with his wife and his memories.

'Kayne.'

The grating voice cut through the air like an edge of steel. Kayne turned, staring numbly through eyes blurred with tears. A scarred face met his gaze. A face he'd been sure he would never see again.

Jerek took a step forward, his twin axes clutched tightly in his hands. The Wolf's expression was stone. There was a darkness in his eyes that was terrible to behold, as if he had walked through hell itself.

*If I ever see you again I'll kill you. That's a promise.*

Kayne met his old friend's stare. For a moment, neither man moved. Then Kayne nodded once, slowly. He turned back to Mhaira's grave and placed the wreath carefully down. The Wolf always paid his debts. Always kept his promises.

He knelt there, listening to Jerek approach. He wasn't going to fight. Not now. He just wished he could have seen Mhaira one last time. He thought of her smile and fresh tears glistened in his eyes.

The Wolf shifted behind him. 'Kayne,' he rasped again.

'Aye,' Kayne replied calmly. It was time.

For a long moment nothing happened. And then an axe fell to the ground either side of him, and a strong hand squeezed his shoulder.

# SPRING

SPRING

# The Fade Prince

THE WAREHOUSE SHOOK as though it were being battered by a giant's club. Dust and ash rained down through the cracks in the wooden roof and Eremul the Halfmage came awake choking and spluttering. Monique, beside him on the floor, did much the same, except somehow she managed it with a lot more grace. As often happened, he tried to climb to his feet only for his brain to catch up with the fact that he no longer had feet, or indeed ankles or knees.

*Thirteen years and still instinct overwhelms memory. Overwhelms rational thought. Then again, I am but a human. Not an immortal fehd.*

'Let me help you,' said Monique, gently lifting him from the floor and assisting him into his chair. He blinked dirt from his eyes and squinted through the cloud of dust. Mard was sitting cross-legged amidst the detritus and staring at Monique suspiciously, possibly with some kind of cock-rot-related anxiety in mind. Ricker was passed out, so drunk that a direct kick to the face wouldn't have woken him.

*So, exactly the same as always. What then is that racket outside?* The building began to shake again and now there was a loud roaring noise, as though a hurricane were tearing through the city. Eremul wheeled himself over to the door and peeped out. He wasn't the only one. Dorminia's many homeless glanced fearfully from the cramped doorways of the Refuge to see what latest terror threatened the city. Everything was coated in ash and dust – the fallout from the colossal cloud that had mushroomed into the sky the day the Breaker of Worlds was deployed to destroy the gholam. Even within the Obelisk, the heat had been near unbearable for a minute or two.

The Halfmage had been relieved to learn that none in the city had perished – at least not as a direct result of the weapon's deployment. The coming days would doubtless bring complications, with the city's water supply becoming polluted. Also, the trembling in the earth caused by the blast had weakened Dorminia's structures, and several had since collapsed, burying their unfortunate inhabitants within.

The Halfmage shook his head. In the last year the city had endured war, a sustained bombardment from the First Fleet's artillery, and now the unleashing of the deadliest weapon ever created.

*The Grey City. An apt name for possibly the grimmest conurbation this side of a metaphorical hell.* It was hard to conceive of a time when he might fondly reminisce about Salazar's rule, but the Halfmage could feel the moment edging slightly closer.

Monique placed a hand on his arm and poked her head out of the doorway for a look. 'Shall we see what the fuss is about?' she asked. He glanced at her in surprise. Monique had seemed largely content to remain in the Refuge since seeking him out. Indeed, she was worryingly quiet most of the time. He imagined the stress and uncertainty of the times – not to mention their decidedly charmless room-mates – would have that effect on a woman.

*When it comes to women, my imagination is all I have by way of experience.*

'Eager for some clean spring air?' he asked wryly, gesturing at the sheets of dust blowing through the streets. It seemed as though the disturbance was coming from the Hook: the large plaza in which the city's criminals were once executed and where Eremul himself had come within moments of doing the hanged man's dance, or whatever the humorous equivalent for a man with no legs could be termed. 'I suppose it is at least fresher than what comes out of Ricker's arse on a morning.'

Monique gave him a scandalized look that quickly became a smile and Eremul felt the unfamiliar warm sensation spreading through him. *To hell with your* hashka. *Forget magic. Love is the most powerful addiction of all*. Or at least it was for those who had gone thirty-five years utterly starved of it.

'Follow me,' he said, wheeling his chair out through the door. 'I can probably work a little something to help with the dust.' He muttered a few words and summoned the meagre reserves of magic within him, shaping it into a warding spell that kept the airborne detritus away from him and Monique. Dirty faces watched them from half-open doors. Many revealed malice or anger, but the Halfmage was beyond giving a shit about the opinions of his neighbours.

Eremul and Monique made their way between crowded warehouses, skirted around heaps of rubbish, dead animals and piles of rotting sewage. The Refuge might provide a roof over their heads and a bowl of foul-tasting soup on an evening, but it was otherwise a lawless, filthy place. A year ago Eremul might have termed it 'hellish'. Not any more.

*Hell is defined by the limits of imagination – and imagination is defined through the limits of experience. True hell cannot be known until it has been lived.*

The orphans in the Warrens, they knew true hell. The Pioneers who had sailed to the Celestial Isles had known true hell, every man and woman, at least for the short time they had remained in possession of their heads. What the homeless were suffering in the Refuge was but a trifling inconvenience in comparison.

As they neared the Hook, the drifting clouds of dust and ash grew thicker, the roaring louder. Eremul had to put his hands to his ears to block out the noise. Dozens of fehd were gathered around the edge of the plaza. Dust and ash swirled around the

Ancients as they formed a circle, Isaac among them beside his sister Melissan. The siblings wore stony expressions. There was an air of tragedy about the two Adjudicators that was almost palpable. The agony Eremul had witnessed on Isaac's face following the death of his half-sister Nym had shaken him for days. It may have been Isaac's emotional projection that made him feel bad for the fehd officer – but Eremul had the oddest sensation that it could also have been simple empathy.

Isaac saw them approaching and gave a tiny nod of greeting. His obsidian gaze lingered on Monique for a second and he seemed to give a regretful sigh before returning his attention to the spectacle in the centre of the plaza. Melissan regarded the two humans as a woman might regard a fresh dog turd turning up on the bottom of her shoe. But she did not protest as they arrived at the Hook and both stared slack-jawed at the huge metallic bird hovering ten feet above the ground.

Or at least it resembled a metallic bird; on closer inspection Eremul concluded it was some kind of fehd relic. It was forty feet from nose to tail, with a wingspan at least twice that.

'It flies,' Monique said breathlessly. 'It must be magic.'

'Not magic,' said the Halfmage with a frown. The roaring seemed to come from somewhere beneath the wings. 'It's a machine.'

'The oldest of machines,' said Isaac behind them. The Adjudicator had quietly joined the couple. 'It is one of the last surviving relics of the Time Before – a smaller brother to the great ship that brought us to these lands. Prince Obrahim has arrived.'

The flying machine was slowly lowered to the ground. The roaring died and the billowing clouds of ash and dust slowly settled back to the earth. A small portal on the side slid open and a short flight of steps was lowered. A moment later a fehd who could only be their mythical prince stepped out.

He was of equal height to General Saverian, and in fact looked similar enough that none could mistake them for anything but brothers. The prince wore a golden cloak and carried a great metal sceptre topped by the largest diamond the Halfmage had ever seen. Unlike the white-haired general, Obrahim had hair as golden as the dawn. It was topped by a silver coronet.

Saverian stepped from the circle of fehd and lowered himself to one knee, the point of his crystal sword resting on the ground. The rest of his kind immediately followed suit. Isaac nodded at Monique to kneel and she quickly obeyed.

Eremul glanced around, feeling simultaneously embarrassed and a little self-satisfied. *I am the only man present, human or fehd, who is not expected to kowtow to this prince.*

'Saverian,' greeted Prince Obrahim, in a voice just as ancient and just as utterly assured as his brother's. 'I crossed the ocean immediately when I heard the news. Seven of our kin have been lost to us, including your own betrothed. We will mourn each of them for a decade. You may all rise now.'

General Saverian rose and sheathed his sword and a moment later the two brothers embraced. 'The gods-forged construct that attacked our kin in the Demonfire Hills has been Reckoned,' said the white-haired commander. 'The gholam is destroyed.'

Prince Obrahim nodded gravely. 'I understand it was kin to the gorgon and the gargantuan. You warned me about them, brother. That they could threaten even us were they ever to be unleashed against our kind. I should have intervened when the gods first thought to release them upon this continent.'

'Yet more confirmation that this crusade is necessary,' Saverian grated. 'Humanity should never have been permitted to flourish unsupervised. Their wickedness cost us two of our kin. Now their recklessness has robbed us of a further seven.'

Eremul saw that Monique's face had taken on a distant look, her eyes strangely vacant. He gave her arm a squeeze and she seemed to snap back to herself. Men and women from the Refuge were beginning to arrive on the outskirts of the plaza, curiosity getting the better of fear.

The prince frowned at the city folk making their uncertain way towards the Hook. 'Tell me, brother. How goes the conquering of this place humans call the Trine?'

Saverian's jaw clenched angrily. 'We have yet to breach the magical barrier the White Lady has placed around her city. The Breaker of Worlds was to offer a solution.'

Prince Obrahim raised his sceptre and the diamond tip flared, so blindingly bright that Eremul had to look away. 'We shall see if this barrier can withstand *me*,' he pronounced. 'Come, brother. I wish to familiarise myself with this land we abandoned two thousand years ago.'

The prince and the general left the Hook, the rest of the fehd slowly filtering out behind them, returning to their enclave in what was formerly Dorminia's Noble Quarter.

Eremul watched their departure. He waited for Isaac and Melissan to leave and then turned to Monique. 'Are you well? You seem distant.'

Monique removed her reading lenses and tried to blow away the dust that coated them. When that failed, she attempted to use a sleeve, which did little save add to the grime. Like Eremul's own robes, her clothes were thick with dirt. 'I'm worried, beloved. I do not wish to die in this place. I travelled north from Tarbonne looking for a better life. All I have found here is misery.'

Eremul tried not to let the pain he felt show. *You found me*, he wanted to say. But he knew that wasn't enough. He had been foolish to believe anything he could have offered her would ever have been enough.

*No. There is something.*

He took a deep breath. 'I may be able to get you of the city,' he said, watching Isaac's departing form and remembering a ploy he had used to sneak him, the barbarian Brodar Kayne and the rest of his companions out of the harbour in similar circumstances. 'It will be risky and exhaust what little power I have – but if I can save a single life, I wish it to be yours.'

Monique stared at Eremul for a moment, eyes wide. Then she threw her arms around him and buried her face in his chest. 'Thank you,' she whispered. 'You are a good man.'

'I'm not sure about "good",' he replied drolly. 'Or even "man". But considering the paucity of compliments I receive, I'll take what I can get.'

Monique giggled and even without her perfume, and smelling as ripe as everyone else in the Refuge, the Halfmage felt himself responding to the woman's presence. He summoned his courage; steeled his nerves and decided to take the plunge. 'I believe there is a washroom in the east part of the Refuge that offers some privacy. Perhaps it might be a good time to relieve ourselves of the city's accumulated filth.'

*Oh, shit,* he thought. *Oh, shit.*

Monique appeared to hesitate for a moment. Then, 'Thank you, but I want to go back and rest now. It is cold and I miss the comfort of walls around me.'

*Shit.*

'Of course,' he replied with a bright and utterly fake smile. 'Why, I, too, cannot get enough of Ricker and Mard.'

# Ruins

'COLE. COLE! WAKE up. You're falling off your saddle.'

His grey eyes fluttered open and Sasha stared at her friend in concern. He hadn't been the same since he'd returned from the Shattered Realms. He hadn't been the same since their ill-tempered parting months ago, in truth, but there was something else in his face now, maybe shame, that she would occasionally glimpse when he let his guard down. It unsettled her. If there was one thing she could count on, it was Cole being Cole. He was her tether to the shores of normalcy in the bewildering storm of the last year.

'I remember this place,' Cole said. He righted himself on his horse and frowned at the glittering waters of Deadman's Channel to their left. 'This is where the *Caress* docked. I accidentally dropped Isaac's lute into the water there.'

'Accidentally? Come on, Cole, fess up. You were jealous of him.'

'*Jealous?*' Cole repeated, sounding offended. 'I was the only one who suspected he was more than he let on! The Fade wouldn't have captured Dorminia so easily if I'd been around.'

Sasha hid her smile. That sounded more like the Cole she knew. They were both silent as they passed the spot where he had tried to kiss her. She'd responded by slapping him across the face. She caught him glancing at her just then, mouth opening and closing as though there was something he wanted to say. Whatever it was, he decided to keep quiet.

'Where's Midnight?' Sasha asked, for no better reason than to break the awkward silence. Against all probability Cole had returned from Tarbonne with a small kitten under his care. Apparently an assassin had attacked Cole aboard the *Caress* and he'd barely escaped with his life. The same couldn't be said for Cole's friend, Ed, who had rescued the cat in the first place. Sasha had been sad to learn of the man's murder; she remembered his surprisingly gentle hands carrying her away from the wreckage of the fallen house on the day the White Lady and Thanates had half torn the city apart.

'Midnight's with a friend,' he replied absently.

'It's not your fault, you know,' she said.

'What isn't?' Cole fired back, too sharply.

'Ed's death.'

'Oh.' The tone of his voice suggested that wasn't what had been on his mind, though now he looked even morose than he had before.

Sasha heaved a sigh and focused on the final stretch of their ride up from Thelassa. It was a pleasant morning. Though the land was unusually barren – a consequence of the nearby Fade ruins – there were still a few flowers eager to open their faces to the early spring sun.

Several weeks had passed since the incident north of Dorminia and the worst of the winter was thankfully over. Sasha knew better than to expect the changing of the seasons to herald a change of fortunes: whatever setback the Fade had suffered had only delayed their assault on Thelassa. Still, it had given the White Lady a little breathing room, some time to explore other ways in which she might be able to save her city. That was why Sasha, Cole and a handful of the Consult were riding north towards the ruins Brianna had first visited back in the summer. Perhaps they would find something that would prove useful against the Ancients, or at least shed light on their strange weapons and abilities.

*Anything is better than sitting in the palace listening to the White Lady and Thanates argue.*

The two wizards fought like cat and dog. Surprisingly, their bickering had yet to descend into another bout of spell-slinging. Sasha did her best to keep the pair from each other's throats. The rest of the time she spent lying on her bed, shaking like a leaf in the wind, drenched in sweat. Fergus was no longer forthcoming with the silver powder she craved and getting her hands on more had so far proved difficult. The *haskha* withdrawals struck without warning and often left her feeling suicidal. Occasionally, such as when she saw the face of the man drawing level with her and Cole just then, it left her feeling downright murderous.

'A clement day for a little exploration,' Fergus said, a small smile fixed to his thin lips as he looked from Sasha to Cole. Her friend hadn't talked about what had happened in Tarbonne, except to say that his mission was a failure. Fergus knew the truth: as a senior member of the Consult he'd been present when Cole had made his report to the White Lady shortly after arriving back in Thelassa. It bothered Sasha that Fergus was privy to information Cole refused to discuss with her. Bothered her more than she could say.

'The ruins are vast,' Fergus continued. 'The Mistress has sent expeditionary forces on two occasions in the past, but they uncovered nothing of value. Let us hope today proves more fruitful.'

'Don't worry,' Cole replied. 'If there's anything worth discovering, we'll find it.' He looked the perfect picture of health now, the white in his hair all but gone and the colour restored to his cheeks. Sasha wanted to ask about the change in his physical appearance, but something stopped her. Perhaps she feared the answer.

*I feel him inside me, Sash. Hungering. Eager for me to kill. I'm not sure I can control it. I'm scared.* Cole's words to her back in the palace, before his ill-fated journey south.

'He seems nice enough. A bit distant, maybe.'

Sasha cast a disbelieving look from Cole to Fergus, who

had returned to his position behind them. 'Him? Trust me, he is *not* a nice man.'

'He offered to help you while I was away, didn't he? You turned him down. At least that's what he said.' Cole frowned at his hands.

*That fucker.* 'What else did he tell you?'

'He offered some advice, that's all.'

Sasha leaned over her mare and spat. 'Don't listen to him,' she said.

A few minutes later they came within sight of the ruins. Such was their immensity that the shadows they cast seemed to swallow them up. The structures were alien in appearance, all harsh lines and winding bridges that connected a hundred feet above the ground. One building had collapsed entirely and another was missing most of its north-facing side. It was a miracle it still stood.

'Let us split up and spread out,' announced Fergus. 'Note anything of interest. We will assemble here at noon and decide how to proceed from there.'

Sasha was about to accompany Cole to the northernmost building when Fergus placed a hand on her shoulder, causing her to shudder involuntarily. 'There is no need for the two of you to explore the same section of ruins. There is a great deal of ground to cover. Perhaps you could start with the westernmost building.'

Sasha opened her mouth to protest, to tell him to go fuck himself, but Cole unexpectedly spoke up. 'I could use the time alone to think.'

He had that distracted look again. Even so, Sasha couldn't help but feel a little hurt. 'Go careful,' she said, flicking her long brown hair out of her face.

*Damn. I could use a hit.*

She watched him walk away. Then, shielding her eyes from the sun, Sasha headed towards the most westerly of the ruins, wondering what surprises lay in store.

The lower levels of the massive building were a warren of corridors, many of which had long since collapsed. The holes in the crumbling walls let in enough sunlight for Sasha to see by, and as she moved through the strange architecture she picked her way around piles of rubble that hadn't been disturbed in hundreds of years. The remnants of strange artefacts littered the smooth floor, many of them utterly foreign to Sasha's understanding, or so rotted with age their original purpose was impossible to comprehend. She picked up a rectangular piece of glass attached to a hard, smooth substance nearly as thin as parchment and turned it over in her hands. She couldn't imagine what use it could possibly have and flung it away. It hit the wall and fell apart, and she glimpsed the silvery sheen of metal within.

There were other objects constructed of the black shiny substance, most incorporating glass in some way. Many had tiny knobs that might have been used to operate the relics, but none of them responded to Sasha's pushing and prodding.

In one room that might have been a study, she spotted a strange sphere resting atop the decayed remains of an ancient desk. She leaned down to blow off the dust and saw that it was blue and green in colour, the former overlaid with several large splashes of the latter. As Sasha examined the object closer, she saw that the green splashes were further divided into smaller segments, all overwritten by the incomprehensible Fade script.

'*Alemania*,' said Fergus from behind her. Sasha jerked in surprise and spun around to find the self-proclaimed 'man of progress' peering over her shoulder. The rest of the Consult were waiting just behind him, blocking the doorway. 'I learned a little of the Fade script,' Fergus explained. 'The language has been lost for centuries. Lost, that is to say, save for the Mistress and one or two of her peers. It is incredibly difficult to learn, but I have never shied away from a challenge.' Fergus took the sphere from Sasha's unresisting hands. 'This is a reproduction,' he said. 'Still, it must be close to two thousand years old. Remarkable.'

Sasha stared beyond Fergus to the men and women lurking nearby. They were dressed in the white of the Consult, but she noticed that several were also wearing gloves. She spotted the glint of metal implements on the belt of one of them. Another had a sack and a length of rope dangling ominously in his hands. 'What's going on?' she said, a terrible suspicion beginning to take hold. 'What are you doing here?'

Fergus smiled his lizard's smile. 'I fear I wasn't entirely honest with you earlier. We did in fact make a rather interesting discovery the last time we explored these ruins. An entire laboratory located beneath this building. It was there I began to formulate the process for the creation of the Unborn. But further investigation yielded much more than that. The Fade built these constructs to house their thralls, though that wasn't clear at the time. What *was* clear was that they had mastered a form of physical modification that could yield results similar to the enhanced abilities displayed by the Unborn, without the undesirable side effects.'

Sasha felt a sudden pricking sensation in her leg and gasped in shock. Fergus quickly withdrew his hand and she was horrified to see that he grasped a needle between his fingers, the end wet with her blood. 'What did you do? *What the fuck is on that needle?*'

'A sedative,' Fergus explained. 'A strong one, in recognition of the remarkable resistance you have likely built up over your years of substance abuse. The very same resistance makes you the perfect subject for my experiment.'

'Does the White Lady know?' Sasha tried to ask, her words slurring. Her body felt heavy all of a sudden.

'The Mistress approved of my past experiments,' Fergus replied. 'For reasons beyond my understanding, she would not countenance any harm to come to you. Rest assured she will never learn of your fate. My assistants have been selected for their discretion. They too are men and women of progress. The trouble with Magelords is that, by their very nature, they represent the past.'

Fergus's words seemed to drift to her from a long, long way away – and then they were gone…

*

'Pass me the scalpel.'

Sasha drifted awake and stared up at the sun – or at least at an object so bright it seemed like the sun. As awareness began to return, she realized it wasn't the sun but rather a glass tube on the ceiling above, emitting enough light to make her eyes water.

She blinked, and then coughed. A narrow face slithered into her field of vision and Fergus stared down at her with bright eyes. There was something dark flecking his cheek. Blood.

'Most interesting. The sedative wore off even faster than I had imagined! This bodes well for the augmentation. Very well indeed.'

Sasha tried to move her body but it felt strange, as though it no longer belonged to her. She opened her mouth to scream – but it was already open, and no sound emerged except a soft gasp.

She heard a *snip snip* and utter terror seized her. She couldn't move but she could tremble, every muscle contracting wildly. She tried to inhale, but the breath refused to enter her lungs.

'She's having a seizure,' came the voice of a woman. One of Fergus's assistants.

'More sedative,' he ordered. He leaned in close and whispered in her ear as the needle entered her arm. 'You are unlikely to survive for long after I complete the procedure. Know that your death will further our cause in more ways than one. It is my hope that your fate will be the catalyst for your young man to finally embrace his destiny. He will become the weapon we need.'

*Cole.* Somehow she plucked the name from the tumbling pieces of her consciousness as it once more plummeted towards oblivion.

*Help me.*

# Death's Embrace

DAVARUS COLE TRUDGED through the northernmost of the Fade edifices, not paying a great deal of attention to the crumbling antiquity surrounding him. History had never much interested Cole. The future was where his mind wandered now, in particular his future with the brown-haired girl he had loved since he had set eyes upon her as a boy of eight winters, being led into Garrett's estate for the very first time.

He knew he had to tell Sasha how he really felt about her. But before he did, he would need to tell her what had happened down in Tarbonne. Tell her the truth about the monster he had become.

And that, he was certain, would end whatever they had.

*I'd rather live the truth than a lie.*

Fergus had told him that the truth could set you free. That he should embrace what he was, instead of rejecting it. The more he thought about it, the more Cole realized the man had a point. He'd lived a lie for thirteen years. Believed himself the son of a legendary hero when he was merely the spawn of a vicious killer and a street whore. The dagger at his belt had taken more lives than the great plague that had ravaged Dorminia years ago, but it was all he had. Magebane defined him. Without it he was worthless.

*Better to be a tool than an insect crushed under the heels of Magelords or worse.*

Lost in his thoughts, he rested a hand against a wall while he opened his trousers to relieve himself. Something clicked beneath his fingers and an instant later he was plunging through a gap that had just opened in the wall, cock flapping wildly, flailing to stay on his feet. He stumbled into what looked like an amphitheatre and almost fell down a flight of stairs, catching himself at the last moment on a rusty railing just to his left.

'Shit,' he breathed. He shoved his manhood back in his trousers and looked around, then stopped and stared in amazement when he saw what waited at the bottom of the stairs.

Rows of rotten benches ran the width of the great chamber, at least a hundred seats facing the wondrous Fade relic covering the entirety of the south wall. It was like staring into another reality – a window into a different time and place. The moving image on the wall was utterly lifelike in every detail.

As Cole stared, transfixed, tall figures with eyes like obsidian and wielding crystal swords clashed with what at first glance appeared to be men, except they were unusually slight and their ears narrowed to points. One of the first group – a white-haired officer of formidable bearing – raised an object that looked somewhat like a miniature cannon and pointed it towards the second group. The end of the strange object seemed to burst into flame and immediately wreaked devastation on the pointy-eared men. They jerked and juddered and dropped like flies, their bows slipping from their dead fingers, dozens of them mown down in seconds. A moment later the image faded, leaving only darkness.

Cole descended the steps, glancing curiously at the skeletons seated on the benches as he passed. They were ancient, half of them already collapsed to dust, the rest likely to do the same in a faint breeze. On a whim he tried to animate one – to order it to rise as he had the dead crew member back on the *Caress,* or the frozen corpse atop the Tower of Stars. Whatever lingering memory of life that was necessary for his power to work had departed the remains long ago, however, and he quickly gave up.

He reached the wall and ran a hand along it, marvelling at how realistic the image had been. The events depicted must have been real at one time. He couldn't imagine how those memories, or whatever they were, could be captured and displayed on a wall. There was nothing except dust when he examined his fingers. He began to turn away when without warning the living memories sprang back to life.

Cole leaped back, yelping in surprise. A great reptilian head appeared, bright red scales glistening like armour. Cat-eyes narrowed with baleful fury and the creature opened its maw, revealing teeth like rows of longswords. Flame suddenly burst from the monster's mouth, turning the wall orange. The fire was so lifelike Cole had to pat himself just to make sure he wasn't somehow being roasted alive without his knowledge. To all appearances the wall was a raging inferno, but there was no heat, no smoke, no sound.

The living memory adjusted itself and the massive reptilian creature spread its huge wings, soaring above buildings very much like the one Cole had found himself in before it had fallen to ruin.

The image seemed to *jump*, showing the monster from a different angle, except now one of the onyx-eyed humanoids straddled the back of the beast. Cole saw that it was the white-haired commander from the first living memory. As he watched, the commander raised his crystal longsword and stabbed down through the monster's sinuous neck, burying it to the hilt. The beast roared a silent death cry and plummeted from the sky. At the last possible moment the humanoid leaped off the back of the dying beast, somersaulting to catch hold of the ledge of an adjacent building and haul itself to safety as it crashed to the earth.

The image jumped again, and this time the foreboding commander was staring up at a star-filled sky. There was something up there in the darkness, something impossibly huge, dwarfing the reptilian monster from the previous living memory, but it confounded Cole's efforts to discern exactly what it was. In the distance, profane shapes were crawling and slithering across the landscape towards the commander. He raised a hand, and hundreds of his tall, obsidian-eyed kinsmen charged past him towards the approaching horde. Just before the armies clashed, the living memory died. The wall went black again.

Cole blinked a few times and gave a rueful shake of his head. Whatever magic this was, it was certainly captivating. It was also certainly a waste of his time. He ought to be searching for traces of hidden knowledge that might help humanity fight against, or at least understand, the Fade.

He turned and climbed back up the stairs, exiting the amphitheatre through the hidden entrance he had somehow activated. He could hear the drumming of rain outside and realized to his shame that a considerable amount of time must have passed while he was preoccupied with the living memories. Was it noon yet? He thought it best to return to their meeting spot and wait for the others.

He emerged outside to dark clouds and darker spirits. The hunger within him had returned again. The relentless voice urging him to *kill them all* had quietened after feasting so heavily back in Tarbonne, but nothing could diminish it for long.

He took a deep breath. He needed to talk to Sasha about what he had become. He couldn't put it off any longer.

He pulled up his hood and splashed his way back to the entrance of the ruins, his boots sinking into puddles that soaked him up to the ankles. It was impossible to hear anything above the roar of the downpour. The sun was hidden behind clouds as dark as sin but he was reasonably certain that noon had come and gone. The absence of Sasha and the others did little to improve his mood. He waited around in the pouring rain, his anger at the world in general growing by the minute. He ought to be lauded as a hero after killing Salazar. All he'd ever wanted was fame, glory and, most of all, the girl.

*Instead it's heartbreak, buggery and betrayal. All because of Magebane.*

All because of some dead man's steel.

He drew his enchanted dagger and glared at it. He itched to toss it in a puddle and walk away, but he knew that he could not. He was as much a slave to the weapon as his Augmentor father had been.

*Like father, like son.*

The bitterness in his mouth was too much and he spat. He turned and was about to go and search the west building for Sasha when the tall figure of Fergus suddenly appeared, trudging through the rain. The senior member of the Consult wasn't wearing his customary small smile. Instead, the man had a concerned expression on his thin face. 'You had better follow me,' he said, dabbing rain off his reading lenses with a sleeve. 'I am sorry to say there's been an incident.'

*

'We found him here, fresh from operating on your friend. I dare say the things he did to her would have been even more horrific had we not managed to overcome him.'

Cole knelt over Sasha, cradling her body in his arms, too numb to do anything but stare at the girl he had loved more than anything in the world. The corpse of the Fade was sprawled nearby, his head smashed in by a blunt object. Cole could hardly bear to look at the dead Ancient. He could hardly bear to look at Sasha, but he forced himself.

Her beautiful brown hair had been shorn, leaving her scalp bare. A three-inch incision in the back of her head had been stitched back together in rushed fashion. Sasha's clothing had been removed and there were tiny holes on her arms and legs, as though someone had inserted various needles into her. Her skin was grey and threaded by visible blue veins. Her lips, so beautiful in life, had turned purple. But it was her eyes that distressed Cole most of all. They were red, filled with blood. The unwelcome reminder of Zatore – the parallel between the only girl he had ever loved and the monster who had recently tried to kill him – was too much. He lowered Sasha's body to the table and then sank to the floor. He curled up into a ball, deep sobs racking his body.

'*Why?*' he tried to ask. His world was in ruins; everything turned to ash.

'We must assume this creature recently returned here,' said Fergus. 'In retrospect, it is no surprise that the Fade would send one of their own to survey a place they once called home. I fear Sasha was simply in the wrong place at the wrong time.'

'At least we managed to kill it,' said the woman beside Fergus. 'Some small measure of revenge for your friend.'

Cole stared through blurred eyes at the corpse of the Fade. 'Revenge?' he spat. 'I'll have revenge on them all. Every one of those bastards. Every single fucking one of them! What kind of creature would do this to her?'

'A monster,' Fergus said gently. 'That is what we are fighting, Davarus Cole. Monsters. It is time for you to embrace your destiny. Submit to the hunger within you and unleash it upon those deserving of your fury.'

Cole took a deep breath. Fergus was right. He wiped away his tears with the back of one hand and climbed to his feet, jaw set in determination. 'Don't worry. I'm not holding back any longer.' He stared at Sasha and felt the world rock around him. 'We'll take her back with us,' he said, voice shaking with grief.

'Of course we will,' Fergus replied. He placed a thin hand on Cole's arm. 'Let us leave here. It has brought you enough pain already.'

Cole stared at the man's sleeve as his fingers gave him a comforting squeeze. There was a speck of blood there. Sasha's words from earlier that day suddenly stirred in Cole's brain. *He is not a nice man.*

Cole focused on Fergus. There was a strand of long brown hair clinging to the bottom of his white coat.

*How did that get there?*

He looked around the room. The Consult were busying themselves packing away various items to take to Thelassa for study. One of them, the woman who had spoken a moment ago, had an anxious look on her face and refused to meet his eyes.

Cole's gaze settled on the corpse of the Fade, and narrowed. The Ancient's skin was greyer than those in the living memories he had witnessed in the ruins to the north. The golden hair was limp and dry and the obsidian eyes were dull and lifeless. He summoned the Reaver and reached out, searching for a spark, that tiny thread of life that had still been present even in the frozen corpse on top of the Tower of Stars. There was nothing at all. The body before him was utterly empty, a husk.

'How long has he been dead?' Cole asked quietly, nudging the corpse with a foot. Something felt wrong.

Fergus looked up from unpacking a large bag. A bag just the right size for Sasha's body. 'We stumbled across him a couple of hours ago. My colleague caught him by surprise and broke his skull before he could commit further crimes against humanity. Come, Davarus Cole. Waste no more time on the dead. Focus now on the living; those Ancients you will shortly send to their graves.'

Cole stared at the Fade's head wound. It didn't look right. There wasn't enough blood, for one thing. It was almost as though the damage had been inflicted some time after the creature's death...

'You're lying,' he said slowly.

'Lying?' Fergus echoed. 'I'm afraid I do not follow.'

Cole concentrated and heard the heartbeats of the Consult suddenly quicken. He narrowed his eyes and looked at the woman, whose heart was racing faster than the others. There was a fresh sheen of sweat on her face. He caught the glitter of metal among the objects she was packing.

*A scalpel. Needles.*

Finally, he understood.

'You killed her,' Cole said, rising slowly from his examination of the Ancient's broken skull. Rising, like an angel of death. 'You found this corpse somewhere and thought you could use it to cover up the truth. You experimented on my Sasha. You murdered her.'

'Now, young man, that is quite absurd—'

He heard movement behind him and whirled, Magebane already in his palm. One of Fergus's assistants was lunging at him, a needle held between his thumb and forefinger. Cole punched out and opened the man's throat, shoved him aside as blood fountained out and lunged forward, stabbing another of the Consult in the stomach and giving his dagger a cruel twist. The vitality of the dying man filled him; made him stronger. Turned him into something else.

*Kill them. Kill them all, child.*

The Reaver's voice boomed in his ears and he gave himself to it, slaying one after another of Fergus's assistants as they fought feebly to escape. They were wicked creatures, no more human than the Unborn. Their heartbeats thundered in his ears and he used the incessant roar to hunt them down, killing without mercy, bloodlust turning the world red. He moved like quicksilver, untouchable, an assassin of supernatural lethality.

Until only Fergus remained. The man's pulse was only slightly raised and his voice was steady – even a little *curious* – as he raised his long-fingered hands in a placating gesture. 'Remarkable! Your efficacy is encouraging. But you must understand I am not your enemy. All this was done in pursuit of a greater goal. You see, one cannot make progress without sacrificing—'

His words became a scream as the Reaver plucked the needle from his hand and plunged it into his left eye. Then Magebane was opening the man's body, crimson droplets raining everywhere. Fergus was dead before he hit the floor.

The Reaver stood there, rasping and covered in crimson. The roar of beating hearts was silenced but the bloodlust remained, driving him, urging him to kill. There was nothing left alive. Nothing left to feed the hunger, except—

There *was* something. It was tiny and fragile, like a newborn chick taking its first tottering steps from a nest a hundred feet above the ground. The Reaver listened and followed the sound until he was standing over the body of a girl. There was hardly any life there – the barest speck. But his appetite was ravenous and even as a flicker of consciousness began to stir, the Reaver exalted in another soul to be consumed...

*Kill them. Kill them all.*

Magebane plunged down, its point aiming at the spot right above the heart.

At the last possible moment Davarus Cole twisted the blade, slamming into the table upon which Sasha rested. He gathered her in his arms and hugged her close. 'Hang on, Sash,' he whispered.

He sought desperately to remember how he'd healed Derkin's mother back in Newharvest. Somehow he had channelled the stolen vitality of the man he had killed into the dying woman, closing her wound and bringing her back from the brink of death. Sasha was even further gone, so close to death's door half of her was already through. But he had to try. He had to try with every shred of willpower he possessed.

He felt his strength departing his own body and flowing into Sasha. It was a horrendous sensation but he gritted his teeth and willed more of the stolen life force of Fergus and his assistants into the body of the girl he loved, giving it all, giving everything he had. Still she didn't respond. He redoubled his efforts. Seconds turned into minutes.

He was close to spent now, weaker even than he'd been before his ill-fated journey to Tarbonne, but he wouldn't give up. He would give it all if he had to.

Even himself.

He felt her twitch beneath him. He refused to relent. He ignored the agony spreading through his own body, fought against the light-headedness threatening unconsciousness at any moment—

Until suddenly Sasha gasped, a sound that could be either the most terrifying or the most beautiful in the world. Cole felt Sasha's chest begin to rise and fall, the breath finally entering her lungs.

He tried to stand and almost fell, his legs as weak as water, dizziness and nausea almost overwhelming him.

He took a deep breath and steadied himself. Now began the hardest part of all.

Davarus Cole bent down and gathered up Sasha in his arms. 'Stay with me,' he whispered. 'I'm getting you out of here.'

# Reunions

'YOU AWAKE, SON?'

Brodar Kayne waited hesitantly by the tent flap, suddenly uncertain of what to say to the boy he had raised to be a man, the boy he had raised to become king of the High Fangs. There were a lot of things he wanted to say. Some things he *had* to say. Three years was a long time, and the news he had brought with him to the tent upon learning Magnar was finally conscious was the kind of news no father wanted to give his child.

'Yes.' His son's voice was as weak as parchment. As weak as parchment, but nonetheless as familiar to him as his own scarred hands. Hands he'd used to lift him from the cradle as a babe. To feed him as a child. To teach him how to wield a sword as a man.

Kayne closed his eyes for a moment and steeled himself for what had to be done. 'Mind if we talk?'

There was a brief moment of silence, and then, 'Come in, Father.'

He entered the tent and came to stand beside Magnar. His son was still desperately weak, half the weight a man ought to be and so badly maimed it broke Kayne's heart to look upon him. 'Does it hurt?' he asked, trying to keep the pain out of his own voice.

Magnar raised a mangled hand. He'd lost two fingers on his left hand and one on his right, and ugly scars disfigured his chest where Krazka had mutilated him. Kayne had an inkling the butcher had done worse things, but he didn't want to ask. Some things were better left unknown. 'Not as much as before,' Magnar said. 'But it hurts.'

'I'm sorry,' Kayne said, feeling utterly helpless. 'The healers say you'll get stronger with time.'

Magnar nodded, a distracted look in his grey eyes. He'd grown a beard since his imprisonment. It only served to highlight the scars around his jaw where no hair could grow and likely never would. 'Stronger,' he repeated, sounding bitter. 'I'm broken. The broken king.'

Kayne stiffened, feeling as though ghostly fingers had just raked him down the back. Like wildfire, the Seer's words ignited in his brain.

*You stood before the Bandit King. You knelt before the Butcher King. And you sent the Broken King to his death.*

He might've stood before Asander the Bandit King and he might've knelt before Krazka the Butcher King, at least after a fashion. But there was no way in hell he would ever send his own son to his death. 'No man's broken till he can't get back up,' he said, more sharply than he intended.

Magnar looked away and Kayne hesitated a moment, dreading what was coming, knowing it had to be done. 'Son,' he began. 'I got something to tell you. It's… it's about your ma.'

Magnar's grey eyes, his mother's eyes, met Kayne's blue orbs, and just like that understanding passed between father and son. 'When?' came his strangled reply.

'A few weeks back.' Kayne swallowed the lump in his own throat. 'She loved us both. As much as any woman can love a husband and son.'

Magnar nodded. His eyes were squeezed closed, and Kayne turned away so as not to see his son's tears. He cleared his throat, took a step towards the entrance to the tent, and then stopped. 'I'm sorry,' he said. 'For thinking what I did about you. That you could do what I thought you did.'

'It's okay, Pa.'

Kayne nodded, suddenly overwhelmed by gratitude that Mhaira had raised a more forgiving man than he himself had ever been. 'Rest now, son. We're already halfway to the Trine. I promise, you ain't seen anything like the city of Dorminia.'

*And I'm guessing they ain't seen anything like us.*

Kayne exited the tent. A brisk wind ruffled his hair and beard and sent the smoke from the many campfires drifting south, towards their eventual objective, still hundreds of miles away. The ruins of Mal-Torrad were behind them now. The spirits had been kind and there was no sign of the gholam as the great train of Highlanders passed through the ruins. Still, the River of Swords was just ahead and fording the waterway was a daunting task at the best of times. With the incessant rain of early spring currently swelling the river to near bursting, now was decidedly not the best of times.

'Your boy all right?' came a rasp behind him and Kayne turned to see Jerek striding over, twin axes on his back and fire-scarred face locked into his perpetual frown. The grimmest and quite possibly the angriest man alive had been in a foul mood since nearing the bank of the great river. He'd been in a foul mood since the day he was born, that was a fact, but whatever a man might say about the Wolf's temperament, he'd been a better friend than Kayne deserved.

'I just told him the news. About his ma.'

The Wolf nodded. Jerek wasn't much for words. He let his actions do the talking, and he did them louder than any man Kayne had ever known.

'Wanted to thank you again. For everything you've done. For forgiving me.'

Jerek turned away and spat. 'Been saving your sorry old arse for years now. Kill you, and what would I do with myself?'

'Dunno,' Kayne replied. 'Maybe find a wife. Time comes when a man has to settle down.'

Jerek spat again. 'Women,' he rasped. He reached up and ran

a hand over his bald head, then over his beard, shot through with grey. 'Ain't got time for that shit.'

'Kayne!'

The old warrior spun as a familiar voice called out his name. Despite all the tragedy of recent weeks, Kayne couldn't help but smile. Those emerald eyes and that shock of red hair were unmistakable.

Brick wore a green travelling cloak thrown over his leather shirt and breeches, and his bow was slung over one shoulder. Beside him was his girl, Corinn, blue-eyed and blonde-haired. Kayne had last seen the two youngsters just north of the Greenwild – the immense forest that marked the southern border of the High Fangs. Brick and Corinn had departed in order to lead Milo, Tiny Tom and the rest of the orphans to the safety of Southaven in the Green Reaching.

Brick threw his arms around Kayne, who returned the hug. 'It's been a while, lad,' he said, giving him a fierce pat on the back.

'Did you find her?' Brick asked, his youthful voice full of excitement. 'Did you find Mhaira?'

Kayne swallowed the despair that welled up and forced a grin. 'Aye, I found her. But let's talk about that some other time. How are the foundlings?'

'Safe,' Brick replied. 'The chieftain of the Green Reaching, Brandwyn, is a good man. He's making sure they're cared for.'

Kayne nodded. Brandwyn the Younger was a different sort of leader to Carn Bloodfist. A leader for times of peace rather than war.

'I can't believe we're heading south again so soon,' Brick continued. 'I thought we'd found a home in Southaven, but I guess it's like you said. "Find someone that makes you feel like you belong and you'll never want for a place to call home again."' He looked at Corinn, who was hanging back, smiling shyly. Suddenly Brick noticed something – or someone – and his grin returned twofold. '*Jerek!*' he exclaimed.

The Wolf was lurking a little apart from the group. He drew back as Brick sprinted towards him, fixed the boy with a scowl. 'Keep your hands to yourself,' he grumbled. 'It's pissing me off, all this fucking hugging. Are we men, or pussies?'

Brick smiled even wider at that, as though he had expected no less. 'I thought you were dead,' he said, voice thick with disbelief. 'When the gholam followed you into that tunnel I thought it was the last time I would ever see you.'

'Well, here I am.'

The flame-haired youngster looked from Kayne to Jerek and back again. 'You were going to kill each other,' he said nervously. 'Are you friends again?'

Jerek scowled. 'We're all right,' he rasped. 'Now stop with the questions. You're doing my head in.'

Brick's grin almost split his face in half.

*

The River of Swords was a surging deluge. Kayne stared doubtfully across the river and turned to regard the vast army of Highlanders making its way towards the north bank. There were thousands – men, women and children, the young and the old and everyone in between. The great snaking line of humanity stretched back for miles – all the way to the bottom of the Purple Hills, where Asander the Bandit King's men had ambushed Kayne, Jerek, Brick and his uncle in the not-too-distant past.

Kayne wondered what Asander would make of an army of Highlanders pouring out of the mountains and crossing his domain. If he had any sense, Asander would mind his own business. The great migration of the people of the High Fangs to the Lowlands would change the shape of the north forever. If the Bandit King or his Seer tried to interfere with the exodus, they would be swept away by sheer numbers.

*Not to mention drawing the attention of the demon horde, the Legion, that's rampaging through the Fangs.*

Kayne could only hope his countrymen from the remotest Reachings had somehow made it out of the mountains. Orgrim and Mace had bought the Heartlands some time, at least. Maybe the Brethren had, too.

Kayne stared again at the river just ahead of him. Would water slow a demon? He reckoned not, or the Icemelt would've done a much better job of keeping them from the East Reaching. He wondered what had become of Watcher's Keep. Ten years he'd served at the citadel as a Warden. Now it most likely lay in ruins. The world kept on changing, that was a fact – but it seemed to him the last year had seen enough change to last a man a lifetime.

'We will need to ferry the provisions across,' said Brandwyn the Younger. The chieftain of the Green Reaching came to stand beside Kayne. 'We cannot afford to lose any more food.'

*We cannot afford to lose any more food.* That was what Brandwyn the Elder had told Kayne when the Sword of the North turned up at his door in Beregund bringing warning of the Shaman's ire. 'How are we for rations?' Kayne asked.

Brandwyn stroked his rust-coloured beard and sighed. 'Already we've less than half of what we brought through the Greenwild. Our foraging in Mal-Torrad turned up nothing. The place is as dead as ash.'

'The Badlands ain't much better,' Kayne said. 'It's near barren down to the Trine. Seems to me it's a dying world we're living in.'

Brandwyn nodded. 'What the world needs,' he said slowly, 'is fewer men good at killing and more men good at growing. At nurturing.'

The barb behind his words wasn't lost on Kayne, who winced. 'Aye. Fewer men like me and your father.'

The chieftain shrugged. 'The people of the Green Reaching decided to follow a different path after the Shaman burned

Beregund and had my father killed. Perhaps where they lead, others will follow.'

'Can't say I got any objections to that,' Kayne replied. 'Let's hope you and Carn can lead us to a place where the farmers can grow and the merchants can trade. Till then, I reckon it's the job of killers like me to make sure we survive that long.'

*

Night had fallen by the time the bulk of the Highlanders had forded the River of Swords. Even with the wooden ferry Brandwyn and his men had overseen the construction of, a handful of unfortunate souls had been lost to the vicious currents. Most were the very young or the very old, swept away into deeper waters where they were dragged under and drowned. They had also lost a tenth of their rations during the crossing, and fully a quarter of their grain supplies had been spoiled. All things considered, though, it could have been a lot worse.

*Small consolation when you're burying a young child. Trying not to stare into empty eyes but feeling so guilty you have to. Arranging tiny limbs, cool and clammy.*

Kayne turned away from the last of the mounds and wiped his forehead with the back of one hand. He had volunteered for the grim duty, along with the relatives of the deceased. Jerek had wandered over and grabbed a shovel as well, got to digging without a single word uttered. The Wolf was sitting alone now, staring into the dancing flames of his campfire. Brick spotted him from where he was sitting with Corinn among Brandwyn's entourage. The youngster hesitated, and then climbed to his feet and came to sit opposite Jerek. The men exchanged a small nod and sat in total silence.

Kayne ambled over to a quiet spot beside an old willow. He knelt down and placed his greatsword on the sodden earth, then reached into the small leather pouch on his belt and removed the lock of Mhaira's hair he kept there. He brought it up to his face, squeezed his eyes shut.

He didn't know how much time passed while he was kneeling and remembering his wife. He heard movement above him and opened his eyes to stare up at the hulking figure of Carn Bloodfist, the hilt of Oathkeeper jutting ominously above one shoulder.

'We cross into bandit territory on the morrow,' rumbled the chieftain of the West Reaching, staring in the direction of the Bandit King's vast town of tents, south and east. 'Can we expect trouble?'

Kayne climbed back to his feet, his knees cracking painfully. 'Not if Asander has any sense.'

Carn's dark eyes narrowed at something off in the night. 'Do you see that?'

Kayne followed Carn's gaze, squinting up at the sky. A few stars peeked out from behind gathering thunderheads. Many miles east, up in the clouds, a dark speck circled.

'The hell is that?' Kayne muttered. He felt a deep sense of foreboding. 'This Herald demon I heard so much about?' he wondered.

Carn shook his head, causing his braided hair and beard to sway. *The Herald is huge, but whatever that is, it is bigger still.*

Brick came to stand beside them. The youngster raised a freckled hand and stared out with eyes unsullied by the vagaries of age. 'It looks like... a flying lizard,' he said in awe.

'A flying lizard?' Kayne echoed, filled with a deep unease.

An orange flash lit the sky below the creature. 'Was that flame?' Brick said, puzzled.

Once again, one of the Seer's prophecies caught fire in Kayne's weary old brain; a prophecy about the red-haired youngster beside him.

*You will bring fire and blood back to the north,* Shara had told Brick.

Blood there was always plenty of – even in times of peace. But something told Kayne that the strange egg their friend Grunt had been carrying – the egg that the Seer had seized when she had taken them prisoner in the Bandit King's camp – and the appearance of a giant, flying reptilian monster in the night sky were somehow related.

The apparition wheeled once and then disappeared, flying east, dwindling until it disappeared from sight.

'An ominous sign,' Carn rumbled. 'Whatever that thing is, let us hope it stays away from us. There appears be no end to the threats plaguing this land.'

'Changing times,' Kayne muttered.

'This is a night of omens,' Carn announced. 'Heavy with portent. A night for fates to be decided.' He reached up and unsheathed Oathkeeper. The runes etched into the steel glowed purple in the light of the campfires. The chieftain of the West Reaching fixed Kayne with an intense stare, dark eyes glittering in his huge skull. 'A night for oaths to be fulfilled.'

Kayne suddenly became aware of the silence that had settled over the camp. Hundreds of faces were watching the two legendary warriors, Finn among them, anticipation bright in his eyes.

'Ready your blade, Sword of the North,' Carn Bloodfist demanded. 'For the thousands of my kin who died at Red Valley, I challenge you now.'

Kayne saw Jerek begin to rise, and shook his head. The Wolf caught his expression and sat back down with a scowl. He wouldn't interfere.

Brick opened his mouth, a hundred questions on his lips, but Kayne placed a hand on his shoulder and guided him gently away. 'This is between us,' he whispered to the boy. 'Don't get in the way, lad.'

Kayne raised his greatsword, feeling every day of his fifty-odd years, aware of hundreds of eyes boring into him, willing him to fail. Willing him to answer for his sins.

'This is for my father,' Carn growled, readying his own celebrated weapon. 'Prepare to die, Sword of the North.'

Oathkeeper came screaming down.

# Child of Murder

'**W**HERE IS SHE?' demanded Davarus Cole, staggering through the throne room of the White Lady's palace as the Consult and the Magelord's handmaidens watched on. He was utterly spent; dragging Sasha onto a horse and keeping her upright for the entire ride back from the Fade ruins had been tougher than anything he'd ever done. He wanted to collapse right then and there, but sheer anger drove him on.

'Turn back, brother,' said one of the Unborn, moving to block his path. The broken throne loomed on the dais ahead. It was empty.

'I'm not your brother,' Cole spat. 'She betrayed me. Fergus and his lackeys tried to kill Sasha. All we've ever done is dance to that bitch's tune and *this* is how she repays us. Well, I'm not taking it any more. Get out of my way.'

'We will not.' Another handmaiden moved to join her sister, and then another. He was outnumbered three to one.

*Fuck this*, Cole thought, impotent fury lending him courage. He lowered his shoulder and charged, expecting to be pounced upon and dismembered – or at least restrained – but as the White Lady's servants began to converge on him, they shuddered and then stopped, held in place by some mysterious force.

Cole didn't pause to question his good fortune. He hurried past the broken throne and through the doorway at the rear of the chamber, then followed ivy-hung marble corridors to where he knew the Magelord's private chambers were located. He would attempt to kill her when he found her. He knew he probably wouldn't succeed. But there came a point when enough was enough.

He gripped Magebane tightly, his hand pale and thin, his body wasting away from having given so much of its own vitality to save Sasha's life.

He reached a set of ornate silver doors upon which the White Lady's likeness was etched, and his anger intensified. If there was one personality trait Davarus Cole could not abide, it was narcissism.

There were noises coming from beyond the door; it sounded like the White Lady was screaming at someone, most probably Thanates. The two mages hated each other with a passion. Cole certainly couldn't blame the Dalashran wizard-king for his animosity. The woman he had once known as Alassa – the woman Thanates had once loved before the Godswar – was pure evil. Thanates on the other hand struck Cole as hard but fair. A man chiselled from a lifetime of intense hardship into a grim angel of retribution.

Cole gritted his teeth and braced himself. *I know exactly the feeling.*

He drove a booted foot into the doors and sent them crashing open with an almighty clang. He took five strides into the White Lady's chambers before he stopped, dumbstruck by the sight before him.

The Magelord was sitting astride Thanates on a great four-poster bed. She was stark naked, her back to Cole, her platinum hair dancing behind her as she moved up and down in a furious rhythm.

'The fuck is this?' Cole rasped.

Thanates peered around the White Lady's undulating figure. Eyeless sockets of black fire somehow contrived to look guilty. 'Child of murder,' he said, somewhat sheepishly.

The White Lady leaped off Thanates, revealing the Dalashran wizard-king to be equally naked. She spun to face Cole, her silver gown rising off the floor to drape itself around her body. Her purple eyes narrowed in fury. 'You dare?' she whispered.

'I dare what?' Cole yelled, meeting her anger twofold. He pointed a trembling finger at Thanates. 'I followed you from the Blight,' he said accusingly. 'You promised to make the White Lady pay for each and every wrong she's done you. And now I find this... this *bullshit*.'

A member of the Consult, an older fellow, suddenly burst into the chamber behind Cole. 'Mistress!' he began, sweat pouring from his brow. 'I came here to warn you. The child of murder—' He stopped when he saw Cole, realizing his warning had come too late. Then he saw Thanates naked on the bed and his eyes almost bulged out of his head.

'*Get out!*' the Magelord screamed. The man was thrust backwards out of the chamber by the force of her magic. There came a thud as he struck the wall in the corridor beyond.

'Is that how you treat all your faithful servants?' Cole demanded. 'You use them, and then dispose of them when the mood takes you? What did Sasha ever do to you?'

'Sasha? What of her?' the White Lady snarled. Even through the heat of his anger, Cole had to admit it was a beautiful snarl.

'You had Fergus experiment on her. She barely survived, and what's left of her...' He trailed off, feeling sick all of a sudden.

'I did no such thing,' the White Lady said, sounding outraged. 'If Fergus disobeyed me, he will answer for it.'

'Fergus is dead. So are his assistants.'

The silence that followed Cole's announcement could have chilled molten iron.

'I *needed* him,' the Magelord said, an edge of hysteria in her voice. 'Without him, I cannot produce more Unborn. I cannot defend my city.'

'Alassa—' Thanates began, but the White Lady was already storming out of the chamber. Cole clutched Magebane tight to his body, anticipating a magical assault, but the Magelord ignored him, not giving him even a single glance.

Cole was left alone with Thanates. He cleared his throat a couple of times and fiddled with his belt. Thanates coughed and pretended to frown at something on the ceiling. Neither man spoke for a long while.

'Look,' Cole said eventually, realizing straightaway that it was an inauspicious way to begin. 'I *trusted* you. She hanged you from her city walls. A crow pecked out your damned eyes because of her!'

Thanates sighed, his chest heaving. The scars from the torture he had endured five centuries ago were still vivid on his skin. 'We loved each other once.'

Cole shook his head in disgust. He was as tired of love as he was of being manipulated and shat upon by seemingly every wizard in the north. 'She's a cold-hearted bitch.'

Thanates frowned again. 'Perhaps not so cold-hearted. Not always. Love and hatred are strange things, Davarus Cole. Fixate on either for too long and it can become indistinguishable from the other.'

'Not for me,' Cole spat. 'I know all about hatred.'

Thanates rolled from the bed and began searching about for his clothes. For all his magical power and forbidding countenance, there was something tragic about this mighty wizard-king running his hands over the marble floor, unable to see the discarded clothing right there beside him. Cole hesitated and then gathered up the mage's trousers and tattered overcoat.

'Here,' he said, thrusting them at Thanates with a big sigh. 'Get dressed.'

*

Derkin's dilapidated little hovel in Thelassa's undercity was part of a cluster of ancient buildings that had survived the razing of the holy city of Sanctuary centuries ago. More recently it had emerged unscathed from the partial collapse of

Thelassa during the White Lady's duel with Thanates. It was easily reached via one of the many cellars that connected to the ruins from the city above. Derkin had shown Cole his home weeks ago, when the young assassin had first returned from Tarbonne and descended the ruins in search of his friend. He'd needed someone to talk to and the hunchback was the only person in the city other than Sasha whom he could trust. It was remarkable that a man who had dismembered corpses for a living and who was so horribly disfigured on the outside could possess such a good heart, but if there was one thing Cole had learned from recent events it was that both heroes and villains came in the most unexpected forms.

He knocked on the door, which hung from a single rusted hinge. Suspicious eyes followed his every move. There were others in the makeshift community; the very dregs of society who had been banished from the city above on account of past crimes, incurable disease or simply grotesque physical appearance. The pitted face of a plague victim stared at him from the shadows. A one-legged woman hobbled by, a wooden crutch in one hand and an old cloth bag overflowing with spoiled food in the other. Despite serving a useful purpose in recycling the city's waste, Cole had learned, those exiled to the undercity faced dire consequences if they dared venture into Thelassa above.

There was no answer from Derkin or his mother. Growing concerned, Cole tested the lock and saw that it was so rotted with age he could likely break it open with his bare hands, or else simply tear the door off its sole remaining hinge and toss it aside. He doubted Derkin would appreciate him showing up and tearing his house apart and so instead he reached into a pocket and withdrew a lock pick. No sooner had he inserted it into the keyhole than the lock clicked open. Nervous at what he would find, Cole pushed open the door.

Sasha was still lying on the table where he'd left her. Bending over her, silver fire dancing around her manicured nails, as out of place in this hovel as a platinum ring lost in a dung heap, was the White Lady of Thelassa.

'What are you doing here?' Cole demanded. Derkin and his mother were cowering in the corner of the room. As the White Lady's purple gaze narrowed and she moved away from Sasha, Cole saw exactly what the Magelord had been doing.

Sasha's skin was a healthier colour, though it still carried a greyish tinge. The blood was gone from her eyes and she was breathing more easily.

'I have healed her wounds,' the White Lady announced. 'I do not know how the Fade implants will affect her when she awakes.' The Magelord clicked her fingers and the silver fire wreathing her hands winked out.

'Fade implants?' Cole repeated, aghast. 'What do you mean?'

'Fergus inserted tiny machines fashioned by the Ancients into her body. I dare not try to remove them lest she dies in the attempt.'

Cole stared at the White Lady, a whirlwind of emotions raging within him. 'You came here to help her?' he managed at last. 'I don't understand you.'

There was a small flurry of movement on the floor nearby and suddenly Midnight was meowing and pawing at his leg, her claws digging painfully into his skin. She was no longer a kitten but a cat, fully grown.

The White Lady stared beyond Cole, her expression unreadable. 'Does a newborn babe understand its mother? It cares not who she is, or what she must do to support it. Only that she *does*.'

Cole wanted to demand how the White Lady could live with herself after the things she had done. He glimpsed the exquisite pain in the Magelord's purple eyes and knew then that she couldn't.

*She's the most powerful woman in the world, an immortal mage without peer. And she hates herself.*

For the first time, Cole found himself pitying the ruler of Thelassa.

The Magelord blinked and the pain was gone, serenity restored in an instant. She turned to Derkin and his mother, who hadn't said a word since Cole's arrival. 'I understand you have some aptitude for nursing the wounded,' the White Lady said. 'The Consult could use your skills in the conflict to come.'

'Us?' Derkin said, his bug eyes blinking in confusion. 'We're not welcome up above. Are we? I mean, look at me.'

'These are times of war. I will use whatever I have to help protect my city. *Whatever I have.*' The White Lady turned to Cole. 'My handmaidens attempted to stop you reaching me and were overruled by your will alone. Thanates informs me that the Abandoned called you "Father" when you encountered them on your way to the Hall of Annals. You are stronger in the Reaver's divinity than I first thought.'

'I want nothing to do with the Reaver!' Cole snapped back, though he knew that was a lie. He felt so very weak now. Pulling Sasha back from the brink of death had taken everything he had.

'The decision is not yours to make,' the Magelord replied. 'The lingering remnant of the Lord of Death resides within you, as his heart still beats within these very ruins. Perhaps it is time to see how the heart of the father responds to the child. If you wish to master your hunger you must first learn its source.'

Cole wanted to refuse, but what choice did he have? If he didn't get help soon he himself would perish. Either way, he had a feeling this wouldn't lead to anything good.

*Then again, when did it ever?*

*

The sanctuary of the Mother that had once served as the Shards' base of operations was a sorry enough sight, but even that paled in comparison to the desecration of the temple Davarus Cole now found himself in. Five centuries ago it would have been truly magnificent – a monument of unsurpassed grandiosity.

Now, marble statues depicting the Mother in her many forms lay broken on a carpeted floor, almost hidden by dust and other detritus. Huge, stained-glass windows that must have cost thousands of gold spires and taken the efforts of the best artificers in the land to craft were shattered beyond recognition.

However, the most damning evidence of the temple's fall from grace lay in the pulsating thing suspended above the ruined altar.

It was a shocking sight to behold: breathtaking and hideous in equal measure. The heart was the size of a horse, a throbbing mass of rotting tissue, dark purple in colour. Such was the stench that a few months ago Cole would have vomited at the first sickening waft to reach his nostrils. He had grown more familiar with death and its sights and smells since, but nonetheless it still made him queasy. Beside him, the White Lady's mouth twisted in distaste.

'The Reaver's heart was discovered in Deadman's Channel in the years following the Godswar,' said the Magelord. 'I thought it ironic to have it brought to this place. Death taking up residence in a temple that once celebrated the nurturing of life. It pleased me to spite the memory of the goddess I once served.'

A vast network of tubes surrounded the heart, running all the way up to the city above. Cole could see dark blood being forced up the tubes with every slithering beat.

As he stared at the great disembodied organ, he felt something stir within him. An unexplained desire to get closer. He took a few steps until he was standing just below the heart.

'What are you doing?' demanded the White Lady, concern in her voice.

He reached up. The heart felt dry and spongy, utterly loathsome. He was about to withdraw his hand when a familiar voice boomed in his skull.

*Child. You have come.*

He leaped back, shocked at the clarity of the Reaver's words. Only while dreaming or in the midst of a killing spree had the

246

god ever spoken to him so clearly. Yet even as his hand left the heart, he felt stronger for the brief contact. He had an overwhelming desire to feel that power coursing through him again.

'It speaks to you, does it not?' said the White Lady. 'Even after five centuries, the Reaver's consciousness refuses dissolution. Perhaps death knows itself too well. Step away, child. The god is too strong for you.'

Cole hesitated – and then, ignoring the Magelord, he reached up and touched the heart again. His skin visibly coloured, the aching in his bones disappearing like mist on a hot summer morning. He took a deep breath, revelled in the restoration of his body. He felt renewed. Rejuvenated. *Alive.* The heart began to pulse wildly and several of the tubes were torn away, spraying dark blood everywhere.

*Embrace what you are,* boomed that voice in his skull. *You are the key that will unlock the door to our return. The Pattern will be restored but this time without the first Decree. The gods will return – and we* will *walk among men.*

'Enough. You are damaging the apparatus.'

The Magelord's hand touched his shoulder and he spun, ready to drive his dagger into her neck. Her purple eyes went wide and she uttered a word. Suddenly she was on the other side of the temple, a hundred yards distant.

The Reaver snarled, the world throbbing red, the woman's heartbeat thundering in his ears. The hunger raged within him, demanded that he slaughter her, absorb her immortal soul and feast upon it. The world was fire but he was shadow as he flowed towards her. He was vaguely aware of strange words being uttered, the dagger in his hand burning his flesh. The pain only sharpened his ravenous appetite, yet more fuel to the furnace of his hatred.

Just before the Reaver could reach her, the woman suddenly melted into thin air. He howled in fury. She reappeared beside a pile of rubble fifty yards to his right and he sprang at her again, desperate to kill. Once more she disappeared just before his dagger could sink itself into her sweet flesh, rematerializing near the altar.

Primal rage filled him and he screamed. He hurled his dagger at the woman in unthinking fury, wanting to see her reduced to a corpse at any cost. Somehow she danced out of the way of the spinning blade. He launched himself at her and again she uttered a word—

Silver fire wrapped itself around his wrists and ankles, jerking him back, holding him fast.

'Regain your senses. Return to yourself or you will die here.'

He spat, thrashed wildly, but no matter how he struggled he could not free himself from his magical bonds. The anger began to dissipate, the burning rage within him sputtering and dying as the shadows wreathing his body fell away. Another minute passed and then Davarus Cole found himself gasping for breath, sweat pouring down his brow. 'I'm sorry,' he panted. 'It's me. You can let go now.'

The White Lady's own face was covered in a sheen of perspiration. 'I think,' she said slowly, 'it is best not to repeat this experiment.' For perhaps the first time in five hundred years, the immortal White Lady of Thelassa – the greatest living wizard in the north – had come within inches of death.

The silver fire that restrained Cole dissipated harmlessly away and he collapsed to his knees. He blinked a few times, trying to come to terms with what had just happened. Initiating physical contact with the Reaver's heart had allowed the dead god to get a hold on his mind almost instantly. This time, it had taken a Magelord to stop him. There was no telling what carnage he might have unleashed in the city above if the White Lady hadn't intervened.

He stared at the giant heart suspended above the altar. The severed tubes were still pumping foul blood all over the temple pews. Cole got to his feet and went to retrieve Magebane, suddenly aware of just how badly his hand had been burned as a result of the dagger heating up while absorbing the White Lady's magic. He was weighing up whether he should ask her to administer some healing magic when Thelassa's ruler jerked as surely as if he had just plunged Magebane into her breast.

'What's wrong?' Cole asked.

'My magic is failing,' the White Lady replied, her voice thick with disbelief. 'The barrier around the city has been breached.'

'Breached?' Cole repeated. 'I thought even the Fade weapons couldn't pierce it.'

The Magelord ignored him. Instead she raised her arms and spoke. Silver fire rose to envelop both her and Cole, and, though it didn't hurt, he felt the world shift.

The next thing he knew he was standing on the docks, staring out over the water towards Deadman's Channel. Ahead of him, the great silver barrier that encased the city in a protective mantle shimmered in the late afternoon sun.

A terrifyingly huge warship was anchored just outside the magical barrier. At the prow of the great metal ship stood two impressive-looking Ancients. Cole squinted against the sun, trying to see their faces. The white-haired Fade looked strangely familiar. With the aftermath of his transformation into the Reaver, and the White Lady's teleportation spell still confusing his thoughts, it took Cole a moment to recognize the Fade from the living memory on the wall back in the ruins.

*Their commander. The monster-slayer. The bringer of genocide. The general.*

His counterpart, the golden-haired and golden-cloaked Fade with a circlet atop his head – a prince? – was holding something before him. It looked like a great sceptre. A brilliant white beam poured from the tip of the sceptre, and where it struck the White Lady's barrier there was an explosion of sparks. The Fade prince directed the beam along the barrier, cutting out a great door in the Magelord's magic.

There was a tense moment in which Cole could see the White Lady's distress visibly growing. Then a huge rectangular section of the magical barrier simply *fell* away, breaking into a thousand shards of silver energy that faded from existence moments before striking the water.

Like a harbinger of doom, the Fade warship drifted through the massive gap that had just been opened, heading straight towards Thelassa's docks.

'They are here,' the White Lady said, her voice husky with grief. 'The Fade have come. And I cannot stop them.'

# Arrivals

SASHA OPENED HER eyes and screamed.

She caught a glimpse of movement above her and there came a thudding sound, followed by a pained grunt.

'Babykins!' exclaimed an elderly female. 'Are you hurt?'

'I'm fine, Ma,' said a reproachful voice that seemed familiar. 'I asked you not to call me that in front of my friends.'

The world slowly pieced itself back together. She was lying on a rickety table covered in several old blankets that had been folded to provide support for her back. She felt *strange*: her entire body tingled and there was a dull thrumming sensation in her brain. The last thing she remembered was a sinister face smiling down at her, a sharp prick in her arm before darkness claimed her...

She sat bolt upright and stared around wildly, utterly disorientated. 'Where's Fergus?' she panicked.

'Fergus?' repeated that familiar voice. A bizarre but kindly face appeared above her and she recognized Derkin, Cole's friend from the Blight. The little fellow pushed her gently back down to the makeshift bed and gave her a comforting smile. 'I don't know anything about him. Ghost – I mean Davarus Cole – brought you here. He said you'd been involved in an accident.'

'Where am I?'

'We're in the undercity. The Mistress herself saw to your wounds. It seems you have friends in high places.'

'Cole?' Sasha asked. She could hear faint sounds from the city far above – shouts and screams and something else. Something harsh and percussive that stirred up memories of the night of fire, when Dorminia had come under attack from rebels hurling alchemical explosives.

*Cannon fire. Are the Fade attacking the harbour?*

'He's up there,' Derkin said, nodding at the wooden ceiling. There was a loud bang from somewhere hundreds of feet above and the little hut shook, dust raining down. 'The Ancients are here,' the hunchback said, confirming her worst fears.

Sudden concern for Cole stirred her into action and once more she tried to stand. Once more Derkin pushed her gently back down. 'It's safer down here,' he said. 'Besides, you need to rest.'

Sasha lowered her head back against the blanket, noticing as she did so that something was amiss. She reached up and, with growing horror, caressed her naked scalp. She felt the puckered flesh on the back of her head, realized with horror that it was a huge scar. 'What's happened to me? *What did they do?*' she gasped.

Derkin shrugged helplessly. 'All I know is that your skin was grey like a corpse. We thought for sure you were going to die.'

Another tremor shook the house, and a small black shadow raced across the dusty floor to leap up onto her stomach. *Midnight,* she realized.

Seeking some form of comfort, she reached out a hand to stroke the cat. As she touched the animal's fur, sparks danced around her fingers and the cat shot away from her with a loud hiss, fur standing on end.

Sasha stared at her hand. Tiny arcs of lightning danced around her palm before disappearing. 'What the hell just happened?'

Derkin's mother tottered over, a mug cradled in her hands. 'Here, dearie, drink this,' she said. Sasha took the mug from the old woman, but seconds later the liquid within began to bubble and steam, spilling out over the cup and scalding her fingers.

'Shit,' she hissed, dropping the mug. It broke, spilling boiling tea everywhere. 'Sorry.'

'Don't worry about it,' said Derkin's mother, with a gummy smile. 'You're still weak, I expect.'

She didn't *feel* weak. She felt… different. 'Is Midnight all right?' Sasha asked. Derkin was stroking the cat and whispering soothing words.

'She's fine. Just a bit shaken up,' replied the hunchback. 'Are you okay? Your eyes look strange. Different to how I remember them.'

The irony of the bug-eyed hunchback's observation wasn't lost on Sasha, but her eyes did indeed feel strange. They were *gritty* – as though there were stray eyelashes or dust stuck in them. She blinked a few times, trying to dislodge whatever it was. 'I feel weird all over,' she admitted. The hut shook again and she made a decision. 'I have to go,' she said. 'They need me above.'

'It's not safe!' Derkin protested.

Sasha remembered the sky lighting up when the Fade fleet had opened fire on the White Lady's magical barrier. The fire storm had blotted out the sun. 'Nowhere will be safe if the Fade make it inside the city,' she replied. 'Besides, Cole is up there somewhere. I have to find him.' She rolled off the table, surprised at how strong she felt. 'Could you guide me back up to the city?'

Derkin sighed helplessly, but a moment later he grabbed his coat and went to retrieve a massive cleaver hanging from a hook on the wall. As Sasha watched him, a revelation suddenly hit her.

The endless craving for her next hit – an ever-present need that had defined her life since her early teenage years – was gone.

*

Sasha emerged onto the streets of the City of Towers to behold a scene of utter carnage. The destruction the Fade cannons had already wrought was extensive. Where once stood gleaming towers spiralling up towards the sky, now only vast piles of rubble remained. Almost a third of the buildings immediately east of the docks had been levelled. The harbour itself was a graveyard of ships: Thelassa's once-mighty fleet, the pride of the Trine, had been utterly annihilated. As Sasha watched, the greatest of the Fade ships – a truly monstrous vessel – lowered a bridge onto the docks. Human thralls of the Fade began to pour down the bridge and onto the streets of Thelassa, armed with all manner of weapons. A unit of Whitecloaks went to engage them and fierce fighting erupted.

The battling figures were too small to pick out details at this distance, but as Sasha strained to see, something strange happened. There was an odd whirring noise in her skull. To her utter shock, her view of the docks suddenly *expanded*. It was as though her eyes had detached themselves and somehow reappeared at the spot upon which she focused. She strained harder and her vision, eagle-like, was somehow able to pick out the individual beads of sweat on the terrified face of a Whitecloak as a thrall tossed a firebomb at him.

Blinding light exploded. Sasha blinked tears from her eyes as her vision returned to normal. Bodies littered the street where the firebomb had detonated. She reached up and felt her eyes, poking at them in an effort to understand what Fergus had done, but no amount of probing revealed anything unusual.

*What am I?* she wondered, hurrying down a side street towards the palace, hoping to catch sight of Cole. *I'm bloody ugly,* she thought wryly, catching a glimpse of her reflection in a fountain. *Hairless, grey-skinned, scarred. I looked like a gods-damned monster.*

There was movement to her right and a trio of Unborn glided past, moving in the direction of the harbour.

The Tower of Stars loomed just to her left, the tallest building in Thelassa and most probably in the Trine. It was beyond the range of the Fade cannons, and she quickly realized that if anywhere would provide the perfect vantage point to seek out Cole, it was the soaring building upon which they had spent the best part of a week imprisoned.

She tried the door and found it unlocked. The interior of the tower was almost black and the steps seemed to go on forever, stair after stair punishing her legs until she began to fear she would never make it to the top.

Finally she reached the iron grate that opened to the roof. She braced herself and pushed, straining every muscle until the grate began to shift. Somehow she opened it far enough to squeeze through and climbed out, dashing across to the west-facing side of the tower and shielding her eyes against the dying sun.

She concentrated, willing her vision to enlarge her panoramic view of the harbour, just as it had earlier. Once again she heard, or perhaps *felt*, a whirring behind her eyeballs. Suddenly she was right there among a group of Whitecloaks as they fought desperately against a large group of Fade thralls. The triumvirate of Unborn who had passed Sasha earlier joined the fray, tearing off limbs and snapping necks, massacring the thralls just as Brodar Kayne and Jerek the Wolf had cut through Dorminia's defenders during the brief siege of the Grey City back in the summer.

One of the Unborn jerked and stared down at the hole that had just appeared in her chest. A moment later a Fade strode into Sasha's view, a smoking hand-cannon raised before him. It was the first time she had seen an Ancient up close and she gasped. The creature was exceptionally tall and graceful. It was armoured in some kind of silvery material that flowed like cloth. With his free hand, the Fade drew a sword that looked to be made of crystal and turned his obsidian eyes on the three handmaidens. The Unborn pounced at the newcomer but the Ancient moved with astonishing speed, cutting one in half with a single swing of his sword and shooting the other in the face in an explosion of black gore. The third handmaiden managed to pull him to the ground, reaching for his angular face, trying to snap his neck. A second later her head fell apart and another Fade entered Sasha's view. This one was even taller than his kinsman and wore a cloak of dark blue.

It seemed absurd but this Fade seemed *familiar*, somehow. Sasha scanned the harbour, realizing with growing concern that if one single Fade could face off against three of the Unborn – creatures that months ago had terrified her with their inhuman speed and strength – there was little hope for Thelassa.

The mechanical sound whirred in her skull and her newly enhanced vision settled on another group of Whitecloaks as they closed on yet more thralls pouring from the colossal flagship docked at the harbour. There was something strange about these Whitecloaks: they walked with a shambling, uneven gait. Closer inspection revealed that they carried terrible wounds on their bodies. Wounds that would surely have killed a living man.

*They're dead!* Sasha remembered the rotting corpse on the roof nearby; the body Cole had somehow raised during his confrontation with the Unborn. Horrible understanding dawned. *He brought the dead Whitecloaks back. He's sending them against the Fade and their thralls. Cole is somewhere close.*

She scanned the docks again until she saw something that made heart leap in her chest. A dead Fade sprawled on the ground, a half-dozen thralls scattered around him. Each of the corpses bore stab wounds or deep slashes on their bodies.

Locked together in deadly combat at the centre of the pile of corpses was a man wreathed in deep shadows and a blue-cloaked female Ancient with eyes like portals into another world.

They moved even faster than Sasha's altered eyes could follow, ruby-studded dagger and crystal longsword thrusting, stabbing, parrying. She recognized Magebane and knew the figure at the centre of the bleeding darkness must be Cole – but her friend looked more demon than man, his face twisted with hatred, mouth locked in a snarl. The Fade whom he fought against wore an expression of intense concentration. Cole moved faster than Sasha had ever seen a man move, but still he could not breach her defences.

She turned and fled the tower, taking the steps several at a time, almost tripping and breaking her neck at least twice. She didn't know what use *she* could possibly be against an immortal swordswoman of inhuman skill – but she had to try, had to do something to help save her friend who had risked himself for her countless times.

She left the tower behind her and dashed through streets that were deserted save for the occasional Whitecloak or thrall bleeding out on the marble paving. Although the artillery had wreaked havoc, the fighting itself hadn't spread much beyond the harbour. As she twisted through an alley near to the inn where she and Ambryl had stayed when they first arrived in Thelassa, Sasha noticed something in the skies above. Illuminated by the rising moon were two figures: a man and a woman, the former wreathed in black flame, the latter in silver fire.

*The White Lady and Thanates.* Unlikely though it seemed, the Magelord of Thelassa and the former wizard-king of Dalashra flew arm in arm... and they were heading for the docks.

Sasha emerged from the alley just as the first streams of black fire roared down from high above. The fire enveloped a score of thralls, melting their flesh away, leaving their blackened skeletons to dance a macabre jig before they collapsed into the smouldering pit that had been blasted in the marble streets.

A Fade soldier took aim at Thanates with her hand-cannon. Tiny metal projectiles zinged through the air, too fast to follow. In response the blind wizard soared even higher, ascending until he was a tiny speck in the clouds above, beyond the range of the weapon. More black fire streamed down, striking the Ancient, who tossed aside the hand-cannon that now glowed red-hot in her hands. A beam of silver fire joined the black and the White Lady appeared in the skies above like an avenging angel. The Fade's ivory flesh began to slough away under the double bombardment. She screamed, a sound that cut through the din of clashing steel and cannon fire and brought a momentary pause in the fighting nearby. Heads turned to see the source of the terrible sound.

Even though she knew it to be the death cry of an enemy, Sasha felt despair wash over her.

There was a pregnant pause and then a ray of blinding light lanced from the great Fade warship, piercing the heavens just where the White Lady and Thanates were readying another assault. The wizard-king of Dalashra suddenly plummeted from the sky, black coat flapping around him. Sasha watched him fall until movement nearby tore her attention back to the street.

A Fade was heading straight towards her.

It was the blue-cloaked Ancient she had espied from the Tower of Stars earlier. She barely had time to register the hand-cannon raised in his slender hand and hear the bang as it fired. Then she was on the ground, a terrible burning pain in her shoulder, warm blood running down her arm.

She managed to roll onto her back as the immortal strode over, his crystal longsword raised to finish her off. There was no sign of Cole. He couldn't save her now anyway. Perhaps he was already dead.

The Fade loomed over her, his implacable obsidian eyes narrowing. For some reason he hesitated.

'Adjudicator Isaac,' said an approaching voice. Sasha tried to raise her head but lacked the strength to do anything except twitch pathetically. 'The general has ordered an immediate withdrawal. Finish this one off and let us go.'

'I know this human,' said the one called Isaac. 'I am hesitant to end her existence in this manner.'

*Isaac,* Sasha thought dreamily, consciousness beginning to slip away. *I once knew an Isaac.*

'With all due respect, Adjudicator, the general would not countenance you sparing her life. I shall end her if performing this task troubles you?'

There was a moment of silence and then, 'On the contrary, Saverian will wish to question her first. Somehow this girl carries our augmentations within her.'

'As you say, Adjudicator. We will take her back to Dorminia.'

She felt herself being lifted off the ground. Then nothing.

*

'*Sasha.*'

Her eyes fluttered open.

'That is your name. Sasha. We had some adventures together, as I recall.'

The face of a Fade stared down at her. She became aware that she was strapped to a chair and fear seized her – fear that turned into pant-pissing terror when another of the immortals marched into view.

This white-haired Fade was unbelievably tall and wore a cloak of deepest black. His angular face was the harshest Sasha had ever seen, and his ancient gaze was that of a god, or something akin to a god. He stared at Sasha as if she were an insect.

'I do not know why you remember the names of these humans,' he said, in a voice like liquid iron. 'They are transient creatures, no more consequential than the rain.' He turned and walked away.

Sasha looked around, trying to get her bearings. She was in a circular room surrounded by glass. The grey granite buildings hunched together on the streets far, far below could only belong to Dorminia's Noble Quarter. In the distance she could make out the harbour. The mighty Fade fleet was arranged in a perfect formation, indicating that a significant amount of time had passed since the battle at Thelassa's docks.

'You are on the highest level of the Obelisk,' said the first Fade. He still seemed oddly familiar to her. What was it he had said?

*We had some adventures together, as I recall.*

'Isaac!' she exclaimed. 'You were the Halfmage's manservant.'

The blue-cloaked Fade almost seemed to smile. 'I'm surprised you remember me. I tried to be as inconspicuous as possible as I travelled with you, the better to keep my true nature hidden. I fear I almost blew my cover once or twice. Empathetic projection can only achieve so much.'

The ivory-skinned Ancient placed a slender hand on her shoulder. Sasha suddenly remembered that she had been hit by the Fade's hand-cannon near Thelassa's docks. The wound surely ought to have killed her, yet there was no sign of any damage save for a bloody tear in her jacket. 'You were lucky I saw you first,' Isaac continued. 'My sister always was the better shot.'

'You should have killed her, brother,' said a female Fade behind Isaac, a scowl on her alien features. Like her sibling, she wore a blue cloak. Something about that detail triggered a memory. Sasha remembered Cole, veiled in shadow, locked in mortal combat. If this formidable Fade was standing here, that meant...

'Cole,' she whispered. 'You killed him.'

'The god-touched? He escaped, more's the pity. Your kind are a poison that must be cleansed at every opportunity. My brother is too merciful.'

'Do not let your anger cloud your judgement, Melissan,' replied Isaac. His voice hardened a little. 'I was being methodical, not merciful. This human carries various pieces of the surviving wonders from the Time Before within her. Somehow she is utilizing augmentation implants.' Isaac turned to the formidable white-haired Fade. He had his back to them and was staring at something in the middle of the room. 'General Saverian. By your leave, sir, I would like to question her.'

'Be quick, Adjudicator,' said Saverian, without turning. 'Greater concerns demand my attention. The rift beneath the Demonfire Hills will shortly open. The energy unleashed by the Breaker of Worlds expedited the convergence.'

Isaac placed a finger with one too many joints against Sasha's chin and tilted her head gently back. 'Where did you receive eye augmentation?' he asked.

'Augmentation?' Sasha echoed. 'You mean like Salazar's Augmentors?'

Isaac shook his head. 'What you carry within you is not magical in nature. Our ancestors used it to grant themselves abilities that superseded their physical limitations during the Time Before. Someone inserted it into your retinas. You also appear to have other implants, but these cannot be ascertained. Not unless...'

'Unless *what?*' Sasha demanded, her blood turning cold.

'Unless we open your skull,' Isaac's sister, Melissan, snapped. 'Answer his question.'

'It was Fergus,' Sasha babbled. 'He ambushed me in the ruins and put me to sleep using some kind of poison. I awoke in a room with a glowing tube on the ceiling. He cut me here.' She pointed a trembling finger at the back of her skull.

'She refers to New Malaga,' said Melissan. 'I thought you said there was nothing of value within the ruins of our former city, brother.'

'I could not cover every inch of *every* building. The ruins are vast and riddled with secret rooms that no longer show on our records. I will send word to Prince Obrahim, informing him that sensitive material yet remains in the ruins. We can conduct a thorough inventory once they have been reclaimed.'

'General Saverian,' interrupted a Fade on the opposite side of the room. 'There is a... *disturbance* near the Demonfire Hills.'

'The rift?' grated Saverian. He moved away from whatever he had been staring at in the centre of the room, and for the first time Sasha glimpsed the platform there. Her breath caught in her throat. Above the platform, replicated in perfect detail, were miniature depictions of several locations in and around Dorminia. The images were translucent and insubstantial but were otherwise utterly lifelike in every detail.

'Not the rift, sir. Humans. A vast army of them, even more savage than the men of the Trine.'

'Show me,' commanded Saverian. He went to stand beside the Fade who had called his attention to the image on the platform. It depicted a blasted landscape. Sasha concentrated on the image, focusing what Isaac had referred to as her 'augmented eyes' on the tiny figures marching over the broken earth. There came that familiar whirring sound and her vision adjusted...

The tiny figures were Highlanders, she saw. Hundreds of them, thousands. Hard-looking men with unkempt beards and bristling with weapons, women with charms woven into their hair and wrapped in thick furs. There were children, too. Many were half-starved and wore haunted looks.

'Who leads these humans?' Saverian demanded, his jaw clenching as he evaluated this latest threat.

His officer pointed at a figure near the front of the marching horde. 'I believe it is this one.'

'Send the vista-sphere in for a closer look,' ordered the general.

The other Fade turned a knob on a strange metallic box to the side of the platform. A hulking figure suddenly appeared on the floating image. He was half a head taller than the warriors beside him and wore his dark hair and beard in oily braids. The warrior's craggy face stared south with grim determination. On his back was a broadsword etched with strange runes.

'Do you know this human?' Saverian asked Isaac, who shook his head. 'Survey the entire area,' the white-haired general ordered. 'I want their numbers in full. Pay particular attention to any that look capable of magic.'

'Wait,' cut in Isaac. 'I know him.' The Adjudicator pointed at a man following the apparent leader of the Highlanders and Sasha's breath caught in her throat. She would remember that bald, scowling countenance until the day she died. It belonged to a man so grim he made the warrior with the rune-etched broadsword look positively effervescent; a man who had threatened to kill her countless times.

A man who, in the end, had intervened to save her life when no one else would.

'I am familiar with that human,' said Isaac. 'His name is Jerek, but others call him the Wolf. A formidable warrior.'

'Formidable,' repeated General Saverian, his voice thick with scorn. Another figure joined Jerek. A taller man, older and not quite as thickset, with piercing blue eyes that spoke of tragedy and regret, but also of death. A man of contradictions.

Sasha remembered that face as clearly as she did Jerek's. There had been a time when the company of those two warriors would have been her very definition of hell.

She'd learned a lot since then.

'Brodar Kayne,' said Isaac. Perhaps it was Sasha's imagination but the Adjudicator seemed genuinely pleased to see the old Highlander. 'A legend among his people. A good man.'

'A dead man,' the general said. 'Like the rest of them.'

Suddenly, the Obelisk shook. One of the floating panoramas distorted, the image flickering. When it steadied, the vast crater it depicted was suddenly awash with an evil green radiance. Sinister shapes began to crawl up out of the crater, reaching towards the surface with nightmarish appendages.

'Sir,' said another of Saverian's officers. The Fade's voice trembled slightly. 'The rift beneath the Demonfire Hills has opened. The children of the Nameless are beginning to cross over.'

# Convergences

'GOT ANOTHER SCAR to add to that pretty face of yours,' raspred the Wolf in a sardonic tone. 'Carn almost had you. You're getting slow, Kayne.'

Brodar Kayne rubbed at his chin with a rueful wince. Oathbreaker had given him a nasty nick on the jaw and he'd only just escaped with his head attached. Carn was as strong as an ox and as quick as a snake. A better fighter than his father Targus had been, by some distance.

In the end, he'd still lost.

It hadn't felt good, helping the beaten chieftain up off the ground. Sparing his life in front of his men. No small part of Kayne had wanted to allow Carn to run him through and be done with it. To give the sons of the West Reaching the vengeance they craved. But Kayne's father had always taught him that a victory that wasn't earned was no victory at all, and the lesson had stuck with him. Carn had accepted Kayne's mercy with good grace, all things considered. One day the Bloodfist would challenge him again and the result may well be different. That was a worry for another time, though. First, they needed to survive the journey south.

'We all get slow eventually,' he said in answer to Jerek's gibe. 'Age never did no one any favours, excepting maybe the Magelords.' He remembered the Shaman's final words to him. *All things die.* 'Maybe not even them,' he amended.

Suddenly the Wolf stopped in his tracks and stared up at

the sky with eyes like flint. 'What d'you reckon that is?' he growled.

There was something floating far above them – a round, metallic object the size of a man's head that turned slightly as they passed below it, as though it were tracking their movements. Every so often a red light flickered on the strange object.

Kayne turned to Brick behind him. 'Reckon you can hit that?'

The youngster pursed his lips in concentration, measuring the distance. 'Not without wasting a lot of arrows. Maybe one of the sorceresses could toss a fireball at it.'

Kayne thought about it and shook his head. 'I reckon they got better uses for their magic.'

Rana and the small handful of sorceresses who had made it out of the Fangs were kept busy treating the sick and injured. They'd lost more Highlanders crossing the Badlands, some to animal attacks, others to disease and a few to mishaps no one could for account for, like one old fellow who had fallen down a ditch and broken his neck. The food had run out yesterday afternoon and everyone was marching on empty bellies, but they'd made it nearly to the Trine without any more disasters on the scale of the river crossing. All things considered, the great migration of Highlanders had gone smoother than Kayne had dared hope. Now his thoughts turned to how they would be greeted once they reached the northernmost of Dorminia's vassal towns. If not with open arms, then Kayne at least hoped they might settle on a wary truce with the Lowlanders while Brandwyn negotiated on his countrymen's behalf. Then again, the recent coup against the tyrant Salazar may well have thrown the entire region into chaos.

*The world never stops changing. Who knows what we'll find once we reach the Broken Sea.*

'There's fucking ash everywhere,' Jerek grumbled, interrupting Kayne's thoughts. The Wolf kicked up a cloud of the black material. 'Where'd all this shit come from?'

They'd begun encountering clouds of ash days ago. The stuff

got everywhere, dirtying their clothes and spoiling what little water they had available to them. As they drew nearer to the Demonfire Hills it became even more of a nuisance, coating everything like a blanket and half-choking those near the back of the great winding line of Highlanders.

'Not much further now,' Kayne said hopefully. He turned to Brick again. 'Where's Corinn?'

'Down the line,' the youngster replied. 'She's looking after the foundlings.'

'She's a good lass,' Kayne said. 'You're a lucky man. She'll make a fine wife, I reckon.' He tried to keep the grief out of his voice. Even so, Brick must have heard it.

'I'm sorry,' the youngster said. 'I know you miss her.'

Kayne clapped Brick on the shoulder and nodded his thanks. The three men said nothing for a time, each lost in his own thoughts.

'How's Magnar?' Brick asked, breaking the silence.

'Better. They reckon he'll be walking soon.'

'I'd like to meet him, when he's well enough to take visitors.'

'I reckon he'd like that too,' Kayne lied.

Corinn joined them, placing a hand in Brick's. 'Tiny Tom keeps asking after Grunt,' she said sadly. 'I told him he wouldn't be coming back.'

'He was a good man,' Kayne said. He thought about it for a moment and then added, 'or whatever he was.'

'Aye,' Jerek rasped. 'He was all right.'

'I wonder what happened to Jana,' Brick offered. Kayne saw the mischievous twinkle in his emerald eyes. 'I hope she got home safe. Do you think she made it back to the Jade Isles, Jerek?'

'Don't give a shit,' the Wolf grunted. 'She can choke on one of her nana fruits for all I care.'

'You don't mean that.'

The Wolf shot Brick a glare. Jerek was in a foul mood. A *fouler* mood, at any rate.

Suddenly the great line of Highlanders came to a grinding halt. 'Trouble ahead?' Kayne asked the fellow in front of him – one of Carn's sworn swords, who eyed Kayne like a man might eye a foul-smelling turd. He spat and shook his head, clearly in no mood to talk. Kayne sighed and picked his way over the carpet of ash to stand beside Carn Bloodfist and Brandwyn the Younger. The two chieftains were staring south. Kayne squinted, following their gazes. There was a sickly green glow on the horizon.

'I don't like the look of that,' he volunteered. Something else was troubling him too. There was an odd but familiar sensation in the air, the indescribable feeling of wrongness that sometimes crept over a man when a demon was nearby.

Brandwyn's mouth twitched nervously. 'The air feels poisoned,' he said, reaching up and wiping sweat from his brow. 'It is warm. Too warm.'

'We cannot turn back,' Carn rumbled. The big chieftain gave no indication that he was ashamed of his defeat on the southern bank of the River of Swords. The same couldn't be said for his followers, like the warrior Kayne had just passed. In particular, young Finn seemed to spend half his days glaring a hole in Kayne when he thought the older man wasn't watching.

'If it's a choice between starvation behind us, or the unknown ahead of us,' Kayne said slowly, 'I know which I prefer.'

Carn nodded his agreement. 'For the time being, we will set up camp. I will send men to the forest west of here in search of food and dispatch a small group to investigate the land that lies ahead.'

'I'll go,' rasped the Wolf. The three men turned to regard him. Jerek's axes were in his hands, his dark eyes scanning the horizon for any sign of danger.

'You are one man,' Carn said. 'Besides, I have my own scouts.'

'You gonna stop me?' Jerek growled. He took a step towards Carn, fire-scarred face darkening in anger, jaw clenched. The two men stared at each other. Though Carn was easily the bigger man, it was he who eventually looked away.

'Your life is yours to risk as you see fit,' he rumbled. 'Report back here before midnight. I plan to be moving on again by then.' Carn stomped off to relay his instructions to his men. The Wolf spat and then set off south without a backward glance, stalking alone towards the malevolent green glow in the distance.

Brandwyn shook his head. 'Your friend is brave to stand his ground against the Bloodfist,' he said. 'Brave or stupid.'

Kayne blinked. 'Eh?'

'Your friend,' Brandwyn explained. 'Carn usually shows no mercy to those who defy him.'

Kayne watched the diminishing figure of the Wolf in the distance. 'What do you know about Jerek?' he asked quietly.

'Only that he served in the Forsaken for many years. That he was exiled for an unspecified violation of the Code, and that he later rescued you from the Shaman's cage.'

'That's all true,' Kayne said. 'But there's something else you need to know about the Wolf. You can't control him. You try to tell him what to do, you make him angry. Carn might not be one for mercy, but Jerek, he don't know the meaning of the word. Those two ever come to blows, it won't be the Bloodfist leaving alive.'

*

Magnar's grip was stronger than it had been the last time, but it was still woefully weak. Kayne put an arm around his son's waist, supporting him as subtly as he could manage. 'One foot in front of the other,' he said. 'Slowly, now. Take your time. There ain't no rush.'

The dancing flame of the torch cast silhouettes on the tent that mirrored Magnar's tottering efforts. He took another step and wobbled.

'Easy. That was good, son. Let's try that again.'

'This is a waste of time,' Magnar said angrily. 'How long has it been now? A month?'

Brodar Kayne shrugged helplessly. 'You almost died, son. Jerek dragged me through the Fangs for the best part of an entire winter after he freed me from the Shaman's cage. The sorceresses can only do so much. It's up to you to build up your muscles again.'

'Build my muscles *how*? When I cannot hold anything?' Magnar flexed his mangled hands as if to demonstrate and Kayne had to look away. His son's suffering was too much.

*Fat lot of good I am,* he thought bitterly. He wished he were a smarter man. Then he might know what to say to ease his boy's pain, to show him a path back to a life worth living. But his talent had always been in taking a life, not giving it.

'We're almost at the Trine,' Kayne ventured. 'Maybe there are physicians in the big cities who can help.'

'Can they restore my fingers? Erase the memory of my imprisonment? Bring back Yllandris?'

'I... I don't reckon they can. But maybe they can fix your body well enough so that you can fight—'

'*I don't want to fight.*' The strangled fury in Magnar's voice stopped Kayne dead in his tracks. 'I'm tired of this, Father. Always striving to be the man you expect me to be. Always trying to live up to your legend. I didn't want any of this. I didn't want to be king. I did it because you wanted it. And now look at me. *Look at me.*'

Brodar Kayne didn't look. Instead he stared at the floor and swallowed the lump in his throat. 'I—' he began, but Magnar cut him off again.

'Get out.'

Shoulders sagging, Kayne turned and left the tent. He paused outside for a moment, staring up at the moon and stars, wondering how everything had turned out like this.

He remembered when he'd wanted to be a hero. Perhaps he had been, for a time. Serving at Watcher's Keep, helping to keep the demons at bay. He was a long way from a hero now. There weren't many things in this world more pitiful than a broken-down barbarian who couldn't move for the weight of his regrets. Several campfires away, Finn chose that moment to look up and met his gaze. The younger man's lips twisted in a sneer.

Head bowed, suddenly longing for a friendly face, Kayne set off thinking to find Brick, only to stop when he realized how pathetic that was.

*My only friend aside from the Wolf. A lad of fourteen winters.* Brick was probably enjoying some alone time with Corinn. The last thing he'd want was Kayne slinking into his tent desperate for some company.

He was about to go and sharpen his greatsword for the umpteenth time that night when a familiar figure stormed into camp. Jerek's bald head was shiny with sweat, and he was covered head to toe in foul ichor. The axes in his hands were dripping with the stuff. 'Demons,' he rasped. 'A fucking valley full of 'em heading our way. Rouse the camp.'

With anyone but Jerek, Kayne might've been inclined to ask questions. Instead he stumbled through the encampment, yelling at warriors to ready their weapons and for women and children to take shelter before the fiends came boiling over the hills. *They were supposed to be coming from the north.*

He didn't have time to ponder the injustice of it all. Before the Highlanders were even half-organized the first of the demons appeared in the night. It was like nothing Kayne had ever seen. The legs and abdomen of a giant spider sprouted a humanoid torso covered in madly staring eyes, while its two arms ended in vicious pincers. Behind the spider demon flowed a tide of gibbering demonkin, as well as blink demons, the latter disappearing and reappearing elsewhere amidst the great throng of horrors surging towards the Highlanders.

Words of power cut through the panic and fire and lightning rained down upon the oncoming demons. Rana and her sorceresses had formed a circle near Carn's tent and were unleashing their combined magical might against the fiends. Kayne found himself standing shoulder to shoulder with Finn and another young warrior from the West Reaching, waiting in a grim line at the camp's southern edge while the assault from the circle thinned the onrushing tide. Thinned, but did not devastate: more demons made it through the magical storm than were slain.

The hilt of his greatsword slick in his hands, Kayne forced himself to remain calm while he mentally counted the yards between the Highlander line and the gibbering, snarling multitude boiling towards them.

*Five hundred. Four hundred. Three hundred.*

Even with the best efforts of the sorceresses, there were still nearly as many demons as men. Kayne knew the line couldn't possibly hold, but they had to try, if only to buy their countrymen time to flee.

When the fiends were fifty yards away the demon-fear hit them. The warrior to Kayne's left suddenly turned and ran. Another man broke, and then another, until big holes gaped in the formation. Finn looked likely to flee at any moment. Kayne met his gaze. '*You hold,*' he snarled. And despite, or perhaps because of, the hatred warring with terror in the other man's eyes, he held.

Seconds later the fiends were upon them.

Kayne hacked at a demonkin, felt leathery flesh split open and warm ichor sprayed all over his face. Claws reached for him and he reversed his swing, severed an arm the colour of raw meat. He heard the snap of dagger-like fangs behind his ear and threw an elbow back, stunning another of the demonkin for just long enough to part its eyeless lump of a head from its neck.

A blink demon pounced at him, razor tongue probing, and Kayne realized he was wrong-footed. He tried to get his greatsword up, knew he wouldn't make it in time. Just before it reached him, an axe spun head over shaft to sink into the fiend's central eye, dropping it mid-leap. Jerek barged past, wrenched his axe out of the fallen demon in a burst of gore. 'Too slow, Kayne,' he grunted, turning and burying his other axe in the skull of a demonkin.

The fighting raged on, chaotic images of the horror playing out around him burning themselves into Kayne's brain as he fought desperately. A warrior was dragged screaming across the ground, entrails hanging out of his belly, black with ash. One man went down under a group of demonkin, their claws and razor teeth tearing off chunks of flesh, pulling him apart while he screamed and screamed, even after it seemed there couldn't be enough of him left *to* scream.

The mass of profane shapes parted. The spider demon scuttled out, gore dripping from its snipping pincers. It reared back on four of its hairy legs, pounced with astonishing speed at the warrior who was attempting to blindside it with a spear and severed his head with a single snap of its pincers. The demon was already turning towards a new target as the headless corpse fell to its knees, blood spraying everywhere. The pincers snapped again and more heads sailed into the night air. The warriors nearest the fiend fell back, overwhelmed by this newest threat. They were brave men, would have faced any human foe without giving an inch, but the spider demon put a terror in them that was utterly primal.

Brodar Kayne's blue eyes narrowed. He raised his greatsword. Alone, the Sword of the North went to meet the demon.

Just as he reached the fiend, an arrow zipped over his shoulder, striking it in the chest, piercing one of the many night-marish eyes that covered its humanoid torso. *Brick,* Kayne realized, admiration warring with horror.

The boy was here, fighting alongside men twice his years, hardened warriors raised on a lifetime of violence. Kayne wanted to scream at him to fall back, to seek the safety of the camp behind him. No sooner had the arrow sunk into the demon's flesh than it was upon Kayne. Pincers snapped out, aiming at his neck. The greatsword in Kayne's hands danced, knocking aside one clicking appendage after another.

Another arrow struck, this time piercing the spider demon's abdomen. It reared back on its backmost legs and suddenly Finn was there, his longsword hacking at the demon's underbelly as it twitched and spasmed above him. 'Die, you fucker!' he snarled, though he might just as well have been talking to Kayne.

'The hell are you doing?' the old warrior yelled, but by then it was too late. The spider demon slammed its front legs back down, engulfing the Westerman. All but Finn's head disappeared beneath its grotesque, bristling bulk. The young warrior's eyes went wide with terror, all his bravado stripped away in an instant. 'Help me,' he pleaded.

Kayne sprang into action, his greatsword plunging into the demon's side. He gave it a vicious twist and ichor spurted out, coating him head to toe. The fiend's body twisted as it tried to reach him but the Sword of the North was already moving, ducking under the snapping pincers, greatsword swinging and shearing off two giant hairy legs. The demon reared again, writhing above the old barbarian.

Kayne thrust with all his strength, driving his blade in up to the hilt. The demon tried to slam itself down on him but he held it off, skewered on three and a half feet of steel. He jerked the sword down, pulling with all his strength, tearing open the abdomen above him. Ichor rained down, until finally the demon's stinking innards slid out of the gaping hole in its underbelly to strike Kayne, warm and sticky.

With a shudder, the spider demon went rigid and it ceased its struggles. Kayne thrust the fiend's corpse away from him. It landed on its side, legs curling up as it died, an appalling sight.

Kayne shrugged off the steaming innards and wiped demon ichor from his face. He went to Finn and knelt down, examined the man's wounds. Finn's exposed flesh had been pierced by hundreds of bristling hairs that covered him like a forest of needles. The young Westerman's breathing was laboured and

Kayne guessed the weight of the fiend pressing down on him had broken a rib or two. 'Hold on,' he grunted, grabbing Finn below his arms. 'I'm getting you out of here.'

Kayne dragged Finn over a field of ash that was scattered with dead and dying Highlanders, praying desperately that nothing attacked him while he was pulling the Westerman away from the fighting.

Finn gagged, coughed up a mouthful of spider-demon hair. 'Why are you helping me?' he gasped, bloody saliva flecking his chin. 'I wanted to kill you.'

'I don't blame you for it,' Kayne said between ragged breaths. 'A man makes his choices and lives with them. I'm making a choice now. You ain't dying this night.'

Finally he dragged Finn beyond the fighting. The circle of sorceresses was still launching spell after spell at the demonic horde. He thought better of disturbing them to ask for help with Finn – the young warrior would survive his wounds and their magic was needed elsewhere. Kayne was about to turn back to the battlefield when he saw a familiar blonde-haired girl watching him. 'Corinn?' he said, dismayed. 'What are you doing here? This ain't no place for a child.'

'I'm not a child,' the blue-eyed girl shot back. 'I couldn't let Brick go alone. He wouldn't stay away. He idolizes you. You and the Wolf.'

'He does?' Kayne said incredulously.

Corinn nodded. She was angry, Kayne saw. 'I'll tend to his wounds,' she said, kneeling to examine Finn. 'I have some healing... skills.'

The old warrior nodded his thanks and turned back to the fighting. He pounded across the earth, knees jarring with every step, but slowed when he saw the latest nightmare approaching from the southern hills.

There were seven armoured figures making their clanking way towards the camp. Each was covered head to toe in black steel plate in the style of the Kingsman, Sir Meredith, whom

Kayne had killed some months back. Sir Meredith had called himself a 'knight'.

These latest horrors might be dressed like knights but the malevolent red glow behind their visors and the fear that washed over him as they strode forward, massive iron flails swinging, confirmed beyond doubt that they were demons. Their movements were methodical and unhurried. They met the first of the Highland warriors and engaged them. Swords and axes, spears and arrows bounced off their armour, turned aside as though they were mere children's toys. The demon knights struck back with brutal force, the metal heads of their monstrous flails hitting home with inhuman strength. Shields exploded, weapons were knocked out of hands and arms shattered. Bodies were lifted off the ground and hurled, broken, through the air. The seven fought as one, a deadly, impenetrable unit. Warrior after warrior fell. Fire and ice rained down on the demon knights without effect and bolts of lightning bounced off their armour as the sorceresses tried and failed to stop their advance.

Kayne went to meet the demon knights. His greatsword shuddered in his hands as one took a swing at him and he caught the flail on his blade. Pain shot through his arms and shoulders. He gritted his teeth and tried to hold onto the hilt of his greatsword as another mighty blow threatened to tear it from his sweaty palms.

Oathkeeper screamed nearby. Kayne risked a quick glance to see Carn locked in combat with a demon knight, the mighty chieftain just about the only man on the battlefield with the strength to go toe to toe with one of the fiends. Even the Blood-fist's magical sword struggled to put a dent in the demon's armour.

Kayne fought on, his breath coming harder and harder. Everywhere he looked the bodies of dead Highlanders littered the ground. An arrow struck the breastplate of the knight facing off against Kayne and shattered. A boy's voice cried out behind him and Kayne broke away from the demon to see Brick on the ground, backtracking desperately, a demon knight bearing down on him.

Kayne's heart felt like it would explode. He couldn't reach Brick in time. He watched helplessly as the demon raised a gauntleted hand and sent the massive iron head of its flail dancing wickedly above it.

A girl screamed, her voice filled with fury.

Ash swept into Kayne's face, temporarily blinding him. Ferocious winds suddenly forced him back, almost sent him sprawling. He cleared his eyes just in time to see the demon knight spinning thirty feet above the ground, caught in the grip of a tornado that had appeared from nowhere, leaving Brick untouched. The tornado pulled the fiend away from the flame-haired archer, carried it away until it was lost in the distance.

Corinn was pointing in Brick's direction, the girl's out-stretched finger quivering, her face a storm of emotion, blonde hair dancing wildly around her pretty face.

*She's a sorceress,* Kayne realized. A mighty one at that: he'd never seen such a powerful spell worked by anyone save a Magelord.

He didn't have any more time to reflect on his surprise. The demon knight was on him again, as implacable as death itself, six and a half feet of sinister intent wrapped in steel and driven by pure hatred. It battered him, drove him almost to his knees.

Kayne fell back, gasping for air. He caught movement out of the corner of his blurring eyes and his racing heart sank further when he saw yet more demons heading towards them. These newcomers looked like exceptionally tall men and women, dressed in silver cloth and brandishing swords made of a glassy substance and a few pointed metal objects that looked strangely familiar.

'On my command,' ordered one of the demons, in a voice that sounded remarkably human. 'Open fire.'

'Yes, Adjudicator,' came a chorus of replies. Kayne parried another swing of the knight's deadly flail, his arms so tired he could barely hold his greatsword aloft. He looked around wildly. Carn was still locked in his desperate struggle. Beyond the chieftain of the West Reaching, standing alone amidst a pile of slain demons, was Jerek. The Wolf was covered in blood and he clutched something in his hands. It was a visored head. At his feet was the armoured body of a demon knight.

'*Fire.*'

The succession of explosions that followed that melodic command almost deafened Kayne. The demon knight opposite him jerked as tiny holes suddenly appeared in its armour, ichor spraying out of its back as it staggered and then collapsed, its armoured corpse sending up a small cloud of ash. Elsewhere, other demon knights were under assault from the newly arrived humanoids. A second knight fell, and then a third, and then the knight facing off against Carn collapsed to one knee, holes peppering its breastplate. The chieftain of the West Reaching brought Oathkeeper sweeping around, parting its head from its neck.

The towering humanoids waded into the remaining demons, crystal swords flashing, their blades cleaving steel-encased limbs as though they were parchment. The humanoid who had given the order to fire approached Kayne, who saw that he wore a cloak of dark blue. There was something oddly familiar about him. Kayne raised his greatsword but hesitated, unsure what to expect.

To his utter shock, the tall, silvery being extended a hand in greeting. 'Brodar Kayne,' he said, in a musical voice that plucked at memories of his time in the Trine. 'Well met again.'

# Uneasy Alliances

'A MUNDANE LITTLE TOWN for such a monumental gathering.' Thanates stood with his arms folded and his black coat flapping around his thin body in the breeze, staring – if such a thing were possible for an eyeless man – at the unremarkable settlement perched on the crag above them. Westrock was home to only a few thousand people, or at least it had been before the recent upheaval.

Davarus Cole had visited the town once before and could hardly recall a damn thing about the place. 'Why here?' he grumbled. 'Why not Thelassa?'

'You know why. Alassa will not open her city to the Fade, no matter what promises they make and dire warnings they offer. She would not even consent to attend this council, lest her absence leave Thelassa undefended.'

Cole squinted up at the hill. It was midday and the sun was hotter than it had been in many months. Weeks had passed since the battle at Thelassa's harbour, and uncertainty over Sasha's fate had continued to gnaw at him until he felt he would go mad. Not only that, but the Reaver's insidious voice in his skull was growing more insistent by the day. The Fade he had killed on the docks had filled him with the vitality of several men, but it seemed even the stolen life force of an immortal eventually waned. 'Can we trust them?' he asked the wizard-king of Dalashra.

The man he had once known simply as the Crow shrugged. 'I don't believe they are lying. Not because I trust their sense of honour – who knows if the Ancients care for such concepts? No, I suspect they simply feel it would diminish them to lie to an inferior race.'

*An inferior race.* Cole had thought the White Lady arrogant, but the Fade emissary – Melissan – who had turned up at the harbour bearing a white flag of truce made the Magelord appear positively humble. All the more galling was the fact that Melissan had every right to be arrogant: she had fought Cole to a standstill on the docks, and likely would have killed him had Thanates not intervened after reversing his plummet from the skies at the final moment.

A great shadow flickered across the grassy slope and Cole glanced up. For a split second, he glimpsed what looked like a giant silvery bird in the clouds above. It was moving so fast he couldn't be certain he wasn't imagining things. 'Did you see that?' he asked Thanates. A second later his brain caught up with his mouth. The eyeless mage gave him a dark frown and together they resumed their trek up to the town in silence.

There was ash everywhere – a thick black coating of the stuff that made everything filthy. The dirt clouds did little to help Cole's mood as he stared at the miserable townsfolk who watched their arrival with faces equal parts fear and despair. Before the Fade invasion, Westrock's principal trade had been in stone mined from the nearby valley: granite and basalt, hauled down the Serpent River in barges and then transported east along the coast to the Grey City. Nowadays, Westrock was almost a ghost town. Many of the houses stood vacant. War and famine had taken their toll, as had the devastating weapon Cole learned the Fade had unleashed on the Demonfire Hills. The towns of Malbrec and Ashfall nearer to the blast were destroyed, ash and dust having entombed the small settlements. The air was reportedly too hot to breathe for any length of time.

There were no merchants on the roads these days; no money changing hands for goods. Everyone had stockpiled whatever food they could get their hands on and locked themselves away to prepare for the bitter end.

The two men slowed as they approached the clearing where once had stood Westrock's market. The stalls had been removed. Cole stared in dumbstruck awe at what now vibrated in the centre of the clearing.

It was the colossal, eagle-shaped construction he had glimpsed flying in the sky high above: a gleaming marvel of metal, the wings wide enough for a dozen men to lie flat upon, with room to spare.

'What is it?' Thanates asked, hearing the roar but unable to see the wondrous sight just ahead of them.

'A miracle,' Cole replied. He couldn't fathom how anything so huge could possibly get airborne, nor move more swiftly than any living creature.

'That does not answer my question,' Thanates growled. 'You test my patience, child of murder.'

'I told you not to call me that,' said Cole. He took a breath to calm his annoyance. 'It's a machine,' he said eventually. 'A machine that flies like a bird.'

The roaring abruptly died. The air buffeting Cole and Thanates suddenly dissipated. An aperture opened in the side of the machine and – despite the nature of their presence at Westrock – Cole placed a hand on Magebane's jewelled hilt as the first of the tall immortals stepped into the clearing.

Thanates' jaw clenched and black fire danced around his hands. The wizard couldn't see them, but he could surely sense them. Could *feel* the aura that surrounded these inhuman creatures. There were five in total. The pair at the forefront of the disembarking group were brothers, that much was clear. One was golden-haired and golden-cloaked. He wore a silver circlet on his brow and carried a metal sceptre topped by a gigantic diamond that glittered brilliantly in the sun. The other brother, white-haired and scowling, wore a cloak of black and rested a massive version of the hand-cannons the Ancients used upon his shoulder. Contempt was etched in every inch of his harsh features.

*The two commanders from the Fade flagship,* Cole realized, with growing dread. The golden-haired brother had somehow cut a great hole in the White Lady's magical barrier in the harbour. Cole remembered the white-haired brother from the living memory in the ruins east of Thelassa – his deeds recorded and endlessly replayed to an audience of skeletons half turned to dust.

The two brothers were followed by a male and female Fade, who also appeared to be siblings. Both were golden-haired and a little shorter than the formidable duo ahead of them, and both wore dark blue cloaks.

Cole already knew the female to be Melissan – but her brother also seemed oddly familiar. As his obsidian gaze met Cole's, the young assassin felt a flicker of recognition pass between them. The Fade who brought up the rear was as dark of skin as the other four were pale, though she shared the obsidian eyes of the rest of her kind. She wore a cloak of deep purple. Cole concluded that the colour of the cloak each Fade wore represented whichever caste or role they served.

The Ancients came to a halt opposite Cole and Thanates. Melissan's brother raised a hand in greeting and then turned and bowed to the towering immortal clutching the diamond-tipped sceptre. 'I present to you his majesty, Prince Obrahim,' he announced in a lyrical voice. 'First-born of the Pilgrims. Eternal Guardian of the People. Undisputed ruler of Terra – the continent you humans refer to as the Fadelands. It is Prince Obrahim who requested this council.'

Thanates sketched a small bow. 'I am Thanates, once wizard-king of the human nation of Dalashra,' he intoned. 'This is Davarus Cole, trusted agent to the White Lady of Thelassa.'

The golden-haired prince did not bow as Thanates completed his introductions, but Obrahim's voice was cordial enough when he spoke. 'As one ruler to another, I greet you. Where are the rest of you? These savage mountain folk my Adjudicator has told me so much about.'

'They prefer to be called Highlanders, my prince,' said Melissan's brother, diffidently. 'I understand they will be here shortly.' He turned to the white-haired Fade next to Obrahim and threw him a salute. 'I present to you General Saverian. Second-born of the Pilgrims, Defender of the People and commander of our armies.'

'Where is the god-killer?' barked the one called Saverian. 'The terms of our truce demanded her presence.'

Even with the Reaver's divine essence lending him courage, Cole felt cowed by the consternation in the iron voice of the Fade general. He knew what Saverian was capable of. He knew that even he – a god-touched assassin – and Thanates – one of the foremost mages of his age – were irrelevancies in the face of this most legendary of Fade.

Nonetheless, Thanates adjusted his tattered black overcoat and held himself as straight as an arrow, meeting Saverian's ruinous stare head-on. 'The White Lady will not leave her city,' he answered. 'She sends us in her place.'

Saverian's eyes narrowed. 'Those were not the terms offered,' he repeated. He shifted the enormous shoulder-cannon he carried, lowering the oversized barrel so that it pointed directly at the sightless wizard, who was unaware of his peril.

Before things could get out of hand, the blast of a horn reverberated and all eyes turned to the north. Several figures were making their way up the crag on the opposite side of town. They were dirty and unkempt and Cole fancied he could smell them every time the wind blew south, but as they neared the clearing he saw a couple of faces he recognized and couldn't suppress a smile.

Brodar Kayne hadn't changed much, though he now sported several inches of grey beard and his face was even more weathered and troubled than Cole remembered. At his side was his constant companion, Jerek the Wolf, a man who never seemed to smile or laugh or do much of anything except threaten and carry out acts of prodigious violence against those who pissed him off, which was basically everyone. Still, Kayne at least had been a boon companion once upon a time. As far as Cole was concerned, any familiar face was a welcome sight.

The figure marching just ahead of Kayne and the Wolf gave a nod of greeting. He was a mountain of a man, though still a little shorter than the Ancients, as rugged as they were smoothly beautiful. He leaned on a great, rune-etched broadsword that radiated the telltale glow of magic and wiped a shovel-like hand against his jutting forehead, which was covered in sweat. 'We are here as promised,' he said in a deep voice. 'I am Carn Blood-fist, and I lead our people in the absence of their king.'

'Magnar ain't well enough to be here,' Kayne added, pain flashing across his scarred face.

Melissan's brother introduced the Fade, while Thanates and the Highlanders finished their introductions. To Cole's faint surprise Kayne grasped his hand in greeting. 'Been a while, lad,' said the old Highlander, grinning.

'It has,' Cole agreed, returning the smile. Something was troubling him, however. He had learned to ignore the endless beating rhythm that filled his ears whenever he was in close proximity to another living thing – a side effect of the Reaver's curse. As he met the old Highlander's blue eyes, he heard that Kayne's heartbeat was weak and uneven.

'The Fangs are overrun by demons,' Carn was saying now. 'We sought to flee south, seeking a new home. Instead we found more demons. More demons, and… whatever you are.'

'We are no demons,' said Saverian angrily, staring at the huge warrior as if he were a worm. 'We are the fehd, and to you, we are as gods among men. The survival of your people is contingent upon our forbearance.'

Mighty as he was, Carn looked suddenly unsure of himself and Cole felt a strange sense of shame that none among them possessed the courage to stand up to this formidable general.

*You don't know what I've been through,* he wanted to shout. He'd killed Magelords, survived the most hellish places imaginable. How dare this white-haired immortal treat him with such disdain!

Melissan's brother was staring at him, a hint of amusement on his ancient face. 'What?' Cole demanded, perhaps unwisely.

'Davarus Cole. You still owe me a lute.'

'I owe you a *what?*' Realization hit him like a hammer blow to the head. 'You're Isaac!' he said, feeling stupid now. 'I thought you seemed familiar.'

'My sister here says you fought her almost to a standstill – and few are her equal with a sword even among our kind. I would say I am shocked, but your race was ever quick to change, to become something else in the blink of an eye. I see that some things about you remain the same, but now you are... formidable.'

*Formidable.* Much as he disliked Isaac, Cole was forced to admit the Fade had a point. 'I *have* changed,' he said. Suddenly emboldened, he gave voice to the question that had been burning inside him since Melissan had delivered Prince Obrahim's offer of a temporary truce to the White Lady. 'Where's Sasha? You took her hostage during the battle at the harbour. If you've harmed her—'

General Saverian took a huge stride forward and suddenly the white-haired commander of the Fade was towering above Cole, who swallowed dryly, his bravado stripped away in an instant. 'You are neither king nor chieftain nor wizard,' barked the general. 'You are a boy. A child, even among your transient race. You will not make demands of us, nor will you threaten us.' The Fade commander seemed to notice something. He reached down and grabbed the golden key hanging around Cole's neck. 'What is this? Give it to me.' Saverian gave the key a yank and the chain snapped.

Cole watched helplessly as Saverian's long fingers brought the golden key up to his otherworldly gaze for inspection. The general's eyes widened in recognition and then narrowed in fury.

'This is the key that activates the gholam,' he growled. 'The god-weapon came here seeking this. I was forced to Reckon it.'

'The key that activates the gholam? Are you certain, Saverian?' asked Prince Obrahim.

'Where potential threats to our people are concerned, brother, I am *always* certain,' Saverian announced. 'This human is responsible for the deaths at our outpost in the Demonfire Hills. For the loss of Nym.'

'Not just at the outpost,' Melissan added, her own voice lowered in fury. 'He also killed Justinian at the docks.'

'Our cousin died in the line of duty—' Isaac began, trying to calm the situation, but Saverian had already drawn his crystal longsword.

'I will end you now,' he declared, an assertion so powerful that Cole shrank back, terror overwhelming him. He tried to reach for Magebane but found his hands were shaking too hard to grasp the hilt. Saverian's aura was like a vice, squeezing all the courage from him.

'Leave him alone,' a woman cried, her voice carrying down from the flying machine. It trembled a little, but nonetheless familiarity eased the panic that held Cole in its grip. He stared up at the wondrous Fade relic and saw her standing there in the doorway. Her face still held a greyish tinge and her hair was little more than dark stubble, but she looked a great deal healthier than when he had left her unconscious with Derkin back in Thelassa.

'Sasha!' he cried.

Saverian's glare shifted from Cole to Sasha. 'You were not given permission to leave the *Seeker*,' he snapped.

Sasha flinched, but did not back away. 'Obrahim gave his word,' she said. 'He said no one would be harmed.'

'You have violated the truce. It no longer holds.'

'Sir—' Isaac began, but the general was already striding towards Sasha, shoulder-cannon raised.

'You dare to protest my justice after what this wretch has done?' he thundered, pointing at Cole with his deadly weapon.

'I was ancient when the tallest trees were saplings. I walked this world in a time of dragons and giants and worse things and I defeated them all. Do you know who I am?'

'Some cunt,' rasped a voice like a wound tearing open. Suddenly, Jerek was blocking Saverian's path, twin axes in his hands.

The Fade general came to an abrupt halt, his eyes wide in disbelief. Then his expression twisted into one of such terrible rage that Cole had to fight the urge to flee. It seemed impossible that any mortal could face the general's wrath and not crumble like sand.

Jerek, however, might have been made of steel.

Saverian and the Wolf stared at each other for what seemed like an age. Neither fire-scarred Highlander nor towering Fade commander blinked. Not when Brodar Kayne came to stand beside Jerek, his greatsword in his hands. Nor when Obrahim joined Saverian, the prince's sceptre raised, the diamond tip flaring brightly.

'Brother.' Prince Obrahim's voice was like a cooling rain on a hot summer day. Calm settled over the clearing. Even Saverian visibly relaxed a fraction. 'I gave them my word,' said the prince. 'We do not break our promises. We do not let our emotions rule us. These are the principles we have lived by since the Pilgrims saved us from the wreckage of the Time Before. We heed them no matter the cost, or we risk repeating the mistakes of the past.'

Saverian grimaced. A moment later he sheathed his sword. 'You counsel wisdom as always, brother,' he said, though his jaw remained clenched.

Obrahim raised his mighty sceptre. 'There will be no more discord,' he announced. The prince gestured at the magnificent vessel Saverian had referred to as the *Seeker*. 'You will join me aboard,' he said. 'I will tell you of the reason I called a truce. I wish to speak of the Nameless.'

# Turbulence

'SASHA TOOK A deep breath and tried to calm her frayed nerves. Not for the first time in recent memory, she had thought she was about to die.

One of Cole's hands closed around hers and gave it a squeeze, and she squeezed back. The two of them stood side by side on the deck of the *Seeker*. The Highlanders were to their left, Thanates to their right. Before them, standing beside a slightly raised platform, was Prince Obrahim. The other Fade were seated before what Sasha had heard referred to as 'the cockpit': a giant array of panels and flickering lights situated below an enormous glass window at the very front of the craft. The dark-skinned Fade, Ariel, was apparently the vessel's captain – or 'pilot', as Isaac had called her.

The interior of the *Seeker* was somewhat cramped with so many in it, but it made a welcome change from the Obelisk dungeons where Sasha had been locked away for the last couple of weeks. At first she had been certain she was going to be executed. The general was insistent that her skull be opened and her brain examined to see what implants Fergus had inserted.

She glanced at Isaac and the Adjudicator gave her the ghost of a smile. She had him to thank for saving her life.

'*We cannot risk endangering our offer of a truce,*' Isaac had argued. He had presented his case to Prince Obrahim logically, leaving no room for sentiment. Even so, Sasha had the feeling Isaac had a personal stake in avoiding seeing her come to harm.

Saverian saw the look that passed between human and Fade and frowned. The general fixed Jerek with an ominous stare. Sasha didn't know if Prince Obrahim would have allowed his brother to carry out his threat, but she was nonetheless grateful to the grim Highlander for stepping in to bar Saverian's path. She still didn't get the Wolf and doubted she ever would – but she now understood why Brodar Kayne, as decent a man as she had met, called him a friend.

Prince Obrahim tapped his sceptre on the deck for silence and then addressed the assembled humans and fehd. 'I have travelled far to be here,' he said, his melodious voice enrapturing all present. 'Across the great breadth of the Endless Ocean. I came in response to the tragedy at the Demonfire Hills, but in truth I should have come sooner. Several months ago I declared a crusade upon humanity. The crimes of Marius required answering with blood.'

*Marius.* The Magelord of Shadowport was dead, crushed by Salazar's magic along with his city. Cole's fingers twitched in surprise as the Magelord's name was spoken, and Sasha resolved to ask him about that later. There were a great many things she wanted to ask him.

Thanates' voice was grim. 'You sent Isaac to Dorminia. He manipulated me into helping him smuggle thralls into the city in preparation for your invasion. You would place humanity in bonds to serve your ends.'

'A race such as yours has no right to freedom,' said Saverian. 'No more than any other animal.'

Black fire blazed around Thanates' hands at the insult, and in response Prince Obrahim raised his sceptre. The diamond tip glowed a brilliant white and a beam shot out towards Thanates, enveloping the mage. He was lifted into the air, floating helplessly several feet above the deck. 'Attempt any more hostile magic and our truce is void,' said the prince. 'You have a singular opportunity to prove humanity worthy of mercy. Do not squander it.'

288

The beam of light winked out and Thanates instantly fell to the deck. He rose, brushing off his tattered coat. With a visible effort, he somehow brought his anger under control. 'I was led to understand your kind had no aptitude for magic,' he said. 'What was that, if not magic?'

Prince Obrahim tapped the diamond at the end of his sceptre. 'Perhaps the final great creation of the Time Before. It is the only one of its kind to survive. With it, certain laws that govern the world can be undone. Reality itself can be altered.'

Sasha focused, willing her enhanced eyes to zoom in on the sceptre. Suddenly she was viewing the metal rod as though she were a fly perched upon its surface. There were dozens of tiny buttons running the length of the rod. Obrahim pushed one, and the diamond tip flared again. Another beam of light shot out, expanding in a cone to illuminate the platform around which they were standing.

Three-dimensional figures suddenly flickered into life upon the platform – a dozen or more Ancients, miniature versions of their counterparts on the deck. They were all washed out, as though the colour had been bled from them. They paid no attention to their audience aboard the *Seeker*.

Sasha recognized the marvel as similar to the one she had witnessed in the Obelisk. Unlike the real-time representations on the platform in the tower, this image appeared to be some kind of living memory recorded in Obrahim's sceptre. Cole, too, didn't appear overly surprised by what he saw. The Highlanders were a different matter altogether. Jerek unleashed a stream of curses and Kayne's eyes widened in shock.

'What sorcery is this?' growled Carn Bloodfist. The big Highlander poked at the figures on the platform with his broadsword, muttering in astonishment as the blade passed right through them.

'They are not real,' explained Obrahim. 'They exist only as memories. What you are seeing now occurred many thousands of years ago, before even I was born into this world. The Pilgrims are about to encounter the Horror Among The Stars for the first time.'

The living memories were milling around the interior of what looked like a vessel similar to the *Seeker,* but on a much grander scale. Without warning, the image suddenly flickered and distorted.

When it finally settled, it revealed a scene like something from one of Sasha's *hashka*-induced nightmares.

Within the living memory, several Fade had sprouted tentacles from their bodies. Arms and legs had been replaced by snaking appendages that slithered out to wrap around the other Fade, tearing off heads and limbs in a spectacularly gruesome fashion. Sasha had to look away. She had seen no small amount of violence in her short life, but the horror of what she had just witnessed made her stomach roil.

Thanates shifted beside her. 'Could you describe what is happening?' the sightless mage asked. The shame in his voice cut through her nausea and Sasha silently admonished herself. It was easy to forget the Dalashran wizard-king was blind. He seemed to 'see' everything, except when he didn't.

Sasha began to describe the horrific scenes playing out on the platform. More Fade appeared in the living memory, and these newcomers were armed. Bursts of silent fire exploded from their hand-cannons and the corrupted Fade were scythed down. Their kin had tears running down their faces as they unleashed death upon them.

'The Nameless takes no fixed form,' said Prince Obrahim. 'At least none that we can discern. It does not dwell wholly within our reality. How and why it attacked the Pilgrims, we will never know. You think us alien, yet the Nameless truly is a thing beyond understanding.'

'I've heard of this "Nameless",' Cole volunteered. 'I ran into a bunch of cultists down in Tarbonne. They weren't a nice bunch.'

The living memory faded to be replaced by another. A

colossal twin to the *Seeker* lay broken on the ground, fire and smoke pouring from the wreck.

'The Pilgrims discovered this land shortly after first contact with the Nameless,' Obrahim continued. 'Their search for a new home lasted millennia. These lands were like and yet unlike the ones the Pilgrims fled, but it was their best hope come the end. The *Salvation* did not survive the landing. In the years that followed, the Void claimed the surviving Pilgrims.'

'The Void?' Cole echoed.

'Even we were not designed to withstand an age among the stars,' the prince explained. 'The bodies and minds of the Pilgrims began to close down. Before they were lost to us, they gave birth to fifty children. The purebloods. I was the first, Saverian the second. We were born of Fehdmann, from whom we took our racial name.'

The living memory shifted again. An army of Fade fought side by side with a pointy-eared, humanlike race against a nightmarish horde. Saverian was there, as was Obrahim himself, his sceptre firing blinding rays that turned the monsters into clouds of billowing ash as they struck.

'Those are demons,' Kayne observed. 'How long ago did all this take place?'

'Three thousand years,' Obrahim replied. 'It took the Nameless horror two millennia to find us. To seek us out among the stars. What you call "demons" are in actuality lesser entities from the same reality as the Nameless. They manifest in this world in forms that mimic the nightmares of the Pilgrims it first encountered. Your Creator did not bring demons into this world. We did.'

'You?' echoed Thanates.

Prince Obrahim had a faraway look in his face as he remembered events from before the dawn of human history. 'It took the combined efforts of the fehd and the elves to seal the Nameless away. Our advanced tools and their magic. The seven greatest elven sorcerers of the age gave their lives in the effort.'

'But we won,' Saverian said. 'I led us to victory.'

'A victory that has been undone since humanity murdered the gods.' Obrahim turned to Thanates. 'Your Magelords broke the Pattern. The great binding spell of the elves has unravelled and now the Nameless is on the brink of returning. In the places of the world where the walls between realities are weakest – in the highest mountains and the deepest oceans – the seals are failing. Soon the Horror Among The Stars will be free to enter the world.'

'The highest mountains,' Kayne repeated. 'Ain't none higher than the Fangs.'

Prince Obrahim shook his head. 'The Demonfire Hills were once named the Mountains of Fire and they rose higher than any place in Terra or Rhûn. It was there we fought a desperate battle against the Nameless. The mountain shook and in the end was shattered before the Nameless was sealed away.'

Cole was frowning at the pointy-eared humanoids. They were almost as tall as the Ancients, but bronze of skin, and instead of hand-cannons and crystal swords they carried bows of wood and blades of iron.

'You killed them,' Cole said accusingly. 'The elves. I saw it happen, in the ruins north of Thelassa. There was an amphitheatre there. These living memories were replayed upon a wall.'

'An enlightenment chamber,' Isaac muttered. 'We abandoned the practice when we departed this continent.'

'The elves grew arrogant,' announced Saverian. 'They threatened the future of our people. In the end, they were Reckoned.'

*They grew arrogant?* Sasha wanted to laugh at the accusation, coming as it did from the supremely proud, white-haired general, but she dared not.

'The elves were long-lived, by your standards,' said Prince Obrahim. 'Yet they were not immortal. They made the same mistakes as our ancestors. We were eventually forced to oppose them.' Despite his words, the prince's voice was tinged with regret. 'Now there is no elven high magic left in the world. There are no gods left to oppose the Nameless if it breaks through. It must be stopped before it is too late. Else, like Old Terra, this world is doomed.'

'How do we kill it?' rasped Jerek, always straight to the point.

'It cannot be killed as we understand the concept, for life and death mean nothing to it. Before the Nameless can enter this world, it first sends its herald.'

'I know of the Herald,' said Carn. 'A nightmare made flesh. Heartstone's circle could not kill it. The Shaman could not kill it.'

'We almost killed it,' uttered Saverian. His voice was filled with bitterness. Bitterness and a terrible anger. 'It escaped. My greatest failure.'

'Brother,' said Obrahim, his voice heavy with sadness. 'You must forgive yourself.'

The living memory of a massive demon appeared on the platform – a towering reptilian monstrosity with three sinister eyes and a set of gigantic, batlike wings folded around its vaguely humanoid body.

'The three-eyed demon,' Cole muttered. 'One of the cultists I encountered down in Tarbonne said it visited his dreams.'

Obrahim nodded. 'It seeks to bend mortals to its will through dark promises. My kind are immune to its insidious nature.'

The demon lord was surrounded by Fade, who were firing upon it with their hand-cannons. The fiend swept up an Ancient in its talons and tore her in half, tossing away the ruins of her body even as the endless rain of tiny metal projectiles sent it crashing to the ground.

'I thought it was finished,' Saverian growled. His jaw was clenched, his teeth grinding together.

Within the living memory the Fade lowered their hand-cannons, apparently responding to some unseen order. They parted and then the living memory of Saverian himself strode to meet the fallen demon, his crystal sword raised. Just before he could deliver the killing blow, the Herald's great wings beat unexpectedly. The demon rose, still clinging to life despite the countless wounds it carried. Saverian sprang at it but the Herald was too fast, taking to the air before the general could finish it off. With another mighty beat of its wings it launched itself beyond reach of the Fade, who were left to unload their hand-cannons at an empty sky.

Obrahim tapped his sceptre on the deck of the *Seeker* and the light from the diamond winked out, the living memories disappearing from the platform.

'I failed,' Saverian grated in the silence that followed. 'I failed our people. If I had not ordered my soldiers to cease firing, the Herald would have perished and the Nameless would have been cut off from this world. The war that followed costs thousands of lives.'

'You made a mistake, brother,' said Obrahim gently. 'One mistake in five thousand years.'

'I underestimated a threat. Never again.'

Thanates cleared his throat. 'You wish for our help. That is why you called a truce.'

Prince Obrahim nodded. 'The Herald acts as the anchor to which the Nameless attaches itself to this world. If it is slain, the Horror Among The Stars may never again be able to find its way back. At least not within a hundred generations of mankind. This is your chance at redemption. Not a *guarantee* – even if you succeed, I may yet decide humanity's crimes are too egregious to forgive. But I will at least consider the justness of our crusade.'

Finally, Sasha dared speak. 'The Herald is a thousand miles away.'

The Fade prince spread his arms, encompassing the flying machine they were standing in. 'A day's travel for the *Seeker*. Ariel will take a small group of you north, to the mountains where the Herald may be found. After that, you are on your own.'

'You won't help us?' Sasha asked.

'I entrust humanity with this mission. Enough of my kind have perished in this land already. I will risk no more of my people unless it is necessary.'

Cole voiced the question on everyone's lips. 'What if we fail?'

Prince Obrahim's ancient gaze narrowed on the assembled humans. 'Then I will do what I must to ensure the Herald is slain, even if it costs more of my people. And after, the crusade against humanity will proceed as planned.'

Thanates wasn't yet finished. 'Your kind crossed the Endless Ocean to see us destroyed. "There will be no exceptions." Those were the words of your general. Why even contemplate reconsidering your decision?' The wizard glanced at Saverian, who appeared deeply unhappy. Melissan, too, looked as though she had swallowed something foul.

The prince nodded at Isaac. 'Shortly after the rift opened in the Demonfire Hills, Adjudicator Isaac approached me and told me something I never expected to hear. Not in a hundred thousand of your human years. He came to me – and he told me his judgement may have been wrong.'

*

Sasha dreamed later that night. She dreamed of her sister. Of the bodies of unformed women floating in glass containers filled with blood. She dreamed of a sinister smile and the *snip* of scissors.

She dreamed of a three-eyed demon, its wings engulfing her, razor talons rending her body apart as she screamed and screamed.

She dreamed of a white-haired giant stalking her down a tunnel while she ran. There was something in the tunnel with her, something made of darkness and fury. It was hidden by a great shadow. She heard the clanking of metal and realized that it wore chains. She flinched away, but it did not move to harm her. Instead it stalked *past* her to block the path of the giant. She ran on, heard growling and the *ra-ta-ta-ta* of an explosive weapon unleashing a stream of projectiles. There was the sound of a chain breaking and then an anguished howl. It made little sense to her, but she kept on running, wanting only to escape. To be free.

But she wasn't free. Instead she was drowning among a thousand slivers of nightmare. They pulled her in and spewed her back out, a whirlwind of fractured dreams filled with the deepest fears, the darkest memories. They did not belong to her and she thrashed wildly, trying to escape, knowing she was still asleep but unable to wake. She felt like she was drowning, that she would never wake up again.

From out of nowhere, a hand grasped her flailing arm. Began topullherup,towardsthelight.Avoicereachedher,growinglouder—

'Sash, wake up.'

Her eyelids fluttered open. Cole was staring down at her, his grey eyes filled with worry.

*Grey like steel,* she thought. Just like a steel frame, he was her support – steadfast, unbending throughout the years.

'You have a fever,' Cole said. He placed a palm against her forehead and it came away damp with sweat. 'Why are you looking at me like that?'

'Like what?' The fire beside them had burned down to embers.

'Your eyes look weird. I thought I heard them... *clicking.*' Cole took a gentle hold of her chin and turned her head so that he could examine the scar on the back of her skull. 'What did that bastard do to you?' he whispered, voice full of cold fury.

Sasha pushed his hand away and rose to her feet. 'I need to clear my head,' she said, ignoring the wounded expression on his face.

She wandered through the great camp, weaving between tents, stepping around sleeping Highlanders. To the south, Westrock perched on its great crag and awaited the morning and all it would bring. The *Seeker* had departed hours ago, carrying Prince Obrahim and the other Fade back to Dorminia. It would return at dawn.

She passed a tent leaking the soft orange glow of torchlight into the night. Within, she could hear a familiar voice arguing softly. It was Brodar Kayne, she realized. Curious, she stopped outside the tent, straining to hear.

'...won't be coming back,' Kayne was saying now.

'Then let me go,' said an angry voice. The voice of a younger man. Magnar, if Sasha remembered correctly.

'I'm old, son. If I die, it ain't nothing that hasn't been coming for many a year now. You've got your life ahead of you.'

'What life?' Magnar's voice was filled with despair – and despair was something Sasha was more familiar with than most. 'Let me do this, Father,' he begged. 'Let me step out of your shadow this one time.'

'You ever fought a demon?' Brodar Kayne demanded. 'Ever felt the demon-fear grab your insides and twist them so badly you can hardly stand straight?' There was a moment's silence and then, 'Can you still hold a sword?'

Magnar's reply was inaudible.

There was a rustle nearby, causing Sasha to jump. Feeling guilty, she bent down and pretended to tie her bootlaces. A freckle-faced boy of around fourteen years emerged from behind some bushes, pulling tight the cord to secure his breeches. He stopped when he saw Sasha, looking vaguely embarrassed.

'Dawn's not far off,' she said, searching desperately for something to say. Teenage boys had always been a mystery to her. She noted his red hair and green eyes. 'You don't look like a Highlander,' she said. 'What's your name?'

'Brick,' he replied. 'I was just taking a piss.' Sasha raised an eyebrow and he seemed to remember himself. 'I mean, I needed to spend a copper,' he said sheepishly. 'Sorry. I've spent too much time with Jerek. I shouldn't talk that way to a lady.'

'Who the fuck said I was a lady?' Sasha replied with a wry

grin, enjoying the way his freckled face turned red. 'You know Brodar Kayne and Jerek?'

Brick nodded sombrely. 'We're practically brothers,' he said.

'Brothers, you say?' Sasha spotted Jerek sitting alone near a campfire. The Wolf was staring off into the night. 'You mean he actually likes you? I thought he didn't like anyone.'

'Everyone says that. I don't think he likes women much. Or most men. But he likes Kayne, and he puts up with me.'

Sasha stared at Jerek, who somehow sensed he was being watched. He turned to stare right back at her and scowled.

'He never married. Never had any children,' she said quietly to herself.

'The Wolf ain't got time for that shit,' said Brick, in deadly earnest.

A tent flap opposite opened and a pretty blonde-haired girl emerged blinking into the night. 'Brick?' she called out, bustling over. 'Who's *this*?' She pouted. Sasha couldn't help but notice her eyes. They were a beautiful shade of blue.

'I'm Sasha,' she said, holding out her hand. After a moment's hesitation, the girl reached out and clasped it.

'Corinn.'

'You need not worry about me and Brick. He's at least ten years too young for me.' *Among other things*. She smiled at the girl. 'I should be getting some sleep now,' she said. 'Tomorrow I fly north to the Devil's Spine.'

'You're going?' Brick exclaimed, shocked.

'Yes. Does that surprise you?'

'Well... But you're not a warrior. You're...'

'I'm a what?' Sasha demanded. 'A woman?'

'Not just that. I mean, Rana is going. But she's a sorceress, like Corinn.'

Sasha stared at Corinn, her eyes widening in surprise. 'Is that true? You're a sorceress?'

'Yes,' the girl replied. 'They say I'm stronger in the gift than anyone since Morgatha the Insane. But Rana was chosen to go.

She's the most senior among us.'

'It ought to be me flying north with Kayne and Jerek,' Brick said. 'They need me.' He turned and spat, clearly trying his best to look tough. Corinn and Sasha exchanged a glance, both women rolling their eyes at the same time.

Brick suddenly noticed the Wolf sitting by his campfire. 'I'm going to sit with Jerek,' he announced. 'I want to say goodbye.'

Corinn seemed annoyed by that. 'Say goodbye? You hardly even talk to each other! All you do is sit there looking angry.'

'You just don't get it,' Brick protested. He walked over to Jerek's campfire and exchanged a perfunctory 'all right' with the Wolf, then proceeded to sit down and say nothing.

'He's right. I don't get it,' said Corinn ruefully. She shook her head. Her blonde hair shone prettily in the light of the fires. She truly was beautiful.

Sasha tore her gaze away from the girl opposite her. 'I think I do,' she said quietly.

*

The *Seeker* arrived back in Westrock just after dawn. Sasha and the rest of the small party that had been chosen for what, in all likelihood, would be a suicide mission made their way up the crag, walking in silence. Thanates took the lead despite his blindness, guided by the drone of the engines above them. Kayne and Jerek followed behind, the Highlanders armed to the teeth. Behind them was a Highland woman of middling years who Sasha assumed must be the sorceress Rana. The woman seemed uncertain, possibly even a little afraid. Cole and Sasha brought up the rear of the group, separated from the plain-faced sorceress by one of the White Lady's handmaidens. Thanates had taken to his crow form and flown to Thelassa in a last-ditch effort to convince the ruler of Thelassa to come with them. She had refused. She would not leave her city with the Fade occupying

Dorminia, no matter what promises they made. The Unborn would be her eyes and ears on this most urgent of quests. The future of the Trine, of humanity in the north, depended on their success.

The fury in Saverian's eyes before the formidable white-haired general had returned to Dorminia had suggested that he would relish their failure. Relish their failure, and perhaps the opportunity to claim his own redemption against the Herald, should they fail.

As they reached the *Seeker*, the door on the side of the craft slid open. An unexpected figure raised a hand in greeting.

'Isaac?' Sasha whispered. The Adjudicator had his crystal sword and hand-cannon at his waist.

Cole frowned up at the Fade. 'Don't tell me he's coming,' he muttered, too quiet for Isaac to hear.

The stairs were lowered and one by one they climbed up into the *Seeker*. Ariel was in the cockpit, adjusting the craft's bizarre navigational controls. She gave them a nod of greeting as they came aboard.

'Well met,' said Isaac. 'The radar reports the weather to be clement almost all the way to the mountains.'

'The what is the what?' Kayne said, clearly puzzled.

'The skies are clear. We should reach the Devil's Spine by evening.'

The old Highlander's brow furrowed in confusion. 'Evening... you mean evening today?' His tone seemed to suggest that wasn't likely.

The Adjudicator smiled. 'The *Salvation* could cover such a distance in the blink of an eye. Compared with the wonders our ancestors left behind in the Time Before, the *Seeker* is a primitive and ungainly thing.'

'What are you doing here?' Cole asked bluntly. 'I thought this was about humanity. Our redemption.'

The old Cole would probably have added *and me* in there somewhere – but the old Cole had been irrevocably changed, if not erased, by whatever he had gone through in the last few months.

*We'll talk once this is over. I need to be frank with him, to tell him the truth about what I was. What I am.*

'I asked Prince Obrahim to allow me to accompany you,' replied Isaac. He hesitated, then added, 'I am to observe and help where possible. The Herald must be killed.'

Thanates cracked his knuckles. Black fire danced between his fingers. 'Demons hold no fear for a wizard-king of Dalashra.'

'The Herald shrugs off magic like none other of its kind,' Isaac warned. 'It is monumentally difficult to kill. Its wounds heal within minutes.'

'Then we'll kill the fucker quick,' Jerek growled.

'Can we trust your prince?' asked Thanates. 'If we slay this Herald, he will reconsider your crusade against humanity?'

Isaac hesitated. 'Obrahim is inclined towards mercy. Unlike his brother.'

'What if he's lying? You ask us to risk our lives on a premise that may be an illusion. Your prince may have already decided our fate.'

'We do not lie,' said Isaac. 'And we do not break our word.'

Sasha closed her eyes as the *Seeker's* engines fired and the craft began to climb into the air. Heights and sea travel were two of her greatest fears. She wondered who, if the gods were dead, she had managed to offend for life to keep throwing this kind of shit at her.

*Don't look. Don't look. Don't—*

'Look, Sash!' Such was the excitement in Cole's voice that Sasha's eyes involuntarily flew open. Through the window at the craft's anterior she could see tiny figures far below, growing smaller and smaller as the *Seeker* rose into the sky.

'Carn looks a lot smaller from up here,' Kayne quipped. The chieftain of the West Reaching had stayed behind to supervise the great camp of Highlanders north of Westrock. More Highlanders were pouring in by the day, many hurt and in need of aid. Brandwyn could have handled the logistical side of things, but the Bloodfist had reluctantly chosen to remain in case the truce with the Fade went south. He was their best choice to lead the Highlanders into a possible war. Sasha thought Kayne a likely candidate but, much to her surprise, it seemed he was not particularly loved by his countrymen.

'Brace yourselves,' warned Ariel from her seat near the cockpit.

The engines suddenly roared and Sasha's stomach twisted into knots as the ship leaped forward. Her body was forced back against the chair, her ears pressed flat against her head. Everyone else looked similarly discomfited. All except the White Lady's handmaiden, who might have been relaxing in a quiet meadow.

'What's the hell's happening?' Sasha tried to ask, but the words came out as little more than an unintelligible moan. Moments later the pressure eased. She took a deep breath, trying desperately not to vomit and reveal herself to be the weak link in the formidable collection of individuals assembled on this mission; the one with little fighting skill and no magic to speak of.

*The girl.*

She needn't have worried. In the seat next to her, Cole leaned forward, his face a peculiar shade of green. He gave her a queasy grin and then promptly puked all over her lap.

\*

Once she got used to the roar of the engines and the dulling effect the altitude had upon her hearing, Sasha found travelling aboard the *Seeker* to be surprisingly pleasant. Eventually she summoned the nerve to wander up to the cockpit and stare out through the glass, marvelling at the wispy clouds passing by. She could see a winding river below. The sun, which was just to her left, made it glisten like blood.

'So, this is what it feels like to be a bird,' she said, filled with wonder. She turned to Thanates. 'Can you see?' she asked him. 'When you take the form of your familiar, the crow. Can you see?'

'I have. a *memory* of sight,' the wizard replied. 'But when I return to my true form I remember little.'

'I don't understand.'

'Tell me, child. Have you ever had something that you treasured torn from you? Sometimes, when you sleep, you think you have it back. But it is merely an illusion.'

'Yes,' she said, after giving it some thought. 'My sister.'

Isaac was frowning out of the window as if troubled. Sasha hesitated, then turned to the Adjudicator. 'You told your prince you may have made a mistake. What changed your mind?'

'A friend.'

Sasha was suddenly overcome by a great sadness. 'A friend?'

*It's him,* she realized. *These are* his *emotions. He's sharing them with me. What did he call it? Empathetic projection?*

'Yes. A friend I fear I am going to break. Worse than break. Shatter.'

They watched the clouds pass in silence. Brodar Kayne came to join them. His blue eyes were wide in disbelief as he stared at the winding river below. 'That's got to be the River of Swords. Took me and the Wolf weeks to reach its banks after we left the Trine.'

Next to Kayne, Jerek stared down out of the window with an uncertainty Sasha had never before seen in the taciturn warrior. She looked from one man to the other and felt a deep sense of sadness for the pair. All that they must have been through, making the journey from their homeland not once, not twice, but three times. All the hardships they had endured. And here they were, making the same journey in the space of a day, from the safety of a flying ship. Magic was one thing; everyone knew wizards could bend reality, but they were few and far between and often so outlandish they almost seemed to live in a different world entirely. The Fade, on the other hand, made the miraculous seem normal, the exceptional seem mundane. She wondered if that diminished men like Brodar Kayne and Jerek the Wolf; shattered their understanding of who they were.

The *Seeker* flew over the river and Ariel veered the craft slightly to the right. Ahead of them rose rolling hills of a striking violet colour that contrasted stunningly with the red landscape of the Badlands to the south.

'The Purple Hills,' Jerek rasped.

'They're beautiful,' Sasha exclaimed. She hadn't realized the world could look so spectacular from up above. All the darkness, all the ugliness that seemed to thrive around her seemed to disappear as she stared down.

She had an idea then. She concentrated, willed her eyes to see as far as they could go. She heard the whirring in her skull – and then she seemed to *plummet* towards the earth. The feeling was so exhilarating she couldn't help but laugh in delight. The hills grew larger until she could make out the individual flowers blanketing them, the flowers that gave the hills their name.

'Dahlias,' she said. Spring held the world in its nurturing grip and for that brief moment she was truly alive, truly happy, fulfilled in a way that, previously, only *haskha* had ever managed to achieve.

'I see you are getting the hang of your eye augmentations,' Isaac observed. 'I am curious to know what other implants you possess.'

'I'd rather keep my skull intact,' Sasha replied wryly. She turned her head, intending to call Cole over, then suddenly spotted a town to the east. 'There's a settlement over there,' she said. 'It looks like a city of tents.'

'The Bandit King's town,' Kayne said darkly. He appeared to remember something then and turned to the dark-skinned Fade piloting the *Seeker*. 'Best fly carefully,' he said. 'There's something out there—'

A monstrous snout suddenly filled Sasha's vision. It shifted until a great yellow orb was staring right back at her, a dark slit running vertically though the centre.

*An eye*, she realized, in utter horror. It regarded her with a sinister intensity. Then it blinked.

She jerked back, accidentally headbutting Jerek in the mouth, blinking her own eyes until her vision returned to normal. The Wolf began to rage at her, but she ignored him. 'Turn around!' she screamed at Ariel.

The Fade frowned at her. 'This is the shortest route to the Devil's Spine.'

'You don't understand,' Sasha cried. 'It's huge!'

'What is?' demanded Ariel, clearly irritated now. Jerek's foul-mouthed tirade wasn't helping matters much and it didn't seem like he would be letting up any time soon – but just then Isaac pointed.

'*That*. Pilgrims help us. A dragon.'

Sasha was flung across the deck as the craft suddenly veered left. She climbed back to her feet, ignoring Cole's questions. She glanced back out through the glass and saw the dragon in its full, terrible glory. The behemoth was green and scaled and possessed a sinuous neck, at the end of which was a reptilian head filled with teeth. Its tail alone must have been the length of the *Seeker*. The monster beat its gargantuan wings furiously. Somehow, terrifyingly, it was gaining on them.

'How fast is that fucker?' Jerek snarled, having finally run out of curses to hurl at Sasha.

'Faster than we are,' Isaac said, his musical voice discordant with dread. 'Dragons haven't been seen in Rhûn for thousands of years. We drove them off shortly after we arrived in these lands. That specimen is a huge example. It is ancient. Perhaps even older than Obrahim himself.'

'Can we kill it?' Kayne asked.

Isaac shook his head. 'The *Seeker* has no weaponry to speak of. Its purpose is to transport, not to fight.'

Suddenly the dragon began to gain altitude, disappearing into the clouds above.

The sorceress – Rana – stared around wildly. She had said little up until now, but the fear on her face told its own story. 'Where did it go?'

There was a tremendous roar and the craft shuddered as if struck. Fire crawled down the glass above the cockpit. The air became uncomfortably hot and Sasha gasped and choked. She stumbled towards the rear of the craft where it was a little cooler.

The *Seeker* shook again and this time the impact was enough to knock her off of her feet. There came the sound of grinding metal from above and the tip of a massive talon punched a small hole in the top of the craft. Cold air immediately screamed through the gap. *I'm going to die*, she thought in utter panic. *I'm going to die*.

Cole wrapped an arm around her and pulled her close to him. 'I've got you,' he said. 'Hold onto me.'

And though a part of Sasha wanted to yell at Cole, to scold him for treating her like a child, she held on.

Thanates suddenly stood up. The wizard-king of Dalashra straightened his coat and stared at the gap above, through which freezing air was whistling a mournful tune. 'Make for the Spine with all haste,' he growled. 'I will join you later, if I survive.'

'Wait—' Cole began, but the mage ignored him. Black fire wreathing his body, Thanates began to shrink, sprouting feathers, nose lengthening to become a beak. Seconds later he had fully assumed his crow form. He hovered unsteadily for a moment and then the bird that was Thanates cawed once and rose towards the gap in the craft, disappearing in a flutter of dark feathers.

'Bring her down closer to the ground,' Isaac ordered. 'We're losing pressure.' Ariel adjusted the controls and the *Seeker* began to descend. Above the whistle of air being sucked into the craft, Sasha could hear the furious roars of the dragon, answered by the thundering sound of magic being unleashed.

Sasha huddled into Cole and attempted to block out the horror of what was happening. Though she no longer needed a hit with the same intensity as before, at times like this she nonetheless longed for a pile of *haskha* to take the edge off her terror.

'What now?' Kayne grunted from where he sat beside Rana and Jerek. The Wolf spat out a mouthful of blood and glared at Sasha. The White Lady's handmaiden was watching the gap through which Thanates had disappeared. She seemed unmoved by the danger they were in.

'Now we get as close to our destination as possible before our air runs out,' Isaac replied. 'Assuming the dragon doesn't return before then.'

'Things can't possibly get any worse,' Cole groaned.

Ariel turned her head to glance back at him. The expression on the pilot's face was unreadable, but if a Fade could manage droll, Cole thought she achieved it just then. 'Don't get too comfortable,' she said. 'The damage to the body of the craft is serious. We're going down.'

'Shit.'

Isaac smiled, perhaps enjoying Cole's discomfort. 'Ariel's sense of humour is legendary in our homeland. While it is true that we are descending, it is a gradual process and we are already nearing the Fangs. I dare say we've made it through the worst of this journey. What was it I once said? You are survivors. With luck, you might even survive the Herald.'

Somehow that didn't make Sasha feel any better.

# Echoes of the Past

'**B**RODAR KAYNE TOOK a hesitant step and winced. His ankles hurt, his knees hurt – for some reason even his arse hurt, but he would be damned if he was going to ask any of the grim-faced men and women who had just stepped off the *Seeker* to check it for bruises. Everyone was too busy nursing their own pains, physical or otherwise.

The flight over Mal-Torrad and the relentless descent over the southern mountains had been dicey. The landing had been even worse. There was something to be said for horseback, Kayne reckoned – chief of which was the general absence of random attacks from giant, fire-breathing lizards. Neither Thanates nor the dragon had yet reappeared.

The Wolf kicked at a pile of rubble and swore. He was even more pissed off than usual, which was to say very pissed off indeed. The others were similarly glum. Ahead of the small party loomed Watcher's Keep – the great citadel in which Kayne had spent most of his twenties. The *Seeker* had given up the ghost barely a mile from the last bastion of the Highland people.

Or at least, it *had* been the last bastion. Now it lay in ruins.

Their grim little company made its way through training yards littered with corpses. Training yards Kayne had once sparred on, practising his swordplay for the day he would join his brothers in the defence of their nation. Now that nation was broken, overrun by the same fiends that had massacred the citadel.

Rana stared at the carnage in horror. 'My nephew was supposed to travel here to become a Warden,' she said. 'Krazka killed him. Perhaps it was a small mercy.'

They passed the corpse of a young man. His head was twenty feet from his body, mashed into one of the citadel walls. The sight was downright gruesome and Rana went white, then turned away to heave. Kayne waited until she had recovered and placed a hand on her shoulder. He had just intended to offer some comfort, but she flinched back. Shame filled him.

*She sees a killer,* he realized. *A monster no better than a demon.* He turned away and spotted the place on the walls where he and Mhaira had stood together to be wed by old Rastagar. He remembered the dazzling smile on her face when he'd first set eyes on her being walked down the aisle, her blue gown making her look like a Lowland princess rather than a simple shepherd's daughter.

He sat down on a broken column and massaged his temples with callused fingers, trying to dislodge the lump in his throat. Sasha came over to sit beside him. 'Everything okay?' she asked.

'Aye.' He coughed, trying to disguise the crack in his voice.

Sasha frowned at him. She looked a good deal different than she had months back, her pretty brown hair shorn right off and her skin blotchy and grey, with dark shadows under her eyes. Nevertheless, she gave him the same disapproving stare she had back in Farrowgate and the memory of it made him smile despite everything. 'I'm here if you need to talk,' she said simply.

'Appreciate it,' Kayne said, climbing to his feet. 'But I'm all right.'

Sasha rolled her eyes and, strangely, Kayne thought he heard a clicking noise.

Jerek was examining the corpses. Most bore terrible wounds: bodies had been torn apart by oversized teeth and claws, and in some cases pincers. Davarus Cole wandered over and began poking around a body near to Jerek, a grim expression on his face.

The Wolf scowled at him. 'Best do that somewhere over there. Don't want you spilling your guts all over my boots.'

Cole stiffened and glared at Jerek with eyes the colour of steel. Just like Magnar's eyes. 'It was something I ate!' he shot back. He looked around, his gaze settling on the most gruesome corpse in the yard. It was bloated and purple, infected with some kind of demonic poison. Cole strolled across to the corpse and grabbed hold of its feet. 'Let's have a look at you then,' he said brightly, giving the legs a good tug, intending to turn the body over. Instead it split apart at the waist. The legs came away in his hands and putrid blood poured out, smelling vile even from where Kayne was standing.

Cole blinked a few times, keeping his face carefully expressionless. 'Just as I thought,' he said neutrally. 'Demons killed him. Excuse me.' He hurried off, disappearing behind a nearby tower.

Kayne sighed, then ambled over to Jerek. 'How long they been dead?' he asked.

'Couple of weeks,' the Wolf replied. 'Reckon the demons have all moved further inland. Might be quieter than we anticipated in the Borderland.'

'I hope you're right.'

Cole reappeared, making a show of adjusting his belt as though he'd just gone for a piss but fooling no one. The others came to join them.

'I wonder how Thanates fares,' Isaac said. 'There is nothing more dangerous in the world than a great wyrm. Nothing except perhaps for Saverian.'

Without warning, a bell tolled. Kayne looked to the east, where the tallest tower in Watcher's Keep loomed over the buildings and training yards. Once, the Shaman had perched upon the clock tower in raven form, watching Kayne getting wed. The grizzled Highlander gave a rueful shake of his head. This place held memories enough to keep his old brain reminiscing all night if he let it, but they had a task to carry out.

'I hear something,' Jerek rasped. 'Bats. Hundreds of 'em.'

Kayne listened. He too could hear it – a great susurration, as of many small wings beating.

'There,' Cole said, pointing to a swarm of creatures flying in their direction. He turned to Sasha and grinned. 'Hope you don't mind a little guano on your head.'

As the swarm got closer, though, Kayne saw that something was terribly wrong.

'Are those… *flying heads?*' Rana gasped, horrified. Kayne's poor vision began to make out details: rotten eyes, desiccated cheeks, sharp fangs crowding gnashing mouths.

'Those ain't no bats,' Kayne said darkly. 'They're demons.'

There was a bang next to him, and one of the heads exploded in a splash of gore. Isaac had his hand-cannon raised – a similar weapon to the one with which Krazka had threatened to blow Kayne's brains out before Rana had stopped him. The barrel smoked gently.

Rana pointed a finger. Lightning burst from the outstretched digit, striking one demon and then another, disintegrating their wings and leaving their blackened heads to tumble to the ground. One of the demons reached the White Lady's handmaiden and clamped its teeth down on her arm, gnawing at her pale flesh. The Unborn calmly reached across with her other hand and squeezed, crushing its skull beneath her fingers.

'There's too many,' Cole said. 'We'll be eaten alive.'

Kayne cleaved in half the first of the heads that reached him, then spun and kicked another into a wall, where it connected with a satisfying crunch. He saw a familiar building and dashed towards it. 'Inside the barracks!' he shouted. The door was already slightly ajar and he kicked it open, nostrils filling with the stench of recent death. Jerek came through after him, followed by Isaac, Cole, Sasha and finally Rana, a shield of blue magic raised before her.

'What about the Unborn?' Sasha gasped.

'Who gives a shit,' Jerek snarled. Kayne was of a mind to agree. He slammed the door shut and pulled the bolt across. He reached down to the pouch hanging on his belt, intending to retrieve some flint and tinder and light a candle, but Rana wriggled a finger and a glowing orb rose from her outstretched palm to illuminate the hall.

'Thanks,' he muttered. He frowned at the door as something slammed into it. 'Ain't never seen a demon like that before.'

'Whatever realm the Nameless inhabits is home to as many nightmares as there were Pilgrims to dream them,' said Isaac, his voice grim.

The barracks were a mess. Beds were overturned and the bodies of young men were strewn all over the floor. Blood covered the mattresses, the sheets, the walls. It looked as though a demon had made it inside the building without anyone realizing and massacred everyone while they slept.

The Wolf knelt down, frowned at a series of bloody prints on the wooden floor. 'Blink demon,' he growled.

'What's that?' Cole asked.

Kayne picked his way through the dormitory, stepping around disembowelled bodies, trying not to lose himself to despair. 'Pray you don't have to find out.'

'Wait a damned minute,' Cole exclaimed angrily, hands on his hips. 'I'm not some wet-behind-the-ears kid!'

'Could've fooled me,' Jerek spat back. 'You're still full of shit.'

Cole leaped across to the Wolf and pressed his forehead into Jerek's bald scalp, chest puffed out, lips peeled back from his teeth. Jerek responded in kind, forcing his head forward, pushing Cole's back. The youngster went for his dagger, his fingers closing around Magebane's jewelled hilt.

'*Stop.*' The command in Isaac's voice caused both men to pause. Jerek glowered, while Cole appeared suddenly uncertain. 'This helps no one,' the Fade officer continued. 'I told Prince Obrahim that you would stand united. I do not care to report to him that one of you killed the other before we had even made it to the Devil's Spine.'

'That what you're here for?' Jerek grated. 'To study us? To squeal to your prince and his prick of a brother? What you gonna do if we fail your test?'

The Adjudicator turned away, busying himself examining bodies. 'There is another ship crossing the Endless Ocean. It carries a Breaker of Worlds. You be will Reckoned.'

'We'll be what?' Kayne asked, but Sasha was already reaching out to grasp the Fade's arm, her face pale with shock.

'You won't,' she hissed.

'It is not my decision,' said Isaac. 'I have advocated for you. All I can do is help you slay the Herald, or at least ensure you do not destroy yourselves before then. I cannot lie to my prince. It is against the principles of our race.'

The door shook again and Rana jumped. 'I do not follow,' she said slowly. 'Reckoned? What does it mean?'

'It means annihilation,' said Sasha. 'To reduce our cities and everyone within to ash.'

A grim silence followed her pronouncement. 'How much farther is it to the Devil's Spine?' Cole asked.

'A few days' march,' Kayne replied. 'Into the Borderland, and then passing the Lake of Mirrors. Never ventured much beyond that when I was a Warden. Don't know many men who did.'

'Perhaps we should wait for the *Seeker*,' suggested Rana. The magical shield on her arm unravelled, ribbons of blue energy fading away as they fell to the blood-splattered floor.

'We don't know how long Ariel will require to complete the repairs,' said Isaac. 'I suggest we wait out the swarm, and then make our way east on foot.'

'Fine with me,' grunted Jerek. 'Rather be marching through demon-infested wastelands than cooped up here with this prick.' He glared at Cole, who returned the stare.

Kayne sat down on one of the beds. It had once been Borun's, he realized with a start. A lot of water had passed under the bridge since then. A lot of blood, too, including Borun's own the final time they'd met in the Trine.

Rana hovered for a moment and then sat beside him. 'Back at Lake Dragur,' she said. 'I left you to die.'

'Aye,' Kayne replied. 'I remember. You told me you were no healer.'

'A lie. I didn't want to mend your wounds.'

He shrugged.

Rana's eyes met his. 'I heard the stories they told about you, Sword of the North. The things you'd done. I thought the world was better served if men like you were allowed to die.'

He looked down at the bed. Remembered Borun's laughter.

Remembered Borun's head striking the ground and coming to rest against an outcrop of granite, his life's blood dripping from Kayne's greatsword.

'Perhaps you were right,' he said quietly.

*

They marched hard, moving ever east through the Borderland. The White Lady's handmaiden rejoined the group just outside Watcher's Keep, not uttering a word, merely falling in behind them. There was still no sign of Thanates.

The morning after they set out from the ruined citadel, they came across a sight that made Kayne's old heart ache. A line of dead Wardens snaked across the grass, their broken weapons scattered around. Opposite them, littering the ground in far greater numbers than the Wardens, were the corpses of demons. Hundreds of them.

'They made a last stand here,' said Rana. 'When Orgrim ordered them to retreat and let the demons pass, these Wardens refused. They came here to die.'

Kayne walked down the line, looking at the faces of the dead, trying to commit them to memory. They were all much younger than him. Some even younger than Magnar.

*Then let me go.*

His son had wished to fly north with the small party. He'd pleaded and begged and threatened until tears flowed from his eyes. He even demanded it as his right as king, though they both knew he had no authority. The Highlanders followed Carn Bloodfist and Brandwyn the Younger now.

Magnar had pleaded and begged and threatened, but Kayne's memory of the Seer's final vision had hardened his resolve to stone.

*You sent the Broken King to his death.*

He wouldn't let the southerner's prophecy be fulfilled, not this time. He wouldn't let his son end up like one of the corpses there on the grass, torn apart by demons, his flesh turning purple. So he'd asked Magnar a question he already knew the answer to; a question he knew would end the discussion right then.

*Can you still hold a sword?*

His son's reaction had broken Kayne's heart – but at least Magnar was safe back in camp. Not here in the Borderland, stuck in the middle of nowhere, on a suicide mission to kill a legendary demon.

Davarus Cole was staring at the corpses. Sasha noticed him and gave a shake of her head.

'What's going on?' Kayne asked, seeing the look that passed between them.

'Do you remember the corpses that rose from the earth that night in Farrowgate? I think you called them strollers.'

'Aye. They sometimes rise when there's wild magic in the air.'

'Yes. Well, Cole has picked up a few new talents in the last year. He carries the essence of the Reaver within him.'

Kayne raised an eyebrow at that, but Cole was already gesturing at one of the bodies. Much to Kayne's horror, it began to move, rigid limbs cracking as it pushed itself up off the ground. Kayne was on it in an instant, his greatsword stabbing down, skewering the skull. The corpse went still.

'What was that for? I had it under control!' protested Cole, but Kayne was already turning to him.

'That ain't no way to respect the dead,' he snarled. 'These men gave their lives to protect their homeland. They ain't tools to be used as you like.'

To his credit, Davarus Cole looked ashamed. 'I thought they might come in handy if we run into any more demons,' he said. 'I'm sorry.'

'Being capable of doing something don't mean you should,' Kayne replied. He softened his voice. The boy had only wanted to help, after all. 'Sometimes the end don't justify the means,' he said gently, giving Cole a pat on the shoulder.

The White Lady's handmaiden watched them with dead eyes that nonetheless seemed to convey a certain amount of regret. Kayne noticed her staring. 'Everything all right?' he asked.

The Unborn crossed her arms and stared east across the Boundary. 'We should move,' she said in her emotionless voice. It was the first time Kayne had heard the creature speak.

'Are you there?' Sasha asked curiously. 'Are you her? The White Lady?'

The handmaiden simply walked away.

\*

The following day the small group arrived on the bank of the Lake of Mirrors. The edge of the lake was overgrown with thistly plants. Isaac stepped gracefully around them and gazed down at the glistening waters with eyes like volcanic glass. Kayne was a tall man, but he barely reached the Ancient's chin. 'My people once had an enclave to the north of here,' Isaac said in his melodious voice. 'None ever spoke of such a lake. I suspect it was formed during the cataclysm humanity refers to as the Godswar. Perhaps it still carries a divine essence within.'

'I don't like the sound of that.' Davarus Cole's tone seemed to suggest he had had some bad experiences with this kind of thing.

Kayne frowned down at the water. 'The *veronyi* – the wise men – they say that if you're lucky, you can see your fate in the lake. I ain't never seen a damn thing the few times I tried.'

Isaac stared into the depths. 'I see nothing at all,' the Fade said. 'Only emptiness. Perhaps its magic does not work for my kind.'

Sasha stared into the water. It might've been Kayne's imagination, but he thought he heard a clicking noise again. 'I see... it looks like a *city*,' she said, clearly confused. 'At the bottom of the lake. It's probably just my imagination. The lake is deep. Unbelievably deep.'

Though the water was crystal clear, the bottom of the lake was not visible to Kayne's eyes. *Mind, my sight's getting so bad I struggle to see my own manhood when I'm taking a piss. When I'm able to piss.* All he saw was water.

The Wolf scowled down. 'Nothing,' he growled. He spat, causing ripples in the lake that disturbed their reflections. Oddly, the Wolf's lengthened while Kayne's diminished.

Davarus Cole was hanging back, a deep frown on his face. 'I'm not going near it,' he said.

Rana peered into the lake. 'It's just water,' she said. 'If there were truly magic within, I would sense it.'

Jerek gave a humourless smile. 'Fuck me. First the boy pukes his guts up at the sight of a little blood and now he's too scared to approach water in case he gets his dick wet. Best get a clean pair of trousers ready, Kayne. He'll need them when we find this demon lord.'

'Oh, piss off,' hissed Cole. He inched towards the lake, as though certain something terrible would happen at any moment. He finally reached the edge and peeked into the water. Apparently seeing nothing untoward, he relaxed and gave Jerek a smug grin, spreading his arms wide. 'You see? You think I'm scared of a little water? Let me tell you about the time I went to the Swell—'

Behind Davarus Cole, the water suddenly exploded. As Kayne and the others watched, dumbstruck, a giant fist emerged from the lake and wrapped liquid fingers around the young assassin, whose expression switched from surprise to utter resignation in the blink of an eye.

A moment later he was dragged into the water and pulled under, disappearing from sight.

# Sacrifice

H E THRASHED WILDLY, fighting desperately against the giant fingers dragging him down. The breath was squeezed from him, and he fought against the impulse to suck a mouthful of water into his lungs. The light began to fade as he was pulled deeper. He stared up with bulging eyes at the surface of the lake receding into the distance, knowing this was the end. He had pushed his luck as far as it would go.

He thought of Sasha, wondered briefly if she would shed a tear for him. He thought of Jerek, saw that bastard's sneering face and was filled with anger. The rage gave him renewed strength. He pushed at one of the giant watery fingers, but it was like trying to shove back against a wave.

*The dagger, child,* boomed a familiar voice inside his skull. The fog in his air-deprived brain suddenly lifted and clarity filled him. He reached down to his belt, drew Magebane and with a monumental effort plunged it into the giant finger wrapped around his chest. A colossal shriek reverberated through the lake, and the grip loosened. Just enough for him to wriggle free.

He stared up at the surface, his momentary elation instantly dulled by the impossible distance there was left to swim. Still he tried, driving himself up through the water, his lungs screaming. He was a killer and a whoreson and cursed with the worst fortune of any man alive – but if there was one thing Davarus Cole knew how to do, it was swim.

Swim, and make love to beautiful women.

And drink. There was no man who could outdrink him, that was a fact.

*I'll drink this whole fucking lake*, he thought maniacally, blinding flashes of colour exploding behind his skull. The rational part of his mind knew it would be fatal to open his mouth and swallow, and so he kept on kicking. Kept on fighting. Just like he'd fought his whole life.

Memories of the Swell came back to him. He'd almost drowned then, twice. Almost, but not quite.

He'd almost died that night in Dorminia, when his mentor had plunged a poison-coated dagger into his stomach. That hadn't killed him either.

Corvac and his men had tried to break Cole in the Blight. Violated him and called him their bitch. And in the end, he'd killed them all.

He was halfway to the surface now. The agony was excruciating. Every second seemed to last a lifetime. He must surely breathe in water at any moment. Take in a lungful of the lake and sink like a turd to the bottom where he belonged. Where the world seemed to think he belonged. Always under the heel.

*Fuck you*, he thought wildly. *I'm Davarus Cole. I'm no one's joke*.

And so he fought on, every muscle screaming. The window of light above grew larger, but within Cole the darkness expanded. He was no longer sure if his legs still kicked. He hardly cared now. Everything seemed so distant. His eyes closed, or maybe he just stopped seeing. Finally he could resist no longer. His mouth burst open and he inhaled, a mighty gulp.

He became vaguely aware that he was lying on his back. Someone was pumping his chest. Water vomited out of his mouth, no end to it, rushing up his throat and bursting from him in great splashes.

*How did that get there,* he wondered. He couldn't remember swallowing any water.

'How long was he under?' someone asked, her voice shrill

with panic. Sasha, he realized.

'Three, maybe four minutes. I ain't ever seen anything like it. Thought he must be a goner for sure.'

Cole opened his eyes and stared up into the bearded face of Brodar Kayne: scarred, world-weary and at that moment the most welcome sight imaginable. 'Welcome back, lad,' said the old barbarian. 'That was a close thing and no mistake.'

'You was babbling all kinds of shit,' said a gruff voice behind Kayne. Jerek appeared, his dark eyes fixed on Cole. 'Telling the world to go fuck itself.' He almost sounded approving.

Cole felt a cool hand squeeze his arm. He turned to see Sasha kneeling beside him, tears bright in her eyes. 'I thought we'd lost you,' she said, leaning forward to kiss him on the cheek. That small gesture filled him with strength. He sat up and took a shuddering breath.

'What happened?' he asked.

Isaac frowned at the lake. 'I believe you disturbed the resting place of a divine entity. There were thirteen Primes, but dozens of lesser gods. Given the nature of this lake, perhaps it was Oma, Lord of Foresight.'

'Don't ask me how but you made it back to the surface,' Kayne added. 'I pulled you out just in time.'

'Why did it attack *me*?' Cole asked, but deep down he knew. He was targeted because of the godly essence residing within him. Magebane lay beside him, gleaming wetly. His salvation and his curse.

'You certainly got a habit of finding yourself in the wrong place at the wrong time,' said Brodar Kayne brightly. The old barbarian reached out a grizzled hand and pulled Cole to his feet. 'We best be moving on,' he said. 'Before this dead god gets any more ideas.'

'I'll catch up,' said Cole. 'Give me a moment.'

Sasha hung back, intending to wait for him, but he gestured at her to join the others. He approached the lake, stared down into the depths.

He reached down, carefully undid his breeches. 'Oma, is it? Thanks for the exercise. I needed that. Here's a little something for you.'

He pulled out his cock and took the most satisfying piss of his life.

*

The following day they reached the outskirts of the Devil's Spine. They encountered no more demons, although the rotting corpses of wolves and bears and other animals that had made their homes in the mountains were strewn throughout the rising foothills. Some bore wounds inflicted by demons, obviously the cause of their deaths. Others showed signs of starvation. The land was silent and oppressed, the birdsong notable for its absence.

Davarus Cole stared up at the monstrous peaks in the distance and felt his heart sink. 'We have to climb those?' he said in frustration. 'Maybe we should have waited for the *Seeker*.'

Brodar Kayne came to stand beside Cole. He seemed to be limping a little but was making an effort to disguise it.

Cole heard the old warrior's heart thumping in his chest and felt guilty for complaining. 'I could use a rest,' he announced, more for Kayne's benefit than his own. He was, after all, thirty years the man's junior.

Kayne bent down and rubbed his knees. 'Getting stiff in my old age,' he grumbled.

'Old age,' echoed Isaac. The Fade stared up at the Devil's Spine. 'My kind will never know the curse of growing old. I fear there are those among us who sometimes forget what you must suffer.'

The White Lady's handmaiden met the Fade's alien gaze with eyes as dead as old bone. 'Immortality is not without its own drawbacks.'

'Perhaps for those who have stolen it,' replied Isaac. 'Humans are born to die. Only the gods were meant to last forever. The gods – and the fehd.'

A few minutes later they set off again. They climbed barren hills skulking under the shadow of the gargantuan mountains in the distance, the land rising all the time. 'The Devil's Spine,' mused Cole. He kicked a stone and it clattered down the side of the hill, making a fair racket. Jerek shot him a glare, but Cole ignored the bad-tempered warrior. 'What's a "Devil", anyway?'

'In the Time Before, the Devil was the embodiment of sin,' Isaac said.

'Was he real?' Cole asked. He found Isaac a lot less annoying when the Fade wasn't trying to impress everyone with his endless array of talents.

Isaac shrugged. 'My ancestors considered him a metaphorical construction. Perhaps they simply needed more faith. Perhaps the Devil was behind the events that brought the end upon us.'

Jerek snorted at that. 'A man takes responsibility for his own fuck-ups,' the Wolf growled. 'He don't go around laying the blame on others.'

Isaac fell silent, apparently lost in thought.

As they were passing under a particularly high ridge, Sasha spotted something above them. 'There's a cave entrance up there,' she said, pointing.

Jerek sniffed. 'I can smell smoke,' he rasped. 'Some fucker's cooking.' They began to notice small objects on the ground. Cole reached down and scooped up what appeared to be a finger bone. There was death in the air; he could sense it.

'Reckon we ought to check that out,' the Wolf growled. He glanced around, searching for a way up to the cave entrance. The White Lady's handmaiden suddenly leaped up onto the rock face and began scaling the nearly sheer wall. In moments she had reached the narrow ledge just before the cave. She ghosted inside, disappearing from sight.

Cole eyed the rock face speculatively. There were tiny gaps in the wall – enough to get a foothold, perhaps. He cracked his fingers and turned to the others. 'I don't know about you lot, but I'm in no mood to wait around,' he said. Sasha shook her head but he ignored her. He braced himself and began to climb, using every inch of purchase on the wall to haul himself up. Around two-thirds of the way he thought his impulsiveness might have got the better of him, but as luck would have it he spotted a handhold just in time. He grabbed hold of it, almost slipping, and dragged himself over the ledge.

Then he stood there, breathing hard, and stared out over the foothills. He glanced down at the others, unable to keep the triumphant grin from his face. 'Who's next?' he mouthed down at them. He doubted any of his remaining companions could manage the climb, except for Isaac.

'Prick,' Jerek muttered. The Wolf spat and set off for an alternative route, Kayne and the others following behind. Cole felt a little guilty at flaunting his youth and athleticism in front of the kindly old warrior, but he was tired of people under-estimating him.

He turned and entered the cave. The smoke grew thicker as he padded silently through the winding tunnel. Suddenly a hand reached out and grasped his shoulder, and he almost jumped out of his skin. He had thought himself a master of the stealthy arts, but somehow he had wandered right by the Unborn without seeing the creature. She raised a porcelain finger to her bloodless lips and pointed at the spectacle ahead of them. It might have been Cole's imagination, but he thought he glimpsed disquiet in her dead eyes.

Six robed and cowled figures were standing around a huge cauldron that rested upon a burning woodpile trailing thick smoke. The men were whispering in a strange tongue Cole did not recognize. As he crept closer, he saw that beyond the cauldron were several large cages packed with men, women and children. When he saw the human bones piled near the cauldron and the sickly sweet scent of burning flesh reached his nostrils, Cole suddenly understood exactly what the men – the cultists – were cooking. Fury filled him.

Cole charged at the nearest cultist and plunged Magebane into the man's back. Feeling vitality flood him, he shoved the body away and it fell face-first into the cauldron. Boiling water splashed out, scalding Cole, but he ignored the pain and turned to the next cultist. The man's hood slipped off to reveal an ancient face covered in grime, a filthy grey beard tangled with twigs and leaves. He muttered something and Cole was lifted into the air and flung backwards by an unseen force. He struck the floor painfully, staring at Magebane in disbelief. For some reason, the dagger had failed to protect him from the cultist's magic.

There was a blur of white and the Unborn leaped upon the cultist's back, wrenching his wrinkled head almost clean off as he twisted the man's neck with a loud snap. That left four remaining cultists. Three began chanting in a strange language, while the fourth darted towards Cole, a pair of tongs glowing red in his age-spotted hands.

Cole kicked out, knocking the man's legs out from under him. He planted his palms on the floor and sprang up, tossing Magebane through the air to strike another cultist dead in the throat. There was an ominous rumble and two massive figures suddenly detached from the cave wall – hulking giants made of stone.

The remaining cultists fell back behind their conjured guardians. Cole wrenched Magebane free of the neck of the man he'd just killed. The cultist's life force flooded into him. The Reaver's voice boomed in his skull. The world turned red.

*Kill them. Kill them all, child.*

The Reaver snarled and sprang at the monster blocking his path. It reached towards him, swinging its arm like a club, and he danced around it, brought Magebane scraping down its huge back in an explosion of stone that did little to slow the creature. The White Lady's handmaiden leaped at the other giant, but she was swatted aside, striking the wall hard enough to snap one of her arms.

The Reaver attacked the stone giant with renewed fury, but it was like trying to fell a tree with a twig.

A loud bang echoed through the cave. Suddenly half the monster's body crumbled beneath it. It sagged forward, swinging its arms wildly. The Reaver rolled under the giant's clublike fists, setting his sights on the two cultists cowering at the rear of the cave. They were chanting, working another spell, but all the Reaver could focus on was the delicious sound of their hearts pumping blood around their bodies.

He drove the dagger into the stomach of one of the cultists, exalting in the flood of warmth that filled him. The other cultist finished chanting, and before the Reaver could reach the man he was restrained by some invisible force. He twisted left and right, trying to free himself, but he was held tight.

One of the stone giants fell apart, exploding into rubble. The other was slowly being dismantled by a tall immortal with a crystal sword and a bald, flint-eyed warrior wielding a pair of axes. The tiny part of his consciousness that was Cole knew them to be friends, or at least allies – but all the Reaver saw was fresh prey.

*Kill. Kill them all.*

A woman appeared, one hand outstretched. Lightning sizzled from her fingers and struck the final combatant, blowing a gaping hole in his chest. He collapsed, stone dead, and suddenly the Reaver was free.

He flowed towards the sorceress, shadows trailing in his wake. 'Rana!' shouted another woman in warning, her voice familiar. The sorceress turned and noticed him. She pointed, tried to work some spell, but the dagger grew warm in his palm and absorbed her magic.

The Reaver grinned savagely. He was death – and he would not be denied.

Suddenly the bald warrior with the twin axes was in his path.

The Reaver snarled and stabbed out, faster than any man could hope to follow, aiming for the heart—

His dagger was somehow batted aside. That scarred face slammed into his, headbutting him full in the nose. He heard a crunching sound and reeled back, blood spraying everywhere. Strong arms grabbed him, locking his hands behind him. He hissed and kicked out and threw back his head in rage, but whomever had hold of him refused to be shaken off.

'Easy, lad. I got you.'

A familiar face bled into view, dark eyes wide with concern. 'Cole,' she said desperately. 'Cole, it's me. What's wrong with you?'

*Sasha.*

Hearing the name of the woman he loved brought Cole back to himself in an instant. He sagged in Brodar Kayne's arms, guilt and shame flooding him.

Jerek stalked over to the sole surviving cultist, who was cowering on the floor. The Wolf bent down and pulled back the man's hood. It was another old fellow, beard caked with mud, broken veins like tiny purple worms beneath the flesh of his bulbous nose. The Wolf hauled him up and dragged him over to the cauldron.

'Why?' Jerek snarled, gesturing at the prisoners trapped in the cages. They were half-naked and half-starved, faces staring out in abject terror.

'The Voice in the Valley,' the elderly man said, his voice as crackly as dried leaves. 'It came to us. It whispered to us.'

'These men are *veronyi*,' Kayne said. 'What the hell they doing cooking innocents?' He released his grip on Cole and went to try the cages. They were locked.

'Here,' said Isaac. The Fade had recovered a large iron key from one of the fallen cultists. He tossed it at Kayne, who almost fumbled it, his hands trembling a little.

Sasha moved to comfort Cole, but he flinched away. This time it was Sasha's turn to look wounded.

*Please don't touch me,* Cole thought bitterly. *I'm a monster.*

Kayne unlocked the first of the cages and helped out a couple of children. 'You're safe now,' he said gently. 'What happened here?'

The eldest child pointed a shaking finger at the cultist Jerek was currently holding over the cauldron. The muscles in the Wolf's arm were knotted with the strain. 'The demons took us from our homes,' he said, his voice trembling. 'They brought us here. And then the wise men...' He trailed off, the horror on his face telling its own story.

'The Herald corrupted them,' Isaac announced, staring at the corpses of the *veronyi*. 'It made dark promises to these men in order to win them to its master's cause. The sacrifice of these innocents helped open the door for more demons to cross over.'

'What did it promise you?' Rana asked the cultist, her voice grim.

'Immortality,' he quivered. 'Eternal life. The greatest gift.'

Brodar Kayne turned to the cultist, blue eyes narrowed in fury. 'Ain't no gift worth more than a life of a child!' he snarled.

'To the Nameless, the sacrifice of a child carries more power than anything else,' Isaac said. 'It feeds upon possibility. Nowhere is potential greater than within a child.' The Adjudicator's expression grew troubled, as though his own words had just given him pause for thought.

The White Lady's handmaiden ghosted over, her shattered arm hanging uselessly at her side. Her gaze fixed on the children. While the others busied themselves helping the prisoners, Cole stared at the Unborn. To his utter shock, something wet rolled down the handmaiden's cheek and splashed onto the stone floor. A tear.

Jerek's arm was shaking with exertion. The *veronyi* began to slip from his grasp. 'Spare me!' he wailed. 'I'll repent my sins! I can change, I promise—'

The Wolf forced the man's head into the boiling water, ignoring his bubbling screams, the terrible smell of cooking flesh. 'A promise from a cunt ain't nothing but wasted air,' he rasped. Then he took hold of the rest of the cultist's body and heaved him into the cauldron.

'What are we going to do with them?' Sasha asked, nodding at the filthy prisoners huddling around the cages.

Isaac fixed them with his immortal gaze. 'They cannot come with us,' he said regretfully. 'They would slow us down.'

'They can't stay here,' Kayne said. 'These poor things need taking somewhere safe. Ain't nowhere safe in these lands, save maybe aboard the *Seeker*.'

'I will take them there,' said the Unborn.

'You?' said Sasha, surprised. 'You're the White Lady's eyes and ears. Why involve yourself in the fates of these prisoners?'

The Unborn did not reply. Instead, the handmaiden began rounding up the prisoners. Just before they departed, the Unborn turned back to Sasha. 'If Thanates returns, tell him... tell him I am waiting for him.'

*

The companions made their descent from the cave along a narrow platform that wound along the side of the ridge. Davarus Cole trudged along at the rear of the group, too ashamed to let anyone see him. Blood covered his leather jerkin, a reminder of the carnage he'd unleashed in the cave. His freshly broken nose was utter agony; every breath he took brought discomfort. He caught Rana glancing at him and saw her flinch.

He'd lost himself again; allowed the Reaver to overwhelm him and seize control. Were it not for Jerek, there was no telling whom he might have killed. Perhaps he would have murdered the sorceress. Brodar Kayne. Sasha.

His fingers brushed against Magebane's jewelled hilt. It had failed to protect him against the *veronyi* – they did not use magic but rather summoned the spirits of earth, fire, air and water to do their bidding. He wondered if it might have been better if they'd finished him off before the others had intervened. Saved by Isaac; he truly had reached a new low.

He heard footsteps beside him and looked up. Brodar Kayne had fallen back to walk alongside him. 'All right, lad?' he asked affably.

'Not really.'

Kayne nodded. 'You lost it back there. I've seen warriors on *jhaeld* do the same – go crazy and start killing comrades until the fire leaves their blood and they're left to ponder what they've done. I reckon you're carrying some kind of curse. All that business with raising the dead.'

Cole had been in no mood to talk – but there was something about this old warrior's manner that made him want to open up. 'It's the Reaver,' he said. 'The dead god within me. It urges me to kill, every second of every day. How can I live with that?'

Kayne thought for a moment. 'You ever killed anyone you regret? That you was certain didn't need killing?'

'I don't think so. I've killed when my life was under threat. But it didn't feel good afterwards.'

'It ain't meant to,' the old warrior replied. 'When it starts to feel good, you know you've crossed a line and you can never come back.'

Cole glanced at the barbarian's knee. 'Is your leg troubling you?' he asked. The old warrior was limping again.

'Ain't no trouble,' Kayne replied, suddenly walking a little more stiffly. 'You remember when I took your dagger off you for a time? You threw a mighty tantrum, as I recall.'

Cole did remember. Brodar Kayne had rescued him from a group of Crimson Watchmen and claimed Magebane as his prize. 'I wish you'd never returned it to me,' he said bitterly. 'I hate this bloody weapon. It's the reason for my curse. The reason for everything bad in my life.'

'Then why not get rid of it?' Kayne asked.

'I can't. Without it, I'm nothing. Just the son of a whore and a murderer.'

'No one is ever born "just" anything. It's what you make of yourself that counts.'

'You don't understand,' Cole said. 'Magebane made me who I am.'

'It ain't the weapon that makes the man,' Brodar Kayne replied easily. 'It's the man that makes the weapon.'

Cole saw Rana staring in their direction again. The woman's mouth twisted in distaste. Her contempt made Davarus Cole feel two feet tall – until he realized it wasn't him her disapproval was aimed at, but rather the man beside him.

# Shattered Things

THE HALFMAGE WATCHED Monique sleeping, the gentle rise and fall of her chest the only movement within the dingy warehouse room. Mard was curled into a ball, staring at the wooden walls. He might have been sleeping or he might not; Eremul supposed it didn't make much difference. The former dockworker hadn't spoken in days and the Halfmage suspected his mind had finally gone over the edge, never to return.

Ricker had somehow managed to get his hands on the vilest-smelling rum the Halfmage had ever encountered in his thirteen years spent living near the harbourside. He was utterly paralytic, sprawled out on the floor with the bottle still clutched tightly in his hand.

*Strange how we cling onto even the emptiest of comforts.* There had been a time when all Eremul had to cling onto was vengeance. Once he had finally claimed it, the Halfmage had come to understand how empty hatred truly was.

Sadly, that epiphany hadn't stopped most of the city from hating *his* guts with a relish normally reserved for tax collectors and kiddie-fiddlers. He could hardly venture outside without being spat on or cursed at. Shit had been smeared across the door of the warehouse, and someone had tried to hurl a firebomb through a window the night before last. The explosive had turned out to be a dud, but it had hardened Eremul's resolve.

He stared at Monique as she slept, his heart seeming as heavy as lead at the knowledge that this would be the last time he woke up beside her.

*Love is sacrifice.*

Eremul had spent many years pondering the nature of love – in the absence of practical experience, theoretical explorations were as far his mind and body had wandered. Love couldn't solely be physical attraction, he reasoned. Something as ephemeral and shallow could not start and end wars, or make a man give his life for a woman he loved, or a woman starve herself so that her children may live.

*No. Love is simply a willingness to reduce oneself in some way, for no other reason than the desire to elevate another.*

The Halfmage reached down under his chair and removed a small wooden box affixed to the bottom of the seat. He reached into one of the deepest pockets of his robe and took out a small silver key, which he inserted into the lock. The box popped open.

He stared at the object within. It was a thin and utterly unremarkable sliver of wood, cut from an elm tree. The Halfmage withdrew it carefully from the box and gave it an experimental *swish*, taking care not to wake Monique. Twenty years ago it had been presented to the young Eremul by the wizard Poskarus – one of Salazar's apprentices and a man who wouldn't know the love of a good woman if he awoke to one straddling his withered old cock. Nevertheless, Poskarus had been a stickler for tradition, and foremost of those traditions in the elderly mage's mind had been the presentation of a wand to new apprentices granted a position within the tower's enclave.

The Halfmage muttered a word and the end of the wand glowed faintly. The power it contained was meagre, enough to evoke only a small burst of fire or spark of lightning. But like most objects imbued with magic, it could be siphoned by those with the gift. The draining of its magic would destroy the wand, but Eremul hoped that doing so would grant him enough power to weave the spell he intended to place on the boat in the harbour.

With a final lingering stare at Monique, he reached out and, filled with regret, gently shook her arm.

'What?' she breathed, her dark eyes fluttering open. For an instant her face filled with fear. Then she realized where she was. Her sudden smile almost broke Eremul's heart. 'My love,' she said, in her lilting Tarbonnese accent. 'Is it morning already?'

'Not morning,' Eremul said slowly, trying to keep the emotion from his voice. 'Not yet. But it's time for you to go.'

'For me to go?' Monique repeated, confused.

'We're going to the docks,' he announced. 'I'm putting you on a boat out of Dorminia.'

Monique's eyes widened. She had run out of the violet paint she used to colour her lips and her once-sleek black hair was as dirty as everyone else's in the Refuge, but to Eremul she was the most beautiful thing in the world. 'You're sending me away from Dorminia?' she exclaimed. The hint of delight in her voice stabbed the Halfmage like a dagger, but he ignored the pain, forced a smile onto his face.

*Sacrifice.*

'Another Breaker of Worlds is on its way. The city is on the brink of ruin. The longer you remain, the greater the danger.'

Monique wrapped her arms around him. 'Thank you,' she whispered. 'But what about you?'

'I'll be fine,' he said, with a brightness that was utterly forced. 'Gather your things. We need to be quick, before the city awakens.'

Monique swilled her face off with the water in the half barrel in the corner of the room, then gathered up her few possessions and placed them in an old cloth bag, which she slung over one shoulder. The Halfmage watched her collect her things, feeling pathetically weak all of a sudden.

*Sacrifice.*

Just before they slipped out, Ricker began to whimper in his sleep. His bottle had fallen out of his hand and rolled across the filthy floor. The Halfmage hesitated. 'Would you mind giving

334

that back to him?' he asked Monique. 'I don't want him kicking up a fuss if he wakes.' She fetched up the bottle and placed it back in Ricker's hand with a tenderness that made Eremul's lip quiver.

Mard was still staring at the wall. The Halfmage placed a hand on the man's shoulder and cleared his throat. 'I'm heading out for a while,' he said. 'Don't wait up.'

Mard didn't so much as twitch in reply.

\*

Dorminia looked almost peaceful by starlight, the ghostly radiance disguising the harsh lines of the grey granite buildings that crowded together like thieves in the night. The pre-dawn chill kept Eremul from sweating too heavily as he pushed his chair down to the docks. The journey from the Refuge was considerable, but he would be damned if he would spend his final hours with Monique having her cart him around.

'Where will I go?' she asked him as they walked – or trundled – towards the harbour.

'The boat I will enchant shall carry you to the very eastern tip of Deadman's Channel,' Eremul replied. 'To the port city of Westgate on the border of the Unclaimed Lands. There you will build a new life for yourself.'

'A life without you?' Monique said. Her voice trembled a little and Eremul's throat tightened.

'A life you deserve,' he replied in a whisper. He hesitated a moment to compose himself. 'Whatever happens in this city after you're gone, I want you to know... I want you to know that you fixed me.'

'I fixed you?' Monique repeated. 'I don't understand. You mean you were broken?'

'In a sense.' Before Eremul could say more, movement ahead of them caught his attention. He placed a hand protectively on

335

Monique's elbow as a gang of men came prowling up the road. They were a ragged and feral bunch, homeless vagabonds out looking for anyone foolish enough to be on the streets at this hour. In another time and place Eremul might have felt sorry for them – but the way they were leering at him, and more to the point at Monique, filled him with dread.

'Evening, gentlemen,' he said, hoping they would pass on by.

'What's a pretty thing like you doing with this Fade-kissing cripple?' the largest of the men growled. Monique's face whitened in fear. The Halfmage's anger blazed in response.

'Get away from her,' he rasped.

The man spun to face the Halfmage, his own face now contorted in rage. 'You filthy turncoat,' he grated. 'You sold out your own city to those bastards. Is she what they gave you in return for your treachery? Only way a legless worm like you could ever get a woman.'

'No one gave me to him,' Monique said, strangely calm in the circumstances. 'I gave myself to him. I love him.'

'Love?' the big man said bitterly. 'My wife loved me. She loved me till the moment I found her corpse all burned up in the ruins of our home. Our kids were in the next room. They were dead too. The firebombs killed everyone on the street.'

Eremul stared into the fellow's eyes, feeling sick. *I'm not a traitor!* he wanted to shout. *I was only the one in the city who tried to head off an invasion.* But there was nothing he could say or do. Sometimes grief could swallow a person so completely that there was only one way out.

One of the gang reached out and grabbed Monique's arm. She tried to twist away and her blouse tore, revealing a pale shoulder beneath. Eremul summoned his magic, feeling it surge through his veins until it danced beneath the tips of his fingers. But he knew that if he spent what little magic he possessed now, he would have nothing left with which to enchant the boat waiting in the harbour and transport Monique to safety.

*Sacrifice. Love is sacrifice.*

'This woman is assisting me to the docks,' he said haughtily, trying to instil authority into the lie he was about to tell. 'I am to meet with the Fade general. If you harm either of us, or so much as touch another hair on her head, my master will hunt you down and have you killed. Your families, too. Everyone close to you.'

'You piece of shit,' the leader of the gang whispered. His hand inched towards the cudgel hanging at his waist – but he obviously dared not take hold of it. 'You're worse than they say. You're a monster.'

'Yes,' the Halfmage agreed, forcing a cold arrogance into his voice, the same tone he'd heard Timerus and countless other sociopaths use during his time on the Council. 'I'm a monster. Unless you want this monster to destroy everything you hold dear, you'll get the fuck out of our way.'

The collective fury that seethed from the gang could have boiled water, but none raised a weapon against him. Love, Eremul thought, held them in check: love for their wives or children or whatever else in the world they still cherished.

*Threatening a man is one thing. It takes a special kind of monster to threaten a man's family.*

The threat seemed to have worked. A moment later the gang departed, casting baleful stares back at the Halfmage as they melted into the night. Eremul turned to Monique. 'Did they hurt you? I can lend you my robe if you wish. It's a little large and, I confess, not exactly the most flattering of clothing, but it will keep you warm.'

'I'm fine,' Monique replied, examining her torn blouse. 'I will have this repaired once I reach Westgate. If I can somehow earn some money.'

The Halfmage reached into yet another pocket and withdrew a small pouch. It contained three golden spires and a few silver sceptres – all the coins he had left. 'Here,' he said, holding it out to her. 'This should last you a while. Now, we should hurry. Morning isn't far off.'

They reached the docks an hour before dawn. Eremul's arms hurt but not as much as the aching in his chest as he gazed out across the harbour and beyond, to Deadman's Channel. The hulking fehd warships were arranged in crescent formation, awaiting the arrival of the ship carrying the Breaker of Worlds. The city's occupiers had made no secret of the fact that they were preparing for another Reckoning.

He saw the boat his contact had arranged for him moored to a wooden post near the end of the docks. It had cost Eremul half the purse he'd just handed Monique and the small cutter was weather-stained and flecked with bird shit, but it looked seaworthy enough. She stared doubtfully at the boat. 'There are no oars,' she observed. 'How will I row it?'

'You won't,' Eremul replied. 'You will relax and let my magic carry you away from this place. My final gift to you.' He frowned at the warships in the harbour. 'My spell will hide you from casual scrutiny, but do nothing to draw attention to yourself.'

Monique looked from the boat to Eremul. 'Why are you doing this?'

'I told you. You have shown me a part of myself that I never believed existed. You have shown me that I can be... whole.' Eremul took Monique's hand. 'All I ask is that when you have established a new life for yourself, you remember me. Remember that I wasn't a monster but a man, capable of goodness. Capable of love.'

'I'll remember,' she promised. She leaned forward and kissed him on the lips.

The moment seemed to last both a lifetime and an instant. Eremul took a deep breath. Squinted up at the sky, where the rising sun was only minutes away. 'Time to go,' he said. 'I wish I could help you into the boat, but I fear that would be unwise. You'll have to do that part on your own.'

He reached into his robes and withdrew the wand stashed within. He closed his eyes, mentally prepared himself. Siphoning was a dangerous undertaking, liable to cause both physical and mental injury to a wizard who attempted to draw too much too soon. He cleared his mind; put aside his grief. He began to probe the wand for the magic he would need to complete his spell.

'I can't go,' Monique said abruptly.

Eremul's eyes snapped open. 'This is what you wanted,' he said, though a part of him was elated. *She loves me too much to leave.*

He knew that was selfishness speaking. He needed to get her out of the city. It was for her own good. 'You must go,' he said, trying to keep his voice firm.

'It is against my instructions.'

There was a moment of utter confusion before Monique's words hit Eremul just as the burning stone from the trebuchets had hit the Warrens during the siege of Dorminia. As a sickening realization began to dawn, it killed the light inside him as surely as the flaming load had massacred the orphans.

'What did you say?' he rasped. 'What did you fucking say?'

'It is against my instructions,' Monique repeated. Her accent was the same – but now her voice was as dead, as lifeless, as those of the White Lady's handmaidens. She was near catatonic, her mouth hanging open, eyes unfocused and unseeing. Eremul's gaze was drawn to something on Monique's naked shoulder, which had been exposed during their confrontation with the gang.

A tattoo.

He wheeled his chair closer and reached out a trembling hand. He grasped her arm, trying to deny the truth of what his eyes were seeing.

It was the Fade script; the same script he had seen throughout the city on the bodies of those who served the Ancients as their unquestioning slaves.

Monique, the woman whom he had loved more than life itself, was a thrall.

Eremul twisted her arm roughly in sudden rage, ignored her

gasp of pain. He placed a finger on the tattoo and channelled his magic into it. The tattoo began to writhe, like a spider lodged in her flesh. But it was no spider. It was a mind-controlling parasite that dictated her thoughts and actions. A mind-controlling parasite that made her someone she wasn't. A slave; a thrall.

*An illusion.*

The tiny mechanical construct popped out of Monique's shoulder, dropping to the deck beneath, where it promptly scuttled off the edge of the docks and into the water of the harbour, sinking without trace.

The woman who had been Monique was now staring at Eremul without a hint of recognition in her eyes. 'Where am I?' she asked. 'Who are you?'

'You remember nothing?' Eremul asked, knowing what the answer would be. Knowing but needing to hear her say it.

'I remember... someone whispering to me. Telling me to watch you. To report on you. To love you.' Her eyes ran down his body, widened when they saw that he had no legs. One final knife thrust into his heart. 'How could I love *you?*' she asked, in disbelief.

Eremul turned his back on the stranger.

*

He found his way back to the Refuge in a daze, not remembering how he got there. Not remembering and not caring. He stopped dead when he saw the flames licking at the doorway of the warehouse he shared with Mard and Ricker.

The door had been blown right off its hinges and lay in pieces. Smoke clogged the interior of the building. A small crowd had gathered outside, a few among them making a futile effort to put out the raging fire with buckets of rainwater.

'Two dead,' said a voice from inside the building, followed by a hacking cough. A burly fellow, perhaps a blacksmith, dragged out a blackened corpse. Eremul stared at the fire-ravaged body, recognizing Mard through blurring eyes. The man went back inside the warehouse and a moment later dragged out another body. Ricker was still clutching the shattered remnants of his bottle in his dead hand.

'I saw who done it,' shouted a woman. 'A gang came prowling through here, looking for the Halfmage. Said they wanted to do to him what he helped do to their families. This is his fault, that Fade-kissing traitor.'

'There he is!' someone shouted.

Eremul saw the finger pointing straight at him through the tears that suddenly filled his eyes. He didn't open his mouth to protest his innocence. Didn't try to flee. Didn't even think to summon his magic to protect himself. Instead he watched numbly as the crowd worked themselves into a frenzy.

'Treacherous fuck!'

'You sold out your kind! We're all going to die because of you!'

'Monster!' someone else screamed. The first stone glanced off his forehead, and he blinked stupidly as blood ran down his cheeks, mixing with his tears. A piece of wood from the shattered door cracked into his chest. That didn't hurt as much as the nail sticking out of it.

Someone grabbed him around the neck from behind and then he was falling backwards, landing painfully on the back of his head, his wheelchair toppling over beside him.

A boot thudded into his chest, stealing the breath from him. Pain shot through his ribs. Another boot struck him in the face, and he could feel its print being burned into his skin as hot agony exploded.

He stared up at the hateful faces above. Clenched fists and booted feet and warm spittle rained down on him from all angles, shattering his body.

*I'm not a monster.* The thought seemed to repeat itself as his head bounced off the street again. He tried to understand how he was still conscious, still so exquisitely aware of every hurt being heaped upon him.

A moment later all thought ceased.

# Unspoken

ASHA WIPED SWEAT from her brow and squinted up at the
mountain ahead. The climb through the lower reaches of the
Devil's Spine had been tough enough – a harsh ascent through
jagged, barren rock hiding deep crevices and plunging drops –
but in the last few hours the terrain had begun to rise even more
sharply. Her hands were scraped raw from dragging herself up
broken ledges of rough stone. Their party's progress had become
agonizingly slow. In particular, the Highlander sorceress, Rana,
and Brodar Kayne were struggling tremendously with the climb.
The latter looked decidedly unwell, gasping for breath and
wincing in pain whenever he thought no one was watching.

Behind her, Cole slunk along at the rear of the group, cutting
a miserable figure. Her friend walked with his head down, and
he seemed unwilling to meet her gaze. What she had witnessed
in the cave had shocked her. Cole had become a creature of
darkness and shadow, the living embodiment of the godly
essence he supposedly carried within him.

She wanted to turn to Cole, to talk openly and honestly about
what was happening to him, but he looked in no mood for
company. Jerek had broken his nose, and his face was caked
with dried blood.

Sasha's own nose was in much better shape now that she
hadn't touched so much as a grain of *hashka* in weeks, though
occasionally she would get a strange tingling sensation in her
hands that she couldn't explain.

At the head of the group, Isaac and Jerek reached the top of a huge protrusion of rock and came to an abrupt halt. The Fade officer cut an impressive figure, blazingly white-skinned against the nearly black rock, beautiful in an utterly alien sense and immeasurably graceful as he raised a slender hand to shield his eyes against the midday sun.

Jerek on the other hand was anything but graceful. Fire-scarred and harsher than the mountains surrounding them, he seemed to contain nothing but iron and fury. He'd barely said a word to her since they'd become reacquainted back at Westrock. He barely said a word to anyone except Brodar Kayne – and even then, he never seemed to say much if a grim nod would suffice. 'Trouble up ahead,' he growled, gesturing with an axe. 'Giants, looks like. Fighting against demonkin.'

Isaac turned to Sasha. 'Perhaps you could take a closer look,' he suggested.

She raised an eyebrow. 'You mean to tell me my sight is better than your own?'

'The augmentation you possess was part of an experimental suite of implants designed to create the perfect human soldier. The project was abandoned when Prince Obrahim declared it to be no longer moral.'

'No longer moral? After you'd already enslaved countless thousands of us?'

'Your species had achieved a level of civilization we could no longer ignore. Only since the murders of Aduana and Feryan has Obrahim once again sanctioned the use of human thralls.'

Jerek seemed to be even more agitated than normal. He tugged at his beard, sent a mouthful of spit perilously close to Isaac's silver-booted feet. 'You two gonna stand there all day flapping your jaws?' he snarled. 'There I was thinking the fate of the world was at stake.'

The Fade fixed the angry Wolf with his obsidian gaze. 'It would be more accurate to say that humanity's fate is at stake. If you fail, my kind will step in. Saverian will not fail again.'

'What if you die here?' Jerek rasped. 'What's your prince gonna say if we drag your corpse back to the Trine?'

'It will not alter his thinking. Unlike your kind, we do not act out of spite or anger.' Isaac's eyes narrowed. 'I trust you do not harbour any unwise thoughts.'

Jerek spat again. 'I told you I would help hunt down and kill this Herald fucker. Till then, I got your back.' The Wolf looked mighty pissed off at Isaac's inference and Sasha decided a distraction might be a good idea.

'Let me take a look at that plateau,' she said, pushing herself between the pair. She stared at the plateau opposite and focused her augmented eyes. The tiny figures almost instantly became towering giants, their long hair braided in knots that hung over naked chests. They were under siege from squat, eyeless creatures the colour of raw meat. The giants were badly outnumbered, covered in bloody wounds from the demons' vile claws. Though their clubs were longer than Sasha was tall – the trunks of trees, torn from the ground and stripped of their branches – the giants' rudimentary weapons did not appear to be greatly effective against the fiends.

'The giants are going to lose,' she said. 'The demons greatly outnumber them.'

'Should we intervene?' asked Rana. The sorceress was an unassuming woman, but she possessed a quiet strength that reminded Sasha of Brianna, the White Lady's one-time apprentice. Sasha stared at the woman, noting her strong jaw, her bright eyes.

'Fuck 'em,' Jerek rasped. 'No giant ever did shit for me. Bunch of pricks.'

Brodar Kayne had finally caught his breath. The old warrior squinted at the battle raging ahead of them and it was obvious to Sasha that he could hardly see a thing. 'I ain't never been fond of giants myself,' he said. 'But they might know something about the whereabouts of this Herald demon.'

Isaac drew his crystal sword. It glittered a thousand shades of red in the overhead sun. 'Let us go to kill demons,' he announced.

They scrambled across broken rock, the sounds of combat growing louder as they neared the tableland upon which the battle was taking place. The harsh crack of Isaac's hand-cannon split the air, and one of the demons was knocked to the ground before the largest of the giants flattened it beneath his mighty club.

Sudden terror gripped Sasha. She slowed, her legs seemingly turned to water. Kayne passed her, half stumbling. 'Demon-fear,' he spat, between gritted teeth. 'Don't let it conquer you, lass.'

Cole caught up with her and grasped her hand. 'Come on,' he said. 'I won't let them hurt you.'

They reached the fighting just as the second-to-last giant fell, his eight-hundred-pound bulk going down beneath a half-dozen fiends, their razor claws pulling his intestines out through his stomach. Sasha raised her crossbow with trembling hands and sent a bolt thudding into the head of one of the demons, killing it instantly. Isaac, Kayne and Jerek plunged into them, sword and axe cleaving apart the fiends. Fire burst from Rana's outstretched palm, roasting four of them, their pink flesh turning a darker shade of red, circular mouths widening in silent screams.

The sole remaining giant wielded his huge tree like a quarterstaff, fending off the demons with both ends. His skin was gouged and bleeding in countless places but he was seemingly immovable, a towering colossus standing head and shoulders above even Isaac. As Sasha watched, Cole sneaked up behind one of the fiends and plunged Magebane into the place where its heart ought to be. The demon twisted around, scything claws raking for Cole's face. He danced back, avoiding the swiping talons by a whisper, and then struck like a snake, once, twice, three times, Magebane tearing gaping holes in the fiend.

In a moment of utter, pant-pissing terror, Sasha spotted one of the demons dashing towards her, its limbs flailing wildly. She reached for her quiver but, overwhelmed by horror, she fumbled the bolt. It clattered uselessly to the ground and she turned to flee, only to trip over a rock and sprawl flat on her face, scraping her cheek painfully. She rolled onto her back just as the demon reached her. Its grotesque head snapped down, teeth gnashing, desperate to tear her face right off her skull. In mad panic she grabbed hold of its head, stopping it mere inches from her, so close she could count the razor teeth bristling in its gaping maw.

Everyone else was busy fighting for their own lives, too busy to come to her aid. She remembered being in a similar predicament outside the gates of Dorminia, the weight of a man pressing down on her as he tried to choke the life from her. She'd saved herself that time, but she'd had a shortsword to hand and besides, that had only been a soldier, not a demon from a place beyond her worst nightmares.

The demon's jaws brushed her nose and she screamed, her arms shaking with the effort of trying to hold it off. She caught a glimpse of Cole, surrounded by a trio of demons. He met her gaze and his face filled with agony. He couldn't reach her in time.

Sasha spotted a jagged rock a few feet away. It was the same rock that had tripped her up. She stared at it, wishing it were just a few inches closer…

It might have been a trick of her panicked imagination, but the rock seemed to shift slightly. She felt that tingling in her body again, just like she had in Derkin's home when the tea Derkin's mother had placed in her hands had boiled out of the cup.

*Am I moving it? Is it possible?* She focused on the rock, willing it to come to her. Again it shifted, further this time, skipping over the ground like a pebble skipping across a pond. Suddenly it jumped, landing near her leg. She couldn't spare a hand, so instead she concentrated on the snarling, biting visage a few inches from her face, willing the rock to crush its skull. It bounced up and struck the demon on the head. It looked stunned for a second or two, but then it attacked with renewed fury.

*Shit.*

In desperation she searched around. This time her gaze settled on the crossbow bolt she had fumbled and she willed it to rise off the ground, to pierce the brain of the nightmarish apparition above her. The bolt vibrated a few times.

*Come on, you bastard. Move. Fucking move!*

There was a soft popping sound.

The demon slid slowly off her, the shaft of the crossbow protruding from its cranium.

Sasha climbed unsteadily to her feet, shocked at what had just happened. Dead demons and giants littered the plateau. Cole and the giant finished off the last of the demons while the others were regrouping, wiping ichor from their faces and their weapons. Isaac walked over and stared down at the dead demon near her feet. 'Telekinetic manipulation,' he said, sounding impressed. 'One of the last augmentations we discovered, and one of the most unstable. You are full of surprises.'

'Thanks,' she muttered, not really sharing Isaacs sense of wonderment.

None of the small company appeared to have been wounded in the fight. The giant, however, bore terrible gashes on both its legs and its stomach. It stared at them suspiciously from beneath heavily lidded eyes, its massive chest rising and falling. Cole stared up at it and frowned. 'Can you speak?'

The giant merely looked down at him.

'You'd better answer me,' Cole snapped. 'I just saved your life.'

The giant grunted and blew snot from its nose. Though it appeared to be accidental, some of it struck Cole in the face.

Her friend reached up and wiped the snot from his forehead, staring at it with an unreadable expression. Then, to Sasha's shock, he leaped up and slapped the massive humanoid across the cheek. 'Don't you disrespect me, you son of a bitch!' he snarled.

The giant gave a furious bellow and took a single lumbering step towards Cole, only for Isaac to block its path. Kayne and

Jerek held Cole back. He seemed as eager to get a piece of the giant as it was to get a piece of him.

'Calm,' the Adjudicator ordered. The giant blinked a few times and then visibly relaxed, pacified by the power of Isaac's voice. Cole looked vaguely embarrassed. Even Sasha found her anxiety melting away as the immortal's command soothed her emotions. 'Tell us what happened here,' Isaac said softly.

'Demons,' the giant rumbled, in a voice like an avalanche. 'Attacked our clan. Other clans all dead or gone. Wouldn't flee. Is our home.' The giant spread its hands and stared mournfully at its fallen comrades. 'Now all gone.'

'We are sorry for the loss of your kin,' said Isaac. 'Tell me. Do you know of the Herald? It is a demon far larger than any other. It has three eyes that see inside your soul, and wings that seem to blot out the sun.'

The giant nodded its massive head. 'It came to us in storm. Many moons past. Offered dark promises. Some giants listened. Not Mighty Oak. Not his clan.'

'You are Mighty Oak?' Isaac asked. The giant nodded. 'Where are the other giants? Those that listened to the Herald?'

'Gone west to smallfolk lands. Gone with demons to slaughter smallfolk. To kill.' The giant nodded at Cole and Sasha. He seemed uncertain about Isaac, treating the Fade with a wary respect that he clearly did not hold for humans. At least not until he saw Brodar Kayne.

'Cold Eyes,' he rumbled, sounding surprised. 'Thought you dead. Many moons ago.'

The old Highlander stared up at the giant. He was a tall man, still an impressive figure despite his advancing years, but compared with the immortal Fade and the towering giant he looked wretched. Wretched and a little broken. 'I ain't dead yet,' he said, though the grimace on his face suggested that he might have some doubts as to how much longer that would remain the case.

'You know this man?' said Isaac.

Mighty Oak nodded once again. 'Cold Eyes famous.'

Kayne sighed at that. The sorceress, Rana, was watching him carefully. 'Why is he famous?' continued Isaac.

Mighty Oak brought an equally mighty fist to his chest in what appeared to be a gesture of respect. 'Cold Eyes killed many giants. Those that tried to cross Boundary. Strong Heart and Long Tooth. Dancing Maiden, too.'

'Dancing Maiden?' Sasha said. 'You mean there are female giants?'

*Of course there are, stupid,* she silently chided herself. *The males don't get themselves pregnant.*

'Dancing Maiden dragged body to mirror lake,' Mighty Oak said. 'Spoke of Cold Eyes as deadly killer. She died well.'

'Didn't realize "he" was a "she" until after,' muttered Kayne, looking at the ground. Rana was staring at Brodar Kayne with a hard expression.

A sudden wind gusted across the plateau. Sasha shivered. The wind felt... strange. Cold, and yet also hot.

Mighty Oak's eyes narrowed. 'Must seek shelter. Killing wind is coming.'

'Killing wind?' Isaac repeated, his melodic voice echoing eerily. The giant nodded. 'Have to go. Not safe here.'

'Wait.' The command in Isaac's voice stopped Mighty Oak dead in his tracks. 'Do you know where the Herald may be found?'

The giant pointed towards the north-east with a finger as thick as a spear shaft. 'In valley beyond mountains. Land is... wrong there. Mighty Oak's kind no go near.'

'You could come with us,' Brodar Kayne said. 'We could use your help.' There was something in the Highlander's voice. A deep sadness, maybe.

Mighty Oak shook his head. 'First shelter. Then I search mountains for kin. Maybe others survived.'

Brodar Kayne cleared his throat. 'Wish you luck with that, friend. Sorry about your fellows.' The old warrior Mighty Oak had named 'Cold Eyes' might have been talking about the fallen giants scattered about the tableland – or he might have been talking about the giants he himself had killed in his younger years.

They watched the lumbering giant depart. 'I hope he finds more of his people,' Rana said. 'There is a certain sadness in him being the last of his clan, bereft of everything he once knew.' Sasha noticed then that the sorceress appeared to have a few specks of blood on her face.

Kayne shook his head. 'He's got the demon-rot,' the old warrior said quietly. 'You saw those wounds on his legs? They were turning black. He'll be dead on the morrow. Maybe the day after.'

A gloomy silence followed that unhappy pronouncement. The wind howled again and this time Sasha felt wetness on her face. She reached up and when she examined her fingers she saw with horror that they were speckled with blood.

'Sash!' exclaimed Cole. 'You're bleeding!' He glimpsed his reflection in Magebane's blade and paled a little beneath the crimson sheen covering his own skin. 'Shit. So am I...'

*

They sought shelter as the wind quickly became a terrifying storm. The companions huddled in a small cave just below the tor on which the battle had taken place and listened to the raging of the killing wind. The howling from outside was otherworldly, like the screams of a mad god reverberating through the mountains. At one point, shards of a hard substance rained down, shattering as they struck the rock. Had the party still been out in the open, the unnatural rain would have cut them all to ribbons.

'What the hell is that?' Sasha wondered aloud. Something shattered just inside the cave and she scooped it up in her hands, accidentally cutting herself. The substance resembled opaque glass, cloudy and rough-textured. It was like nothing she had seen before.

'We are very close to a rift,' Isaac explained.

'A rift?' Cole asked, half-heartedly. He seemed distracted.

'A doorway to whatever dark dimension the Nameless and its kind reside within. The barrier between realities is weakest near a rift. What is happening outside is a result of this convergence.'

'And you're saying we've got to get even closer to this rift in order to track down the Herald?' Kayne didn't sound impressed. 'Can't say I'm keen on the prospect.'

Sasha wasn't keen on the prospect either. Once again she wondered why she had volunteered for this suicide mission. In truth, though, she already knew the answer. He was sitting just opposite her, gloomier than she'd ever seen him. Cole met her eyes for an instant, then glanced away.

There came the fluttering of wings from outside, barely audible above the storm. A large bird suddenly skipped across the cave's surface, shedding dark feathers from its body, so bedraggled it was a wonder it could still fly. It came to a halt just before Cole.

Sasha stared at the bird. It was a crow, she saw.

The bird began to glow. Magic wreathed its avian form and it began to change shape, growing arms and legs, becoming a man—

'*Thanates,*' she gasped.

The wizard-king of Dalashra looked as though he had been through hell. His face was even gaunter than usual, and his black overcoat, tattered at the best of times, was almost falling off him, and was torn and singed in countless places. He had a fresh scar running from the top of his head down to the bottom of his cheek.

Thanates raised a gloved hand and ran it through his receding hair. Flakes of ash tumbled out, drifting down to the ground. 'Now *that*,' he said darkly, 'was unpleasant.'

Isaac rose majestically to his feet, obsidian gaze watching the mage intently. 'The dragon?'

'I lost it. Eventually. It proved more stubborn than I had anticipated.'

Jerek looked up from where he was starting a fire. 'You mean you didn't kill the bastard?'

'I doubt there is a human alive who could slay such a beast. I include the Magelords in that. Even Alassa.'

Alassa was the White Lady's true name. Sasha remembered the Unborn's parting words in the cave of the cultists.

*If Thanates returns, tell him... tell him I am waiting for him.*

Sasha rose and went to sit by the wizard as he attempted to dry himself by the fire Jerek had just kindled. 'She misses you,' she said. 'The White Lady. She told me to tell you that.'

Thanates seemed taken aback. 'She did?'

'Yes.' An awkward silence followed. Sasha looked across the fire to Cole, who sighed and rose to his feet.

'The storm's stopped,' he stated coolly. 'I'm going for a walk.'

'Do not be long,' Isaac said. 'You need to rest. Tomorrow we enter the Valley of the Nameless.'

'You're not my father!' Cole shot back. He spun and stalked out of the cave, pulling his hood tight up over his head.

Jerek spat. 'He's pissing me right off,' the Wolf rasped angrily.

'I'll go and speak with him,' said Sasha. She got to her feet and hurried after her friend, ducking out of the cave. The storm had left the terrain battered and blasted. Broken shards of the strange substance littered the ground. Up on the plateau, the bodies of the giants had been stripped of flesh and a good number were torn apart, limbs scattered everywhere. The demonkin were already dissolving into puddles of putrid gore.

Sasha caught up with Cole and placed a hand upon his shoulder to slow him. 'What's got into you?' she demanded. 'You've been acting like – well, like an arsehole ever since the *Seeker* went down.'

'Thanks for the insult,' he replied petulantly. 'Last time you called me an arsehole I didn't see you for months. Maybe you're hoping the trick will work again.'

'Cole, don't be like this. I thought you were finally starting to grow up.'

He rounded on her, the fury in his grey eyes stopping her dead in her tracks. 'Don't talk to me about growing up! You have no idea of the shit I've been through. The only thing keeping me going, the only thing keeping me sane—' He seemed to catch himself, thought better of what he was about to say. 'Look, don't worry about it,' he said, softening his tone. 'I've got a lot on my mind. Tomorrow we face the Herald. I don't know why they chose us for this stupid mission—'

'They didn't choose me,' Sasha said quietly. 'I volunteered.'

'You what? Why would you do that?' Cole's brow creased in puzzlement.

'Why do you think?' Sasha fixed him with a stare. 'You, you fucking idiot,' she finished, when he continued to say nothing. 'You're the only thing I have left.'

He continued to stare at her.

And then, very slowly, he leaned in, eyes closed, lips pursing together.

She stopped him six inches from her face, pressing a gentle finger against his mouth. 'No,' she said softy. 'I don't want this. I'm sorry.'

The hurt on his face made her want to scream. 'How can you say that?' he said, in a strangled voice. 'After all we've been through! We grew up together! We're meant to be! Even Thanates and the White Lady are together now and she tortured him for a thousand nights! For fuck's sake!'

'Cole, listen—' Sasha began, but he was already storming off. She watched him go, heaving a big sigh. Then she turned back to the cave.

Jerek was watching her from the entrance, his dark eyes revealing nothing. 'What?' she demanded.

The Wolf scowled right back at her. 'Can't a man go for a quiet piss?' he snarled. 'Fucking kids and your bullshit. Some of us got bigger worries to think about.'

Sasha considered asking Jerek what he meant, but deep down she already knew.

# The Valley of the Nameless

THERE WAS SOMETHING comforting in the simple act of sharpening a sword. The routine of running a whetstone down a familiar blade. The familiar shape of a well-worn hilt in your palm. The act of sharpening a sword seemed to suggest that everything could endure forever, if only you paid it the right mind and gave it the right amount of care. It seemed to hint that a man, like a sword, would never grow old so long as he kept himself sharp.

It was all a lie, of course. The fact of the matter was that the world kept on changing. Nothing endured forever, not a sword and especially not a man. Eventually all things broke. All things died.

He was unwell. That'd been obvious for a while. Lately, though, the pain in his chest had grown worse. He was so damn tired all the time. It might've been age – the endless years of travelling and fighting and killing, claiming their price at last. But he knew it was more than that. Brodar Kayne reckoned he had maybe one fight left in him, and it would be the biggest of his life.

The climb over this latest ridge was the toughest so far. His breath rattled in his chest like the wheezing of his friend Braxus's bellows back in the day. They were almost at the top now. Soon they'd begin the descent into the unknown – a place the giant, Mighty Oak, had referred to simply as 'wrong'.

*Mind you, ain't too much right with anything that's happened over the last year.* Getting to know Brick had definitely been one of the high points. The reunion with Magnar, too, though he wished it had been in better circumstances. He prayed that they might be given time to heal – both physically, and to rebuild the relationship between father and son.

'You're in pain,' observed Rana. The sorceress didn't talk much, though she was forthcoming enough with dirty looks. He knew why and he couldn't blame her for it. As far as Rana was concerned, he was a cold-blooded killer. A weapon with no other purpose. No better than the greatsword on his back.

'I'm old,' he said. 'Pain's pretty much a given when you're dumb enough to keep doing this shit at my age.'

'You are not much older than me,' Rana replied. She might've been somewhere just short of her fiftieth winter. She looked a hell of a lot better than he did, that was a fact.

'Age maybe ain't so much what you have to show in years,' he said slowly, 'but what you have to show in the wounds you've picked up along the way.'

'I assure you,' Rana said curtly, 'I have plenty of scars of my own.'

'Sorry. I didn't mean to suggest otherwise.' The two of them trudged along in that uncomfortable silence of folk who had been brought into the same vicinity by coincidence rather than design. At least though they weren't the most awkward pairing on this expedition deep into the heart of demon territory. Just ahead of them, the youngsters, Davarus Cole and Sasha, were pointedly ignoring each other. Jerek and Thanates seemed content enough exchanging grimaces, while at the head of the small party Isaac navigated the tricky terrain with an ease the others could only dream of, his slender arms and legs belying a surprising strength.

'Seems odd to be talking about getting old when you're travelling with an immortal,' Kayne offered, having searched for something to say.

'Do you think we can trust him?' Rana asked.

'Don't reckon it matters. You saw how their weapons cut down the demons north of the Demonfire Hills. If the Fade want to wipe us all off the map, ain't much we can do about it.'

'I wonder if the men at Red Valley felt the same way. Or all the other men you've killed. Men who knew they were no match for the Sword of the North.'

Kayne's head sagged. 'Maybe they did.'

'I hope,' continued Rana, 'that if we succeed, and the Fade prince grants us leniency, the future will be decided by men like Brandwyn the Younger and not Brodar Kayne. I wonder what will become of you and your ilk. Where you will stay in a world where your skills are no longer relevant.'

'In the past,' Kayne muttered. 'Where we belong.'

The companions finally crested the summit. They paused for a moment to catch their breath and then went to stand together to gaze out over the valley below. The ground fell sharply, black rock devoid of any semblance of life descending into a deep basin that was wholly obscured by an evil fog. The miasma swirled with unholy lights and crackles of dark energy. Malevolent fingers of alien matter occasionally swept through, only to collapse in giant bursts of sickly green light.

'You want us to climb down into that shithole?' Jerek rasped.

'What you see is but a ghost of the reality to which the Nameless belongs,' Isaac explained. 'It will not harm us. The rift itself is far, far below the earth. When the demons cross over, they crawl their way to the surface. Somewhere below that fog the Herald awaits.'

'How do we kill it?' Rana asked. 'My sisters and I were twelve in number, a powerful circle by any standard, yet even we could not destroy the demon when it attacked Heartstone.'

Isaac looked at each of the companions in turn. 'You are the most formidable humans these lands have to offer,' he pronounced. 'The greatest of mortal wizards; the most powerful sorceress in the north; the carrier of a dead god's essence; a girl augmented with the powers of my own kind; and two warriors who together have overcome every obstacle placed before them. A grim company, but one united by fate; tied together by Pattern. One that will not quail in the face of a demon lord.'

'Save the poetic shit,' the Wolf snarled, Isaac's final utterance obviously having proved one grandiose proclamation too far. 'How do we kill the cunt?'

The Fade had the grace not to look put out by Jerek's interruption. 'With magic. With sword and axe and bow. Its scaled hide is as strong as chainmail, but it can be pierced. It can be defeated. Follow me, and keep your eyes open – there is no telling what lies ahead of us.'

They began the climb down, Kayne picking his way slowly over the broken rock in case he fell and knackered his knees more than he already had. The faces of the others were by turns apprehensive and determined. About halfway down, Thanates slipped and Kayne had to place a steadying hand on the arm of the blind mage to stop him plunging to the valley floor below. 'Reckon you could make this a lot easier on yourself if you turned into a crow,' he said.

'Perhaps,' replied Thanates. 'But I wish to conserve my magic for the Herald.' Kayne nodded at that. Thanates seemed like a good sort for a wizard and in other circumstances he might've enjoyed getting to know him. But it was clear that Thanates had only one thing on his mind – the challenge before them.

'At least you can take to the wing if things go poorly,' Kayne said, half in jest. Thanates shook his head. 'A wizard-king of Dalashra does not abandon his comrades,' he said grimly.

An hour later they reached the bottom of the valley. The ground was as barren as the rocks above them. There was an eerie green light emanating from the surface that mirrored the light they'd glimpsed on the horizon north of the Demonfire Hills. 'What happens if the Herald's not here?' Kayne grunted to Isaac.

'The Herald must remain in place while the Nameless attempts to cross over,' Isaac explained. 'The Herald is its connection to this world. To this reality.'

'And if we kill it, the link will be cut?'

Isaac nodded. 'Once the Herald is slain, no more demons will be able to pass into this world.'

'What about those already here?'

The Fade shrugged. 'We will deal with them the old-fashioned way.'

Kayne's hands tightened on his greatsword. The pain in his chest was bothering him again, a sharp and unpleasant sensation akin to an invisible hand twisting his insides. He needed to vomit. He needed to piss. He tasted bitterness in his mouth and realized he needed a drink. All things considered, he was eager for the fighting to commence, if only so he could forget his aches and pains and concentrate on the one thing he was good at.

He saw Rana watching him. The sorceress knew the truth. She'd known it all along.

*I'm a killer. A reaper, not a sower. Ain't never brought nothing good into this world.*

That was a lie, he realized. He'd brought Magnar into the world. And he'd brought his love for Mhaira, who in return had made him a better man than he had a right to be. He owed it to her not to feel sorry for himself. To make the best of what he could in the time he had remaining to him. He smiled back at Rana, who seemed confused by his abrupt change in manner.

The intensity of the green glow increased as they delved deeper into the valley. Above them, the strange fog continued to broil and flash crazily, lit by all manner of phantasmal energies. It became impossible to tell the time of day. At one point they encountered a demonkin. The fiend was easily dispatched by Kayne's greatsword and Jerek's axes. As they were nearing a pool of purplish water, however, a pit suddenly opened in the ground ahead of Davarus Cole. The youngster leaped back with a yelp as a sickly green radiance burst from the hole. Moments later, a pair of clawed feet reached out and gripped the earth, dragging the blink demon from the rift and out into the world of men.

Isaac moved like quicksilver, his hand-cannon sending a projectile into the demon's central eye with a bang that reverberated through the valley. The demon's paws slid from the earth as it fell lifelessly back into the rift, tumbling from sight.

Kayne walked to the edge of the pit and stared cautiously down. The hole seemed to go on forever.

'Take care,' warned Isaac. 'You do not wish to fall into the realm of the Nameless. I suspect it would be a fate very much worse than death.'

They continued on. The sense of unease grew stronger, the fog overhead more erratic. They narrowly avoided an encounter with a gigantic swarm of the flying demons they'd first seen back in the ruins of Watcher's Keep, taking cover behind an outcrop of boulders veined with the same shiny substance that had fallen from the sky and torn up the earth during the unnatural storm the previous night.

When it finally seemed like they could go no further, Sasha slowed and raised a hand to her eyes, shielding them from the luminescence that bled from all sides of the valley. Kayne heard that odd clicking sound again. It seemed like it was coming from Sasha's skull. Davarus Cole glared at her. Behind the anger was a great and terrible hurt.

Kayne had seen something similar in Magnar's eyes, the night he'd refused his son's request to fly north with the small party. 'What's wrong, lass?' he asked, wondering again what had occurred between the two youngsters.

'There's something out there,' Sasha said, dread in her voice. 'Something *huge*.'

# The Herald

'THE HERALD?' WHISPERED Brodar Kayne.

Sasha stared and for a long while said nothing, the sheer horror of the apparition in the distance robbing her of the ability to speak. The demon lord was even more nightmarish in the flesh than its living memory aboard the *Seeker* had hinted at. It crouched in a shallow depression, its gigantic bat wings wrapped tightly around its body, twenty feet of scaled, fiendish monstrosity that made her stomach lurch to gaze upon. Though it wasn't on the same colossal scale as the dragon that had attacked them in the skies above the Purple Hills, there was an ineffable *wrongness* about the demon that poked at primal fears even the sight of the great wyrm had not agitated.

'The Herald,' she whispered, finally finding her voice. 'It's kneeling, with its wings folded around it. I don't think it knows we're here. It seems like it's sleeping.'

Isaac nodded. 'It is communing with the Nameless,' he said. 'We have stumbled upon it when it is at its most vulnerable. Let us not waste this opportunity.'

'How much further?' Kayne grunted. The old barbarian appeared utterly exhausted. Sasha looked at the demon lord far in the distance.

'Another hour, maybe.'

'Then we had best hurry,' replied Isaac grimly.

The last thing Sasha wanted to do was get any closer to the Herald than she was already. But as her augmented vision returned to normal and the grim little company made their way towards the centre of the valley, she caught Cole looking at her and reminded herself why she had volunteered for this suicide mission.

*I have to keep him safe. Whatever he feels towards me now, whatever words were exchanged outside the cave last night, he's the reason I carry on fighting. The only thing I have left.*

Cole scowled and looked away and she sighed. One day, she would tell him the truth. She glanced at Jerek and noted how he hung back to keep pace with Kayne.

*Perhaps some truths are better left unspoken.*

The last stretch of their march took them gradually down into a vast basin. As they walked, skeletal remains began to speckle the dark rock beneath their feet. They grew more numerous the further the group pushed on, until their boots were crunching over bone.

Isaac was the first to spot the demon lord. The Fade raised an ivory hand. 'Slowly now,' he said. 'We are almost upon it.'

Surrounding the Herald was a sea of bones, human and giant and those of creatures larger still – great cave bears and even a few that appeared to have once belonged to some kind of giant fish.

'Those are whale bones,' Sasha whispered. 'The Herald must have hunted them in the Frozen Sea to the north. How many creatures have died beneath its claws? Thousands? Tens of thousands? The demon kills everything it comes across.'

'Even the local wildlife has some measure of potentiality to be harnessed,' Isaac explained. 'The Herald spent decades – centuries – harvesting life in order to bring others of its kind into this world in order to anchor the Nameless to this reality. I only wish we had learned of its presence before things were allowed to progress this far.'

'Fucker's huge,' Jerek growled. His axes were in his hands, his dark eyes narrowed to slits as he stared at the demon towering above them.

'The bigger they are, the harder they fall,' Cole said grimly. He turned and spat, almost hitting Isaac in the face by accident.

'Bullshit,' the Wolf rasped. 'They bigger they are, the harder they hit. The harder they are to put down.'

'It is a formidable opponent,' said Thanates. 'But I have fought a dragon and survived. Let us see how it fares against a wizard-king of Dalashra.' He spread his palms and black fire flickered down his arms to dance around his fingertips.

The presence of the forbidding mage opposite gave Sasha some small hope. She had witnessed him battling the White Lady almost to a standstill. If this mightiest of mortal wizards could stand toe to toe with a Magelord, perhaps they might yet have a chance against the Herald.

Isaac drew his hand-cannon with one hand and his crystal sword with the other. 'Before we attack, we must first trap the demon,' he said to the wizard-king, and to Rana beside him. 'Use your magic to incapacitate rather than kill. If the Herald takes to the skies, our task will become doubly difficult.'

Rana turned to Thanates. 'Do you know anything of circle magic?' she asked.

'I've heard rumour of it,' the wizard replied. 'A pooling of magic, in order to achieve effects greater than would otherwise be possible.'

Rana held out a hand. 'I will show you how,' she said. 'You must direct the spell. Your power is twice that of my own.' Thanates took her outstretched fingers in his gloved fist, and together wizard-king and Highland sorceress began exchanging whispered words. Sasha and the others waited patiently, exchanging meaningful looks – all except her and Cole. He refused to meet her gaze.

'We will begin our spell now,' growled Thanates. 'Move quickly once the demon is trapped and bring every weapon you have to bear against it. I do not know how long our magic will hold.'

Together, Thanates and Rana began to chant. The tang of magic rippled through the air. Ahead of them, the surface of the vast pit of bones vibrated, clinking together, creating an eerie tune that drifted through the valley like a ghostly lullaby. The Herald shifted and then straightened to its full, colossal height, its gigantic wings folding back to reveal a reptilian body covered in large black scales. Tiny bones stuck between the scales fell away as the Herald shifted its dark bulk. A trio of sinister eyes flickered open and Sasha felt utter terror grab hold of her. They seemed to strip away her sense of self, exposing her soul – all the rawness, all the ugly truths of the things she'd done writhing up like a host of maggots bursting from a corpse. Cole was similarly affected. Magebane shook in his trembling hand.

Hundreds of bones rose up from the ground, forming a massive chain composed of thighbones and ribs and giant vertebrae all held together by magic. The chain coiled like a snake and then wrapped itself around the demon lord, holding the Herald fast, binding its wings to its body.

'Now,' Isaac thundered. The command in the immortal's voice cut through the demon-fear, and Sasha found her legs moving, carrying her towards the Herald. Jerek was ahead of her, axes in his hands, Cole beside him. Together they scrambled over the sea of bones. Isaac and Cole skipped nimbly across the shifting surface; the others had a tougher time of it, stumbling and sliding.

The Herald thrashed, trying to free itself from the gargantuan chain. Its snakelike tail lashed out, pulverizing bone, sending up great clouds of white dust. Its grotesque maw opened wide, revealing teeth like daggers, but the demon lord made no sound. At least, no sound audible to the ears. Sasha somehow had the sense of a thousand sibilant voices screaming deep within her skull.

The crack of Isaac's hand-cannon echoed time and again. The Herald's body twitched, ichor spraying from the holes that appeared in its hide. The Fade Adjudicator was the first to reach the demon, jumping and spinning through the air, crystal blade shearing through midnight scales. Cole and Jerek reached it next, Cole's dagger plunging into the Herald's taloned legs, Jerek attacking the opposite side, the two working surprisingly well in tandem.

Sasha suddenly slipped on the uneven surface and skidded, landing painfully on her knees. She rose and was reaching into the quiver on her back for a bolt, preparing to cock her crossbow, when the Herald's triumvirate of burning eyes met her own. Terror overwhelmed her once again. The crossbow fell uselessly from her nerveless fingers and she sank back to her knees, sobs racking her body.

\*

*The damn thing'll be dead before I reach it at this rate,* Kayne thought, pounding across the pit of bones. Deep down he knew his optimism was misplaced. For all that Isaac together with the Wolf and young Cole were laying into the fiend, he reckoned it would take more than sharpened steel or even crystal to down a demon lord.

He passed Sasha, who was overcome by demon-fear, brown eyes wide in panic and body shaking like a leaf. It couldn't be helped. He plunged on, knees creaking, heart thundering like hell. He was almost at the demon when its tail whipped out, catching Isaac and Jerek glancing blows and sending them sprawling. With a mighty flexing of its knotted muscles, the Herald shattered the chain of bone restraining it into a thousand pieces.

'Shit,' Kayne whispered.

He heard fighting behind him, turned to see Rana and Thanates beset by a pair of demon knights. The armoured fiends had likely climbed out of the pit that had just appeared nearby, an evil green glow leaking out of the hole to bathe the combatants in a baleful radiance. Evidently the spell the wizards had cast to bind the Herald had been disrupted by the appearance of the demons.

Kayne wavered, torn between joining the attack on the Herald and going back to help Thanates and Rana. The demon lord took a mighty step towards Isaac and the Wolf, both of whom lay stunned. Much to Kayne's surprise, Davarus Cole was suddenly scaling the demon's back, his dagger plunging into it again and again while the Herald tried to shake him off.

Rana's agonized scream made up his mind for him. He turned and sprinted back across the bones, reaching the fallen sorceress just as the demon knight towering over her was preparing to crush her skull. Thanates was locked in mortal combat with the other knight, wielding a staff of black fire, parrying the demon's monstrous flail with surprising skill.

Kayne blocked the demon knight's overhead swing, his arms screaming with the effort. They exchanged blows, the old warrior rocking back with every punishing parry of the demon's weapon. Rana shifted slightly and Kayne saw that she bore a deep wound in her shoulder, blood leaking out to soak her robes. Nonetheless, she somehow raised a finger and pointed it at the demon. Lightning crackled from her extended digit, striking the fiend. It jerked and smoke drifted from its visor, behind which two crimson pinpoints flared in malignant fury.

The demon knight might have been finished or it might not. Either way Kayne wasn't taking any chances. He recalled Jerek, near the Demonfire Hills, clutching the decapitated head of one of the fiends, and knew what he had to do. Between the helmet and the breastplate he spotted the gap. He lined up his greatsword, swung, and decapitated the demon in a single stroke. The killing blow was inch-perfect, despite the weakness in his arms.

He reached down, intending to help Rana up. Suddenly a sibilant sound exploded in his skull.

*Sword of the North.*

Kayne blinked, nausea rising in his gut. It was as though a score of voices assailed him all at the same time.

*You are dying, Sword of the North. I hear your heart groaning. The end draws near for you.*

'What do you want?' he rasped, trying to catch his breath. The pain in his chest was growing worse.

*I can offer you life. You are a killer. Nothing less and nothing more. Do not sacrifice yourself. Not for them.*

'Get out of my head,' Kayne whispered.

The Herald's words seemed to expose his inner fears, stroked at his doubts – those hidden and those not so hidden. *The sorceress hates you. Your own people hate you. You have nothing. No place in this world. Join with me. Accept my master's blessings and make a place. Embrace your true nature, Sword of the North.*

Brodar Kayne hesitated. Rana stared up at him, reaching weakly for his hand.

He made no move to help her.

\*

*Kill it. Kill it, child.*

The Reaver's voice pounded in his skull and Cole lunged again, driving Magebane into the fiend's scaled body, revelling in the life force that flooded through him. For a moment the fear that had gripped him had threatened to squeeze the life from him, but then the god had spoken. Its divine command had cut through his paralysis like a hot knife cutting through butter. Like a magical dagger cutting through a demon's hide.

He saw Sasha on her knees, face pale with terror, but whatever feelings Davarus Cole might have towards the girl who had scorned him were lost in the wild bloodlust of a dead god's fury. He grinned as another deep thrust sent warm ichor splashing over his cheek. Once he was finished with the demon, he would end her life, too. And the lives of the others. A cacophony of sibilant voices tried to plead with him, tried to bargain with him, but they were overridden by the endless booming refrain of the god within him.

The Reaver felt no pity.

*

Thanates had his back to Kayne. It would be no effort at all to strike down the wizard-king of Dalashra while he was occupied with the demon knight. Kayne was the Sword of the North, and he saw death in every possibility.

*Kill her*, came the voice of the demon lord. *Kill her and then kill the Dalashran. None will judge you when the Legion has scoured the land. You are a weapon, and a weapon has only one purpose. To kill. Serve your purpose.*

He raised his greatsword, angled the edge towards Rana's neck. She met his eyes, not comprehending.

Her stare reminded him of a look Mhaira had given him once. When she was in the worst throes of her sickness and he thought he would lose her. He remembered the moment when the storm broke and familiarity dawned in her gaze. Her smile, drawing him back from the brink of despair.

'I'm not a weapon,' Kayne grated. 'I'm a man.' He pulled Rana up gently and put a hand around her waist to stop her falling. Thanates had plunged his black-fire staff through the visor of the demon knight. It was kneeling now before the mage, armoured body sagging, slowly dying.

Kayne turned to face the Herald just as the demon lord succeeded in dislodging Davarus Cole, who was wreathed in shadow, looking half demon himself. The boy fell near twenty feet, struck the bone pit at an awkward angle and went still. The Herald raised a mighty foot and prepared to crush its helpless opponent.

Sasha huddled on the ground, unable to move. Unable to do anything except sob uncontrollably, so overcome with dread she could barely think. She glimpsed Isaac and Jerek being flattened by the Herald's flailing tail, saw Cole somehow scramble up the demon's back and stab it repeatedly, lost to the unnatural fury driving him, as terrifying in his own way as the fiend whose shoulders he straddled.

*You're worthless*, said a tiny voice inside her. *The others fight, while you cower. You're nothing. Nobody. They're heroes. You? You're just the girl.*

Suddenly, Cole was hurled to the ground. He hit it hard enough to kill any other man, and though the shadows that wreathed him softened his fall somewhat, he lay still, winded. The Herald's trio of burning eyes fixed on her fallen friend. The demon lord raised a massive, taloned foot. In seconds Cole would be crushed to a bloody pulp. Isaac and Jerek were still shaking off the effects of the Herald's lashing tail. There was no one else to help him.

Sasha scrambled to her feet, a deeper terror than that which paralysed her spurring her into action. In desperation, she sought out the only weapon she could possibly use against the colossal demon. The effort of moving it with her telekinesis caused her to scream and a moment later she blacked out.

*

The Herald staggered back. As Kayne watched, the gigantic jawbone of a whale rose from the ground nearby and launched itself like a spear, piercing the demon's chest, going right through to emerge from the other side. Sasha staggered and fell, blood pouring from her nose.

Grievously wounded, the Herald beat its gigantic wings, seeking to escape. Thanates turned from the demon knight and hurled his staff of black fire at the ailing demon lord. It struck the fiend, scorching its flesh and – more damaging for it – ruining its leathery wings. The demon plunged back to the ground and in an instant Isaac and Jerek were upon it, crystal sword and steel axe dealing wound after wound. In what appeared to be a last desperate gambit, the Herald fixed Jerek with its trio of sinister eyes, seeking to hypnotize the Wolf with its ruinous gaze. Seeking to bend him to its will like it had attempted to bend Kayne. Its greatest mistake.

The Wolf split the fiend's face in half with a snarl.

It took a minute or two for the demon lord to perish. For its thrashing to eventually cease and its massive body to settle on the bones of the countless creatures it had killed over centuries of ruthless slaughter.

Kayne watched the Herald's death throes, attempting to catch his breath. Once he was somewhat recovered, he left Rana with Thanates and went to check on the others. Sasha was helping a shaky Davarus Cole back to his feet. The girl's nose dripped blood and dark veins stood out on her face. Cole looked to be in some pain but had no visible injuries. Jerek glared at the boy and then, unexpectedly, gave him a small nod. Davarus Cole perked up immediately, his chest visibly swelling.

'We did it,' Kayne rasped, scarcely believing his own words. 'We killed the bastard.'

Not only that, they'd slain the Herald without taking a single loss. The only one of the party in any real danger was Rana. 'Can you heal her?' Kayne asked Thanates.

The wizard gave a grim shake of his head. 'Restorative magic is not my domain.'

'Let me take a look at her.' Isaac inspected Rana's wound. It looked deep, but at least the flow of blood had slowed. 'She will survive until we make it out of this valley,' he announced. He paused to look each of them in the eye. 'You've done a remarkable thing this day,' he proclaimed. 'I will confess that I had my doubts—'

He was interrupted as a gaping pit suddenly appeared behind him. Another hole appeared beside Kayne, and a third opposite Davarus Cole. The earth beneath their feet began to fracture, tearing apart, green radiance spilling out.

'What's happening?' Sasha asked. She sounded dazed and confused, the effort of spearing the Herald with the whale's jawbone having exhausted her utterly.

Isaac looked concerned. 'The Herald's death has broken the connection between this world and the realm of the Nameless. The rift beneath the Devil's Spine is beginning to collapse in on itself.'

'What does that mean?' Cole asked.

'It means we should get the fuck out of here,' growled the Wolf. He was already stalking back the way they had come.

Isaac sheathed his weapons and turned to follow Jerek. 'What he said,' the Fade called back.

*

The escape from the valley was more hellish than any of the companions could have imagined. The world was literally collapsing around them, gaping holes appearing in the ground without warning, hundreds of tons of stone breaking and falling into an abyss in which dwelled the darkest of nightmares.

If there were any positives to be taken, Kayne thought as his abused knees screamed in protest, it was that no more demons climbed up out of the tunnels to add to their woes.

They were almost to the edge of the valley, preparing to begin their ascent, when a vast chasm opened right in front of them. Isaac stumbled, his legs giving way beneath the collapsing rock. He flailed wildly for a second, and then the earth started to swallow him. For the first time Brodar Kayne saw utter terror in the otherworldly gaze of the immortal.

Isaac would have been doomed were it not for Jerek's lightning reflexes. The Wolf sprang forward and grabbed one of the Fade's slender arms, his muscles bulging with the strain. Jaw clenched, Jerek dragged Isaac up and away from the hole.

The Fade stared down into the depths, his obsidian eyes wide in shock. He turned back to Jerek, began to offer his thanks, but the Wolf merely spat and turned away. 'I told you I got your back,' he grated. 'A man says a thing, a man does a fucking thing.'

They began the long climb out of the valley. Rana leaned on Thanates, the blind wizard and the wounded sorceress doing their best to support each other. Davarus Cole and Sasha were just ahead of Kayne. They still hadn't said a word to each other. Whatever had gone on between them had seemingly formed a rift as deep as the abyssal holes tearing apart the valley below.

As they dragged themselves up a particularly steep incline, the numbness Kayne had been feeling in his arms for weeks returned with a vengeance. He slipped off the rock he had hold of and landed painfully. He rose shakily, his body bruised and cut – but the pain of those minor scrapes was as nothing compared to the sudden, intense cramping in his chest. Cole slid down the incline, concern for Kayne plastered all over his face, and the old warrior forced himself to smile, to make light of the situation. 'Getting too old for this shit,' he tried to say –but a spasm sent him stumbling to his knees instead.

'What's wrong with him?' someone shouted. Kayne could hardly hear over the pounding in his ears. His throat seized up. He tried to breathe, but every inhalation was burning agony.

'It's his heart,' someone shouted. The world went dark.

'Kayne,' rasped Jerek beside him. 'Where the fuck's the *Seeker*?'

He tried to open his eyes, but they were heavier than sin.

The last thing he remembered was being lifted up into the air, a great roaring sound filling his ears.

# SUMMER

SUMMER

# New Beginnings

THE SUN WAS finally setting in the west, delivering a blessed relief from the early summer heat. The vast Highlander encampment stretched out on the plains below as far as Davarus Cole could see, though the campfires had remained unlit now for many weeks. If everything went as hoped, soon the monumental gathering of mountain folk would pack up their tents and abandon the temporary refuge, moving west and east and north and south to settle in the Trine and its surrounding area. The Year of Upheaval, as the scribes had begun to refer to the events of the last twelve months, had wrought immense changes in the region. Magelords had been toppled; cities destroyed; entire peoples displaced. An ancient master race had returned to the continent bringing ultimate judgement, and it was this last concern that had brought Cole here, to Westrock.

He turned to face the town, and took a deep breath. Everything depended on the outcome of the meeting that was about to take place. Isaac had delivered his report to the Fade prince weeks ago. According to the Adjudicator, Obrahim was inclined to grant humanity mercy. Davarus Cole had learned the hard way that assumptions tended to be the seeds of disaster, however. If the answer wasn't the one they anticipated, Carn Bloodfist and the White Lady of Thelassa had already made preparations for war.

Thanates was waiting for him halfway down the dirt road that led into town. Even now he could hear the *Seeker's* engines throbbing. It still struck him as a little absurd that such an inconsequential place should play host to such momentous events – a visitation that would likely decide humanity's fate. The Fade prince ought to be delivering his final judgement in some exotic locale on the very edge of the world, as befitted the occasion. Not the boil on the arse of the Trine that was Westrock.

*This is no fairy tale*, he reminded himself. *This is real life*. He himself was living proof that the Pattern the Creator wove cared not for any sense of decorum. He'd returned from the Devil's Spine a hero, and yet here he was, slowly dying, withering away under the Reaver's curse. To add to the injustice, the girl he loved had broken his heart. He'd once thought that accomplishing great deeds would be enough to make him happy; make him the man he'd always dreamed of being. But it seemed that life was more complicated than that. The news about the impending marriage between the young bandit and the pretty Highland sorceress hadn't exactly boosted his spirits. It wasn't their fault, but to Cole it felt like yet more salt rubbed into his wounds.

'Davarus Cole,' Thanates greeted him. At least the wizard-king of Dalashra had stopped referring to him as 'child of murder'. 'Are you ready?'

*I was born ready*, said a tiny voice in his skull. A voice that belonged to his past. 'Not really,' he said instead.

The mage's mouth set in a grim line. He still wore his long black coat, though the most egregious holes had been patched by Thelassa's seamstresses. Cole had asked Thanates why he didn't simply buy a new coat. The wizard had replied that it was part of who he was. 'Ready or not, it would be unwise to keep Prince Obrahim waiting.'

'I doubt if turning up five minutes late will cause him to change his mind about whether humanity is beyond redemption,' Cole muttered. 'Not unless he's a *really* petty bastard.'

The two men made their way through the empty town. Westrock had been evacuated ahead of the arrival of the Fade.

The tension was so thick Cole almost fancied he could reach out and cut it with a knife, or better yet, Magebane.

The *Seeker* was just ahead of them, taking up the lion's share of space in the clearing. Occupying the rest of it was Prince Obrahim and his officers, Isaac among them. Cole's heart sank when he saw General Saverian beside his brother. The commander's jaw clenched and unclenched as though he was chewing rocks. Whether or not that was a good sign, Cole couldn't be sure.

'Prince Obrahim,' said Thanates, kneeling before the legendary Fade ruler. Cole followed his lead. He still felt awed by Obrahim, perhaps the most formidable being in the world with the possible exception of the white-haired general beside him.

'Rise,' said the prince. 'I have made my judgement.'

Cole didn't dare breathe. The world hung in the balance, the great cosmic scales tilting one way and then the other. On one side waited salvation. A chance to rebuild all that had been destroyed: cities, alliances, faith.

And on the other side, utter annihilation.

Prince Obrahim's primeval gaze glittered. 'Adjudicator Isaac made an impassioned defence of mankind. I have never seen him so animated.'

The look General Saverian gave Isaac could have cracked stone. A muscle in the commander's cheek twitched furiously.

'Your people murdered your gods,' Prince Obrahim began, filling Cole with dread. 'You broke the Pattern. You murdered two of my kind. And yet…' The prince paused, and Cole felt every moment of that silence as though it were an age. 'You are a young race, and not yet beyond forgiveness. Our truce holds.'

Cole sagged with relief. Even Thanates wiped sweat from his brow and released a deep breath he'd been holding.

'Brother,' barked Saverian, turning to Obrahim, the shoulder-cannon trembling where his body shook with anger. 'You cannot grant mercy to these humans. The danger they pose—'

'Enough,' ordered Obrahim. He was unaffected by his brother's terrifying fury. 'I have made my decision. You will abide by it.'

General Saverian seethed silently, but he threw his prince a salute nonetheless.

Prince Obrahim beckoned Isaac forward. The Adjudicator carried a scroll case in his hands. 'Upon this are written the terms of our armistice,' Obrahim pronounced. 'In summary, we will retain control of the city of Dorminia. The ruins of New Malaga north of Thelassa will be ceded back to us. I wish to establish an outpost there with a view to re-founding what was once our westernmost city. Furthermore, you will agree to provide assistance in countering any demon threat from the northern mountains: the Legion yet runs amok in the High Fangs. One day they shall turn their attention to the south. We must be prepared. You must be prepared.'

'We shall,' replied Thanates. 'You have my word. With the White Lady's blessing, I give you hers, also.'

Prince Obrahim nodded. 'In return, I give you my promise that so long as the terms are fulfilled, we will not bring you further harm. You will relay the details of this meeting to your mistress as well as the leader of the Highland people. I will require their signatures to seal the accord.'

Cole doubted that Carn Bloodfist knew which end of a quill to hold, let alone how to sign his name, but he was wise enough to keep his mouth shut. He took the proffered scroll from Isaac, who gave him a nod that he found strangely satisfying. All his life Cole had been handed the easy route to girls and riches and glory – but the one thing he truly craved, he realized, was respect.

'Prince Obrahim,' said Thanates. Cole had never heard the wizard-king of Dalashra sound so uncertain, not even in the face of Obrahim and his forbidding brother. 'In recognition of our new alliance, I would extend to Your Highness and those of your choosing an invitation. Alassa – whom you know as the

White Lady – and I are to marry. We would be honoured if you would attend the event.'

Cole stared at Thanates in shock, feeling as though the Dalashran had just betrayed him. The wizard had said nothing to Cole of his intentions. *That's just fucking perfect,* he thought, bitterness rising in his throat. *First a couple of kids get everyone worked up by announcing they're getting married. Now two immortals who only months ago tore Thelassa apart trying to kill each other have decided to tie the knot.* It made no sense to Cole. *It should be me and Sasha,* said a pathetic voice inside him.

Prince Obrahim almost smiled. 'I will see what can be arranged,' said the golden-haired prince. He gestured to Saverian. 'My own brother is finally going to lifebond. He and Melissan will join their bloodlines in the ruins of New Malaga, in memory of Nymuvia, who was born there.'

*Hang on a damned minute!* Cole wanted to scream. *I thought he and Nym were betrothed for a thousand years! Now that arrogant son of a bitch is getting married, or lifebonded or whatever you call it, to Nym's goddamned sister?*

It was all too much. He turned away, not wanting these tall, immortal, *perfect* bastards to see his tears of frustration.

*What happened to the hero getting the girl?*

*

Sasha finished braiding Corinn's hair and took a step back to admire her handiwork. The young sorceress wore a green silk gown that Thanates had brought back with him from the City of Towers. It was a perfect match, impeccably complementing her blonde hair and remarkable blue eyes.

'You think Brick will like me?' Corinn asked. Her tone betrayed her nervousness.

'Brick is fourteen years old,' Sasha replied sardonically. 'He'd like you if were wearing nothing but a cloth sack, and a fishing net on your hair.'

'I want to look beautiful for our joining ceremony.'

'You *are* beautiful,' Sasha said, giving the girl a hug. She caught a glimpse of herself in the silver mirror on Corinn's dresser – a gift from the White Lady – and smiled wryly.

*Me, on the other hand, I'm anything* but *beautiful.* She had grown bored of waiting for her hair to grow back to a manageable length and had taken a razor to it again. The effort of using her telekinetic implant to save Cole's life during the battle with the Herald had ruptured something in her face. She had dark veins running across her head and cheeks. Sometimes her nose would bleed for no apparent reason.

A few of the sorceresses in camp had taken a look at her, but their physical and magical ministrations hadn't helped with either her appearance or the blinding headaches that crippled her without warning.

*I can live with it,* she told herself. The strange dreams sometimes kept her awake at night, fragments of a hundred nightmares leaving her reeling and disorientated upon waking, but she knew that, compared with Cole, she had it easy.

He ducked into the tent at that precise moment, looking worryingly pale and gaunt. He barely glanced at her but she saw the pain in his eyes before they flicked away. 'All right,' he muttered. He turned to Corinn, presenting his back to Sasha, and gave the young sorceress a long whistle. 'You look stunning,' he said. 'Brick's a lucky man.'

'Thank you,' Corinn stammered. Sasha frowned.

*Is he really trying to make me jealous?*

'The wedding begins in a few hours,' she said. 'You should probably change out of those leathers into something more presentable.'

'Why?' Cole shot back. 'These Highlanders don't place much stock in appearances. Besides, Thanates won't bother to change. Neither will Jerek.'

'You're not Thanates. Or Jerek.'

'What's that supposed to mean?' Cole bristled, insulted.

'Nothing. Look, do you have a reason for being here? In case you hadn't noticed, we were having some private time between us girls. For all you know, Corinn might have been undressed when you barged in.'

Cole frowned. 'Fine. I'm leaving. I just thought I'd stop by to tell you we're invited to the White Lady's wedding in a couple of weeks. You should probably bring a helmet.'

Sasha remembered the ferocious battle in the skies between the Magelord of Thelassa and Thanates. It scarcely seemed possible that they could put their hatred behind them and rediscover their affection for each other after five centuries of enmity. 'After everything that's happened?' she said in disbelief.

'It's good to know *some* of us can learn to love,' Cole shot back. He turned and stamped out of the tent before Sasha could respond, leaving her with her mouth hanging open, a hundred angry retorts on her tongue.

Corinn met Sasha's gaze. 'What's going on with you two?'

Sasha sighed. 'You really don't want to know.'

Half an hour later she left Corinn's tent to go and get ready herself. She made her way through the camp and towards the hill that led up to Westrock, where she and Cole were staying – in separate rooms – at the last inn in town. Highlanders nodded as she passed them, gestures of respect in recognition of her part in securing a future for their people.

The specifics of exactly what had happened in the Devil's Spine were unknown to most. The strange bard, Shakes, had already been to visit her on a couple of occasions. He'd promised to pen an epic that would see her name live forever in legend. It all felt surreal, as though this were happening to someone else. After all the hardship she'd endured, it seemed impossible to believe that things were finally taking a turn for the better, even if she herself was a freak: an unstable, physically altered mutant who might manifest powers that could kill herself and everyone around her at a moment's notice.

She spotted Brick just ahead and made her way over to him. The flame-haired youngster was chatting with a group of Highlander men, laughing and joking as though he'd grown up among the mountain folk rather than having been introduced to them scarcely six months past. He was a charming boy and would no doubt be a good husband to Corinn. The rumours flying around camp suggested that Carn Bloodfist and Brandwyn the Younger, the two chieftains who jointly ruled the Highland people, had big plans for the young couple.

'Sasha!' he greeted her, taking her hands in his own. He gave her a big grin, his green eyes bright with pleasure. He reminded her of Cole, back when he was a younger man. A happier man. She suddenly felt guilty.

*It's not my fault.*

Brick was dressed in a blue tunic, and wore a new pair of leather pants, high black boots and a belt that seemed a little ostentatious. He caught her staring at it and blushed.

'It was my Uncle Glaston's,' he said. 'He had his faults, but I wanted to wear something that belonged to him.'

She gave him a small hug. 'You must be nervous.'

'A little,' he admitted. 'You know, I wish Kayne could have been here to see us wed. At least Jerek will be there.'

Sasha nodded sadly. 'He'll be watching you in spirit,' she said comfortingly.

'Aye,' replied Brick. He'd already begun adopting Highlander words and expressions. 'I guess I should begin making the final preparations. We're going to wed just outside Carn's great pavilion. Something called a "varoogi" will perform the service.'

'A *veronyi*,' Sasha corrected him. She shivered, remembering the corrupted *veronyi* in the cave in the Devil's Spine. The things she'd seen over the course of those few days would stay with her forever.

She bid Brick farewell, reaching out and giving his red hair a tousle for good measure. 'You'll take good care of Corinn, won't you? She's a sweet girl.'

*I guess some of us have to be.*

*

'You sure you can do this? The sorceress told you not to move. I told her you was a stubborn cunt.'

He gritted his teeth and pushed himself up from the pallet. 'I ain't missing this,' he said. 'You'd have to hold me down to stop me.'

Jerek scowled at him. 'I ain't touching you. You fucking stink.'

Brodar Kayne couldn't disagree. He'd been confined to bed for weeks now, too weak to do much of anything except push food into his mouth and sip water from a pitcher with trembling hands. According to the healer who was overseeing his recovery, he was extremely lucky to be alive. The heart attack he'd suffered ought to have killed him. A lot of things ought to have killed him, he thought ruefully.

Despite his harsh words, the Wolf reached out a hand and with surprising gentleness pulled Kayne to his feet. The old warrior took a tottering step, testing his legs. They were as shaky as a leaf in the wind but at least his knees no longer felt like they were on fire. He lifted a hand to his chin and felt the beard bristling there. 'Reckon I should shave for the ceremony?' he asked.

Jerek gave him a look that made it abundantly clear he couldn't give less of a shit if he tried. 'How's Magnar?' Kayne asked, deciding to change the subject.

He vaguely remembered his son coming to visit him once or twice. He couldn't recall what they had said to each other.

The Wolf shrugged. 'He don't get out much,' he grunted. He was sitting on a wooden stool near the entrance to the tent, watching Kayne with his dark eyes. According to the woman in charge of Kayne's recovery, Jerek had spent more time with him than anyone else. Davarus Cole, who'd been to see him a few times, had told disbelievingly of how the Wolf had hauled Kayne up the side of the valley single-handedly, carrying him to the *Seeker* as though he were a child rather than two hundred pounds of hard muscle and harder regrets.

'You know if he's coming to the ceremony?' Kayne pressed. 'You ask him?'

'Ain't none of my business.'

Kayne scrubbed the dirt from his skin over the small washbasin in the corner of the tent and tried not to let his spirits sink. He and Magnar needed to talk. He wished there was some way he could help his son. At least now he had time to try. For maybe the first time in his life he had no obligations. Nothing to run from. No one upon whom he'd sworn bloody vengeance.

*I'm free*, he thought. *Free at last.*

Then he glanced down at the silver wedding band on his finger and was grateful that the soapy water on his face hid his tears.

*

A great crowd had gathered outside Carn Bloodfist's crimson pavilion. A small wooden platform had been erected, and upon it stood the oldest *veronyi* Kayne had ever seen, a wheezing old relic bent double by age. Brodar Kayne stepped through the mass of Highlanders, Jerek beside him, searching for some sign of Brick and his wife-to-be. Curious faces turned to stare at him, the young and the old and everyone in between. He saw Finn watching him, the lad's face an angry mask. Rana was there too, flanked by sorceresses from her circle. She met his gaze and frowned. He had to admit to finding her continued distaste for him disheartening.

'You saved that bitch's life,' Jerek rasped. The Wolf was never one to mince his words. 'Least she could do is show a little gratitude.'

Kayne shook his head. He hadn't saved her life in an effort to change her mind about him. He'd saved her life because it had been the right thing to do.

'Brodar Kayne.' Brandwyn the Younger's cultured voice hailed him and the old warrior turned. 'It is good to see you back on your feet.'

'Only just,' Kayne replied. 'Don't reckon I'll be undertaking any more epic quests any time soon. Or ever, if I'm being honest.'

'I have heard tales of your heroics,' the young chieftain of the Green Reaching said, with a toothy smile. He reached up and stroked his rust-coloured beard. 'The young man from Dorminia, Davarus Cole, was eager to spread the story of how your small band of heroes slew the Herald. Together you have given our people a chance to rebuild. You recall our conversation on the bank of the River of Swords?'

Kayne frowned. 'Aye. I've played my part. Reckon it's up to you now. Time to plant some seeds and see how they fare with a little watering.'

Brandwyn nodded. 'We have an agreement with the White Lady to settle the towns and villages north of Dorminia, as well as founding our own settlements in locations we deem advantageous. The Lowlanders have been decimated by war just as we have. Together we can forge a new future of peace and prosperity. Though some among us seem keen to coerce rather than cooperate. To seek further expansion instead of solidifying what we have.' The chieftain frowned at the great tent behind them. His meaning was clear.

Kayne looked around. 'Where *is* Carn?' he asked.

'He left with a handful of his most trusted men. He has business of some kind to the south. I believe he will return in time for the ceremony between this "White Lady" and her lover.'

'Thanates,' Kayne clarified. 'You know if he's here?'

Brandwyn nodded towards someone in the crowd. Kayne followed the movement and saw the wizard standing a little apart from everyone else, sweat beading his furrowed brow in the afternoon heat. Kayne and Jerek made their way over to him. 'Well met,' Kayne greeted him.

'The Sword of the North!' exclaimed Thanates. 'It is good to hear your voice.' The two men clasped hands. Even Jerek deigned to offer a grunted 'all right' – always a sign that a man had managed to earn the respect of the grim warrior.

'I hear congratulations are in order,' Kayne ventured. 'You're following young Brick down the aisle shortly.'

Thanates bobbed his head, a gesture that reminded Kayne of the crow familiar whose form the wizard so often took. 'It is a strange thing,' he said. 'I hated Alassa for what she did to me. I promised I would make her pay tenfold. Yet vengeance takes no account of love.'

'Love's a powerful thing,' Kayne said.

'There are other reasons for us to marry,' Thanates admitted. 'I wish to reclaim my throne. Once I rule Dalashra again as its rightful king, an alliance through marriage with Thelassa will be of immeasurable benefit to us both.'

'Politics,' Kayne said ruefully. 'I ain't got time for that shit, as a rule.'

'Consider yourself blessed,' said Thanates, with a wry twist of his mouth. 'Some of us lack that luxury. Ah – the young lovebirds arrive.'

Kayne turned to see Corinn and Brick making their way towards Carn's tent. The crowd parted for them, cheers and the occasional bawdy comment accompanying the nervous girl and her grinning husband-to-be. Corinn's gown reminded Kayne of the dress Mhaira had worn during their joining ceremony. He felt a tear roll down his cheek and wiped it away with the back of his hand.

*You're getting soft,* a voice said inside his head. A moment later he realized it no longer mattered. He was done fighting.

The Sword of the North was a weapon that no longer had a purpose. Perhaps it was time he allowed his edge to dull. Though the scowling warrior standing next to him might have something to say about that.

'Kayne!' Brick exclaimed in delight. Much to his shock, and against all etiquette, the smartly dressed youngster wrapped the old Highlander in a hug as he came close to him. 'I thought you weren't coming!' he said excitedly.

'I weren't going to miss it was I?' Kayne replied, with a big grin. Jerek gave Brick a nod and offered up an 'all right' that might even have held a bit of warmth, if you closed your eyes and listened really carefully.

Corinn still looked very nervous. Nervous, and maybe a little bit unsettled. 'Something wrong?' Kayne asked gently.

The young sorceress stared down at the grass. 'My father always wanted to give me away,' she said. 'He wanted to accompany me down the aisle. But he's dead and I have no one.'

Kayne knew what he had to do then. He held out a hand, ignoring the numbness in his arm. Most likely it would never be quite the same, would never allow him to wield a sword as he once had, but that was okay. He was no longer a man of violence. 'I'd be honoured to stand as your Spirit Father,' he said. 'If you'll have me.'

Corinn stared at him with her blue eyes, and then her pretty face broke into a smile. Her soft hand took hold of his weathered palm and together the three of them made their way to the *veronyi* waiting on the platform.

The wise man conducted the sacred rituals of earth, fire and water, offering up prayers to the spirits of the land and sea. Brick looked shocked when he was asked to take the flame from the *veronyi*'s wrinkled hand, but Corinn smiled at him and Kayne threw him a wink and the boy did it with only a slight hesitation, delight spreading over his freckled face when he realized it didn't hurt but rather filled him with a warmth that symbolized the brightness of their love burning throughout the years.

Finally, the wise man presented the new couple with a wreath moulded from the branches of trees felled in the forest to the west. 'Let this wreath remain forever untouched by the passing of the seasons,' the *veronyi* announced. 'Just as their marriage grows stronger, so shall this symbol of their love grow harder. May it never break.'

Brick and Corinn held the wreath up between them to a chorus of cheers. The ceremony was brought to a close, and Kayne was suddenly overwhelmed by memories. A lifetime passed before his eyes in an instant.

The demon attack on his village, massacring his entire family, leaving only a terrified boy to escape, his brother's screams following him through the years.

Joining the Wardens. Spending a decade at Watcher's Keep helping to defend his homeland.

Meeting Mhaira for the first time. Her smile, which could light up a room. Marrying her, surrounded by friends and comrades.

Many years spent in darkness, doing his best to cling to the light. Always it lay within her – within Mhaira and a second light within his son. One was extinguished now, never to light his way again, but the memory of it would keep him warm until the day he died. The other was dimmed, struggling to stay alight. It was his responsibility to nurture that light, to make it burn brilliantly once more.

He remembered the Seer's vision.

*You sent the Broken King to his death.*

The vision had proved false. Magnar was here, and he was safe. He and his son had been given a second chance. An opportunity for a new beginning. Kayne vowed silently that he would seize it, and do the best that he could in the years remaining to him. He would do it for Mhaira.

'You're crying,' observed Corinn. She and Brick had exchanged rings, and now both wore gold bands on their fingers.

'Tears of joy,' he said. 'Congratulations, lass. You chose well.

Prophecy or no prophecy, this one's destined for big things, I reckon.' He embraced the young sorceress, and then it was Brick's turn for a hug. 'You take care of her,' he said.

'I will,' Brick promised. 'Will you come and visit us? After you're back from the City of Towers?'

'Course I will,' said Kayne.

'And Jerek? What about you?'

The Wolf was hanging back, never one for open displays of affection – or hidden displays of affection, or just affection in general. But, much to Kayne's shock, Jerek reached out a hand and patted Brick on the shoulder. 'Aye,' he grunted. 'I'll visit you.'

Kayne bid a final farewell to the newlyweds. The effort of standing as Spirit Father for Corinn had left him exhausted, and so he wasn't entirely pleased to see the bard, Shakes, hurrying towards him, a sheet of parchment in one hand and a quill in the other.

'Brodar Kayne!' he called. 'A moment of your time! I'm hard at work on that poem I told you about.'

'Maybe later,' Kayne grunted. 'Stop by my tent if you like. I could use the company. Right now I need to rest.'

'I quite understand.' Despite what he'd just said, Shakes hovered for a moment as Rana went to offer Brick her congratulations. The flame-haired youngster said something and turned to point at Kayne, who saw the sorceress glance up at him.

'Something the matter?' Kayne asked Shakes.

'No. It's just ironic, that's all. The last thing any of us expected was a happy ending.'

'Life is full of surprises.' Kayne glanced over at Brick again, expecting to see Rana glaring at him, perhaps remonstrating with the youngster to steer clear of the ageing killer across the way, the infamous Sword of the North. A man who had nothing left to offer anyone, especially not a bright young boy with the world at his feet.

Instead, she met his eyes and held his gaze. A moment later, she smiled at him.

# The Grim Company

THELASSA, THE CITY of Towers, shone like a pearl in the brilliant sunshine.

Sasha had never fully appreciated just how beautiful the city was. Perhaps it had taken a journey through hell, both personal and very almost literal, to allow her to see the good even among all that was wrong. The streets were teeming with people all the way to the palace. She remembered walking this very same avenue at night alongside her sister, hearing ghostly instruments plucking notes out of thin air. On this occasion, the music they were playing was joyous rather than the hypnotic swell that had preceded the Seeding. Under a perfect summer sun and surrounded by smiling faces, it was easy to forget the horrors the White Lady had inflicted upon her city to keep it safe.

The marble palace melted out of the shimmering air ahead. It was there the White Lady of Thelassa and Thanates, wizard-king of Dalashra, would seal both a marriage and an alliance five hundred years in the making.

She saw the Highlander contingent waiting by the palace gates. Carn Bloodfist and Brandwyn each headed up a small retinue of warriors. A little behind them lurked Brodar Kayne and Jerek, together with a younger man who might have been Magnar, Kayne's son. The old warrior noticed her and gave her a wave. She smiled and waved back. It was good to see him up and on his feet.

Davarus Cole, however, wasn't faring so well. He'd swapped his leathers for a pair of fresh trousers and a white linen shirt with flared cuffs. He looked dashing, though the forlorn expression on his disturbingly pale face slightly spoiled the effect. The glistening sweat on his brow appeared to be the result of something more than just the heat. He was shaking his head, as though listening to something only he could hear and not liking what it was saying.

She leaned in to whisper to him. 'Are you feeling okay?'

'Do I look okay?' he snapped back.

'No. That's why I'm asking.'

'Don't pretend you care.'

Sasha stopped dead in the middle of the avenue. 'You know I fucking care,' she hissed. 'This isn't about you, Cole. If you were going to be an arsehole, you shouldn't have come.'

The look he gave her chilled her blood. It wasn't just the fury in his eyes that disturbed her; there was a *hunger* there. Of all the things Cole had made her feel over the years, threatened had never been among them.

'The Reaver hasn't fed in months,' he said, his voice a ragged whisper. 'I love you, Sasha – but you need to know that I want to draw Magebane and shove the sharp end through your chest. I want to turn on this crowd and slaughter them all. Make these marble streets run red with blood. This is my curse. Don't ever confuse me being a monster with me being an arsehole.'

She struggled for words, overwhelmed by what he'd just told her. 'I'm sorry—' she began, but he was already turning, storming into the mass of city folk. She watched him go, guilt and fear waging a war in her mind.

As she contemplated chasing after him, there was movement at the palace gates up ahead. They swung slowly open and a member of the Consult stepped out and politely asked the assembled Highlanders to move away from the entrance. A gong sounded from somewhere in the city, so loud it must have been magically amplified.

A squad of armed Whitecloaks came marching towards the palace. The crowd cleared the avenue, and Sasha found herself bundled to the side along with scores of onlookers. A moment later she understood why. Making her serene way towards the palace, utterly resplendent in her wedding dress – a work of art that had apparently taken several of the best seamstresses in the city a month to create – glided the White Lady of Thelassa.

Behind the Magelord trailed her handmaidens. Sasha gasped. There were hundreds of them, a winding snake of porcelain-skinned dolls following their mistress in a great line that wound all the way back to the city.

The White Lady reached the gates of the palace and turned to the assembled crowd. There she waited as the Unborn formed three great ranks behind her.

The Magelord of Thelassa slowly raised her hands towards the heavens. Sasha was a good distance removed and didn't have the best view. She focused on the ageless wizard, her augmented eyes adjusting themselves until the White Lady's unearthly beauty filled her vision. The immortal wizard spoke, and in her voice was a great regret. A regret so deep it rivalled the waters of the city's great harbour.

'I stand you before you on this most joyous of days to offer an apology,' she said, her voice carrying down the long avenue like a soothing wind. 'For five hundred years I have sought to make this city a beacon of light in the darkness. Yet, where there is light there is also shadow. I have done things – terrible things – to preserve the autonomy of our city. I cannot take back those actions, or the unreasonable sacrifices I have demanded of you.'

Silence followed the White Lady's words. Then a murmur began, confusion spreading like wildfire. *They don't know,* Sasha reminded herself. *The Consult poisoned the city's water supply and erased their memories. Why is she telling them this now?*

She remembered the White Lady's handmaiden – her proxy? – in the cave of the Nameless cultists. The disquiet on her face. Was that the moment when the city's Magelord had understood the extent of her crimes? Did she seek to unburden her guilt before she wed? Or had the love she had apparently rediscovered fixed something broken within her? For some reason, Sasha felt guilty. She searched around for Cole, but even her enhanced vision could not pick him out among the crowd.

'To you, my subjects, I offer an apology,' the White Lady continued. 'An apology and a promise for a better future. The magical barrier around the city is no more. When the sun rises tomorrow, Thelassa will be open for trade with Dorminia, and with the Shattered Realms to the south and the Unclaimed Lands to the east. Together we will make Thelassa the most prosperous city in the north. But first a great injustice must be addressed.' Below the Magelord's purple eyes, tears streaked her cheeks. She turned to face the ranks of the Unborn. 'You have suffered enough,' she announced. 'I now release you from your servitude.'

The handmaidens began to crumble. One by one they disintegrated, collapsing into a fine dust that rose and floated out to hang suspended above the avenue, sparkling in the sun's rays. The first rank of Unborn was destroyed, and then the second, and then the third, until eventually Thelassa's Magelord stood alone, her army of unnatural servants all reduced to dust, only the great golden cloud above the city giving any indication they had ever existed.

The Magelord lowered her arms. There was a pregnant pause and then the cloud fell from the sky, covering the crowd below, which reacted with a mixture of horror, surprise and eventually amusement when it became clear it would not harm them.

Sasha scooped a handful of the dust from her scalp and stared at it. She half expected it to be vile to behold, but it resembled nothing more than fine golden sand. It glowed and then began to dissipate, its magic fading away.

'Soon the memories I stole will return to you,' the White Lady announced. 'I will offer no further explanation at this time, except to say that I will accept your wrath. I will accept your fury. But I will not accept your judgement, for none but those charged with the responsibility of shepherding their people through a godless world could understand my burden. I leave you now to enjoy the celebrations. Tomorrow we begin again. A new age for humanity.'

With those words, the White Lady turned and swept into the palace. Sasha shook her head, dislodging the remaining dust. The day had already offered up a host of surprises and it wasn't yet noon. She met the eyes of the woman opposite her, a lower-ranking member of the Consult. Sasha gave her a smile, trying to be friendly, but she received only a blank stare in return. The woman's face seemed strangely vacant.

Sasha left the avenue to search for Cole again, but a moment later she stumbled, unfamiliar thoughts and memories invading her waking mind, bringing a chaotic assortment of images that made little sense. They passed quickly, but the experience left her badly shaken. She had experienced such episodes more frequently of late, but this was the first time they had occurred during the day.

'I hope the augmentations aren't troubling you.'

She spun and stared up into the face of a familiar Fade. He smiled down at her, the dark blue cloak he wore hanging lazily over his shoulder.

'Isaac!' she exclaimed.

'Well met. I feared I might be late for the wedding.'

'Don't worry about that. Thanates hasn't arrived yet. What are you doing here?'

The Adjudicator raised a hand to shield his face from the sun. 'Prince Obrahim is running late and so I come in his stead. He is making preparations for his brother's lifebonding ceremony. Saverian and my sister will shortly arrive in New Malaga, having finished their work in Dorminia. It seemed proper that at least one of my kind be present to witness this marriage between our new allies.'

Isaac noticed he had golden dust flecking his cheek. He wiped it off and examined his fingertips with a wry smile. 'You know,

396

this reminds me of a ritual our kind practises upon the completion of our lifebonding ceremony – a tradition that dates back to our ancestors in the Time Before. Our records of that epoch are almost non-existent, but from what little we do know it is surprising just how many echoes of Old Terra can be found in these lands.'

'Perhaps that is why your Pilgrims chose this place to settle,' Sasha ventured. 'It was familiar to them.'

'Perhaps,' Isaac agreed. 'Or perhaps these lands and those belonging to my ancestors share a common Creator. He went by several names in the Time Before, all of which are now forgotten.'

'That is the fate of all things,' Sasha said. 'To be forgotten.'

'A dark thought for such a glorious day,' Isaac replied drolly. His expression shifted and suddenly he looked pained. 'I would have liked to have shared it with another.'

'Another?'

'Yes,' Isaac replied. 'The Halfmage. I looked for him in Dorminia. I thought to bring him here to witness the wedding. But I was too late. He was already gone.'

'The Halfmage?' Sasha repeated. '*He* was the one who made you change your mind? About humanity being beyond redemption?'

'He was.'

'How?' she asked. It hardly seemed credible. The Halfmage she remembered was a bitter husk of a man.

Isaac was silent a moment before replying. 'I saw in him a truth about mankind. That the ugliest among you are capable of surprising beauty. That no matter how your short lives may seek to break you, there is something within the best of you that will not shatter. He showed me that a hero may be found in the most unlikely of forms. That no imperfection cannot be tolerated when a heart is good.'

Sasha listened to Isaac, growing more agitated with every word. She saw Brodar Kayne place an arm around his son and guide him into the palace. 'Excuse me,' she said, turning away from the Fade, towards the harbour where Cole had slipped off, lost in the depths of his own personal nightmare.

'You're leaving?' came Isaac's voice behind her. 'What about the wedding?'

'They'll manage without me,' she called back. 'I need to find someone.'

*

The White Lady's palace was unlike anywhere Kayne had ever laid eyes upon. The opulence beggared Heartstone's Great Lodge; the glistening marble and golden statuary put to shame the musty furs and tarnished suits of armour that had stood so proudly in the king's chamber. Up on the dais in the centre of her throne room, the White Lady looked every inch a goddess made flesh. Thanates cut a decidedly ragged figure beside her, though he wore a new overcoat and had decided to cover his eyeless sockets with a strip of black silk. Above the throne, sunlight bleeding through a window set in the arched ceiling above bathed the couple and their assembled guests on the benches before the dais in a warm radiance.

Just like the *Seeker*, this city and its palace made all that Brodar Kayne had once thought grand seem trivial. At one time that realization might've unsettled him, made him question himself and his place in the world. Now he found himself not giving a damn. He had everything he wanted right beside him.

'You all right, son?' he asked for the third time. It'd taken a mighty effort to get Magnar to agree to accompany the Highlander party, but agree he had – eventually. Magnar didn't look at all comfortable, but the mere fact that his son had taken such a big step was a sign he was on the road to recovery. Just looking at him sitting there filled the Sword of the North with pride.

'How much longer is this going to last?' Magnar whispered. Kayne grinned, sharing his son's sentiments. First they'd sat through a droning Consult minister reading out the terms of the marriage. Then the two wizards had been presented with copious amounts of parchment to sign. Thanates had needed someone to recite them for him. There weren't many lettered men among the Highland people, but Brandwyn had volunteered to help. Kayne wondered where young Davarus Cole and Sasha had got to. Chances were they'd been bickering again and were off cooling down somewhere.

The wedding between the two mages was a far cry from the joining ceremony between Brick and Corinn. Honouring the spirits took pride of a place in a Highlander wedding. The Lowland folk did things differently. In ages past they'd apparently said their vows in front of the gods, but given that at least one half of the couple on the dais had taken an active hand in wiping them out, Kayne could understand why the gods no longer merited much of a mention.

He remembered his own joining ceremony. The happiest day of his life, save for the day his wife had brought his son into the world.

The documents were finally signed. Jerek shifted beside Kayne and made a poor job of stifling a yawn. The Wolf looked even more uncomfortable than Magnar. He had barely said a word since they'd disembarked the small ship that had brought them across the channel. It was a minor shock to the old Highlander that the Wolf had chosen to come at all. Maybe he'd done it as a favour to Thanates, whom he seemed to have decided was all right.

*Or maybe he just wants to make sure I don't overdo it and keel over from another heart attack.*

On the benches opposite them, Isaac met Kayne's gaze and gave him a small nod. It'd been a surprise to see the Fade among the guests. It was tempting to think they were not so different from mankind.

*Except when you remember that they're ageless and seven feet tall and smarter than any living man. And they got weapons that can break worlds.*

One of the Consult rose to present the mages with their rings, which they exchanged. Then two great silver goblets were filled and the same woman presented them to the White Lady and Thanates. The former drank deep, but the latter fumbled his chalice as it was placed into his hands and spilled the contents over the marble floor. Wine ran down the steps from the dais and the blind wizard looked embarrassed by his clumsiness – but the smile the Magelord of Thelassa gave her new husband was the same kind that Kayne remembered Mhaira giving him countless times, and all was well in the world.

'Fucking waste that is,' Jerek rasped, shattering the moment as only the Wolf could.

'There'll be plenty of time for drinking afterwards,' answered Kayne. 'Plenty of time for feasting too, I'm guessing.' He pointed to the tables in the great dining hall beyond the throne room. They were piled high with all manner of Lowland delicacies: roasted pigeon and jellied fruits and more varieties of cheese than he had known existed.

Jerek looked as though he were about to spit, but in a landmark moment of self-control closed his mouth and made do with a scowl. 'Ain't much for all that fancy shit. Give me warm stew and a heel of bread any day.'

The wedding official returned to take her seat near to Kayne, who noticed that she seemed a little vacant. Chances were she was as tired of the drawn-out wedding as everyone else. Thankfully, the ceremony was swiftly brought to a close and they were led out of the throne room and into the dining hall. Kayne picked at a few platters of meat, but he had no stomach for drink and in any case he had been given strict orders to avoid everything except water. Magnar drank enough wine for the pair of them, downing cup after cup with the determination of a man eager to find oblivion sooner rather than later.

Kayne was frowning at an apple-filled tart when one of the Westermen barged into him. It could have been accidental, except several of his comrades were watching the scene with big grins on their faces. Kayne managed to steady himself on the table, though his tart ended up smeared all over his hand. The warrior who'd shoved him was red of face, clearly half drunk already. 'Sorry, old fellow,' he said, a cruel grin revealing yellow teeth. 'Looks like I slipped—'

Jerek grabbed his shoulders and spun him around. The Wolf's head shot forward, flattening the warrior's nose and dropping him like a stone.

'Ain't that a coincidence,' the Wolf rasped. 'Looks like my head slipped as well.' He glowered down at the man, whose comrades reached for their weapons. Carn intervened, ordering them to stand down in a deep growl that bore no argument. The chieftain of the West Reaching turned to Kayne.

'Your friend knows how to hold a grudge,' he said ruefully, meeting the Wolf's gaze. 'In that I believe we are alike.'

Kayne cleared his throat and wiped warm apple tart from his shaking hands. 'I was hoping we might've put all that behind us.'

'I made an oath,' Carn growled. 'I do not break my promises.'

Jerek's eyes narrowed. He turned away from the groaning warrior at his feet. 'I'm going for a walk,' he declared, storming out.

Kayne watched him go, confused by the Wolf's sudden exit. *Probably for the best*, he decided. The last thing he wanted was to be the cause of a fight breaking out at the wedding of the two most influential mages in the north.

Brandwyn and his small entourage watched the scene in silence. At least the Greenmen had the sense not to drink. Kayne gave the chieftain of the Green Reaching a friendly nod and Brandwyn returned the gesture. Isaac seemed unimpressed by the bounty on offer. 'Not hungry?' the old warrior asked.

'I cannot help but recall the homeless and the starving in

Dorminia,' Isaac explained. 'It seems perverse to partake of this bounty when thousands go hungry.'

'Ah.' Kayne stared at the tart he was just raising to his mouth and placed it carefully back down on the table.

Isaac began to say something else, but a loud explosion suddenly shook the room, cutting him off. 'The hell's that?' Kayne muttered.

Isaac's obsidian eyes narrowed. 'It came from the avenue,' he said.

They hurried out of the dining chamber and into the throne room. Screams were coming from outside the palace. Moments later the harsh percussive *ra-ta-ta-ta* of a Fade weapon reverberated up the avenue. It seemed to go on forever, an endless snarl that cut off the screams until only silence remained.

Kayne joined the surge of men and women emptying the throne room and hurrying down the hallway to the palace gates. Magnar lurched along behind, the effects of too much wine obvious in his wavering steps. 'Stick close to me,' Kayne whispered.

They exited the palace and stopped dead, staring in shock at the carnage on the avenue before them. The celebrants were fleeing the palace, a vast tide of city folk scattering in all directions. Dozens of bodies were twitching on the ground amidst spreading pools of blood. The Whitecloaks had been ruthlessly slaughtered, mown down by the terrifying white-haired Fade and the blue-cloaked female making their determined way down the avenue towards the palace.

'Saverian,' whispered Isaac beside Kayne. 'Melissan.' The dread in the Adjudicator's voice as he spoke their names made the old Highlander's blood turn cold. Saverian's shoulder-cannon was raised before him, smoke pouring from the barrel. Melissan held a hand-cannon in each of her hands.

'General, what is the meaning of this?' Isaac demanded. 'This... this is *murder*.'

'Stand down, Adjudicator,' barked Saverian, continuing his advance. 'This is not your concern.'

402

Despite the immense power in that ancient voice, Isaac took a step towards his commander. 'Prince Obrahim promised no harm would come to these people,' he said.

Saverian's mouth twisted in anger. 'In this, my brother's judgement is flawed. I am the shield that defends our people from harm. I am the sword that has vanquished every threat for five thousand years.'

Like moonlight and shadow, the White Lady and Thanates emerged together from the palace beside Kayne. Carn Bloodfist suddenly loomed behind him and he could hear the other Highlanders readying their weapons, steel sliding from sheaths. Kayne reached over his shoulder, unsheathed his own greatsword.

'Look at them,' Saverian continued, contempt flowing from him like poison. 'God-killers. Genocidal old men. A crippled wizard who ought to have died long ago. I do not see the child of murder or the mutant girl among this sorry gathering – but know that they too shall face judgement. They are all monsters.' Saverian tossed aside his shoulder-cannon and reached down to draw his crystal sword. 'For five thousand years I have protected our people,' he proclaimed. His voice was as sharp as the blade in his hand. 'I do not parley with monsters. I slay them.'

'Sir,' Isaac tried again. 'Prince Obrahim gave his word. *Our* word.'

'This is not a course I choose lightly, Adjudicator,' grated the white-haired commander. 'Before even my prince's wishes, my responsibility is to keep my people safe. I will not suffer a potential threat to live. To grow stronger. To one day bring us harm. Get out of my way.'

'I will not.' Suddenly, Isaac had his own crystal sword in his hand. He looked beyond Saverian to Melissan, who trailed a few feet behind the general. 'Sister,' he pleaded. 'You cannot do this.'

Melissan hesitated for a second. Then her eyes narrowed. Her voice was heavy with spite. 'Humanity is poison – and those you seek to defend are the most virulent poison of all. Do as Saverian commands, brother. Stand aside.'

'No.'

'Then you leave me no choice,' said Saverian. 'It seems I must add betrayer-of-kin to this grim company of which you are so enraptured. Defend yourself.' The general raised his sword.

Everything seemed to happen at once. The two Fade came together in a deadly dance, crystal swords blazing red in the light of the sun. The White Lady began to utter words of power – but as she raised her hands, the silver light wreathing her fingers flickered and died. Kayne turned to his countrymen, began to yell at them to move forward and protect the two wizards.

Just then the White Lady jerked. The bloody end of a sword emerged through her stomach. Holding the other end of the weapon was none other than Brandwyn the Younger.

The Magelord stumbled back, staring at the hilt protruding from her waist in confusion. She raised her hands, but once again her magic flickered and died. 'Powdered abyssium,' said Brandwyn calmly. He took a step to the side and a dozen members of the Consult came forward. Each held a knife that must have been concealed in their robes. Among them was the woman who had handed the White Lady and Thanates the goblets back in the throne room. 'We slipped it into your wine,' Brandwyn explained. 'A gift from General Saverian. As were these thralls.'

As one the Consult assassins closed on the Magelord of Thelassa, knives raised. Without warning, the warriors loyal to Brandwyn began to cut down their opposite numbers from the West Reaching, many of whom were too drunk to offer much resistance.

'You treacherous fuck!' Carn growled. Oathkeeper was in his massive hands. 'Why?' he asked, the shrieks from the weapon echoing his rage. He tried to reach his opposite number from the Green Reaching, but several Greenmen blocked his path.

Brandwyn fell back, slipping behind a huge warrior with a double-headed axe. 'Peace,' he hissed. 'This land needs peace, not war. Men like you, men like the Sword of the North – you bring nothing but death. Magelords, wizards – they bring nothing but disaster. This is a new age, and you and your ilk have no place in it.'

Half the Consult assassins were suddenly wreathed in black fire, their clothes burning away, the flesh beneath melting like hot wax. Thanates faced them, utter fury twisting his features. He staggered as an arrow appeared, quivering, in his back. There was an archer among Brandwyn's men. He was already reaching for another arrow.

Kayne saw a warrior dashing towards him. He turned aside the man's thrust, reversing his parry and hamstringing his would-be killer in a single motion. He was about to finish him off when Magnar cried out.

His son was on the floor, a sword sticking out of his back. As if in a dream, or a nightmare, Kayne watched helplessly as Brandwyn's man tugged his sword free with a wet sound, crimson droplets raining down.

The bottom seemed to fall out of the world. Kayne stumbled towards Magnar, cut down the warrior standing over him without a second thought. He bent down and gathered his son in his arms.

Magnar coughed, blood flecking his lips. All around them the fighting raged but Kayne cared not for any of it. He held Magnar close, tears blurring his eyes, every ragged gasp from his son's chest breaking his heart that little bit further.

Finally he looked up. Saw the White Lady on her knees, her wedding dress in bloody tatters. She'd been stabbed a dozen times and still the assault continued, knives plunging into her again and again, splashes of her blood painting the white marble, the white robes of the thralls dressed as her servants, whom Saverian had somehow planted among the Consult.

Thanates stumbled towards his new wife, three arrows sticking out of him. Black fire burst from his hands, incinerating the remaining assassins.

He was too late. The Magelord of Thelassa blinked once, her purple eyes uncomprehending. Then she sank to the ground, her head striking the marble softly, ruined wedding dress settling around her like a shroud. As graceful dying as she had been in life.

The wizard-king of Dalashra knelt over her body as it began to crack. Golden light spilled from the last Magelord of the Trine, just as it had from Salazar and the Shaman. Returning to the heavens from where it had been stolen five centuries ago.

Like a bell tolling their doom, Isaac cried out. Kayne saw Saverian's crystal blade burst through the Adjudicator's body. The general thrust his dying officer aside and stalked towards the blind wizard kneeling over the White Lady.

Despite the arrows sticking out of him, somehow Thanates rose. A wordless roar escaped his lips and he hurled a raging stream of black fire at the implacable general. It would have burned any mortal man to a crisp in an instant, yet General Saverian did not slow. His sneer turned into a grimace as the magical assault singed his ebony cloak and caused smoke to rise from his white hair. But it could not touch his flesh. He was beyond magic, it seemed.

The stream of fire died. Saverian calmly knelt and retrieved his shoulder-cannon, aiming it at the eyeless mage. As if sensing what was about to happen, Thanates began to shift shape, changing into his crow form, rising into the sky on midnight wings.

He was a fraction too slow. The *ra-ta-ta-ta-ta* of Saverian's terrible weapon split the air and feathers exploded from the shapeshifted mage, who plummeted back to the earth and began shifting back into his human form.

Beside the body of his wife, the bloody and torn figure of Thanates twitched. Tried to raise his eyeless face.

Saverian's booted foot slammed down on his neck, choking the life from him. With a final spasm, the wizard-king of Dalashra died.

Kayne knelt, Magnar's head in his lap, staring numbly at the carnage. Burned and butchered corpses littered the ground. Carn's men were all dead, only the mighty chieftain himself left standing. He was hopelessly surrounded by eight of Brandwyn's warriors, though two were dead at his feet. Magnar's breathing was growing weaker by the second.

Brandwyn met Kayne's eyes. There was something like shame there.

Then Saverian's voice rang out.

'Let this chieftain face me,' the general ordered, gesturing at Carn. The warriors surrounding Carn fell back and the huge chieftain slowly turned, massive chest rising and falling. He frowned at the white-haired immortal.

Saverian sneered and raised his crystal blade. 'Show me,' he growled. 'Show me the best of what humanity can offer.'

Carn's dark eyes narrowed. He approached Saverian cautiously, Oathkeeper held in a defensive posture. The Fade general's own stance was casual, almost lazy in comparison. Suddenly Carn moved, as swift as a snake, aiming a powerful thrust at Saverian's chest.

Saverian's counter was too fast to follow. His sword flashed once, twice. Carn stumbled back, blood blossoming on his stomach. On his arm. He tried again, attacking with all his ferocity, all his prodigious strength, but skilled though he was, the chieftain of the West Reaching was completely outmatched. Soon he was covered in wounds, red ribbons dissecting his leather armour, carving open his flesh. Oathkeeper dropped from his nerveless fingers, clattering to the bloody marble. He collapsed to one knee, gasping wetly.

Saverian towered over Carn. 'Your best,' he said contemptuously, 'is predictably worthless.' The general's crystal sword flashed and Carn's head fell away from his shoulders, his corpse hitting the avenue with a loud thud. Then the general bent down and retrieved Oathkeeper, staring at the runes carved into the blade with something like amusement. 'A child's toy,' he announced.

With a mighty grunt, he broke the sword over his knee.

'I'm finished here,' the general announced, tossing away the shattered blade. He gestured to Brandwyn, and then pointed at Kayne. 'Finish off your countryman. I will waste no more time on empty legends. As agreed, you will be named chieftain of your people, provided you remember your place.'

Kayne was only dimly aware of the warriors spreading out to surround him. All he could focus on was his son dying in his arms.

'I'm sorry,' he whispered brokenly. 'I made you come here.'

He saw the Seer in his mind's eye then, heard her voice echoing in his skull. *You sent the Broken King to his death.*

He reached down into the bag at his belt. Felt the lock of Mhaira's hair and wrapped his fingers around it. Pulled Magnar close.

He hardly saw the steel blade flashing towards him. Was only vaguely aware of the axe appearing at the last instant to knock it aside.

'Get up, Kayne. Get the fuck up. We ain't dying here. Not without taking as many of them with us as we can.'

The rasping voice seized him as firmly as a strong hand on his shoulder, offering him comfort in his greatest hour of need.

Jerek was beside him, axes in his hands. Kayne met the Wolf's eyes. The two men exchanged a look they'd exchanged a hundred times before.

Brodar Kayne laid Magnar gently down and got to his feet. Lifted his greatsword. 'One last time,' he whispered.

'One last time,' rasped Jerek. The Wolf spat, raised his axes.

Then Brandwyn's warriors were upon them.

They were outnumbered four to one, Kayne only weeks recovered from what could've been his deathbed. His arms shook with every swing, his eyes blurry from grief. He was old, weary and broken-down. A man who had lost everything.

And so he shed the man and became the weapon. Became the Sword of the North once more.

He knocked away thrusts from spear and sword, hacked out at unprotected limbs. Steel whispered past his ear, missed him by a fraction. A few glancing blows landed but he shrugged off the pain, ignored the fresh blood running down his arms and thighs. His own greatsword answered the nicks tenfold, cleaving off limbs, shattering arms and legs. He ran one warrior through, the big bastard with the double-headed axe. Another dashed in, seeking to take advantage of Kayne's temporary distraction, spear point aimed at his chest. Kayne heaved, tearing his own greatsword free in a burst of gore. Suddenly Jerek was there, one axe batting the spear away, the other cleaving through the man's skull.

The two friends fought back to back as they had countless times before. Relentless fury and lethal precision. Fire and ice. Twin axes and greatsword. The fifth warrior went down with a scream, Kayne's sword opening his chest. He glanced up to see Brandwyn watching the fighting, concern etched on his face, the treacherous chieftain too much of a coward to find a weapon and involve himself in the dark deeds he'd helped plan. Beside him, the archer who'd stuck three arrows in Thanates was lining up his bow for another shot.

'Archer,' Kayne hissed to Jerek. The Wolf spotted him at the last second. His biceps bulged as he lined up an axe and sent it spinning steel over shaft. The archer's head burst open like a melon, brains spraying all over the shocked face of Brandwyn next to him.

'Draw your sword, betrothed,' General Saverian ordered Melissan, who until then had been watching events unfold beside the commander. 'Bring them to heel. Prove that I chose wisely.'

As Jerek bent to retrieve another axe from the one of the fallen warriors, Kayne saw Melissan advancing up the avenue. She'd holstered her hand-cannons and had her crystal sword raised, hatred twisting her angular features.

Kayne blinked sweat and blood from his eyes and exchanged a grim nod with the Wolf. He and Jerek fought with renewed fury, knowing they had to improve the odds to stand any kind of chance. Another two of Brandwyn's men fell just as the towering, white-skinned Fade officer stepped over the bodies now piled up around them.

Both Highlanders were covered in blood, Kayne so exhausted he could hardly stand. Age caught up with everyone sooner or later – everyone, that is, except the Fade. On the face of it, the odds were better than before – but there were odds, and then there were damn lies.

This Fade was no Highland warrior. She was a superhuman immortal, better trained and more experienced than any living man. Doubt began to eat away at Kayne's resolve, but just then he saw Magnar shift on the ground. A tiny movement, but one that stoked the fire within. His son was alive.

Like water into a burst dam, purpose rushed in to fill his empty muscles and wounded heart. The promise he'd made to Mhaira flared, hotter than the sun in the sky above.

He blocked the first thrust of the crystal sword. Ducked away from another. Melissan was fast, faster than anyone or anything he had ever fought in his fifty-odd years. Kayne grimaced as her sword cut a deep gash in his thigh. He threw his head forward and felt bone break, and Melissan stumbled away clutching her nose. He too fell back, bleeding heavily from the wound in his leg. One of the two remaining Greenmen Jerek was currently fighting collapsed to the ground, blood pumping from the gaping hole in his neck. Kayne noticed then that none of the blood covering Jerek appeared to belong to the Wolf himself.

Melissan was suddenly in Kayne's face again, mouth locked in a snarl, blue cloak whipping around her as she shifted this way and that, thrusting and slashing with incredible speed. He winced as her sword scored a deep cut in his arm. Even at his best he might not have been her match, and his best was twenty years and about a half-dozen wounds ago. He lost a finger on his left hand as he launched an awkward parry, watched it fly away. The greatsword loosened in his maimed grip.

He did the only thing he could do. He let go of the weapon. Took a quick step forward and punched Melissan hard in the face, a right hook. She was taken by surprise and dropped instantly, hitting her head on the marble floor and lying still.

Agony blossomed as something sharp entered his back and he gasped. He twisted to see Brandwyn preparing to stab him again, the chieftain's shortsword crimson with Kayne's blood. There was no time to retrieve his own greatsword. Instead Kayne reached down, plucked Magnar's knife from his belt and slammed it into Brandwyn's shoulder, giving it a cruel twist. The chieftain of the Green Reaching dropped his weapon and fell back screaming.

A loud bang shattered the silence that followed. General Saverian held a smoking hand-cannon pointing at Kayne.

'Enough,' the Fade commander barked. In a daze, Kayne prodded at the hole in his back. Poked at the gaping wound Brandwyn's back-stab had left. He felt the warm blood leaking between his fingers. The blood might be warm but he was cold now. Cold and getting colder.

Jerek positioned his body in front of Kayne's. The Wolf stared at General Saverian with a fury like nothing Kayne had ever seen. Not even when he'd learned the truth about his family's murder in the ruins of Mal-Torrad. 'Face me like a man,' he rasped, terrible rage in his voice. Terrible rage, and terrible grief.

General Saverian watched the Wolf stalk towards him. Their gazes locked. Instead of reaching for his sword as he had with Carn Bloodfist, the Fade general hesitated and then levelled his hand-cannon. 'I am no man,' he replied coldly. 'I am a fehd.'

*Bang,* went his terrible weapon.

Jerek stumbled. Stumbled, but kept on walking.

The hand-cannon fired again. This time the Wolf went down to one knee, crouching beside the headless corpse of Carn, the patter of his blood drumming on the marble avenue.

'I am no man,' said Saverian again. 'I am a legend.'

411

Jerek's eyes closed. The Wolf began to waver, his axes trembling in his hands. Despite his own agony, Kayne swallowed, tears rolling down his face as he watched the most loyal friend a man could ever wish for about to die trying to defend him. The Wolf swayed once more.

And then his eyes snapped open. Somehow, impossibly, Jerek rose again.

'Die!' Saverian snarled. His hand-cannon fired twice more, the booms reverberating down the avenue.

The Wolf jerked, blood flowing freely from the holes in his chest. He spat crimson drool. Rocked back and forth on unsteady legs. And still he took another step towards Saverian.

The hand-cannon roared again and finally Jerek fell, his axes slipping out of his hands to clatter to the street. The Wolf crawled on his hands and knees towards the edge of the avenue, every inch of his tortured movements a supreme effort of will. He left a trail of blood behind him.

'Yes,' Saverian sneered. 'Crawl away and die. Like the dog you are.' He tried to unload his hand-cannon again, but it just made an empty clicking sound. The general tossed it away and drew his sword. He walked straight past Jerek, who managed to twist his head to meet Kayne's gaze one final time, his dark eyes seeming to offer an apology.

Saverian loomed above Kayne, a white-hired angel of death standing bright against a world beginning to grow dark. 'The traitor, Isaac, once referred to you as a legend among your people,' said the Fade commander. 'But there is only one true legend. Retrieve your sword, if you can.'

With agonizing slowness, the Sword of the North tottered over to where his greatsword rested, almost falling with every step. He stumbled past the bodies of Highland warriors piled high, their weapons scattered around them; the unconscious figure of Melissan; Brandwyn, sobbing like a child as he stared at the knife buried in his shoulder.

Brodar Kayne bent down, sucking in air, clinging to

consciousness by his fingertips. He lifted his greatsword from the ground. Turned to Saverian and raised the weapon. One final act of defiance.

'Why keep fighting?' the Fade commander asked. He seemed genuinely confused. 'You are beaten. Broken.'

Kayne tried to speak, blood spilling over his chin. 'No man's ever broken till he can't get back up,' he whispered.

General Saverian frowned. Then he moved, a silver blur, his crystal sword catching the sun as it dove towards Kayne, faster than the eye could follow.

What happened next was a haze in Kayne's fading mind. Saverian reached up with his free hand to touch the shallow wound on his cheek, disbelief on his face. 'Two thousand years,' he uttered. 'No one has laid a mark upon me for two thousand years.'

Saverian's other hand still clutched the hilt of the sword buried in Kayne's chest.

The Sword of the North sank to his knees and collapsed beside Magnar. The last thing he saw was his son's eyes. Mhaira's eyes. Grey like steel. Silver like the ring on his finger.

He raised his wedding band to his lips. Then he died.

*

Davarus Cole was sitting on the steps of a tavern a mile west of the palace when he heard the screams. He looked up from where he'd been holding his head in his hands, and stared in confusion at the panicked faces of the city folk as they scattered like ants. 'What's going on?' he asked a passing woman.

'Death!' she screamed back at him. 'Death has arrived.'

Cole leaped to his feet. He placed a hand on the jewelled hilt of Magebane and hurried through the crowds, back in the direction of the palace. A dozen thoughts danced through his skull, each more terrible than the last.

*Has the Herald somehow returned? Or... is it the dragon? Please don't tell me it's the dragon.*

'Cole!' He glimpsed Sasha rushing towards him, his anger forgotten when he saw the fear on her face.

'What's happening?' he asked.

'I don't know. I came looking for you, and then I heard something that sounded like Fade weapons. I thought I glimpsed Saverian.'

'The Fade general? What the hell is he doing here?'

Sasha shrugged helplessly. Together the two friends shouldered their way through the crowd until they reached the avenue leading to the palace. There they stopped in disbelief.

Ahead of them lay utter carnage. Dead Whitecloaks were sprawled all the way up the avenue, their bodies punctured by hundreds of tiny holes. But it was the bloodbath just before the steps of the palace that caused Cole to break into a sprint, hurdling the corpses in his desperation to reach his fallen friends.

Thanates lay in a pool of blood, arrows and tiny holes shredding the new coat the wizard had donned for his wedding. Beside Thanates rested the body of the White Lady of Thelassa. Deep cracks covered her withered skin, her youth and beauty fled the moment her stolen immortality had departed her body. The headless corpse of Carn Bloodfist sprawled nearby, the great chieftain's magical sword broken in half. Smeared across the avenue in a ragged line was a trail of blood. It disappeared just before one of the great cracks in the streets that was still awaiting repair.

'Those are Jerek's axes,' said Sasha, pointing to the weapons resting on the ground near the bloody trail.

A moment later they spotted Brodar Kayne.

The old Highlander lay surrounded by fallen warriors. Cole ran to him, bent down and examined his wounds, hoping beyond hope that there might be a glimmer of life left somewhere within the old warrior. But there was none.

Brodar Kayne, the seemingly indomitable barbarian who had survived demons, giants and Magelords, was dead.

The wound that had killed him had gone straight through his chest. His blue eyes stared sightlessly ahead. The expression on his face seemed strangely peaceful.

'Who did this?' Sasha whispered.

Cole stared around him at the bloodbath. The bodies that surrounded Kayne were Highlanders killed by him and Jerek – in a monumental battle, judging by the wounds they bore. But no human blade could have severed Carn's head so cleanly, nor shattered Oathkeeper like a wooden toy. No human could have slain both the White Lady and Thanates, the greatest wizards in the land. No human could have mown down scores of Whitecloaks.

'The Fade,' Cole growled. 'They betrayed us. After all we went through. After all their promises.'

'Look,' exclaimed Sasha, her voice heavy with grief. 'It's Magnar. Kayne's son. They killed him too...' She fell to her knees, cradling the head of a young man in her lap. He was around their own age, Cole saw. Eyes the colour of iron. Just like his own.

He felt something then. A flicker of life.

'Wait,' Cole said urgently. He squatted down beside Sasha and placed his hands on Magnar's chest. 'His heart's stopped,' he said. 'But he's not yet gone. Not completely.'

As he had with Derkin's mother, and Sasha back in the Fade ruins, Cole summoned the essence of the Reaver. Instead of absorbing life, he surrendered it, sacrificing his own vitality, channelling it into the body of Magnar Kayne. He was already weak – the Reaver hadn't been fed in many weeks, and he had little enough strength of his own.

'Stop!' Sasha exclaimed, panic in her voice. 'You're killing yourself.'

'I'm not going to let them win,' he rasped.

Just as he was about to pass out, he felt it. A small tremble from Magnar, like the first green shoots poking through the soil after a flood had passed. A tiny heartbeat, weak and fragile, but growing stronger.

Cole gasped and began to topple, utterly overwhelmed by exhaustion, weaker than a newborn kitten. Sasha caught him at the last moment. He remained in her arms for several minutes, summoning his strength. 'Help us to the undercity,' he gasped.

'The undercity?' Sasha repeated. 'You think we'll be safe with Derkin?'

'Not us,' Cole replied. 'Him.' He nodded at Magnar, who was now breathing steadily.

There was a roar from above and a monstrous shadow engulfed the scene of carnage before the palace gates. Cole glanced up, his heart sinking at the sight.

The *Seeker* lowered itself to the ground, its metallic body gleaming a brilliant crimson in the sunshine.

'Prince Obrahim is here,' whispered Sasha.

At that precise moment, General Saverian stepped out of the palace, the blue-cloaked Adjudicator Melissan beside him.

\*

'Brother. What is the meaning of this?'

Obrahim and Saverian faced each other on opposite sides of the palace approach. The prince took in the devastation with an expression that hinted at great sorrow.

'Treachery,' Saverian said, gesturing at Cole and Sasha. 'The humans betrayed us.'

Even hot with fury at the massacre before them, Cole quailed slightly before the formidable commander. He quickly recovered himself. 'Treachery?' he spat back. 'You killed dozens of innocents! You murdered the White Lady and Thanates during their own damned wedding! You killed Brodar Kayne – as good a man as any I've ever met.'

'You speak of retribution!' thundered Saverian. 'My betrothed and I thought to visit your city before we travelled to New Malaga – a conciliatory act in recognition of our new alliance. When we arrived, we found the city's rulers had murdered Adjudicator Isaac. Just as the ruler of Shadowport, Marius, murdered Feryan and Aduana.'

Saverian beckoned to Melissan. The Adjudicator entered the palace and returned a moment later pulling a pallet. Lying atop it, hands folded over his chest, the shroud covering him stained with blood, was Isaac. 'Witness,' said the general. 'Cut down by the one named Brodar Kayne.'

Cole hesitated. He looked from Prince Obrahim to Saverian. The prince's mouth was a thin line. The diamond at the end of his sceptre flickered for the briefest of instants.

*Could the White Lady have turned on Isaac?* In Cole's experience the Magelord of Thelassa could be as cruel as winter when the mood took her. The eyeless face of the man she had so briefly been wed to, his body sprawled beside her own, was proof enough of that.

Next to Cole, Sasha stirred. 'Kayne wouldn't have harmed Isaac,' she said. 'He liked him.'

Saverian sneered. He turned and pointed to Melissan's face. Her nose appeared to be broken and she had a huge lump on her head, marring her otherwise perfect features. 'Observe what this "Brodar Kayne" did to my betrothed,' the general growled.

He raised a hand and pointed to a thin, bloody line on his own cheek. 'He cut me and I was forced to slay him for his audacity. He and his wretched sidekick, the one who called himself the Wolf. I will give them some credit. For mortals, they were remarkably hard to kill.'

'The Wolf?' Sasha said quietly. 'Jerek never broke his promises. Not when it came to the important stuff. For all his faults, he was true to his word.'

Saverian's laugh was as rough as grating steel, and just as humourless. 'Your kind do not know what it is to be *true*. You are creatures of instinct – a fickle, impetuous race of children concealing your true natures in falsehoods and pretentions. Perhaps it is time the two of you learned the hard edge of the truth.' The Fade general drew his crystal sword and took a single step forward.

Cole drew Magebane, his sudden terror warring with the Reaver's endless urging to kill and neither wholly winning out. He and Sasha were over-matched by this Fade commander. If they were forced to fight, there was no way they would leave this place alive.

Fortunately, a fight never came to pass. Prince Obrahim raised his sceptre. Golden-haired brother turned to white-haired brother and uttered a single word – and there was such great sorrow in Obrahim's voice that Cole himself was moved to tears.

'*Why?*'

General Saverian frowned. 'Why what, my brother?'

'Not "my brother",' Prince Obrahim said hollowly. 'Never again "my brother".'

'I do not understand.'

'You broke your word. You broke *our* word.' Obrahim closed his eyes for a moment. When he opened them again, the dismay in his voice brought tears to Cole's eyes. 'Tell me true, Saverian. Did you murder Isaac?'

The silence that followed was deafening. The general looked from Prince Obrahim to the dead Adjudicator. His mouth twisted. 'You do not believe me,' he said eventually.

Prince Obrahim raised his sceptre. 'The final great invention of the Time Before allows me to read the truth of all things.'

'You never told me this,' Saverian said. He seemed uncertain now, disquieted by his brother's reaction. Perhaps Obrahim was the only being in the world that could so unsettle the legendary general.

'I never had cause. You were my brother. You did not lie to me, nor I to you. But you have forgotten the principles the Pilgrims established when they arrived in these lands.' The Fade prince's eyes filled with sadness deeper than the oceans. 'I loved you, Saverian. For five thousand years you kept our people safe. But for this crime – for the murder of kin – there can be no forgiveness.'

'I did what I had to!' Saverian hissed. His grip tightened on his sword. 'These humans could not be trusted! One day they would have turned on us. I am the shield that defends our people from harm. I am—'

His words became a grunt as the crystal on Obrahim's sceptre flashed. Suddenly he began to drift up into the air, a legend – perhaps the greatest legend of them all – made helpless in the blink of an eye.

Cole was struck by the enormity of the events playing out before him: the final exclamation point to a year of titanic upheaval. Thousands of years of trust, the soul of a people, had just been irrevocably shattered.

'I should end your existence,' Obrahim announced, tears rolling down his cheeks now. 'But I cannot. For I, too, fall short of what our ancestors expected of us.'

The diamond at the top of Obrahim's sceptre flashed again and Saverian fell, somehow landing in a crouch. He rose and faced the prince. 'Listen to me, brother! Humanity is beyond redemption. Let me prove it. I will show you—'

'*No*. It does not *matter*, Saverian. From this moment on, you are no longer of the People. You are never to return to Terra. You are banished.'

'Prince Obrahim,' Saverian pleaded, making one final appeal. 'You cannot do this—'

'It is done,' the Fade prince announced. 'The First and Second Fleets will accompany me back to Terra. Those who wish to remain will join you in exile. You may keep the Breaker of Worlds to ensure your protection and the protection of those who choose to stay behind. Do not ask me for anything else. Never again.' The Fade prince turned to Cole and Sasha. 'I remember now why we departed this continent two thousand years ago. We cannot live among humanity. Perhaps you *are* poison. Or perhaps you merely hold a mirror to our kind that we are wiser to avoid.'

Cole put an arm around Sasha. She was weeping. 'What of us?' he asked. 'What will become of us?'

Prince Obrahim turned away. 'Whatever you make of yourselves in your short lives. Perhaps in a thousand years I will once again take an interest in the fate of this continent. Until that time, mankind is on its own.'

# The Aftermath

THE SUMMER MONTHS passed and Sasha, together with Cole, did her best to help the City of Towers recover from the events of that most traumatic of days. With the White Lady murdered, Thelassa's rule fell to the surviving members of the Consult. Sasha spent many a morning arguing fruitlessly with men and women who had no concept of how to go about wiping their own arses, let alone attempting to rebuild a city whose foundations had been both metaphorically and literally shaken to the point of collapse.

A month after the massacre outside the palace gates, Brandwyn the Younger arrived seeking an audience with the Consult. Aside from Magnar, the young chieftain was the sole survivor of Saverian's assault. He claimed to have been wounded during the attack, and had returned to the Highlander camp near Westrock seeking sanctuary. The scar on his shoulder was consistent with his story, though it seemed uncharacteristic of the ruthless Fade general to permit anyone to survive the coup he had so meticulously planned. Nonetheless, Brandwyn helped arrange the transportation of Brodar Kayne's body, as well as that of Carn Bloodfist and those of the other Highlanders, across Deadman's Channel so that they might be buried nearer their kin. Like the Consult assassins, the warriors Brandwyn had brought with him to Thelassa had been thralls of Saverian. It struck Sasha as curious that the wily chieftain had allowed himself to be so easily manipulated. Perhaps it was her imagination, but he had appeared relieved upon learning that Magnar remembered nothing of the events of that day. Kayne's son remained in the care of Cole's friend, Derkin, and his mother, who had been moved from the undercity to a house not far from the palace.

Arranging the funerals of the White Lady and Thanates in addition to everything else had kept Sasha so busy that she had not been able to accompany the ship carrying the bodies back to the sprawling Highlander encampment. Cole, however, had been insistent that he wanted to go. To say goodbye to Brodar Kayne one last time. When he returned a few days later, he reported that, while thousands had turned out to pay their respects to Carn Bloodfist, only a few dozen had attended Kayne's burial, which took place beneath an old oak tree in a secluded spot below Westrock. Brick and Corinn had come to say farewell, the former crying until his eyes were raw. More surprising was that Rana had paid her respects as the Sword of the North was laid to rest – as had a young warrior with a wine-coloured scar on his face who called himself Finn.

Brodar Kayne's greatsword had been buried with him. No one knew what had become of Jerek's body: Brandwyn recalled seeing the Wolf being shot to pieces by Saverian and insisted that he must have perished in the assault.

As the days went by, it became clear that Brandwyn was exactly the leader the Highlanders needed. The two major surviving clans, as Sasha understood them, quickly rallied behind his leadership. His was the vision that drove his people to begin putting down permanent roots in the region, organizing irrigation systems and food supply chains. He sent impressive plans south via raven to Thelassa, outlining exactly where he planned to establish new settlements once the Fade departed the continent. The question on everyone's lips was when exactly that would be.

Early one clear morning, just before the rising sun burned the mist off the water of the harbour, a messenger arrived at the palace claiming a fisherman had espied the vast Fade fleet on the move. Sasha quickly got dressed and hurried down to the docks, having convinced the fisherman to take her out to Deadman's Channel. There she sat and watched the fleet of hulking gunmetal behemoths sail down the channel to the Broken Sea, and beyond to the Endless Ocean. She used her augmented vision to get a closer look at their decks, to seek a better understanding of how many of the immortals yet remained in the Grey City, but it was a hopeless task. All she knew was that Saverian still ruled Dorminia. While the disgraced general remained in the Trine, no human would ever be safe. The harsh truth was that, with its fleet destroyed and its Magelord dead, Thelassa was more vulnerable than ever to outside aggression. The Unborn might have granted some small measure of confidence in the city's ability to repel an assault, but they too were gone. It was up to mortal men and women, poorly trained for the most part, to withstand whatever Saverian would eventually throw at Thelassa.

Sasha was about to ask the fisherman to return to the city when a shadow passed swiftly overhead, leaving a long trough in the water. She glanced up to see the sleek metallic shape of the *Seeker* winging its way west. Aboard the craft, she knew, was Prince Obrahim. Departing these lands, perhaps never to return. Never to see his brother again.

She wondered how that must have felt, for two siblings who had been so close for five thousand years to be torn apart in such harrowing circumstances. Then she realized she knew exactly how it felt. They'd only spent a few months together during their adult years, but the death of her sister Ambryl had left a void in Sasha's life she knew could never be filled.

She thought of Kayne and Jerek. The two men had been brothers-in-arms, as close in their own way as any blood relatives. They had died as they had lived – fighting side by side against overwhelming odds. In the end, they'd survived everything except betrayal. It occurred to Sasha that maybe that was the only way Brodar Kayne and Jerek the Wolf fighting together could ever have been defeated.

That night, the dreams came again. Glimpses of lives she had no knowledge of, no understanding, as though she shared her mind with a host of strangers. She awoke covered in sweat. Unable to go back to sleep, she got up and lit the candle by the bedside table, then crossed to the small mirror in her private chambers and stared at her reflection. Her skin had a greyish tinge. Purplish veins spidered across her cheeks and forehead. She had dark circles under her eyes. She kept her hair shaved down to dark stubble now, but even that had begun to turn grey. The last few months had changed her as surely as it had the political shape of the Trine. As surely as it had Cole, whom she sometimes heard crying out in his sleep in the room next to hers. She hadn't mentioned it to him. It would only make him angry. He seemed to spend a lot of time angry these days.

The third night after the Fade departed for the west, General Saverian launched his assault on Thelassa.

The alarms sounded out across the city as the first of the ships sailed into harbour. There were no Fade vessels among the invading force, only the remnants of Dorminia's creaking fleet, warships constructed of oak and cedar that had seen better days. Though they lacked the devastating artillery of the Fade warships, they did not require superior weaponry to sail through Thelassa's undefended harbour. The City of Towers no longer had any ships to speak of.

Sasha and Cole were among the first to arrive at the docks, joining the bulk of Thelassa's force of Whitecloaks, who were already arranged in formation. Before them were barrels filled with arrows dipped in oil, ready to be ignited and launched at the approaching vessels at a moment's notice. Just before the ships came within range, they opened fire with their cannons. Rudimentary though they were in comparison with the Fade artillery, their initial volley nonetheless broke the Whitecloak line. The soldiers fell back, unprepared for dealing with death being rained down upon them from the ships. As she stared at the broken bodies smoking on the docks, Sasha understood just how vulnerable the city was without its ruthless mistress.

*We live in a world in which immortal wizards wield godlike power. Where demons inhabit the darkest places and dragons roam the skies. Where a supreme race decides who lives or dies using weapons beyond our understanding. How can any ruler face down such threats and retain their humanity?*

For the first time, she began to feel sympathy for the White Lady and Salazar. In a world filled with monsters, you became a monster too, or you died.

Her moment of introspection was quickly shattered as another regiment of Whitecloaks arrived. The city's soldiers took cover behind hastily erected barricades and Sasha and Cole joined them, listening to the explosions, praying the barrier would offer some kind of protection from the iron shots smashing down around them.

Finally the cannons ceased. Sasha poked her head out to the unwelcome sight of a ship about to dock. She emptied her mind and focused, attempting to utilize what Isaac had called her 'telekinetic manipulation'. She felt the tingling in her body and she *pushed*, willing the ship to topple over and dump its passengers into the churning waters of the harbour. Though it creaked and lurched ominously, the ship proved beyond her ability to capsize. She was quickly exhausted, her hands shaking, the effort of activating the implant in her skull claiming its price from her body.

Rope ladders were tossed over the side of the ship and then a human crew began climbing down and leaping onto the docks, utterly fearless. They brandished knives and swords and cudgels, but they lacked the manner of professional soldiers and Sasha realized they must be thralls. Each of the ships carried hundreds of the enslaved men and women, all of them subject to Saverian's will courtesy of the tiny metallic parasites inserted in their bodies. Having been exiled by his kin, the Fade general was utilizing every tool available to him in an effort to conquer the City of Towers.

The first wave of thralls marauded up the docks and the Whitecloaks went to meet them. Though they were better trained, the Whitecloaks lacked the single-minded aggression of Saverian's mentally enslaved army. Sasha raised her crossbow and tried to pick out a target, but the knowledge that these were innocent people, puppets dancing to a ruthless master, made it tough to pull the trigger.

Cole noticed her hesitation. He drew Magebane and took a deep breath. 'If we don't fight,' he said slowly, 'we die.' But he didn't sound convinced. Nonetheless, he rolled out from behind the barricade and sprang into action, his magical dagger cutting and slicing, killing with terrifying ease. The boy she'd once known, the cocky cutpurse and thief, had become a master assassin to rival his mentor, the Darkson. The realization hurt Sasha more than she could explain.

A cloaked figure launched itself from the deck of the foremost ship and landed on the very edge of the dockside, thirty feet covered in a single leap. Time seemed to stand still.

General Saverian rose and raised his deadly shoulder-cannon. The terrible *ra-ta-ta-ta-ta* of the weapon tore through the air as it unleashed a storm of projectiles upon the combatants. Whitecloak and thrall alike were mown down. Cole somersaulted away, trailing shadows, taking shelter behind a stack of crates, the deck splintering around him.

*Saverian's gone mad*, Sasha thought, staring at the mighty Fade. He had a crazed glint in his obsidian eyes, as though something in him had broken following his exile. *That's what happens when you cannot bend. You break.*

The towering general took a single step forward, his jaw clenched. He seemed to bite off every word as he spoke it. 'Surrender your city and I may suffer some of you to live. To serve me and my kin.'

In answer, several Whitecloaks unleashed a volley of arrows. Saverian exploded into motion, his cloak sending the arrows skittering away, deflecting them in mid-air. One or two struck his silver armour and bounced off, unable to penetrate the Fade-forged material. He raised his shoulder-cannon once again. 'So be it,' he growled. 'You shall all die.'

Sasha focused on the devastating weapon in Saverian's hands. She reached deep within herself, summoning all the strength she had left.

The shoulder-cannon was torn from Saverian's grip. It hung suspended in the air for a moment, before Sasha tossed it into the harbour, where it made a small splash. The general roared his outrage, but the Whitecloaks were already melting out from behind their cover, closing on the exile, who was all alone. The cannons on the ships were unable to fire for fear of hitting Saverian.

*This is the moment*, Sasha thought, hope blossoming. The other ships had yet to unload more thralls onto the docks. Saverian was surrounded, a victim of his own hubris. The general had decided to lead from the front, for no other reason than he believed himself invincible.

But then Saverian drew his sword, and hope was quickly extinguished.

He moved like a whirlwind. Whitecloak after Whitecloak died, limbs sliced off, their bodies cut clean in half. Blood sprayed everywhere, drenched the docks until it was dripping into the harbour in a steady patter.

'Witness,' thundered Saverian, as one of Thelassa's soldiers seemed to fall apart right in front of him, his head soaring in one direction, his arms in another. 'I am the sword that has vanquished every threat for five thousand years! None can stand against me!'

Cole stepped out from behind the crates.

Sasha's heart hammered in her chest. *No*, she wanted to shout. *You'll die, Cole!*

But he was no longer the Cole she remembered. Just as in the cave of the Nameless cultists in the Devil's Spine, her friend had become a living embodiment of the Reaver.

He stalked towards Saverian, seeming to glow from within, a crimson radiance suffusing his skin, while behind him shadows crawled and leaped. The Fade general seemed entirely unmoved by the sight. He merely waited, his jaw clenching and unclenching, the illusion of iron self-control slipping by the second.

Glowing dagger and crystal sword came together in a deadly dance, too fast for her to follow. Once more, Sasha dared hope.

And, once more, hope died. Magebane skittered across the docks and Saverian emerged from the melee with one hand around Cole's throat, holding him a foot off the ground.

'Child of murder,' thundered the general, as more thralls began to drag themselves onto the docks, dripping dirty water from the harbour, weapons glistening in their hands and on their belts. 'You thought yourself my match because a god resides in you? The gods had their chance to challenge me millennia ago. It is too late for them. And now, it is too late for you.' His hand began to squeeze. Cole thrashed wildly, the shadows falling away like shredded fabric as the Reaver abandoned him. He met Sasha's eyes, all Cole again, pure terror on his face.

In sheer panic, Sasha raised her crossbow and fired. The bolt bounced off Saverian's silver armour. He shot her a glare as his thralls closed on her hiding place. 'Ah, the mutant girl. Once I am finished with this one, it will be your turn. I wish to see for myself the implants you stole from us.'

Sasha screamed as she was dragged out from behind the barricade by a pair of thralls. As they laid their hands on her, however, something strange happened. Visions suddenly exploded in her mind. She saw the thrall to her left tilling fields on a hazy summer morning. Something moved in the long grass behind him. She tried to yell out a warning but then a hand clamped around her mouth and the world went dark.

The next thing she knew, she was strapped to a chair in a

darkened room while a sliver of metal was inserted into her arm. It clamped into her flesh and her brain seemed to explode, awareness fading until she could see only a towering, white-haired being whose voice filled her world...

Sasha returned to herself just as one of the thralls raised his cudgel, preparing to smash her skull in. Cole was twitching in Saverian's grasp, his strength almost spent.

Her skin was tingling. She watched the thrall – a big, burly fellow – pull his arm back. 'No!' she screamed, knowing this was the end, her voice cracking with grief.

The thrall hesitated. He looked from her to Saverian. 'Kill her!' the general barked. 'You have your instructions.'

Something burned in Sasha's skull, like a tiny fire had been lit. An implant being activated. The thrall readied himself to attack again.

'No,' she said, calmer this time—

And the man lowered his cudgel. He stared at her, a blank expression on his face... almost as though he were awaiting further command.

Finally, she understood the nature of the implant Fergus had inserted into her skull; the memories she had no knowledge of that plagued both her dreams and her waking hours.

They belonged to the thralls. Somehow, she was mentally connected to them all.

More than connected – she was the *nexus*. The centre of a vast network of men and women enslaved by the Fade-created parasites implanted in their flesh.

And somehow she was the controller, able to override Saverian's instructions.

'Stop him!' she shouted, pointing at the towering general. The thralls on the docks immediately turned on Saverian, who released Cole and raised his sword to defend himself, pure rage twisting his alien features.

Cole was sprawled right in the path of the thralls as they converged on Saverian. Sasha dug deep, summoning the dregs of her strength, using her telekinesis to pull him back and away from Saverian and the men and women converging on him with weapons held high.

The thralls fared no better than had the Whitecloaks. Saverian's crystal sword danced, slicing through muscle and bone, so far beyond their skill that no numerical advantage could possibly make any difference to the outcome.

In desperation, Sasha stared beyond Saverian to the ships bobbing in the harbour. She could *feel* the thralls aboard the ships; see glimmers of their suppressed minds, like fireflies flickering in the night.

She concentrated, reaching out with her thoughts, ordering those aboard the ships to adjust their targets. The carrack closest to Saverian shifted position slightly. The figures operating the cannons shoved fresh iron shots into the barrels...

Just as Saverian cut down the last of the thralls, the cannons roared. A second later the deck exploded beneath the Fade general, fragmenting into a shower of splinters. Sasha caught a glimpse of the Fade commander diving away, his features ruined, his black cloak in tatters. She thought she heard a splash as the cannons died, and then the night fell silent.

Sasha ran to Cole, knelt down beside him. Saverian's fingers had left red marks around his throat, but he appeared more shaken than badly hurt. 'Is he dead?' he managed to rasp. 'Did we kill the bastard?'

She gazed out over the water. She thought she could make out a shape moving north towards Dorminia. No human could possibly swim all the way back to Dorminia from Thelassa – but Saverian was no human. 'I wouldn't count on it,' she said grimly. She stared at the ships in the harbour. Ships packed with thralls, now under her command.

'But,' she added. 'Unless he has another army... I think we've *won*.'

# Monsters

'THEY WILL SUFFER. They will all suffer.'

A terrifying and familiar voice dragged him awake and the Halfmage's eyes fluttered open. Or at least, they tried to flutter open. His face was still swollen and bruised from the vicious beating he'd received outside the Refuge. The sunlight filtering in through the open doorway made him squint and he blinked away tears.

He ought to be dead. The Collectors had scooped him off the streets and had been about to cart him away with the bodies of Ricker and Mard when Isaac's sister, Melissan, had turned up and had brought him to an abandoned storeroom near the docks. A Fade physician had come to administer some healing, setting his broken arm, bandaging his cracked ribs. Sewing his scalp back together.

*Good job I lack legs or no doubt I would also be nursing broken knees.*

Weeks locked up in solitude had given the Halfmage plenty of time to reflect on the injustices done to him. The simmering resentment that had come to define his adult years had become a burning desire for revenge.

He fucking *hated* this city. These people.

His eyes finally adjusted enough to see General Saverian staring down at him. Eremul shrank back in his wheelchair. The Fade commander's features were utterly ruined: half his hair had been scorched away, revealing the blistered scalp beneath.

Terrible burns covered his face. There was a fevered look in his obsidian gaze.

'What happened to you?' the Halfmage whispered.

The general ignored his question. Behind Saverian, Melissan lurked in the doorway. 'The others are ready to depart,' she said to her disfigured commander. 'I shall be glad to leave this accursed backwater.' The hatred in her voice made the anger Eremul had felt for Salazar seem pitiful in comparison.

General Saverian gestured at Eremul with a fire-scarred hand. 'We're taking this one with us.'

'Him?' Melissan's voice was thick with contempt. 'Let this human excrement perish with the rest of them! He is a broken, wretched thing. Unworthy of breathing the same air as you and me. Never mind sharing space aboard the *Retribution*.'

'The *Retribution*,' Saverian growled. 'The name is apt. As for this human, he is my proof that your brother was wrong. My vindication.'

'I do not understand, betrothed,' said Melissan.

Saverian leaned in to Eremul. 'Tell me,' he grated. 'Why did your kin do this to you?'

The Halfmage's eyes narrowed. 'They think me a monster.'

'Are they right?'

He remembered the glee on the faces of the gang as they punched him, kicked him, spat on him. He remembered Monique's final words in that soul-destroying moment at the docks.

*How could I love you?*

'I am what they made me,' he rasped. 'Everything I ever wanted, they denied me. Everything I ever cherished, they broke. Everything I ever loved... was an illusion.'

'What do you want done to those who wronged you?' Saverian's eyes glittered.

'Right at this moment, I'd like to see them burn.'

Saverian turned to Melissan. 'You see, betrothed. Your brother was a fool. His judgement a lie.'

'Judgement? Where is Isaac?' Eremul demanded. 'Where are you taking me?'

'Forget Isaac. You will receive answers soon enough.' Saverian gestured to Melissan. 'Take his chair.'

Melissan looked as though she'd just been asked to hold a slimy turd in her delicate hands. 'I am to play helper to this poisonous little half-man?'

'Only until he is safe aboard the *Retribution*.'

They left the cramped storeroom and emerged into glorious sunshine. The Halfmage fancied he could hear Melissan's teeth grating together as she pushed his chair down the cobbled streets. The Adjudicator hated him, that much was obvious.

*No more than I hate myself. Or you. Or this city.*

He stared down the thoroughfare and noticed with some surprise that the harbour was completely empty save for the single huge vessel carrying the Breaker of Worlds.

*Where are the First and Second Fleets? Where are Dorminia's ships?*

He looked around. The streets were unusually busy compared with what had become the norm these last few months, but they were notably absent of the city's immortal invaders. Men and women crowded together to watch them pass, and for the first time in a long while Eremul saw smiles on the faces of some. Smiles, and expressions of relief.

'Good riddance to you,' one woman muttered under her breath. Saverian turned to stare at her and she ran back inside her house, slamming the door behind her. Something Melissan had said echoed in Eremul's groggy brain.

*Let him perish with the rest of them.*

'You're going to Reckon the city,' he gasped. 'They don't know it – but they are all doomed.'

'Not just this city,' answered Melissan. This whole wretched Trine will be annihilated.'

Eremul grabbed Melissan's wrist and she pulled away from him with a snarl. 'You cannot!'

'Why do you care?' Saverian growled. 'These people hate you. They do not deserve your pity.'

The Halfmage met the general's gaze. 'Maybe they don't. Yet some are innocent.'

'You confuse *ignorance* with *innocence*,' hissed Melissan. 'Every human, even a newborn babe, is poison. A poison that is merely biding its time before it becomes toxic. Your kind corrupt everything you touch. Even the People are not immune to it. Even my own family.'

It took a moment for the meaning behind Melissan's words to sink in. 'Where's Isaac?' Eremul asked again. The pain on Melissan's face all but confirmed his suspicions.

Saverian's ruined jaw clenched. 'He spent too much time among humanity. Sometimes a smaller evil must be suffered so that a greater good may flourish.'

Melissan's fingers dug painfully into Eremul's bruised shoulder. 'Cease your questions. Be grateful you are to be spared the same fate as your kin, for you surely deserve it.'

Eremul sat in silence for another minute or two. Then he said, 'I wish to remain here.'

Saverian stopped abruptly. The Fade general turned to Eremul, his mouth twisting in fury. '*What* did you say?'

'I wish to remain here.'

*You fool! What are you doing? Save yourself!*

'You will die!' barked Saverian.

'That's humans for you. We tend to make a habit of it.'

The general reached for his sword. 'I could kill you now,' he said coldly. 'Piece by piece.'

The Halfmage shrugged and smiled a horrible, humourless smile. 'Ah, that old chestnut. Look at me,' he said, pointing to his stumps. 'Such a threat carries less weight than you might expect when directed at a man with no legs. I suppose you could delve further into the realms of banality and threaten my cock – but I must you warn you, that too would be no great loss.'

Saverian's face filled with such rage that for a moment he looked as though he was going to follow through with his threat. Instead, he sheathed his sword. 'Very well,' he said, his voice seething. 'You will be Reckoned.' He walked away. Melissan shot Eremul a hateful stare and followed after him, leaving the Halfmage alone.

Eremul closed his eyes and let out a deep breath, wondering what to do next. There was little to be gained by warning his fellow citizens. They wouldn't be able to evacuate in time. It would simply create panic on the streets and turn Dorminia's final few hours into a living hell.

He was still wrestling with his conscience when the first mouthful of spit splattered over the back of his head. 'Treacherous prick!' screamed a woman from the window of a building above. He realized with growing horror that a mob was beginning to form.

A stone ricocheted off his broken arm. The agony caused him to bite down hard on his tongue and he tasted blood. He tried to draw upon his magic, to summon a barrier to ward against further projectiles – but when he reached for his magic, there was nothing there.

He stared at his hands in shock.

'Abandoned you now, have they?' someone shouted. 'Even those black-eyed bastards can't stand the cripple!'

Curses and insults rained down upon him. Those Eremul could tolerate, but the spit and then the shit tossed from buckets that followed were another matter. Soon he was covered in filth. 'Traitor!' a man screamed. And then, 'Monster!'

*I am no traitor*, he wanted to shout back. *I am no monster! I'm just a man. A man you reject for being different. For being born with magic.*

'Fuck you,' he screamed. 'Fuck the lot of you.' He was shaking now. He stared around, looking for a side alley to lose himself in. A place where he could wait out the last miserable hours of his life before the Breaker of Worlds burned all the pain away.

A small boy looked up from playing in the dirt and met his gaze. The child had been poking at a damaged wall with a stick, trying to scoop out the cement. When he saw Eremul, he reached into his filthy trousers and pulled out something small and green. It was an apple. He tossed it to the Halfmage, who caught it in his good hand. The skin was a little bruised, but beneath it the fruit was still fresh.

'Don't pay them no mind,' the boy called out. 'Olly and the others said you was sound. They used to run errands for you at the depository. I always liked books. When I grow up, I wanna be like you.'

The orphan waved and scampered off. Eremul watched him go while around him the abuse continued. He stared at the apple and frowned, then placed it in a pocket.

Gritting his teeth against the pain in his injured arm, he wheeled himself after the two immortals in the distance. 'Wait for me!' he yelled.

\*

Eremul sat beside the towering figure of General Saverian near the starboard rail of the *Retribution* and watched Dorminia vanish into the distance. The general turned to him, his arms crossed over his chest, and fixed the Halfmage with a contemptuous stare. 'I knew you would return,' he said. 'It is an imperative of your race to save yourselves at any cost. You know nothing of unity. Of sacrifice for the greater good.'

The Halfmage was silent for a moment. 'Where is Prince Obrahim? There are barely twenty of you aboard this ship. Perhaps the fehd are not as unified as you claim.'

Saverian's eyes narrowed. 'You think yourself clever, half-man. Perhaps Isaac was enamoured of your wit. I am minded to cut out your tongue.'

'That's *Halfmage*,' corrected Eremul. 'And cutting, *again*?

After five thousand years, I had imagined you might possess more creative means of threatening a legless cripple.'

The look Saverian gave him should have chilled his blood and loosened his bowels, but the Halfmage was beyond fear. Monique had broken something inside him.

'Disrespect me again, and you will drown in these waters,' said Saverian. 'That is a promise.'

They were silent for a time. When the *Retribution* was halfway to Thelassa, the ship dropped anchor and the Ancients began inspecting the giant cannon that took up the bulk of the ship's deck. It began to move slowly, the mechanisms that operated it responding to directions presumably issued from below decks.

'Dorminia will be obliterated,' said Saverian. 'The Breaker of Worlds aboard this vessel is twice as powerful as that unleashed upon the Demonfire Hills. The creeping sickness that follows the blast will kill the populace of Thelassa slowly. They will suffer before they die. Suffer like none before them.'

Eremul stared at the great cannon piercing the sky. In minutes it would unleash a Reckoning upon the Trine.

*I have no magic. No allies. I cannot even walk. I have nothing. Nothing except my anger.*

'I want to ask about something,' he said abruptly. 'Isaac's judgement. You said he was wrong. About what?'

Saverian's scarred face twitched. 'He believed he saw something in you that proved your race could be redeemed. Instead he allowed himself to become corrupted.'

'You killed him.'

'I did what was necessary to protect my people. As I have always done. Even now I sacrifice for them. The Breaker of Worlds was to guarantee our security. Instead I shall employ it against the Trine so that humanity may never again sail west and threaten our homeland. My sword shall conquer the lands to the south. In time, this continent will be mine.'

*So said every other tyrant. Is this why your brother*

*abandoned you? You became enamoured of your own legend, Saverian. Blind to your own hubris.*

The Halfmage stared at the sea far below the ship. It looked beautiful in the afternoon sun.

*Peaceful.*

He took a deep breath. 'This isn't about sacrifice,' he said. 'This is about *vengeance*. Your people abandoned you. Conquering Thelassa proved beyond you. Now you seek to salve your ego by murdering countless thousands.'

Eremul summoned all his bitterness; all the anger that had lived inside him for so many years. He summoned it, and spat it right back in the face of the legendary Fade before him. 'You're the fucking monster here, general. The worst kind of monster. A *hypocrite*.'

Saverian was across to him in an instant, a hand around Eremul's throat, his voice bubbling like molten iron. 'Insolent dog,' he thundered. 'You dare judge me? You abandoned your people to die! You cowardly, snivelling little worm! Don't think your magic will save you now. The water you've been drinking was spiked with powdered abyssium.'

Both the Halfmage and his chair were lifted bodily off the deck by the Fade commander. Saverian held him over the edge of the railing, above the sea.

'*You are nobody*,' Saverian growled. 'No one ever loved you. No one will remember you. Your life of pain will be as a passing breeze. Hardly felt. *Inconsequential*. But I – *I* will echo through eternity.'

Saverian let go of him.

Eremul fell, hit the water hard. It was colder than he'd imagined. Out of instinct he began to flail around, but the air trapped in his robes kept him afloat and he forced himself to calm. His chair struck the water right next to him, one of the wheels coming loose. It didn't matter. He wouldn't need it any more. Not ever again.

He fumbled for the box below the chair as it began to sink

into the sea. Managed to get it open and remove the thin sliver of wood within. He pointed it at the hull of the *Retribution*.

Though Eremul could not access his own magic, the wand was its own repository. White-hot energy leaped from the tip. Not as hot as the beam from Obrahim's sceptre, that had somehow sliced through the White Lady's magical barrier – but hot enough. Hot enough to cut through steel.

He didn't let go of the wand. Not when its magic sputtered and died, leaving a hole in the ship above him, which water was already rushing to fill. Not even when the air in his robes finally departed and he began to sink below the surface. He panicked then. He remembered wondering how it would feel to drown.

He thought he saw movement on the railing of the *Retribution* and heard a muffled bang as his head went under. More muffled bangs sounded as Fade hand-cannons fired down upon him.

*Maybe they'll all miss*, he thought, oddly calm as he was pulled under. *I'm only half a man. It can't be easy to hit half a—*

# AUTUMN

AUTUMN

# Loose Ends

SASHA HURRIED THROUGH the carcass of Sanctuary that lay below Thelassa, growing dread like a writhing worm in her stomach. Derkin stumbled along behind her. The pair of them picked their way through the skeleton of the dead city, heedless of the threat of crumbling buildings and the misshapen Abandoned that still haunted the ruins.

Three months after Saverian's defeat at Thelassa's harbour, and Sasha was still struggling to come to terms with her place in the world. With the title the people of the City of Towers had bestowed upon her.

The Grey Sister. First among the Consult. Defender and ruler of the most powerful city in the north.

She could have sent a group of Whitecloaks on her behalf when she learned of Cole's plan – but this was personal. She had to do this herself.

The dilapidated temple of the Mother melted out of the darkness ahead of her. Rays of light cut through the ruined ceiling far above, illuminating the lone figure kneeling before the shattered altar. Above the altar hung the heart of the Reaver. Every beat of the grotesque organ forced blood into the tubes that connected it to Thelassa above, though the towers in which the White Lady's handmaidens had been formed were nailed shut now. It had been Sasha's first act upon assuming her new title. There would be no more Unborn under her rule.

Cole's hood was pulled up tight over his head. Sasha beckoned

Derkin to wait and then made her slow way up the central aisle, stepping around fallen masonry and sections of rotting pew.

Cole's head shifted slightly as he heard her approach. 'You should leave,' he rasped. 'This place won't be safe for much longer.'

'What are you doing?' Sasha asked, although she already knew. She'd known as soon as Derkin had brought her the news.

'Fulfilling my destiny. I can't run from it any longer. The Reaver won't let me.' He turned to stare at her and she gasped. His face was ghostly pale, his thin skin pulled tight over his skull.

'You'll become a monster,' she said, trying to hold back tears.

'The monster we need,' Cole replied grimly. 'Saverian won't stop until we're all dead. We can't defeat him. Not unless I embrace what I am fully.'

'What you are is my *friend*,' she replied. 'My best friend. The only friend I have.'

'I'm sorry,' he said. He reached up and placed a hand on the organ. Immediately his skin gained colour and his cheeks grew fleshier as his vitality was restored.

'We can beat him,' Sasha pleaded. 'We beat him once – we can do it again! Please, Cole, stop.'

'He murdered them all,' Cole rasped. His voice began to change, becoming colder, sinister. A red radiance suffused his body, the shadows writhing around him, shrouding him in darkness. 'Kayne and Jerek. The White Lady. Thanates. We can't hold out forever. It's time to end this.'

'Cole—'

'You and Derkin need to get out of here. Once I lose myself, I'll be gone forever. I can't predict what the Reaver will do.'

'You promised me,' Sasha said, tears in her eyes now. 'You promised you would never abandon me.'

Cole jerked as if stabbed. 'You're the ruler of a city now. You don't need me.'

'You're wrong,' Sasha said urgently. 'I need you more than ever.'

Cole removed his hand from the Reaver's heart and Sasha knew she was too late. Her friend was gone, only the briefest flicker of recognition remaining in his grey eyes. '*Kill them all,*' he snarled, and the voice no longer belonged to Cole but rather echoed from somewhere beyond the grave.

Derkin let out a terrified cry as the thing that had been Cole drew Magebane and made straight for Sasha. She watched him surge towards her, nothing but murderous intent on his face, and a hundred thoughts raced through her mind. She could attempt to use her telekinetic power to toss him aside, but that would not stop him. She could hurl fallen masonry at him, bury him beneath a pile of rubble, break his body so that he might never leave this temple.

But she couldn't do any of those things. Not to him. She would die herself, first.

'I love you,' she whispered instead, and waited for the end.

Suddenly, the apparition that had been Cole hesitated. With a strangled cry, he spun and plunged Magebane into the Reaver's heart, slicing it open, a torrent of blood gushing out to flood the altar. A disembodied scream roared through the ruins as the shadows fell away from Cole, the sinister light dying within him.

Until he stood before her once again.

*

The docks were quiet at this early hour. The heat of summer still lingered and Cole had discarded his cloak while he stared out at the harbour, enjoying the peace and solitude. It made a welcome change from the madness of recent months.

The ships Thelassa had commandeered from Saverian floated beyond the docks, silent sentinels in the night. They were crewed by the army of thralls Saverian had brought to the city. Surprisingly, Sasha had yet to release them from their servitude.

Cole closed his eyes and enjoyed the feel of the sea breeze on his face. Somehow he had resisted the Reaver's possession.

*She said she loves me.*

He'd destroyed the disembodied heart of the Lord of Death. The god had fallen silent since, though he knew the Reaver wasn't gone for good – he still felt its essence within him. He knew that, without the heart to restore his vitality, he would have no option but to kill if he wanted to survive. The thought sickened him. He didn't want to kill. Not ever again.

Something bobbed along in the water below him. He reached down to retrieve it and stared at it curiously. It was a wheel. He felt like he ought to recognize it.

'The Creator certainly has a sense for the theatrical. The Pattern never ceases to surprise.'

Cole turned. An old, rotund man in black robes had just appeared behind him. He wore a kindly smile and had a grandfatherly countenance – but there was something discordant about the stranger. Cole felt ill at ease all of a sudden, as though a thousand tiny, invisible spiders were crawling over his flesh.

'Where did you come from?' he demanded.

'Nowhere in particular,' replied the stranger. The rising sun bathed his face in a red light.

'Who are you?' Cole asked.

'I have many names, all of them false. Names can be dangerous, for knowing a thing bestows power over it. You may know me as Marius.'

'*Marius?*' Cole gasped. 'The Magelord of Shadowport? I thought you were dead.' He stared at the wheel in his hands. A droplet of water hung suspended in mid-air, caught in the act of falling. In the sky above, a seagull was frozen in time.

'A man such as you surely understands the virtue of keeping to the shadows,' Marius said. 'Indeed, it is your nature that informs my visit.'

Cole stared more closely at the stranger's eyes. 'You're a blood mage,' he hissed. 'You sent Wolgred to kill me!'

'I sent Wolgred to *test* you. You are, after all, the Reaver's chosen tool. Every tool requires sharpening on occasion.'

'I'm no one's tool,' Cole snapped.

'We are *all* someone's tool, boy. Your choices are not defined by you but by those greater than you. The weavers; the architects; the conductors. Most go through life blissfully unaware they dance to tunes they cannot hear. For centuries the Trine has danced to mine.'

'What do you want with me?' Cole said angrily. He wasn't going to dance for anyone ever again.

'I want you to play your role,' the Magelord said genially. 'The seeds of the Reaver's return were sown centuries ago. Death is what shall empower his rebirth and the return of the gods. They will restore this world and end this age of ruin. But first the slate must be wiped clean, you understand. The Ancients and the Nameless did not generate the deaths I had hoped for, and yet everywhere one looks conflict is boiling over. My apprentices have done well. There is yet more to be done – which is where you come in.'

'You want me to kill for you?' Cole demanded. 'I won't!'

'A better question might be whether you wish to *live*. If so, I believe you have no choice in the matter.' Marius nodded at Magebane, sheathed on Cole's belt. 'You will kill again. They always do.'

'A life of killing is no life at all. I refuse to be a tool.'

Marius squinted up at the rising sun, his eyes redder than the dawn. 'Unlike certain of your friends, you are not so important in the grand scheme of things. We will see if your resolve remains firm when the Reaver's essence begins to consume you.'

Without warning, Marius stepped off the edge of the docks and disappeared. There was no splash, no great burst of magic; one instant he was there, and the next he was not.

Cole drew Magebane and stared at it for a long while. He remembered something Brodar Kayne had told him.

*It ain't the weapon that makes the man. It's the man that makes the weapon.*

'I think it's time I made a new weapon,' he whispered.

He drew his arm back and, with all of his strength, threw Magebane into the harbour. Then he watched it sink beneath the water.

\*

'I have something to tell you.'

Sasha turned and stared at Cole with tired eyes. She was sitting at her desk in her private chambers in the palace, reading a missive that had just arrived from Westrock. 'Brandwyn's dead,' she said in astonishment. 'They found his body chopped to pieces. What do you need to tell me?'

Cole didn't meet her gaze. 'I'm not going to be around for much longer.'

'What do you mean?'

'I thought I should see the world. While I still can.'

'Does this have something to do with what happened earlier? Because—wait, where's Magebane?'

'Gone,' Cole said. 'Somewhere I'll never find it again. I threw it in the harbour.'

'You did *what?* Cole! Without it you'll waste away. You'll die—'

'We all die,' Cole cut in. He forced himself to relax. 'Really, it's fine. I'm not going to be a slave to that weapon any longer. I spent years thinking I had to be a hero because of Magebane. Then months thinking I had no choice but to be a killer. But there's always a choice. From now on, I'm just going to be me. Who knows – maybe I can find some way to lift this curse before it devours me.'

'Where will you go?' Sasha asked. She wanted to cry, but it wouldn't do for Thelassa's new ruler to show such weakness. She was a girl no longer. She was the Grey Sister – the head of the Consult and ruler of the greatest city this side of the Unclaimed Lands.

'I'm thinking of heading south. I have some scores to settle.' Cole hesitated and Sasha knew what was coming. 'Back in the ruins, when you said you loved me—'

'Yes.'

'Why did you reject me before, when I told you how I felt? I still don't understand.'

Sasha stared at her reflection in the mirror across the room. Cole followed her gaze. He took in her cropped hair, prematurely greying. The dark veins threading her skin.

Understanding finally dawned. 'Sash,' he said gently. 'I don't *care* how you've changed. True, you're not the same girl you once were. But you'll always be beautiful in my eyes. You shouldn't feel you're not good enough for me just because you've changed physically.'

Sasha stared at him for a long moment. 'What the fuck, Cole?' she spluttered.

His smile stayed fixed on his face but Cole had the feeling he'd just said something utterly foolish. 'I only meant—'

'I know what you meant! I love you – *as a brother*. The only way I can love any man. Do you understand me?'

Cole scratched his head. 'I'm not sure I follow.'

'I like girls, Cole.'

'Ah.'

'I haven't been with a man in years. Did you never wonder about that?'

'I assumed you were waiting for me.'

'That's sweet. But I'd never wait for any man. Not even you.'

'So, what you're saying is—'

'What I'm saying is that the hero doesn't always get the girl,' Sasha said, exasperated. 'And sometimes it has nothing to do with the hero and everything to do with the girl.'

*I'm not a hero*, Cole wanted to say. Then he remembered that he *had* helped slay the Herald and saved the life of Magnar Kayne. 'Maybe I am a hero,' he wondered aloud.

Sasha gave him a funny look. 'That wasn't really the point I was trying to make,' she said slowly. 'But, yes, I suppose you are.'

'I understand now,' Cole said gently. 'You like girls. That makes things tricky but I dare say not impossible. Just one more challenge for Davarus Cole to overcome.'

'Cole,' she hissed angrily. 'You fucking—'

But he was already moving towards her. Wrapping his arms around her, a big grin on his face. 'I'm just joking,' he whispered. And a moment later, she smiled too.

'When are you are going to free the thralls?' Cole asked gently. 'You have to, Sash. They're slaves, just like the Unborn. They don't deserve this.'

'Soon,' she replied, not meeting his gaze. 'First we need to be certain they aren't dangerous. That they can adapt to life in Thelassa. It will take time.'

'You know,' Cole mused, 'it's strange. Fergus was an evil man, but the things he did may ultimately have ended up saving the city. He gave you the tools to fight off Saverian.'

Sasha met Cole's iron gaze. *I became the Grey Sister. I will be the ruler Thelassa needs in order to survive.*

'I think the lesson is that good men can be capable of evil deeds,' she said slowly. 'And evil men can unintentionally do good. There are no absolute heroes or villains.' *No black or white*, she thought. 'Only people who try to do the right thing and those who don't.'

'Except for Saverian,' Cole said. 'He's just an arsehole.'

'Arseholes can often surprise you.' They exchanged a grin.

'Do you think Garrett would be proud of us?' Cole asked, and despite her earlier resolve the question brought tears to Sasha's eyes.

'I know he would,' she said. 'And so would the others who didn't make it this far. Brodar Kayne. Isaac. Even Jerek. They all died for what they believed in. Trying to do the right thing.'

'But what *is* the right thing?' Cole asked. 'How do we know?'

'That,' whispered Sasha, 'is the hard part…'

# Epilogue

GENERAL SAVERIAN STARED *out of the window panel at the very top of the Obelisk and cast his gaze over the trees in the parks far below. They were already turning gold and brown. Autumn was his favourite season, for it reminded him that while all things born of the Pattern died, he did not. He would endure forever.*

*His body had already healed from the damage he had taken from the cannon fire back at Thelassa's docks. His kind possessed remarkably fast powers of recovery in comparison with humanity, and though he had lost the* Retribution *and the* Breaker of Worlds *thanks to the actions of Isaac's wretched pet, he was calm now. After all, the most valuable thing the fehd possessed – apart from time – was self-control.*

All things die. But we endure.

*Three of his kin had perished when the* Retribution *had capsized. There were now barely twenty of the People remaining this side of the Endless Ocean, but Saverian was not overly concerned. One of his kin was worth a hundred of humanity.*

*The recently installed elevation chamber chimed behind him and Melissan stepped out. His betrothed approached and placed a hand on his shoulder. 'Thelassa's new ruler proves an obstinate foe,' she said. 'The implant in her skull that allows her to control the thralls is beyond my ability to override. The army cannot be recaptured.'*

*Saverian's eyes narrowed. 'The Grey Sister has been lucky so far. Her luck will run out.'*

*Melissan nodded. She hesitated a moment. 'Do you... do you regret any of this?'*

*'Regret?' Saverian growled.*

*'We are so few, trying to hold onto a city of thousands. The things we have done—'*

*'Were necessary,' Saverian finished, biting off both words. 'This is my duty, betrothed. My duty to my people! First, Thelassa will fall. The rest of the north will follow in time. We will wipe mankind from the continent. My brother may have exiled me, but I will not fail him. I will not fail my people. None shall ever again threaten us!'*

*He realized he was spraying spittle and raised a hand to wipe his mouth clean.*

*Melissan stared at him with an unreadable expression. Then she turned and took the elevation chamber back down without a word. Saverian watched her go. He turned back to the window. He narrowed his eyes and then drove a fist through the glass.*

*'I am General Saverian,' he whispered, forcing his fury under control. 'I killed the elf king in single combat. I drove the wyrms from this continent. I broke the grim company that defeated the Herald. I always win.'*

*He stood there, staring out over the city. Black clouds gathered and a fierce wind picked up, buffeting him, sending his cloak dancing behind him. A flash lit the sky. There was a great rumble of thunder and moments later the first drops of rain struck the glass to either side of the broken window. The gathering storm mirrored the storm raging within him.*

I am the shield that defends our people from harm. I am the sword that has vanquished every threat for five thousand years.

*The elevation chamber chimed again. He heard the doors slide open but did not bother to turn. If Melissan were so displeased by his earlier outburst, she could approach and make her feelings known. He gave no quarter to anyone; not even his own betrothed.*

*Something landed on the rain-swept floor beside him. He stared down at it.*

*It was the head of Asharoth, the guard on duty.*

*Saverian spun. A burly figure stepped out of the elevation chamber. A flash of lightning outside lit the room for an instant, revealing a bald head dripping with rain, fire-scarred jaw clenched in utter determination. Dark eyes promising death.*

*The grim warrior stalked towards him, a bloody axe clutched in each hand.*

'*You should be dead,*' *Saverian growled.* '*I shot you a half-dozen times.*'

*The human known as the Wolf was covered in wounds that had yet to completely heal. Somehow he had made it through the enclave and inside the Obelisk, killing an experienced fehd officer along the way.*

'*You seek to challenge me?*' *the general grated as the warrior did not slow his advance.* '*You are no immortal! You are no wizard! You are not even god-touched. You are just a man. A dead man walking.*'

*The human didn't reply. Did not waver. He kept on coming, the expression on his scarred face so intense that Saverian felt a flicker of unease. He considered drawing his hand-cannon – but the raging storm within him demanded something more.*

*His crystal sword whispered from its sheath.*

*The rain was pounding down now, the beating of it against the glass drowning out the ragged breathing of the bald warrior and Saverian's own measured breaths. He had witnessed this human fight back at the palace. This* '*Wolf*' *was good, remarkably so – better than any mortal had a right to be.*

*But he was the general.*

*The warrior sprang, unleashed a flurry of slashes that would have ended many Fade soldiers, perhaps even an Adjudicator. Saverian blocked them all, driven back only slightly by the sheer fury of the berserker's assault. He launched a counter-attack, felt his sword cut flesh, felt warm blood on* his face as it sprayed out from a deep gash in his opponent's arm.

The man known as the Wolf didn't falter. Instead he punched out with an axe, caught Saverian in the mouth with the haft. The general staggered back and the human warrior rushed him, headbutting him in the face, shattering his nose before Saverian hurled him away. The commander stood there in shock, tasting his own blood as his opponent climbed back to his feet.

The Wolf was relentless. He stormed straight back in, right axe swinging, an overhand slash followed by a low slash from his left axe. He pivoted and launched a reverse strike with his right axe and Saverian parried all these attempts, but the Wolf immediately launched into another combination even more intricate than the last and this time one of his axes glanced off Saverian's chest. The general's armour held – but he felt a rib crack beneath the force of the blow.

The bald-headed warrior was bleeding profusely from several wounds. Saverian spat out crimson and narrowed his gaze on this remarkable human. 'Who are you truly?' he demanded. 'Tell me so that I may add your name to the list of foes I have vanquished.'

'A cunt talks about what's he's gonna do,' the grim warrior replied. 'A man does it.'

Saverian sneered. 'A man dies. Just like everything else that is mortal. But I am no mortal.'

He dove forward, leading with the tip of his crystal sword, the same killing blow that had ended the blue-eyed warrior who called himself the Sword of the North. He moved faster than any human, faster than anything living or dead. He was the general, and for five thousand years his sword had vanquished every threat against his people.

He felt his sword enter the human's stomach. Heard the man's sharp intake of breath, the clatter of his axes striking the floor. 'Now you know how your friend felt in his final moments,' Saverian said. 'Die now. Die like he died.'

*He pushed, attempting to drive the sword deeper into the warrior's body, expecting to feel it burst through his back at any moment.*

*It would not budge.*

*Saverian glanced down. Saw the Wolf's hands around the blade, his biceps straining with the effort of holding it back.*

*The general felt hot breath on his skin and looked up just as the warrior's teeth closed around his cheek. The Wolf jerked his head viciously back and half of Saverian's face seemed to tear away. He screamed, stumbled back, his crystal sword pulled away from his grip.*

*He felt the blood pouring down his neck, the empty space in his cheek where flesh ought to be. He blinked the tears from his obsidian eyes just in time to see the weapon – his weapon – bursting through his chest. It punched through his silver armour like paper, sharper than any steel, sharper than anything that could be found in the earth. This time it was Saverian's turn to gasp, blood filling his mouth, bubbling out.*

*The Wolf snarled crimson drool, began to push him backwards by the hilt of the sword in his shaking hands. Backwards, towards the gap in the broken glass.*

*'You should be dead,' Saverian tried to say, bloody spittle spraying all over his chin.*

*He tried to slide the weapon out of him like his opponent had, to tear the blade free of his body – but he could not. All he could do was focus on that pitiless stare. Eyes like flint, refusing to dim despite the countless wounds covering his body.*

*With a mighty grunt, the Wolf flung him backwards and then Saverian felt himself falling, shards of glass raining down around him, his own sword sticking out of his chest like an exclamation point. As he fell, he watched the dwindling warrior sink to one knee on the tower's edge, seconds from toppling over the precipice himself.*

*He would never know if his killer did indeed fall. His final thought was that none of this should have been possible. For*

*five thousand years he had been the shield that had kept his
people safe. For five thousand years he had been the sword that
had overcome all threats.*

*Yet as the ground rushed up to meet him, a single inevitable
truth echoed in his mind. All things die...*

## A letter from the publisher

We hope you enjoyed this book. We are an independent
publisher dedicated to discovering brilliant books,
new authors and great storytelling. Please join us at
www.headofzeus.com and become part of our
community of book-lovers.

We will keep you up to date with our latest books, author
blogs, special previews, tempting offers, chances to win
signed editions and much more.

If you have any questions, feedback or just want to say hi,
please drop us a line on hello@headofzeus.com

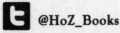 @HoZ_Books

HeadofZeusBooks

www.headofzeus.com

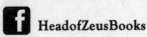 HEAD *of* ZEUS

**The story starts here**